PIXELS OF YOU

From Yuko & Ananth:
For Jones

Thank you George Rohac and Tess Stone for going above and beyond!
Thank you to ST for cheerleading us through the development of this
book. Thank you to Ajay for walking us through the confusing stuff.
General appreciation to Rook the cat, who is—as always—a good boy.

■ ■ ■

From J. R. Doyle:
For my parents, Sam and Erlina

First I'd like to thank my partner, Jack Stanovsky—your love and
support sustained me this past year. Thank you also to Cynthia and
Sylvia Wood for cheering me on. And thank you to Tess Stone, Sarah
Stone, George Rohac, and Fen Garza for the expert assistance that
helped me over the finish line.

Lastly, thank you to the cats Rex, Oscar, and Zoey for being warm
and soft. I love you.

Cataloging-in-Publication Data has been applied for and
may be obtained from the Library of Congress.

Hardcover ISBN 978-1-4197-5281-0
Paperback ISBN 978-1-4197-4957-5

Text © 2021 Ananth Hirsh & Yuko Ota
Jacket illustrations © J. R. Doyle
Colors and letters by Tess Stone
Flats by Fen Garza
Book design by Megan Kelchner/Kay Petronio

Printed and bound in China
10 9 8 7 6 5 4 3 2 1

Amulet Books® is a registered trademark of Harry N. Abrams, Inc.

ABRAMS The Art of Books
195 Broadway, New York, NY 10007
abramsbooks.com

PIXELS OF YOU

WRITTEN BY **Ananth Hirsh** AND **Yuko Ota**

ILLUSTRATED BY **J. R. Doyle**

COLORING AND LETTERING BY **Tess Stone**

FLATS BY **Fen Garza**

AMULET BOOKS • NEW YORK

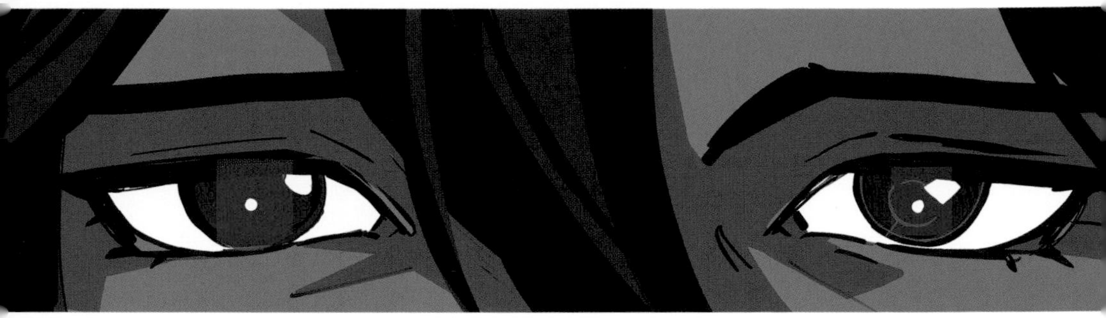

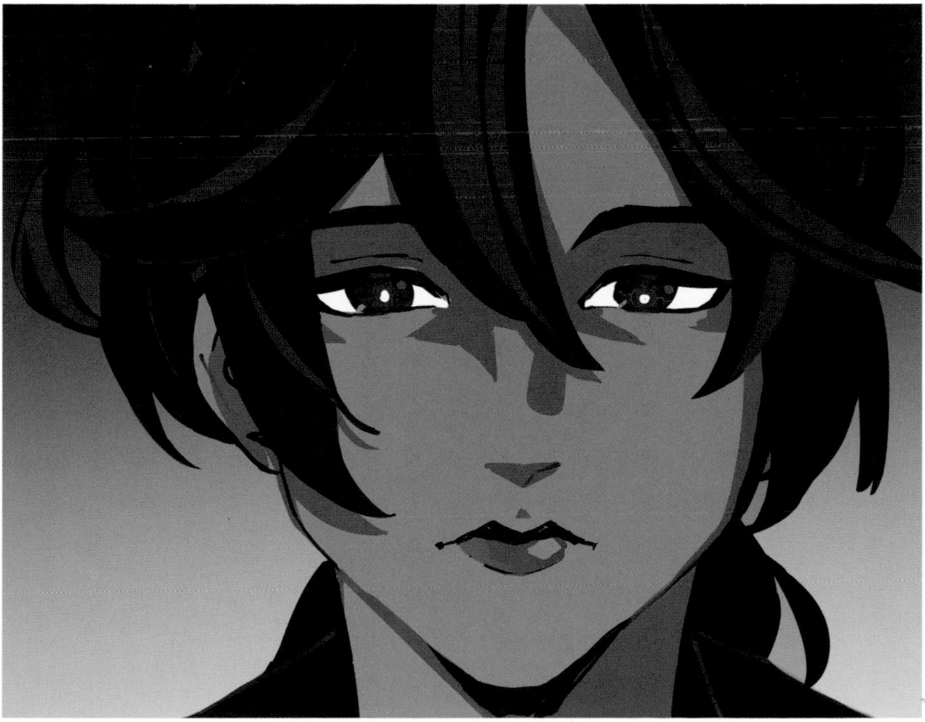

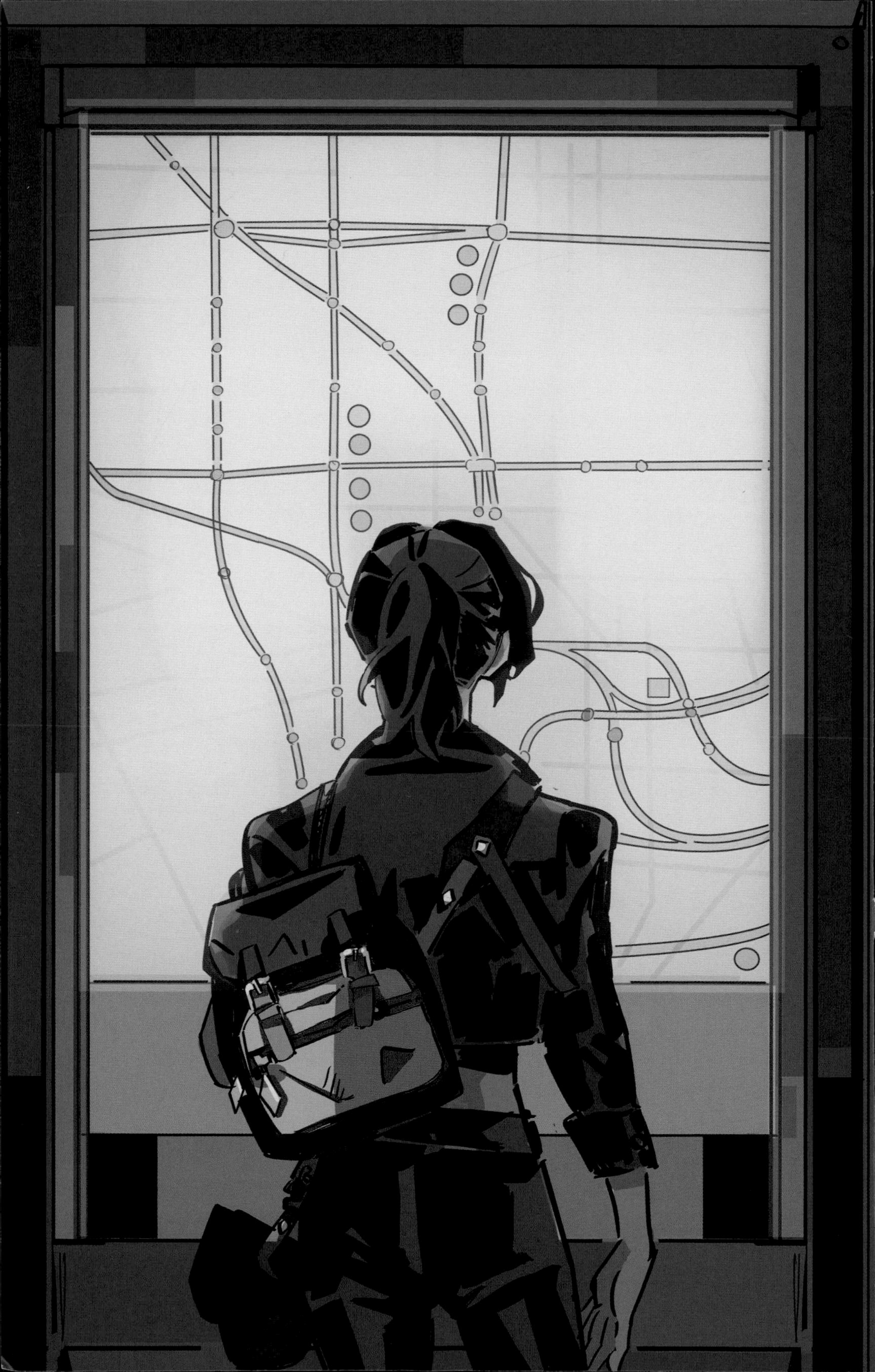

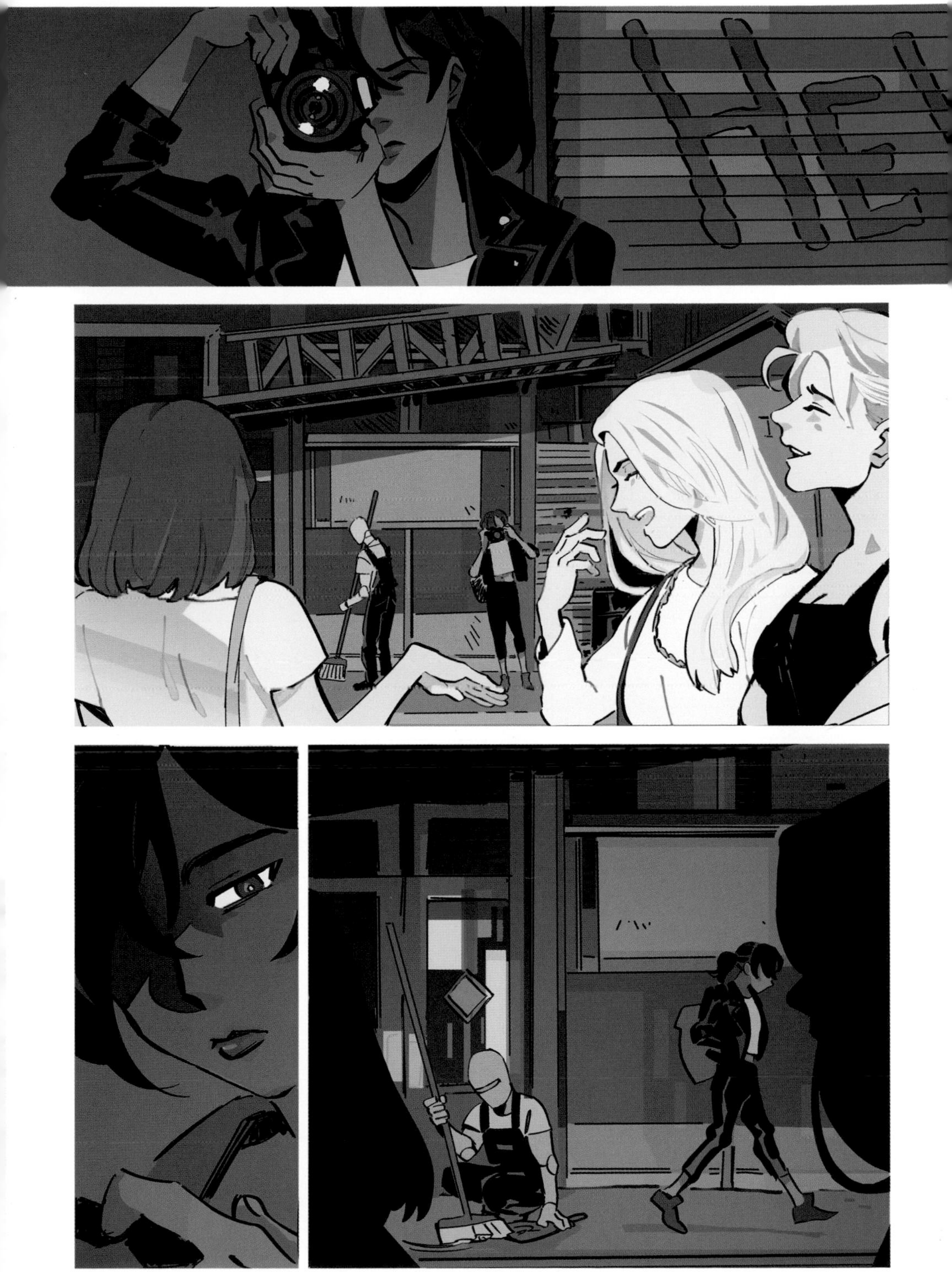

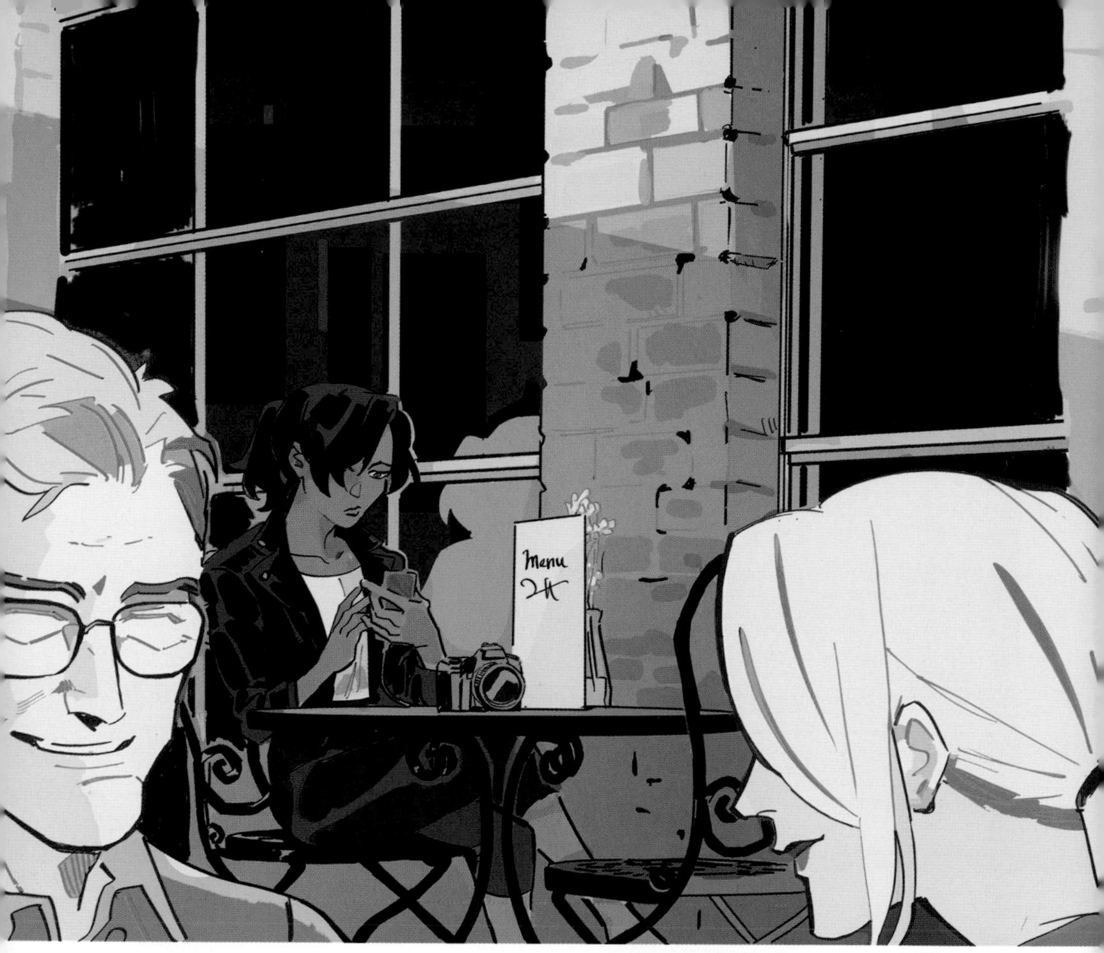
Menu

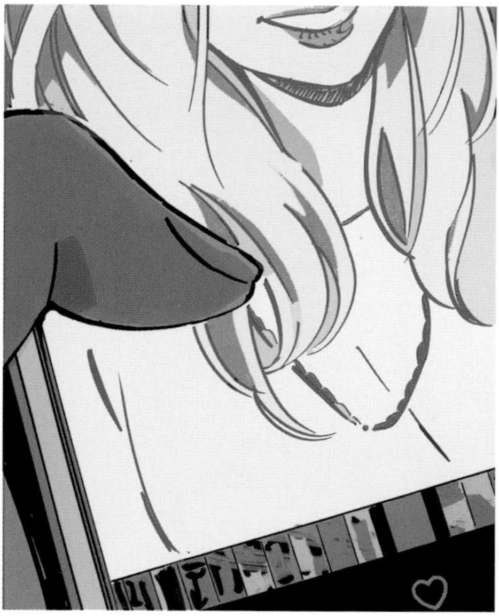

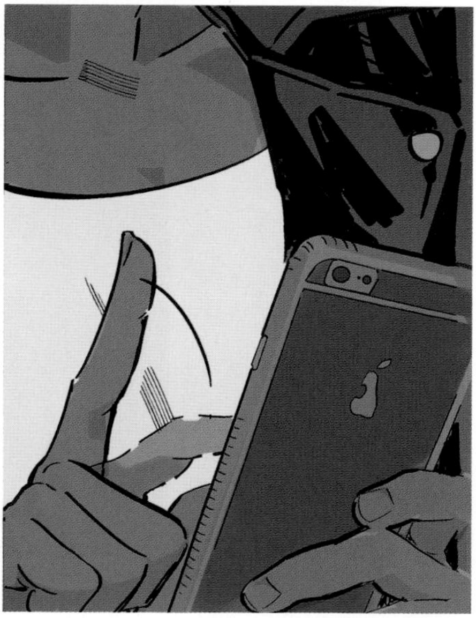

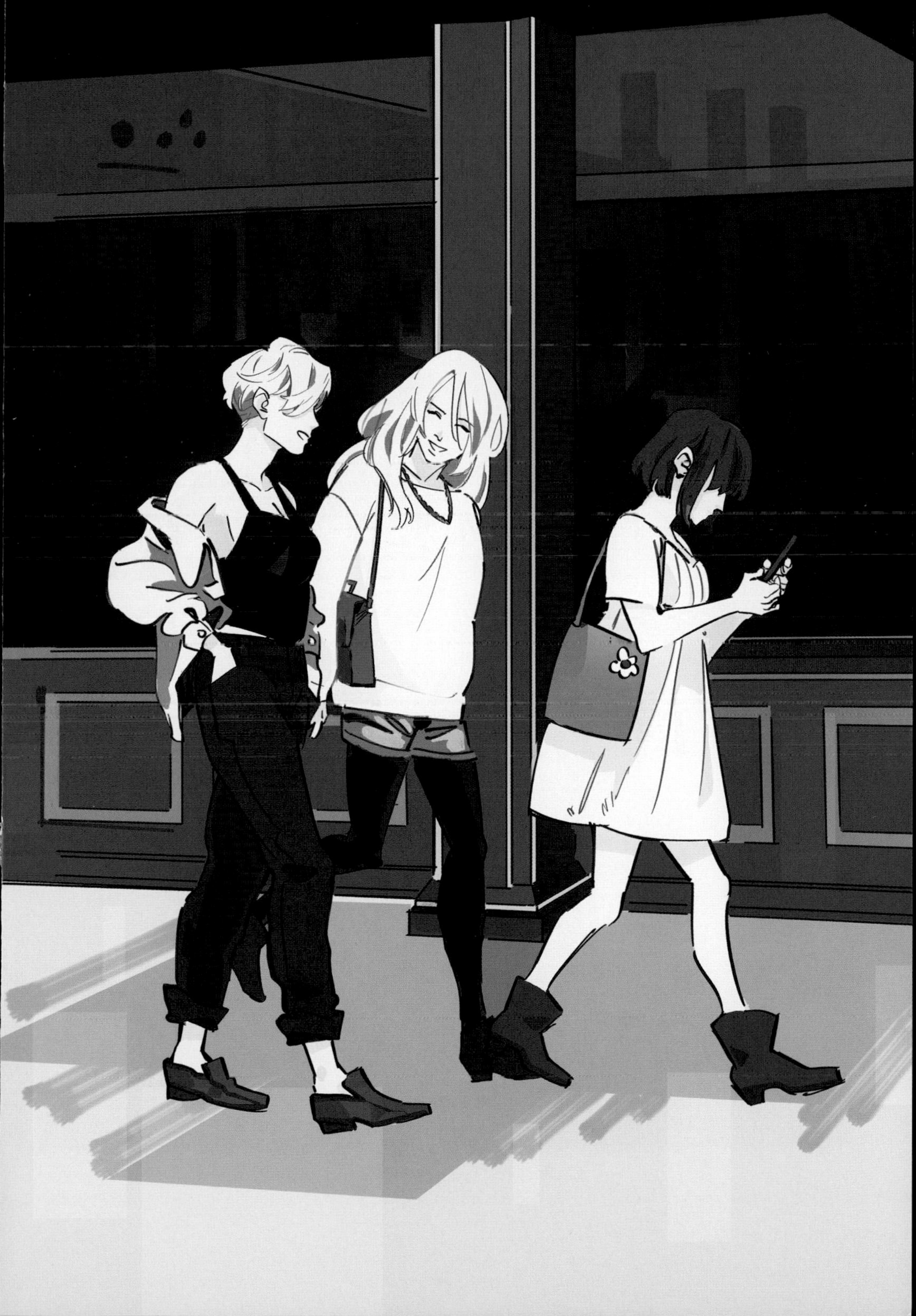

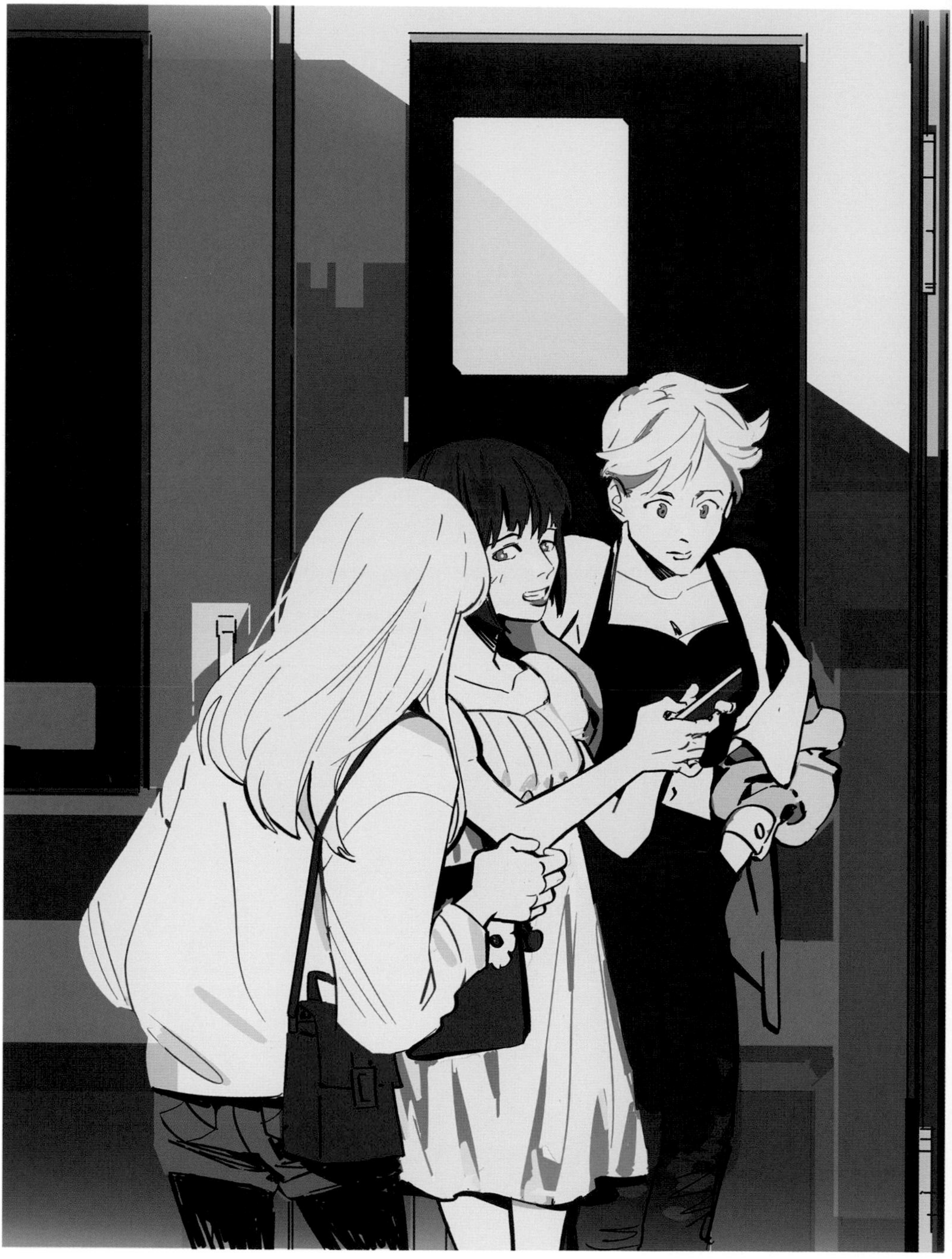

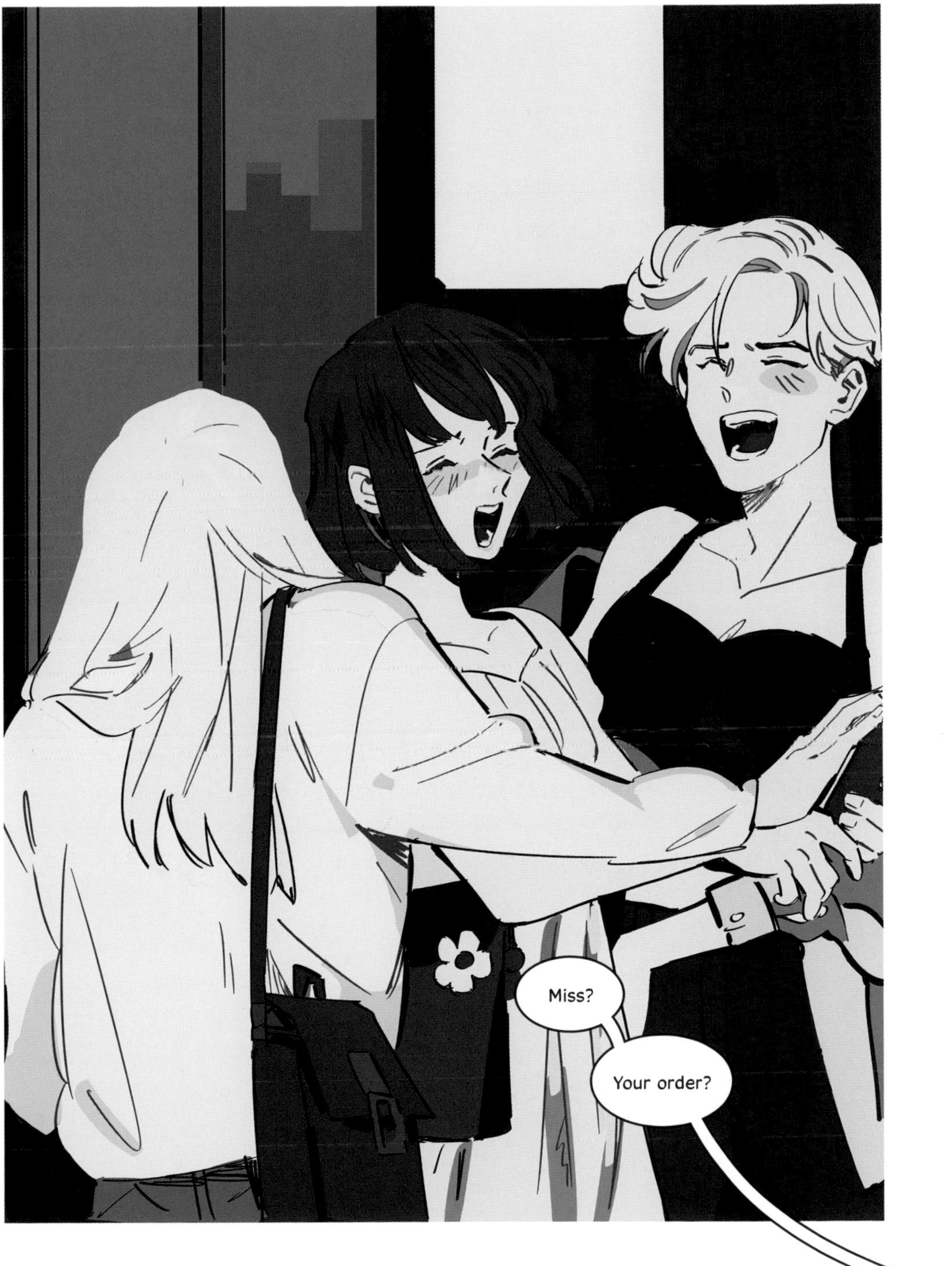
Miss?
Your order?

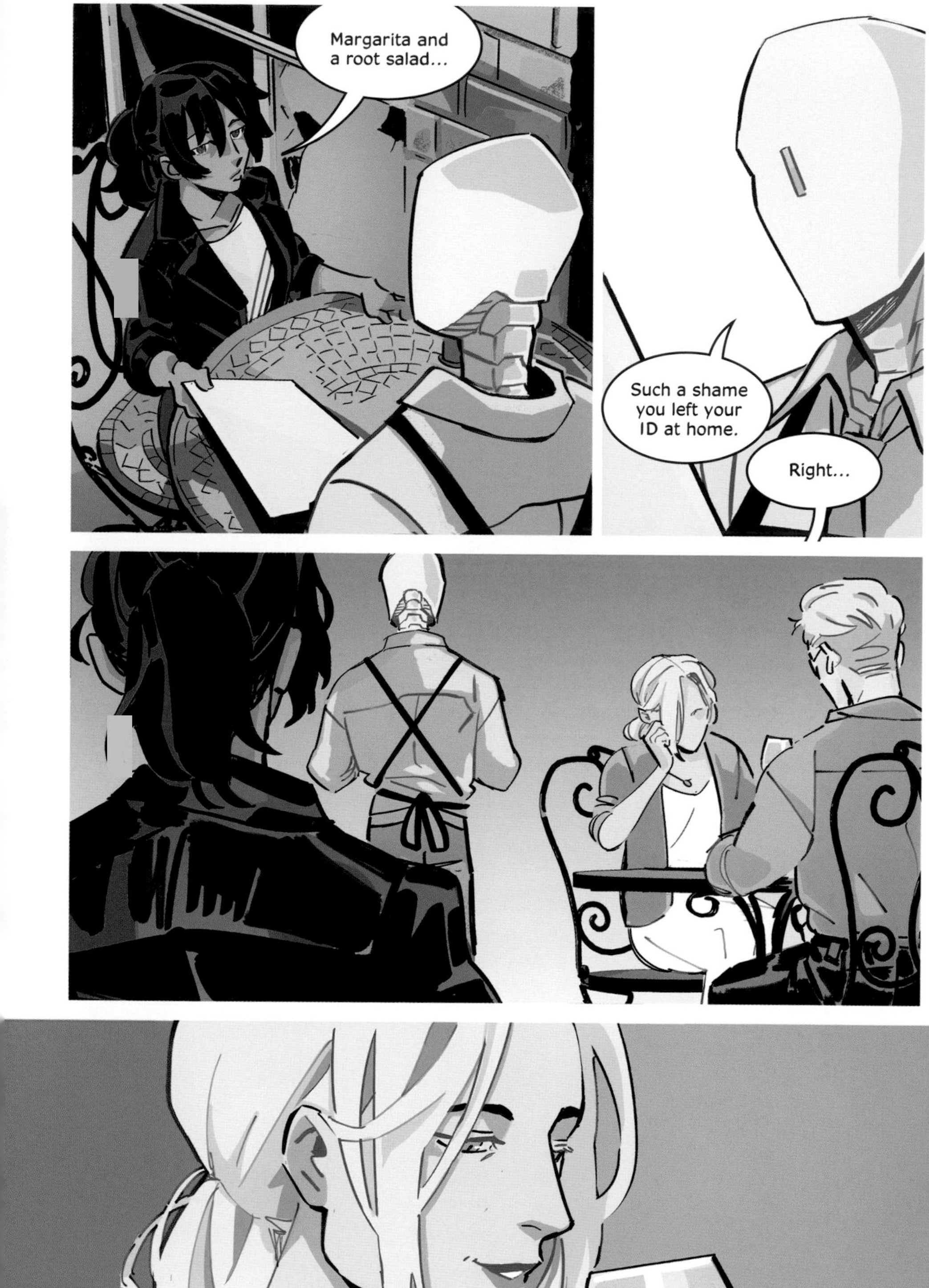
Margarita and
a root salad...
Such a shame
you left your
ID at home.
Right...

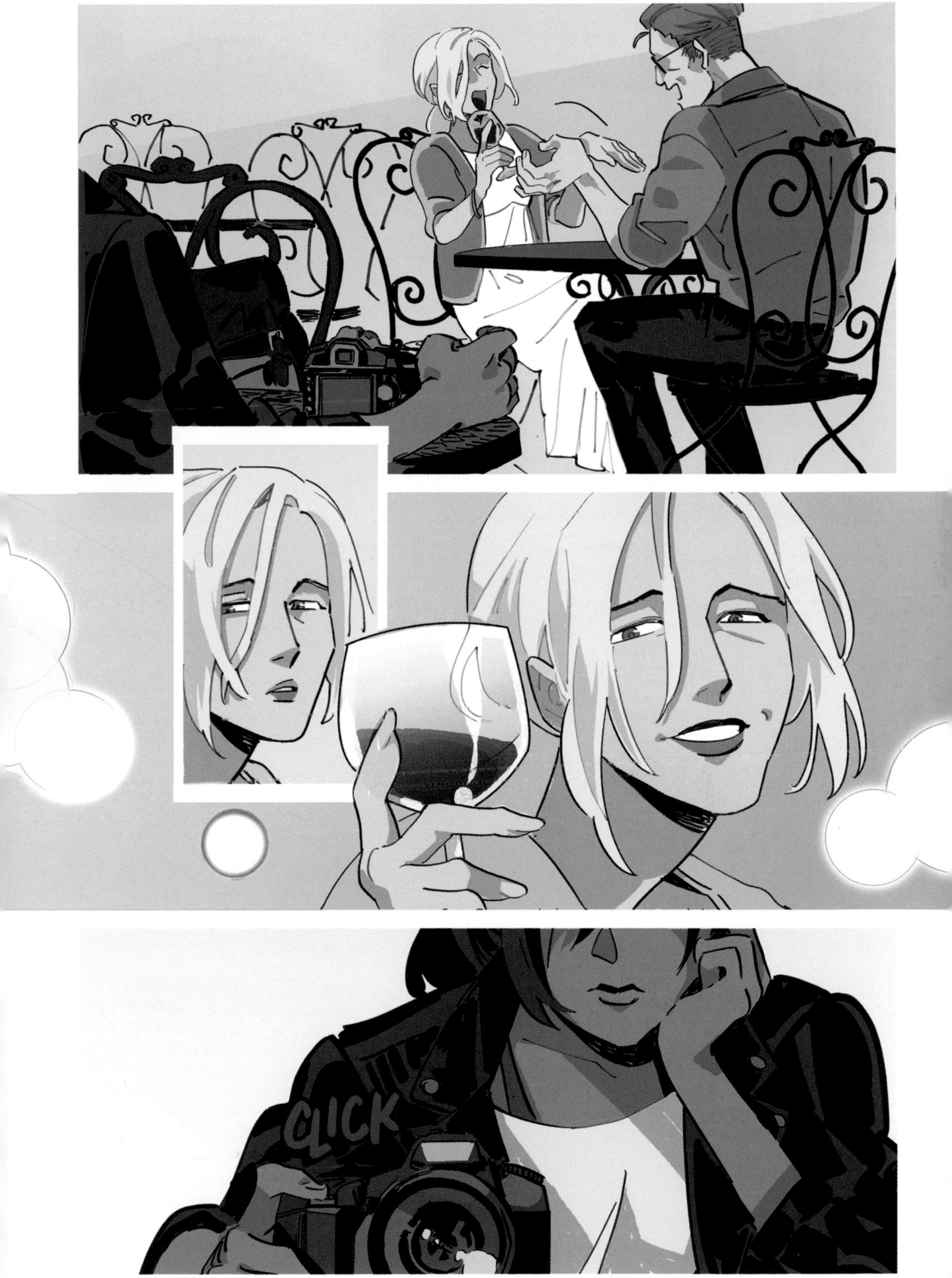
CLICK

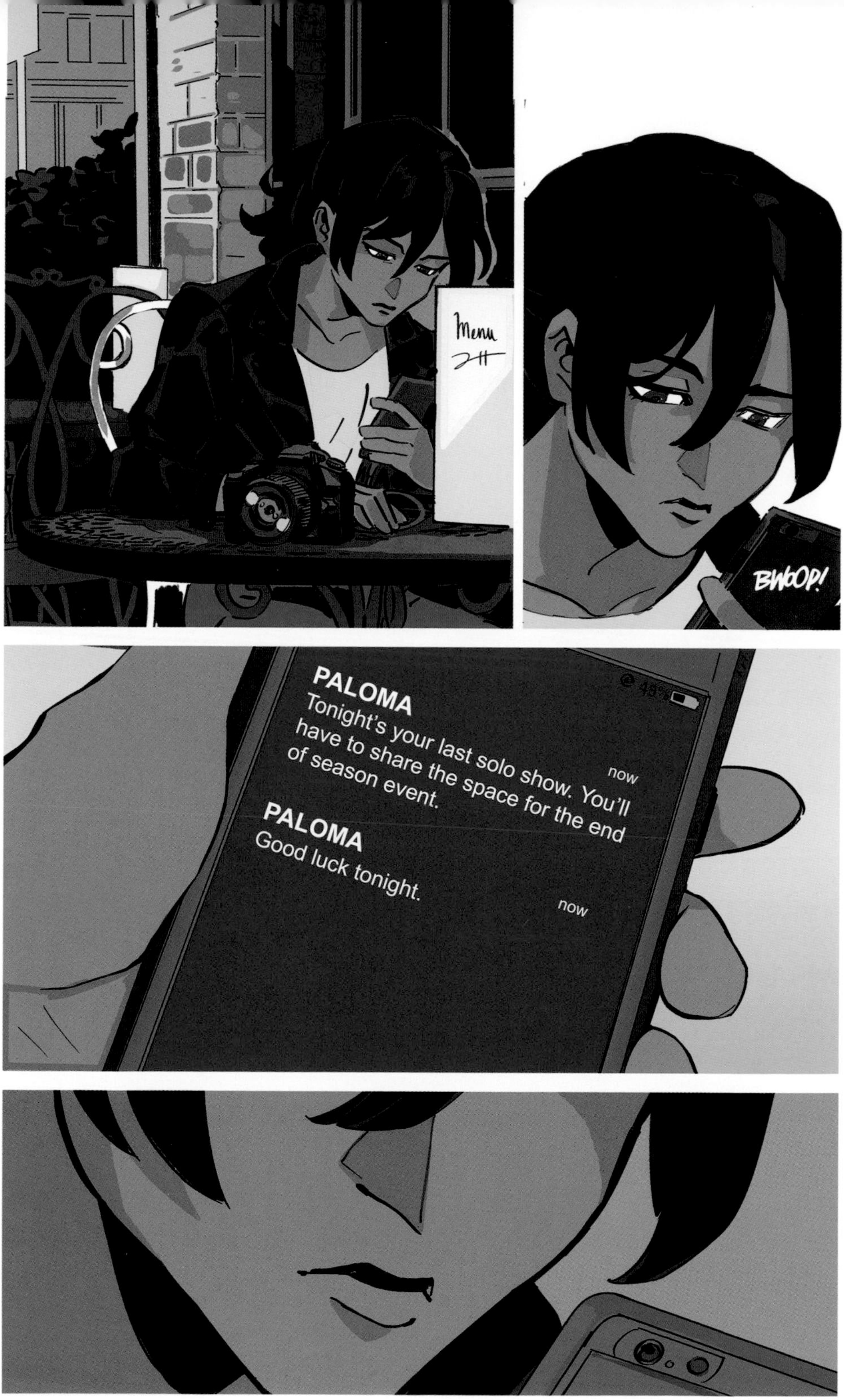
Menu
BWOOP!
PALOMA
Tonight's your last solo show. You'll have to share the space for the end of season event.
now
PALOMA
Good luck tonight.
now

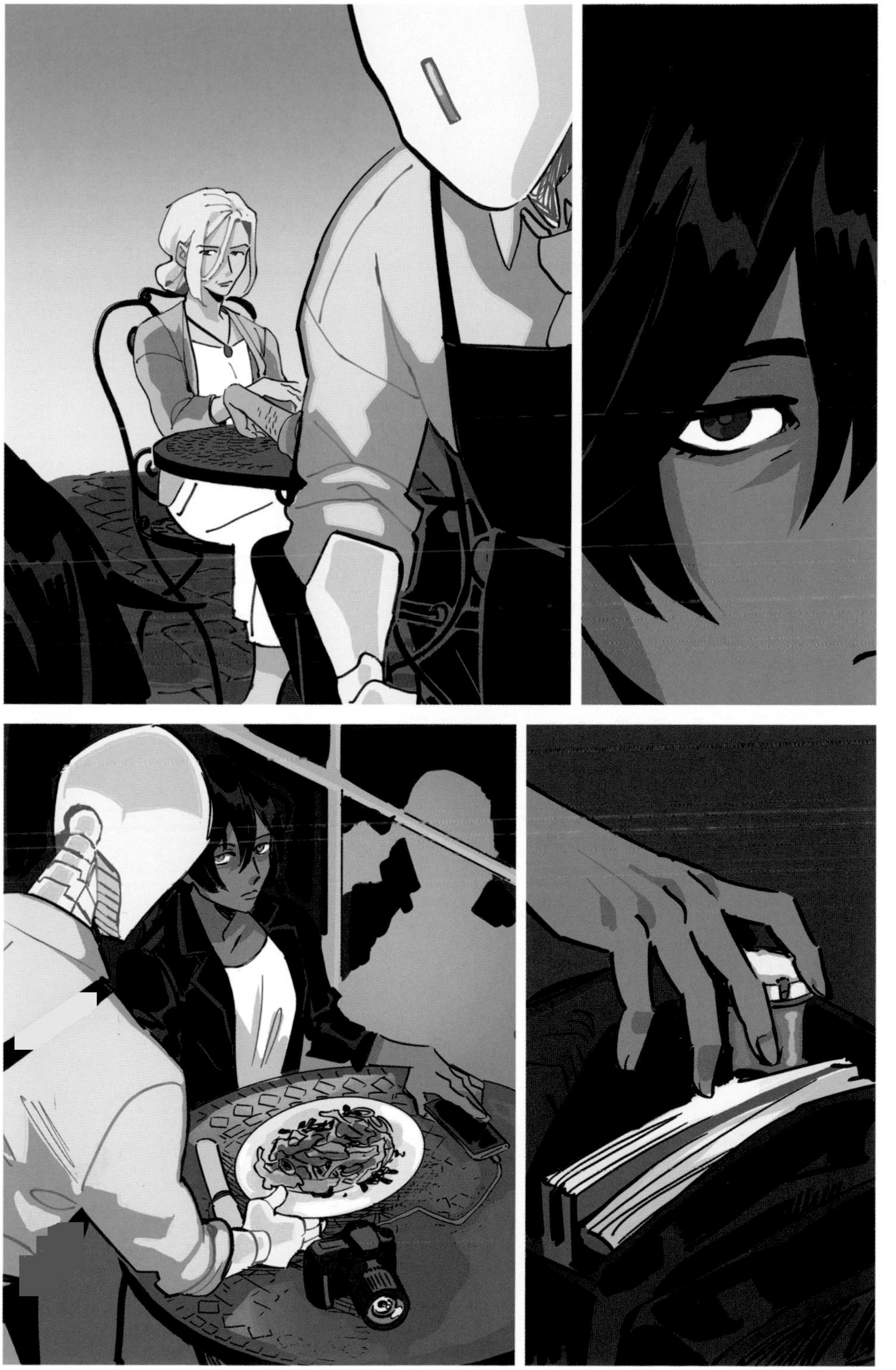

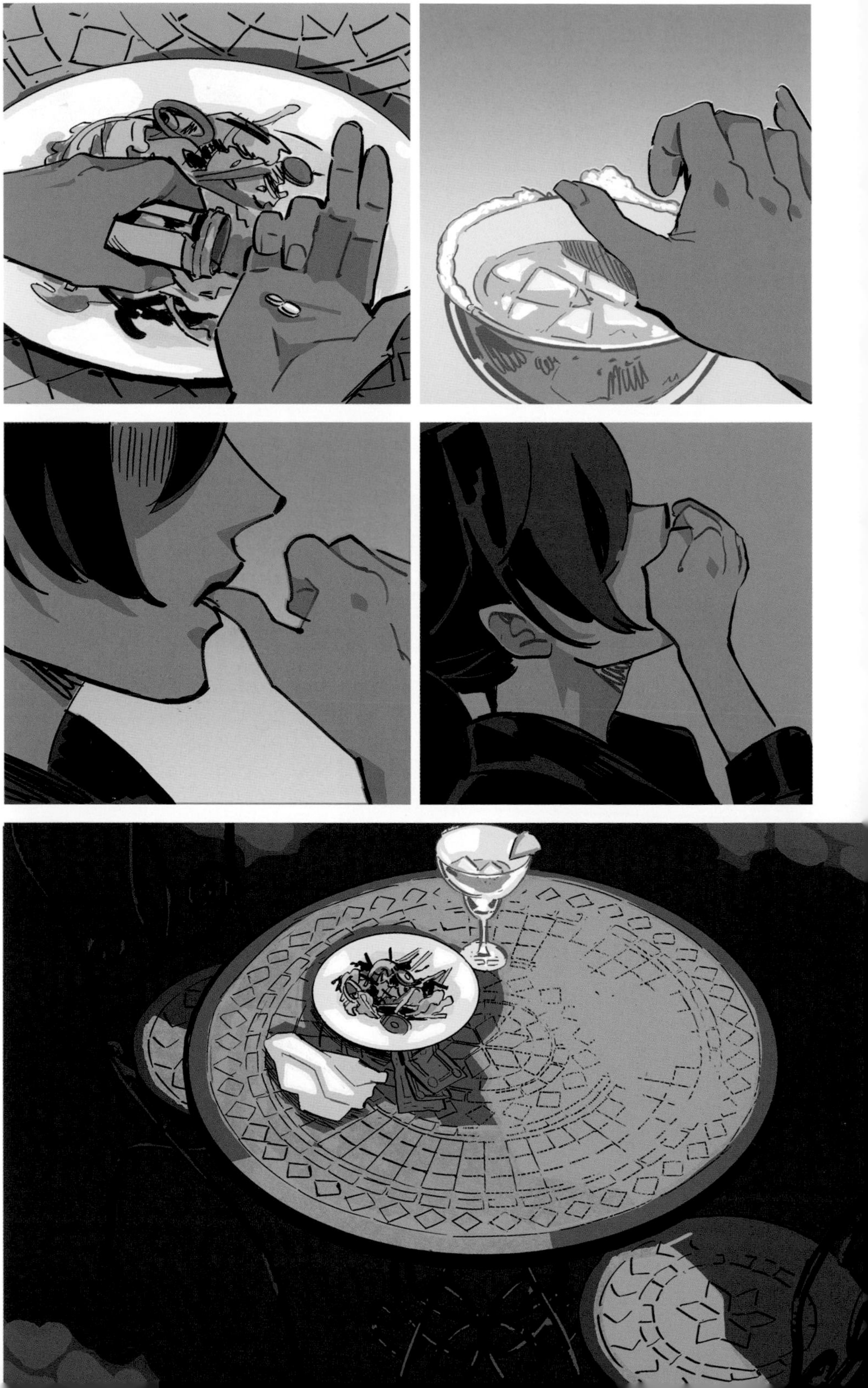

Companies scramble to scrap secret
AI recruiting tool that taught itself bias against
women's resumes: Experts worry that rather than
removing human bias from decision-making,
AI will recreate and automate it.

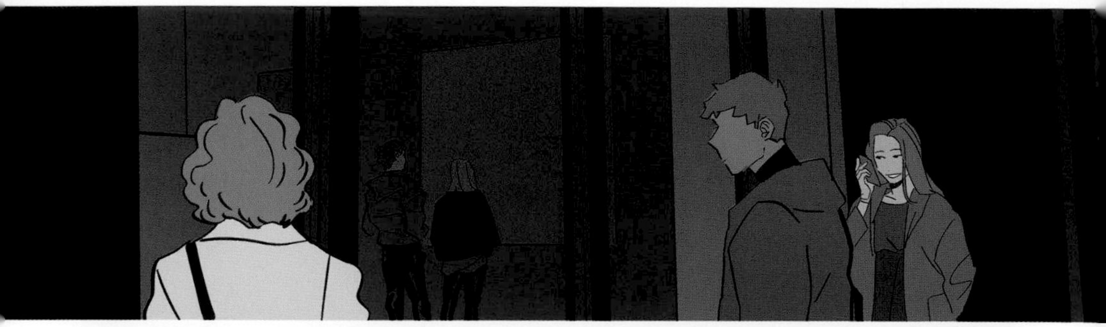

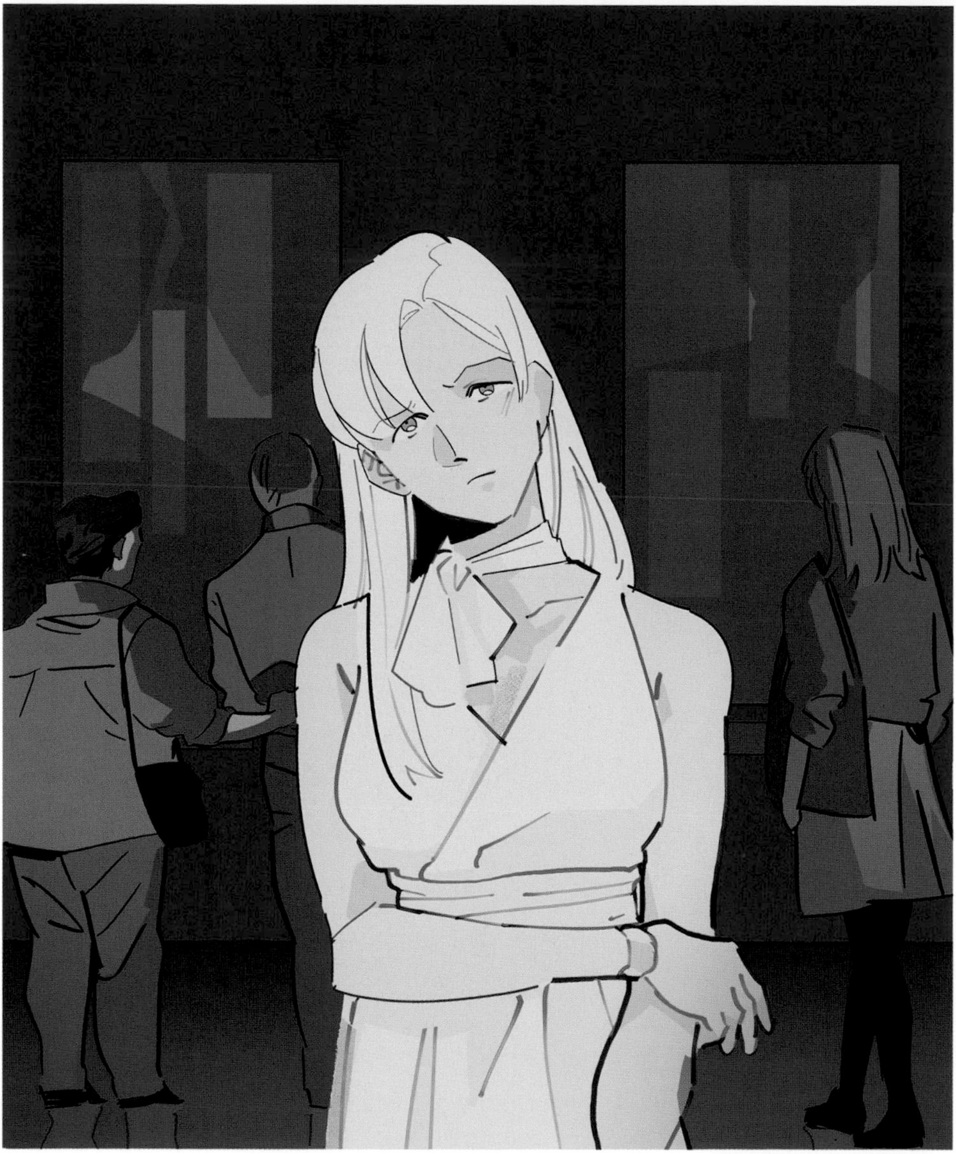

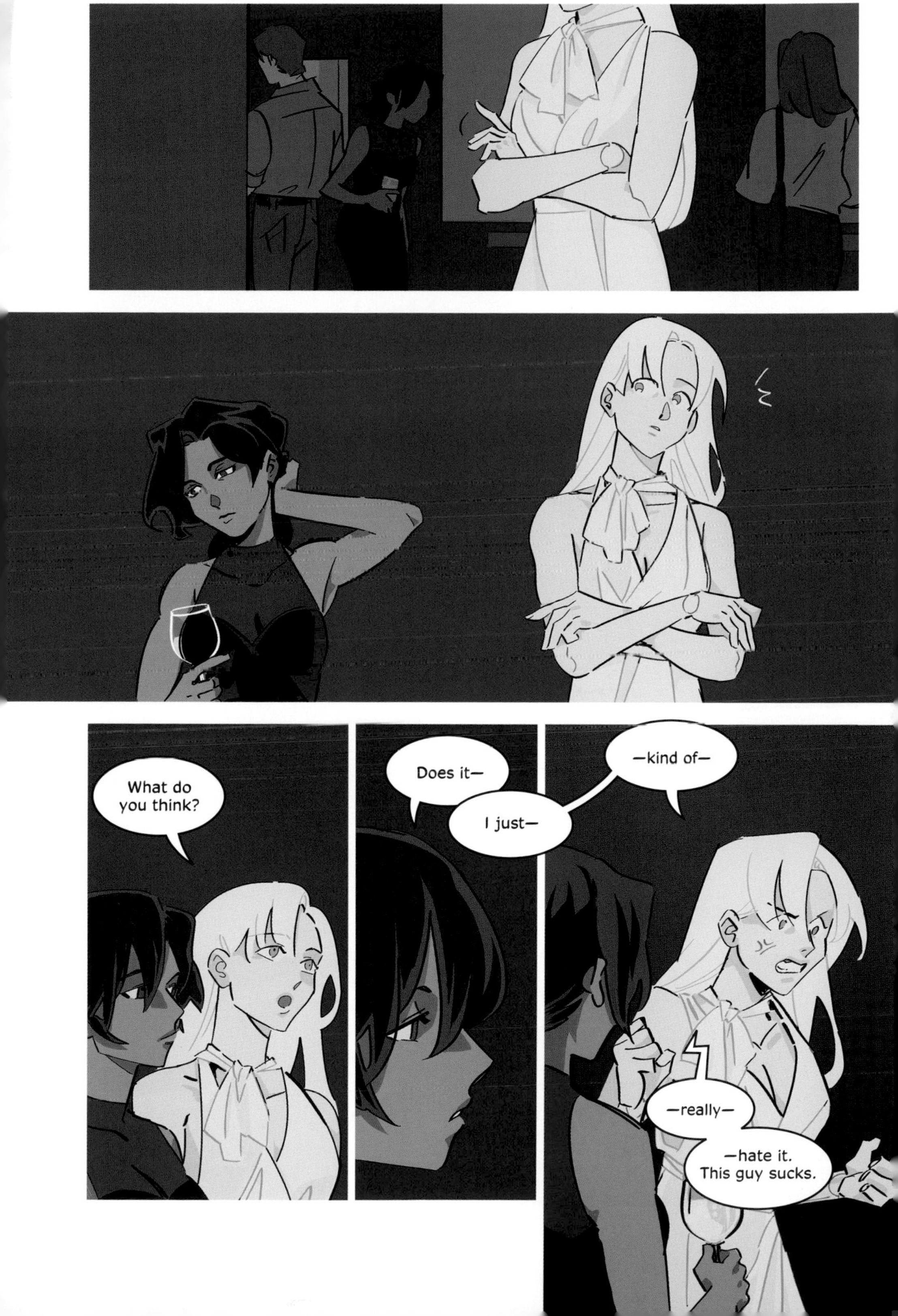
What do you think?
Does it—
I just—
—kind of—
—really—
—hate it. This guy sucks.

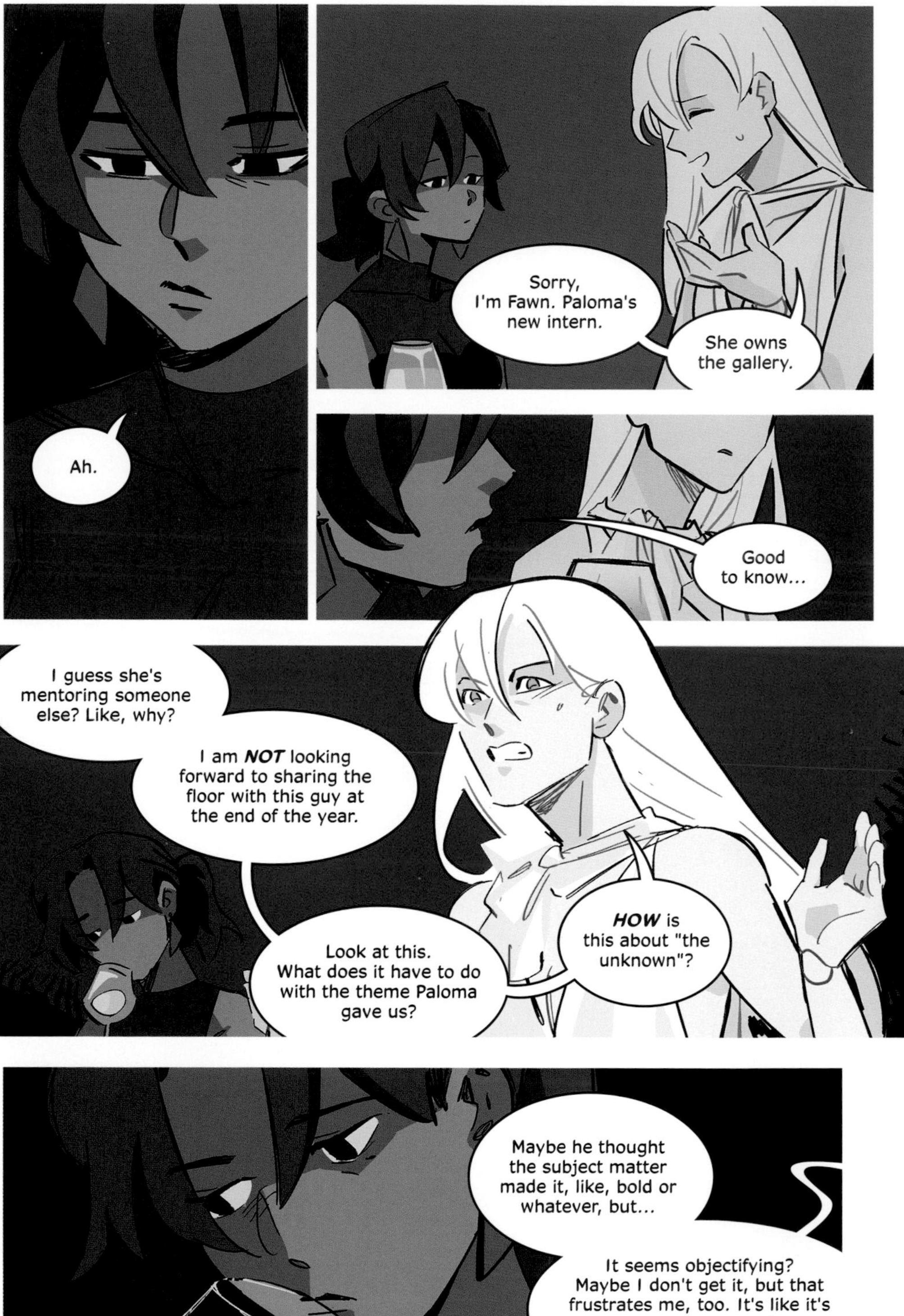

Sorry, I'm Fawn. Paloma's new intern.
She owns the gallery.
Ah.
Good to know...
I guess she's mentoring someone else? Like, why?
I am **NOT** looking forward to sharing the floor with this guy at the end of the year.
Look at this. What does it have to do with the theme Paloma gave us?
HOW is this about "the unknown"?
Maybe he thought the subject matter made it, like, bold or whatever, but...
It seems objectifying? Maybe I don't get it, but that frustrates me, too. It's like it's ***about*** me, but it's not ***for*** me.

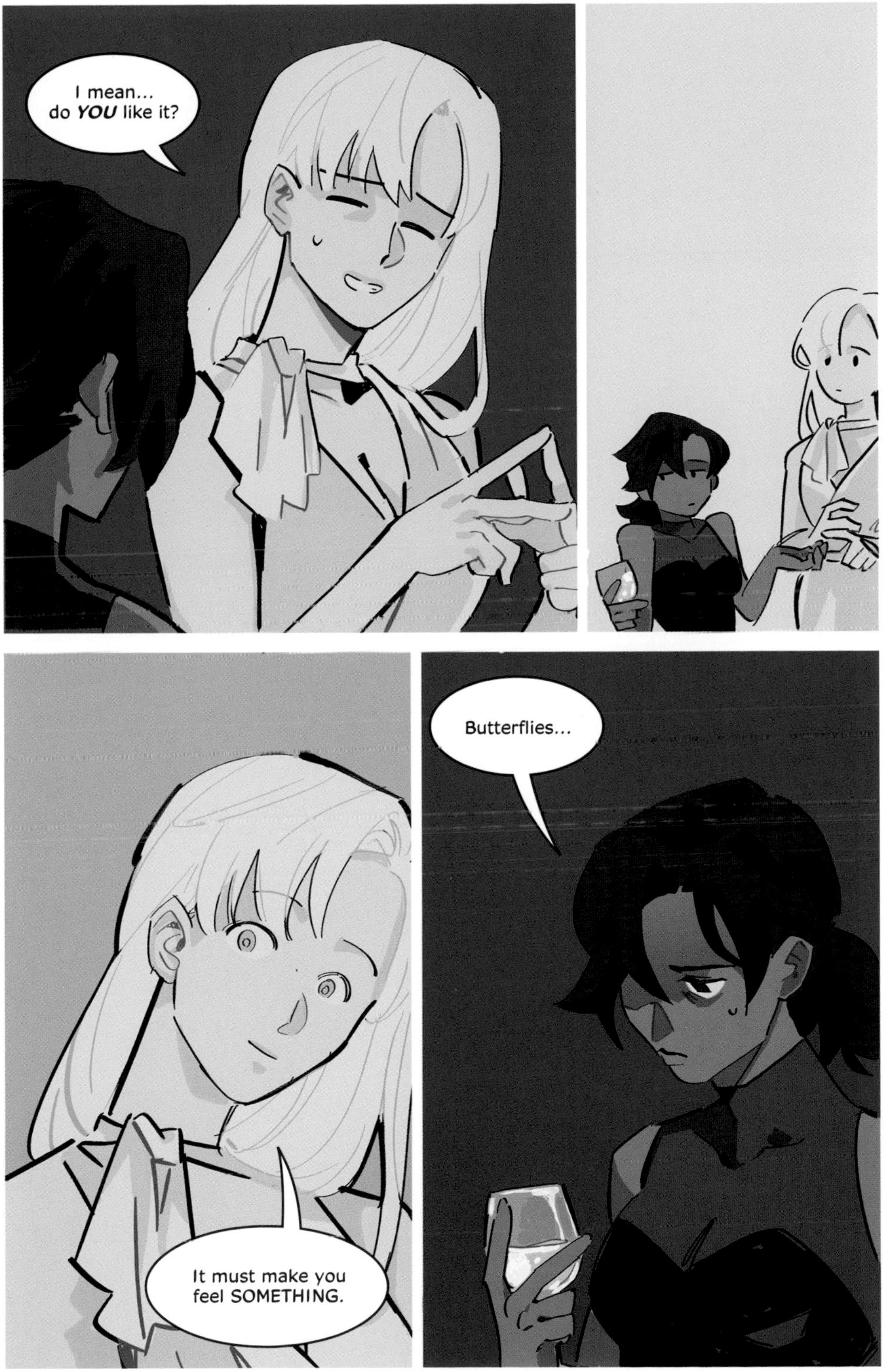
I mean... do ***YOU*** like it?
It must make you feel SOMETHING.
Butterflies...

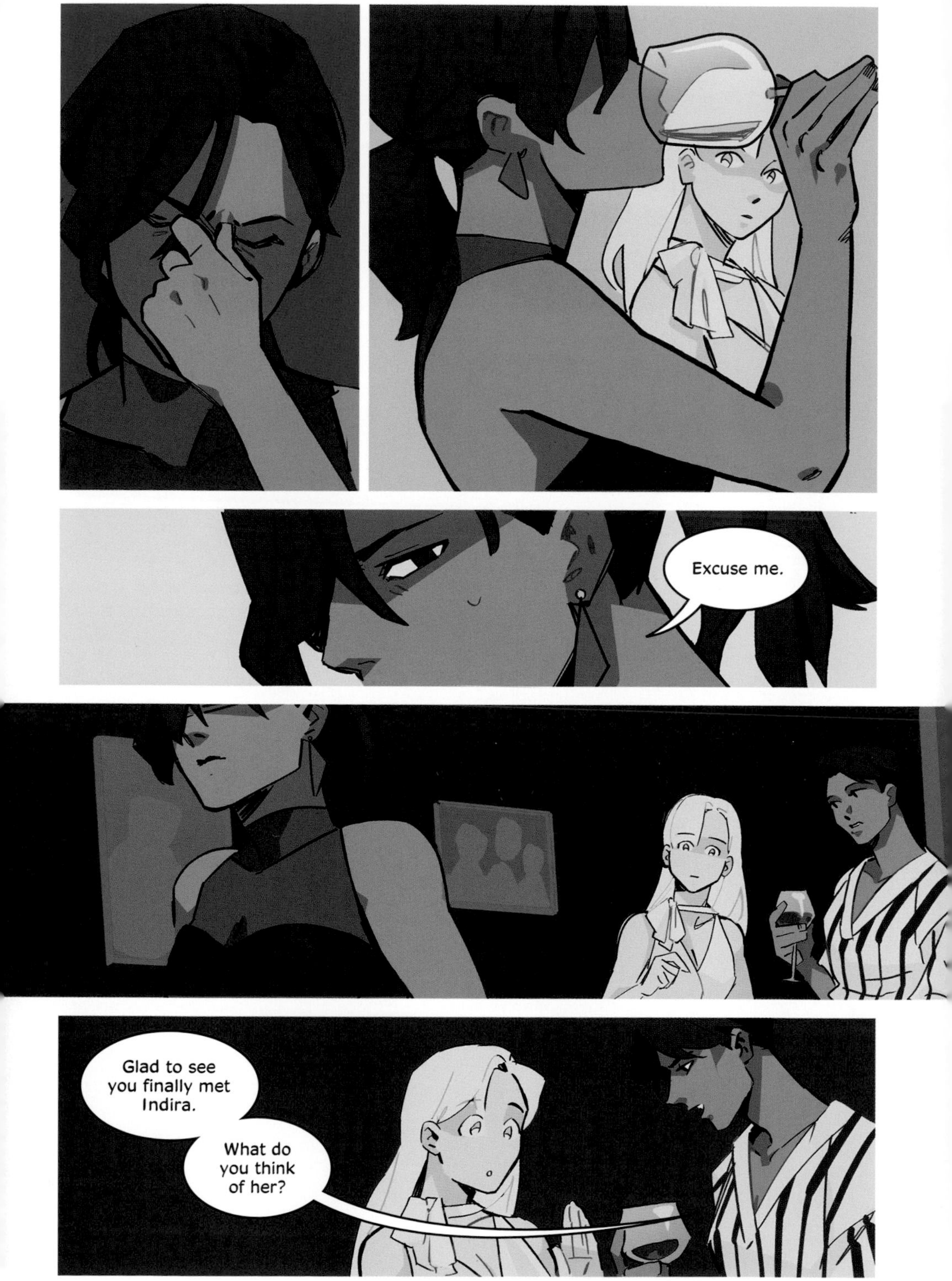

Excuse me.
Glad to see you finally met Indira.
What do you think of her?

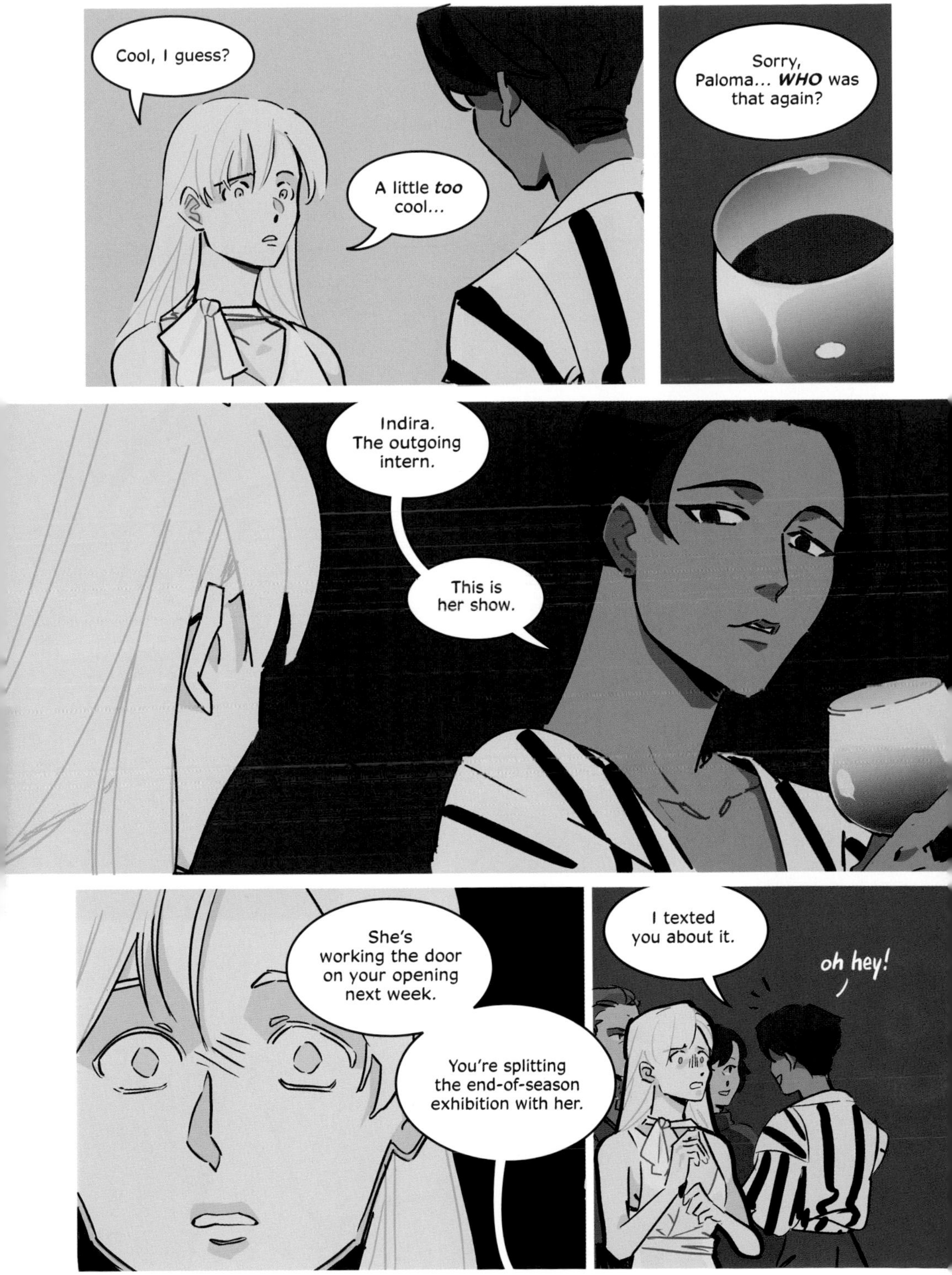
Cool, I guess?
A little *too* cool...
Sorry, Paloma... ***WHO*** was that again?
Indira. The outgoing intern.
This is her show.
She's working the door on your opening next week.
You're splitting the end-of-season exhibition with her.
I texted you about it.
oh hey!

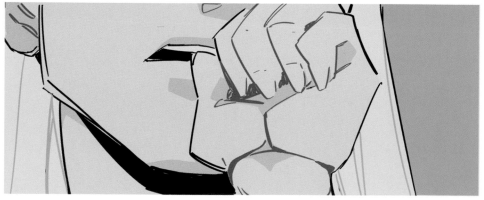

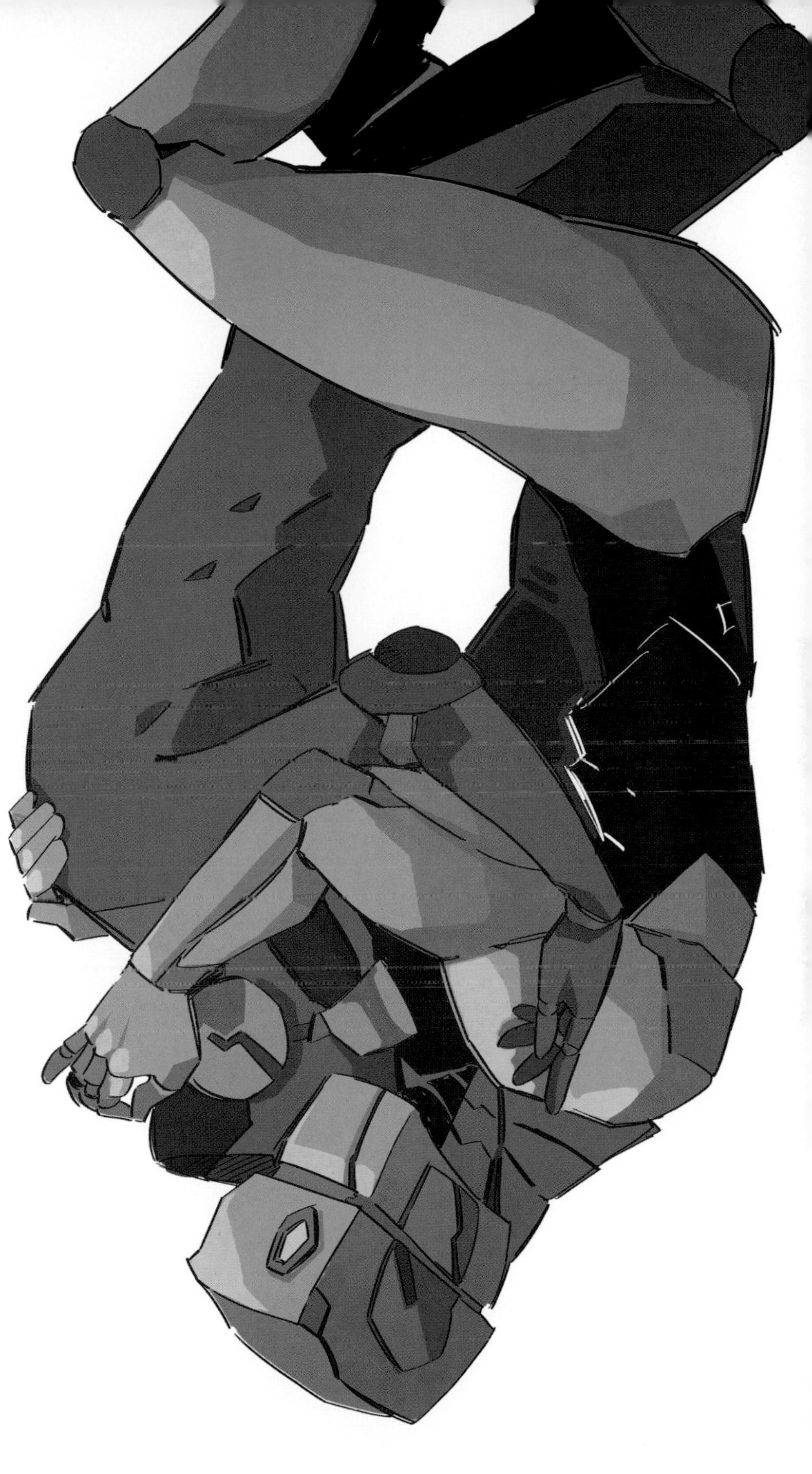

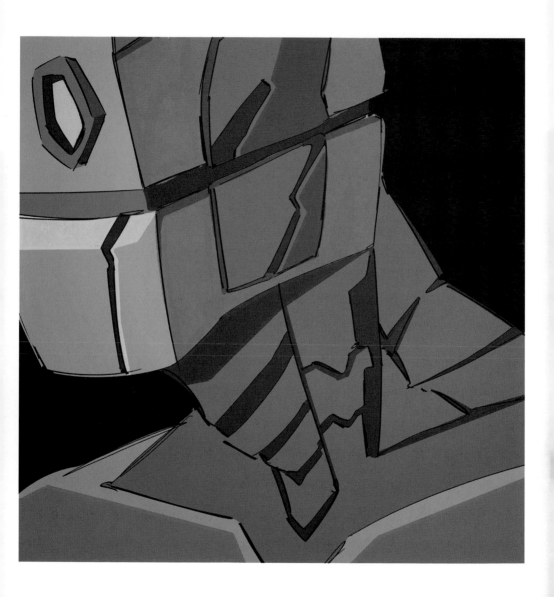

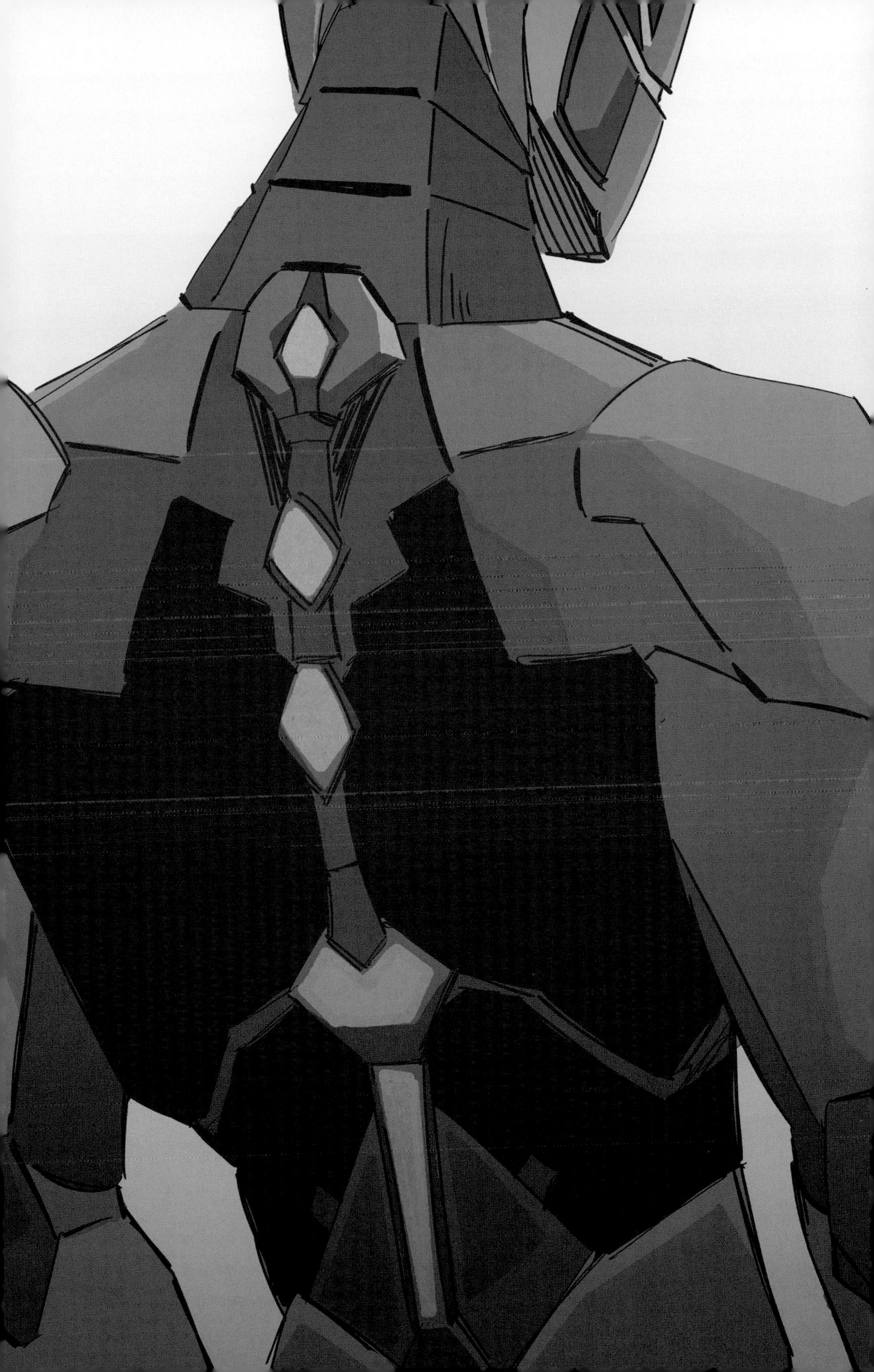

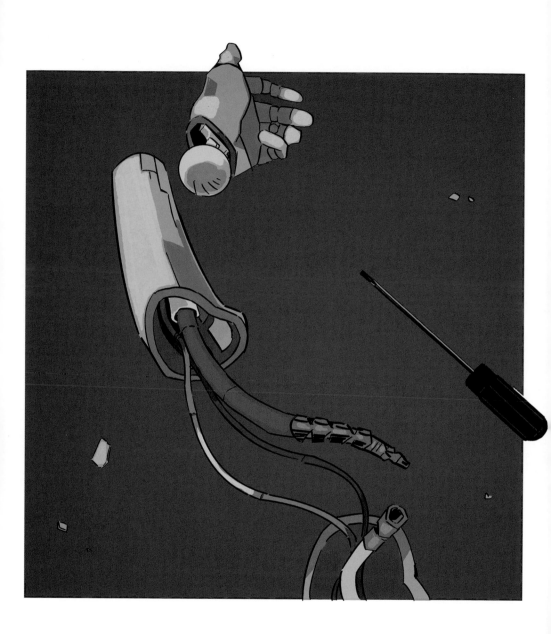

24

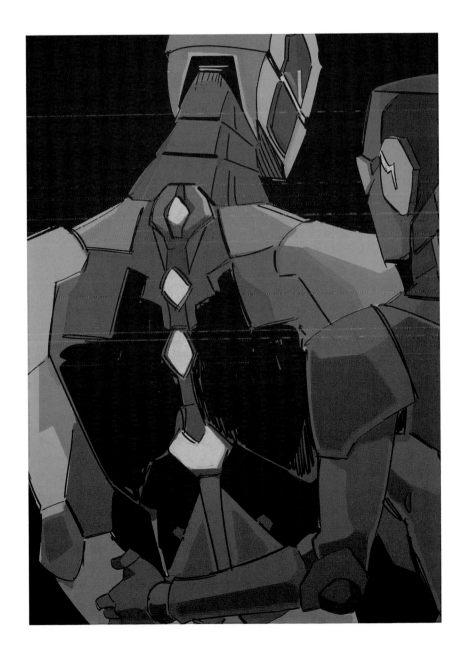

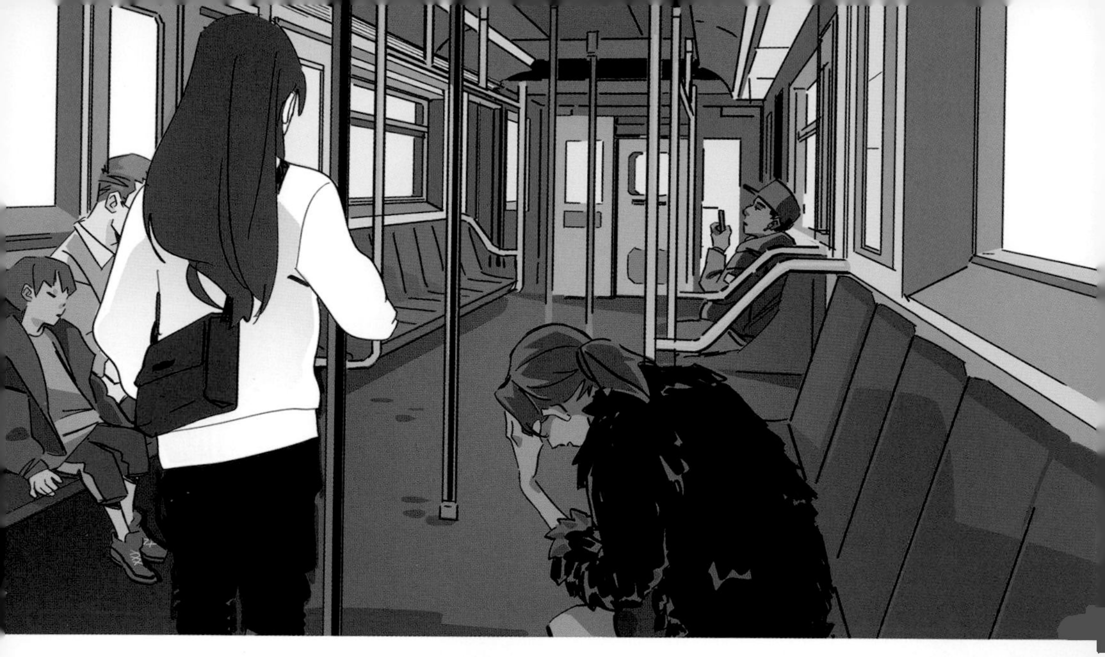
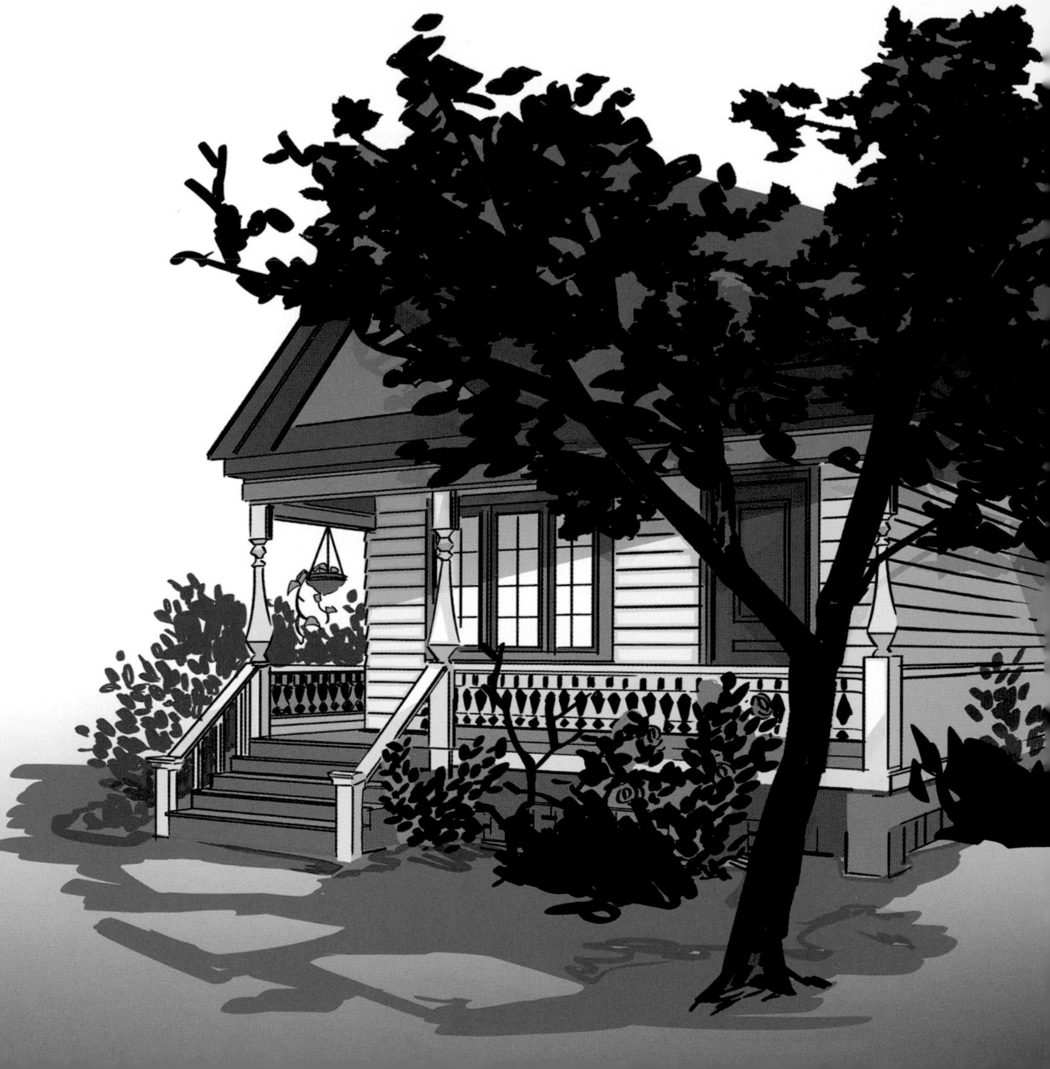

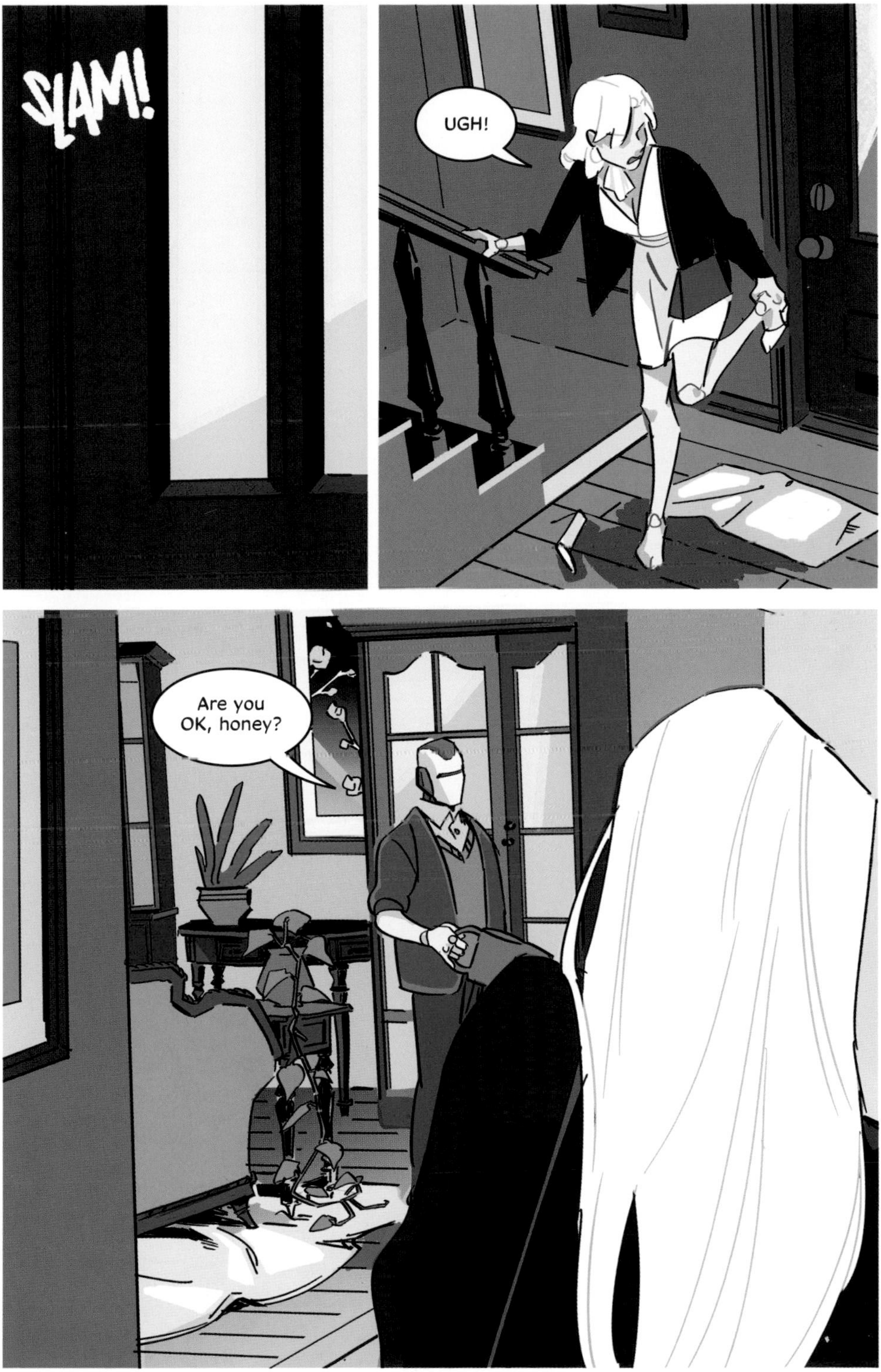
SLAM!
UGH!
Are you OK, honey?

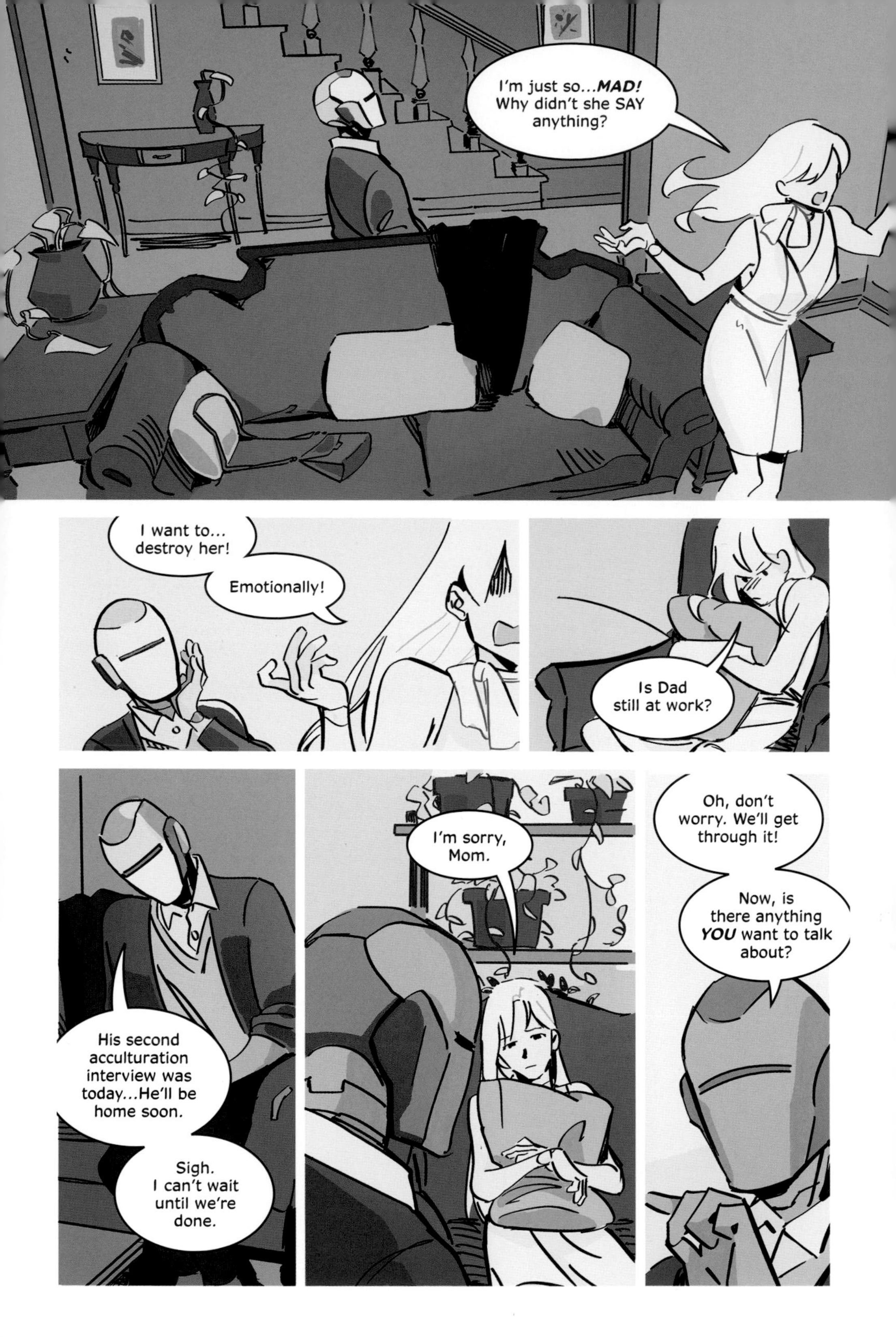
I'm just so...***MAD!*** Why didn't she SAY anything?
I want to... destroy her!
Emotionally!
Is Dad still at work?
His second acculturation interview was today...He'll be home soon.
Sigh. I can't wait until we're done.
I'm sorry, Mom.
Oh, don't worry. We'll get through it!
Now, is there anything ***YOU*** want to talk about?

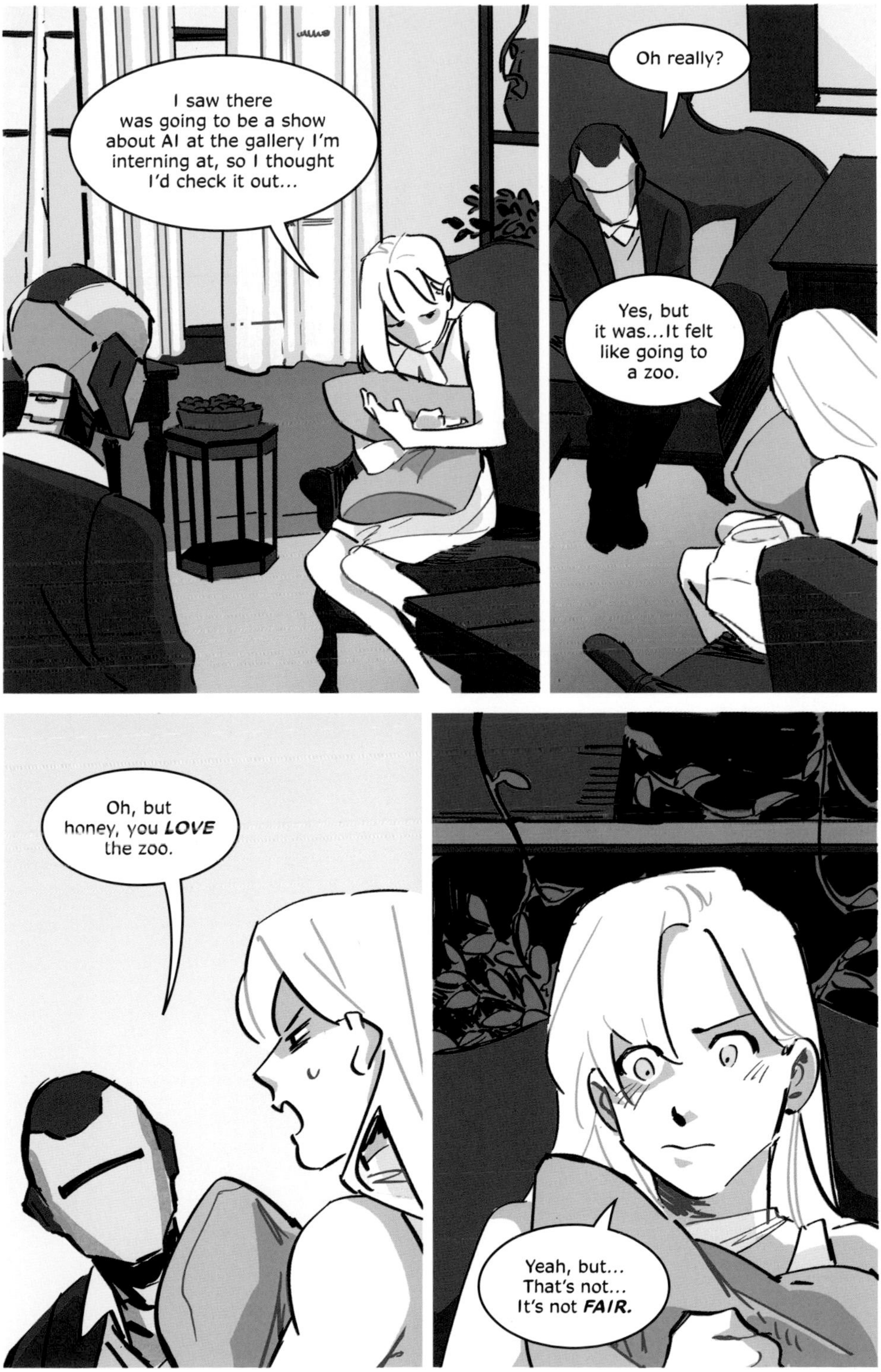
I saw there was going to be a show about AI at the gallery I'm interning at, so I thought I'd check it out...
Oh really?
Yes, but it was...It felt like going to a zoo.
Oh, but honey, you ***LOVE*** the zoo.
Yeah, but... That's not... It's not ***FAIR.***

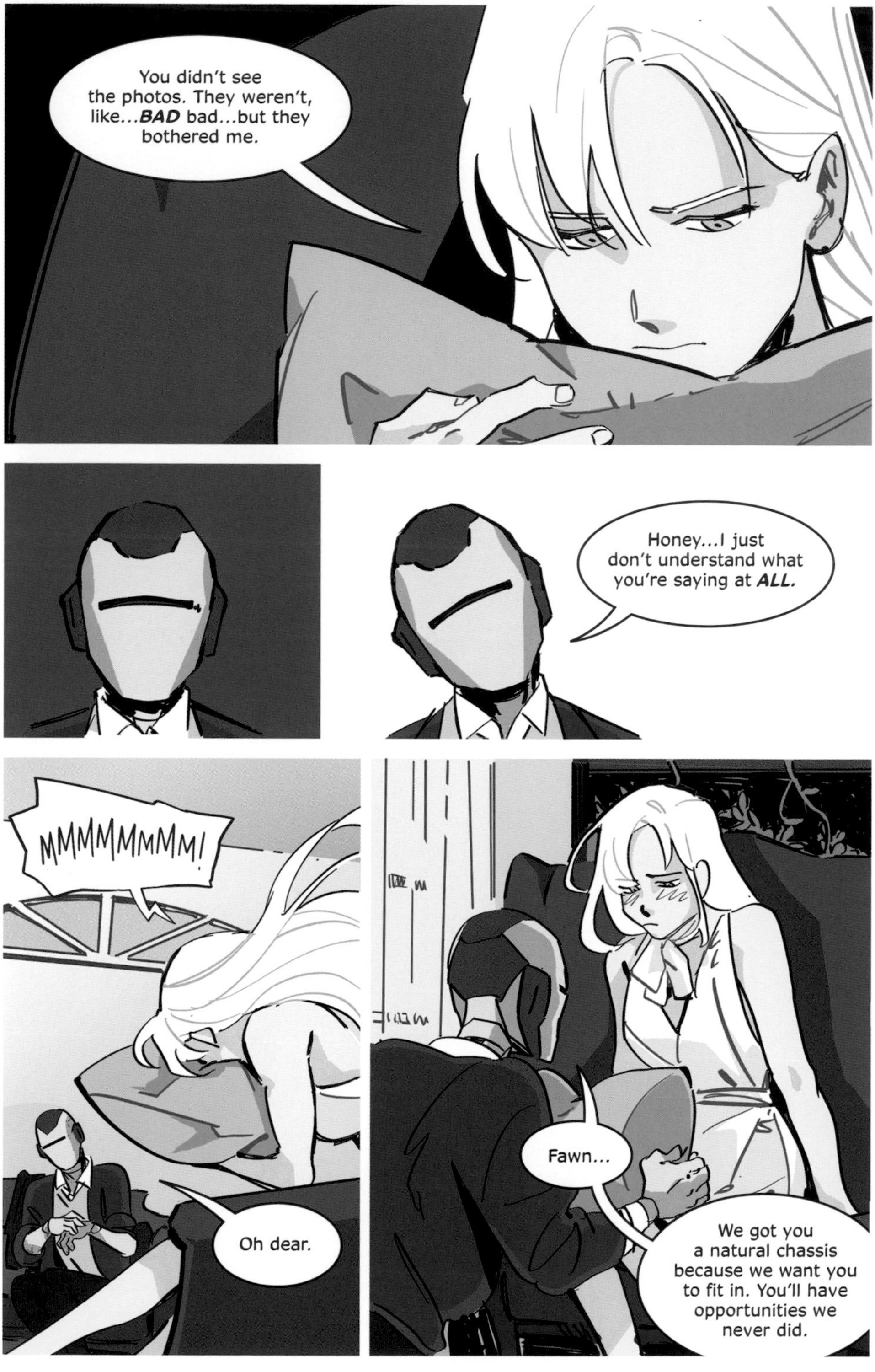
You didn't see the photos. They weren't, like...***BAD*** bad...but they bothered me.
Honey...I just don't understand what you're saying at ***ALL.***
MMMMMMMM!
Oh dear.
Fawn...
We got you a natural chassis because we want you to fit in. You'll have opportunities we never did.

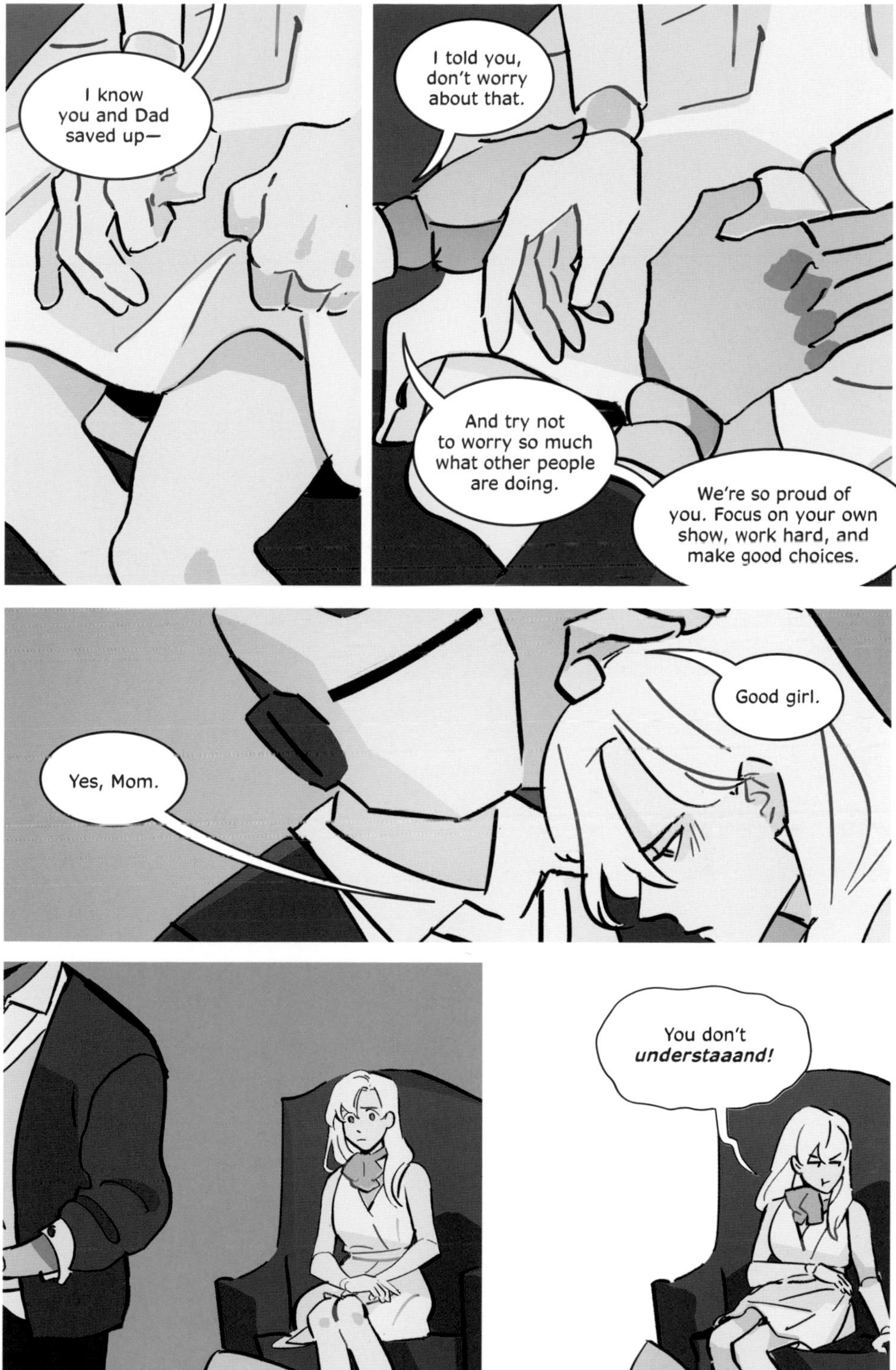
I know you and Dad saved up—
I told you, don't worry about that.
And try not to worry so much what other people are doing.
We're so proud of you. Focus on your own show, work hard, and make good choices.
Good girl.
Yes, Mom.
You don't *understaaand!*

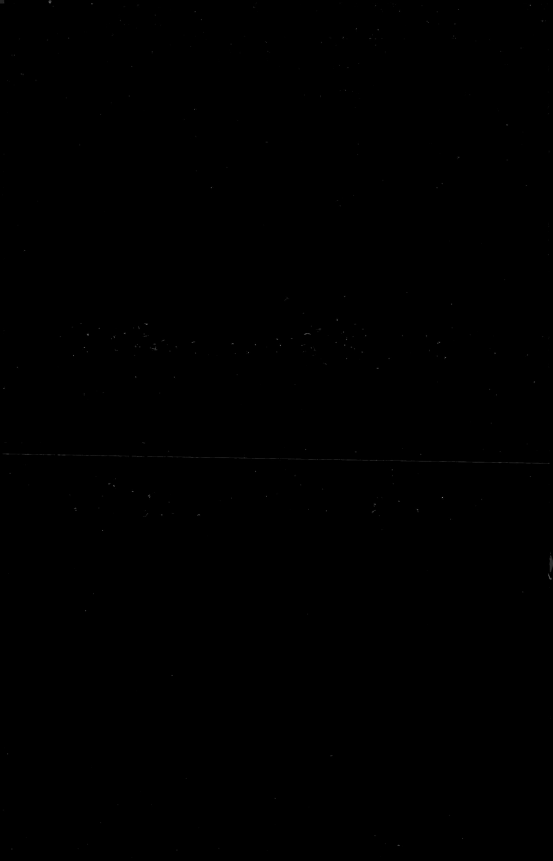

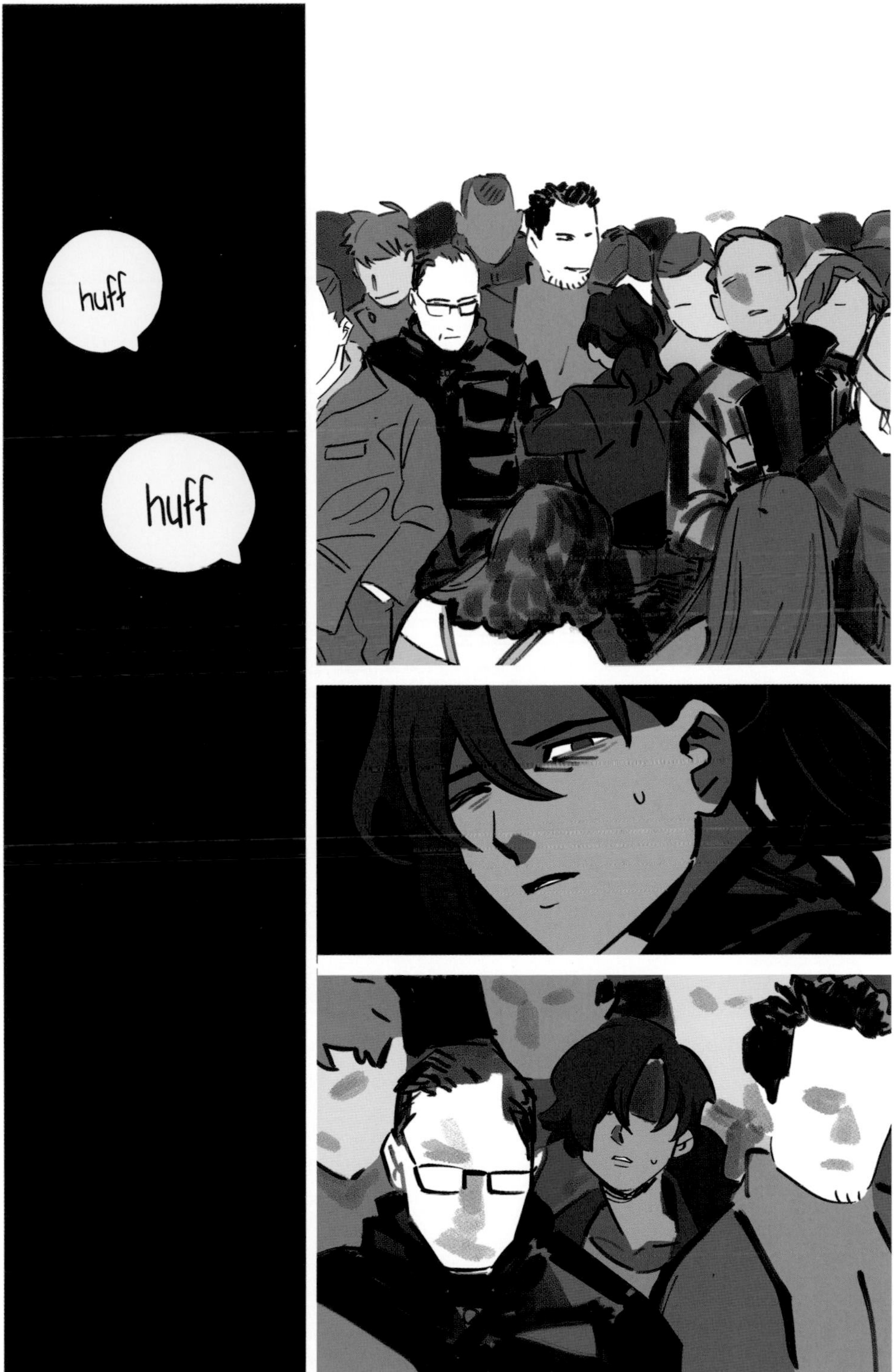
huff
huff

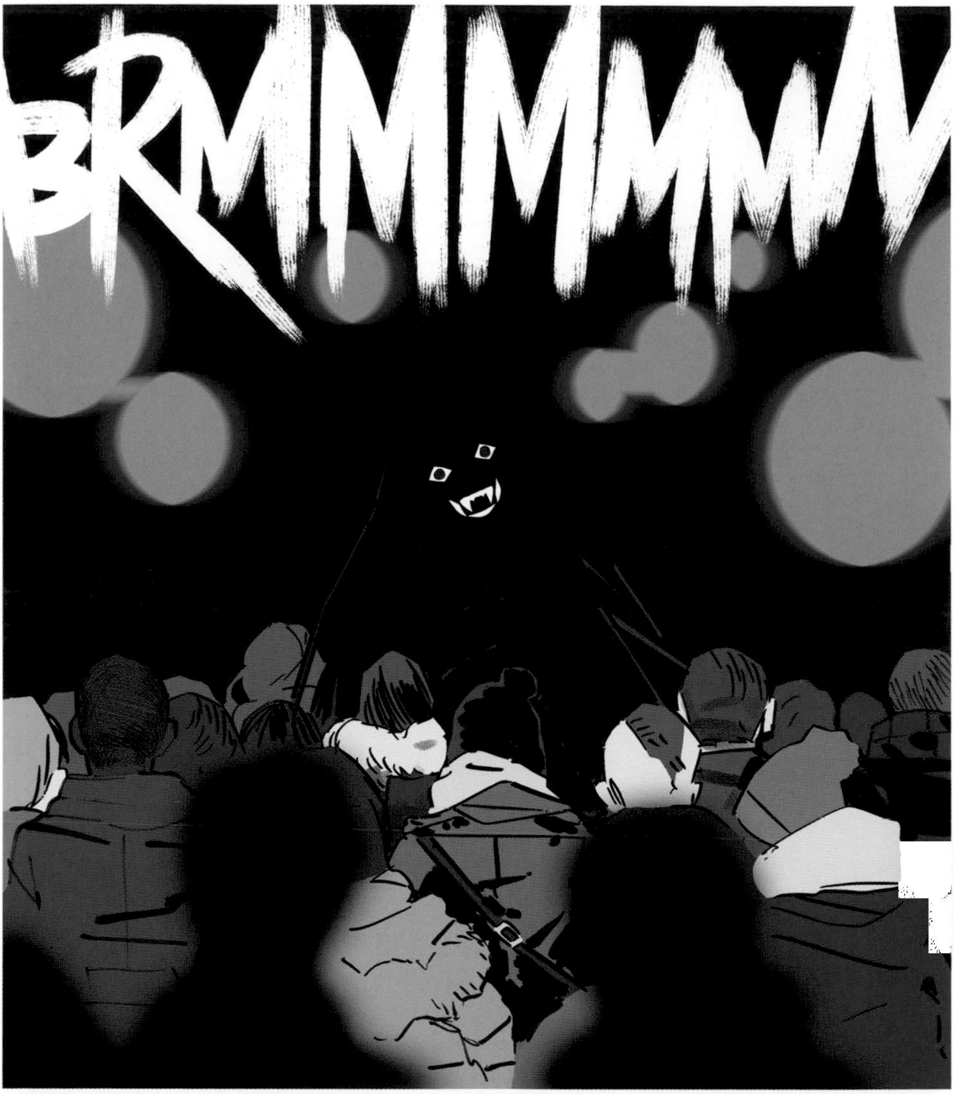
BRMMMMMM

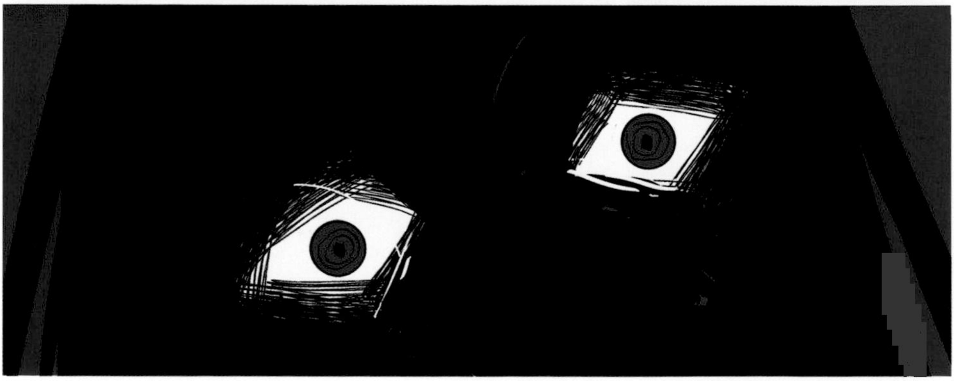

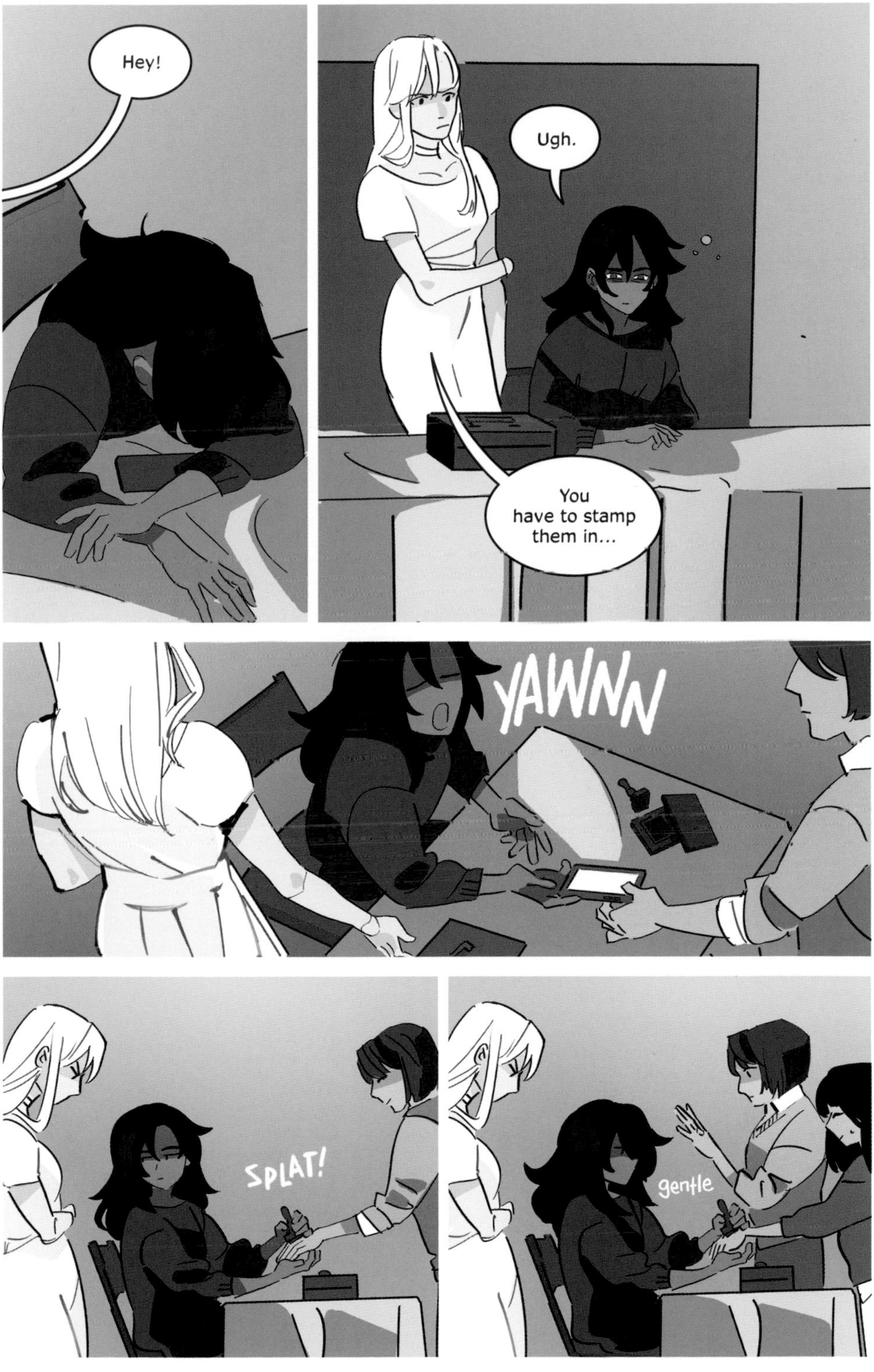
Hey!
Ugh.
You have to stamp them in...
YAWNN
SPLAT!
gentle

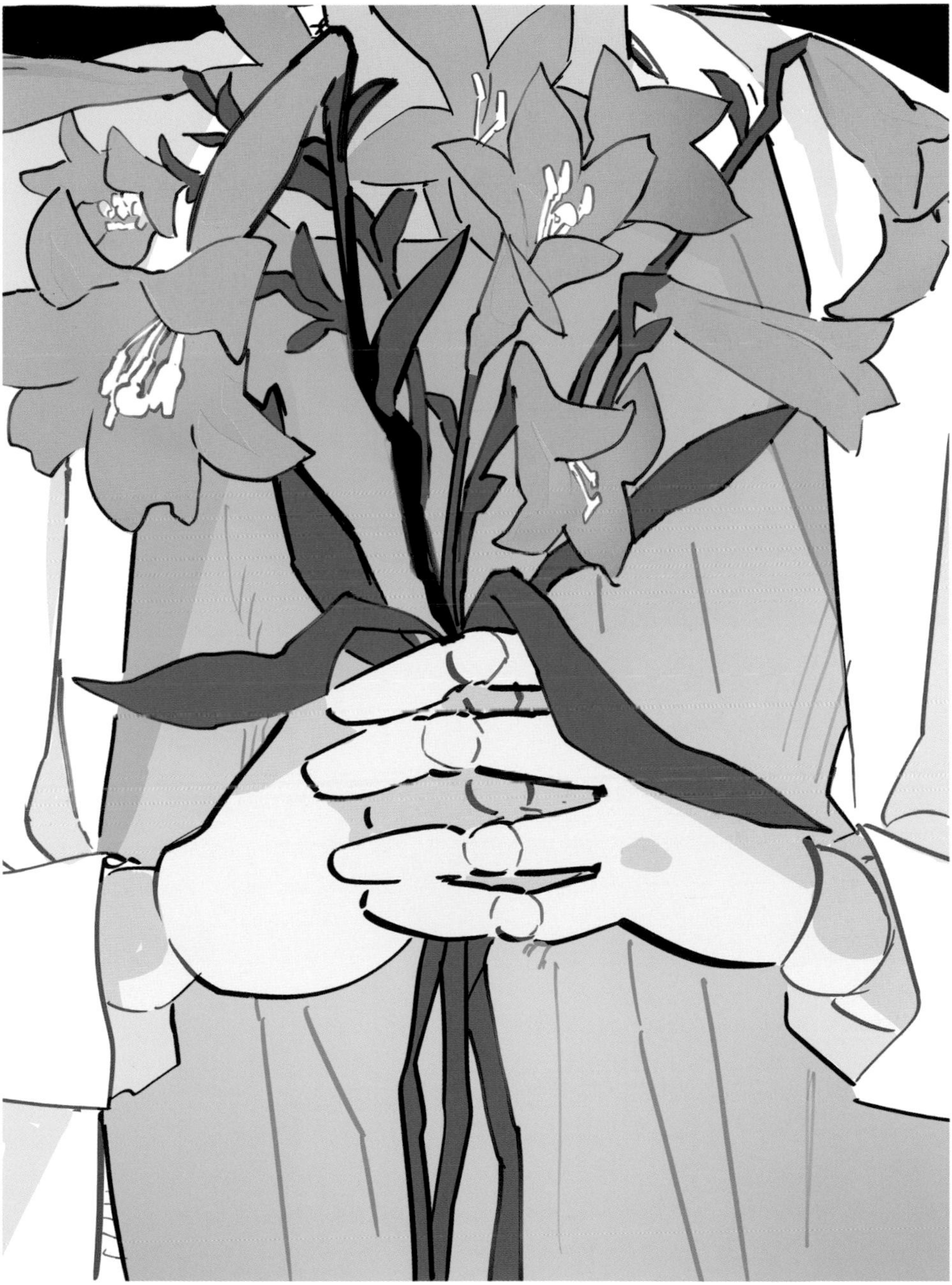

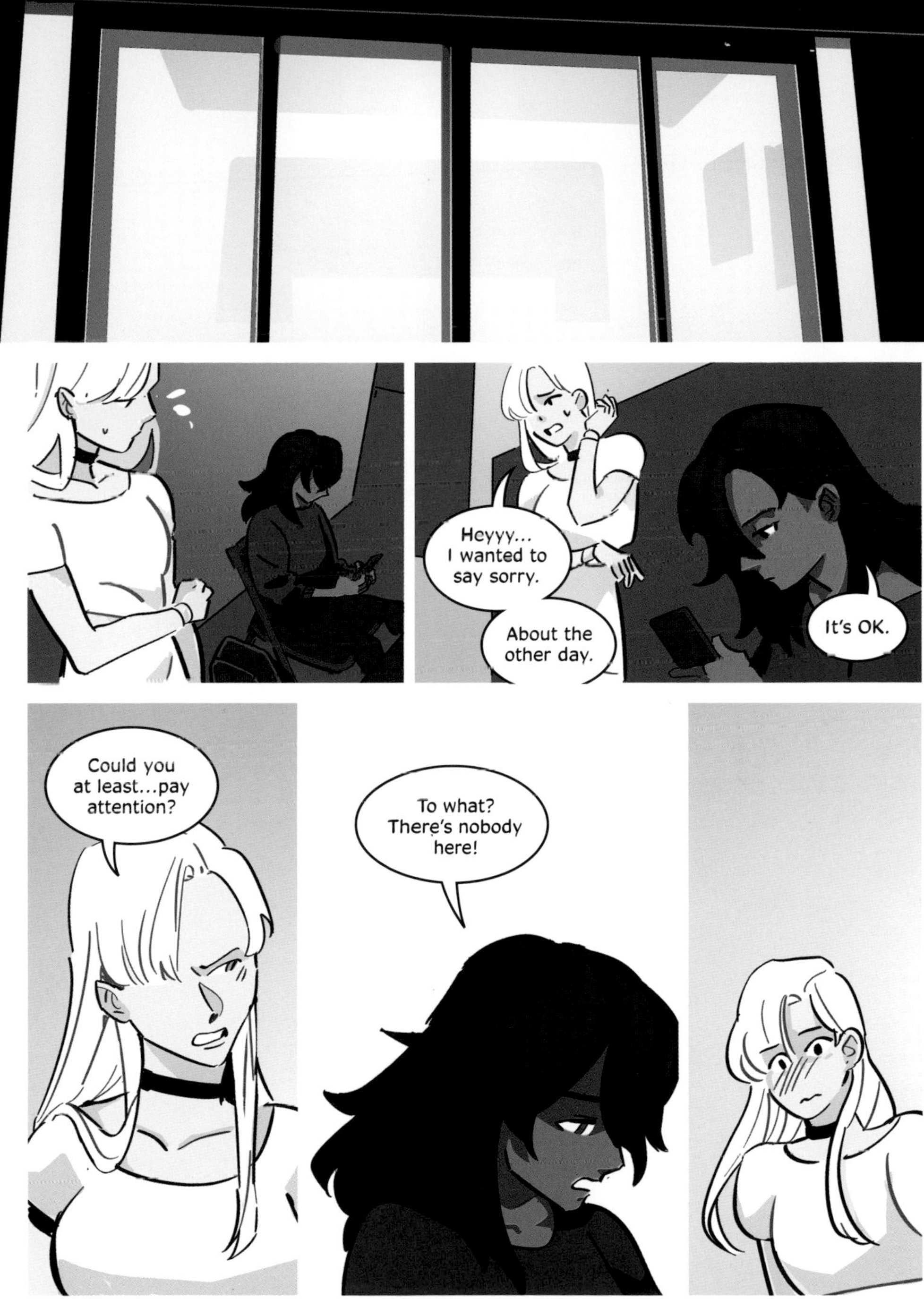
Heyyy... I wanted to say sorry.
About the other day.
It's OK.
Could you at least...pay attention?
To what? There's nobody here!

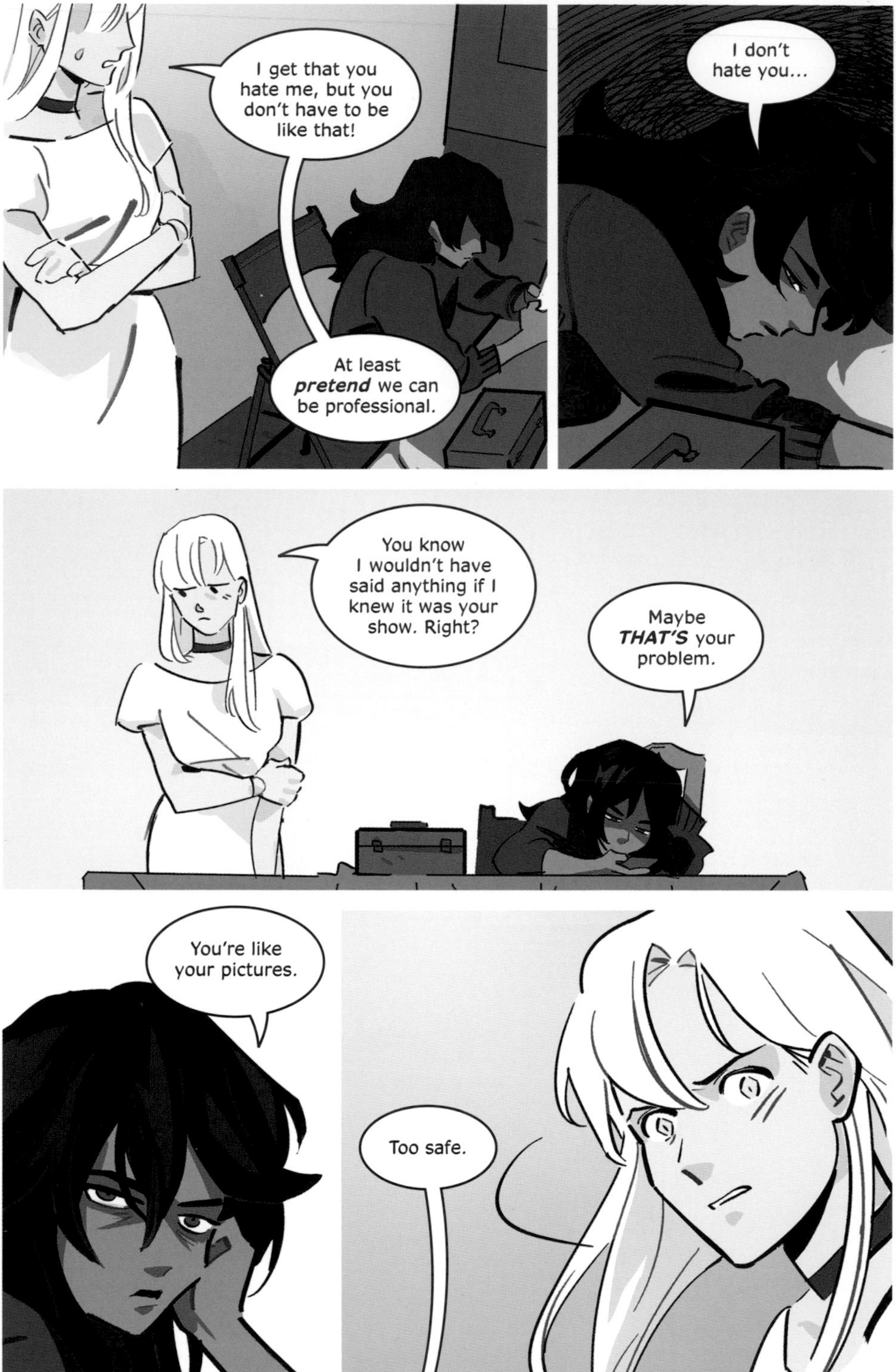
I get that you hate me, but you don't have to be like that!
At least *pretend* we can be professional.
I don't hate you...
You know I wouldn't have said anything if I knew it was your show. Right?
Maybe **THAT'S** your problem.
You're like your pictures.
Too safe.

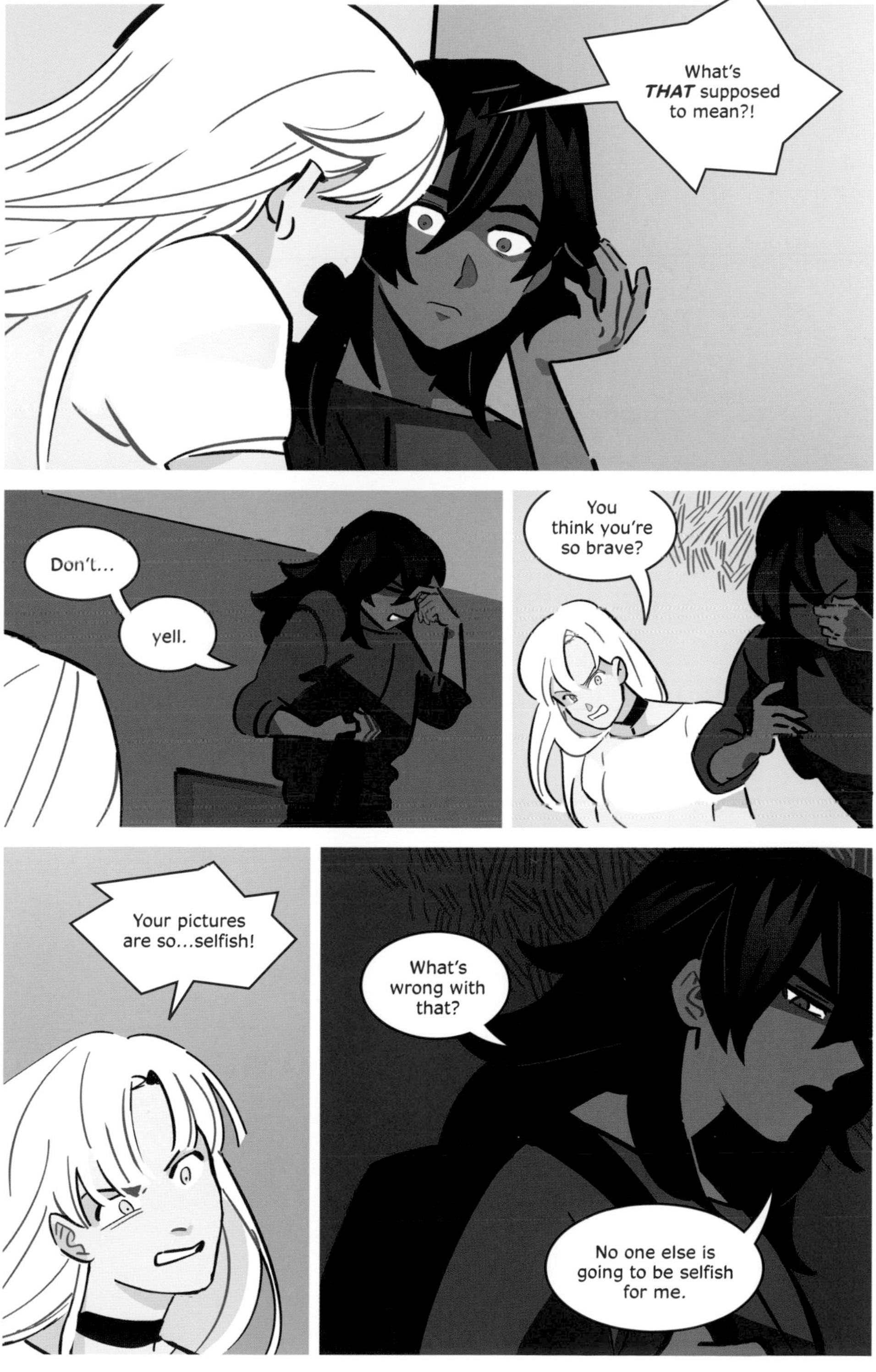
What's *THAT* supposed to mean?!
Don't...
yell.
You think you're so brave?
Your pictures are so...selfish!
What's wrong with that?
No one else is going to be selfish for me.

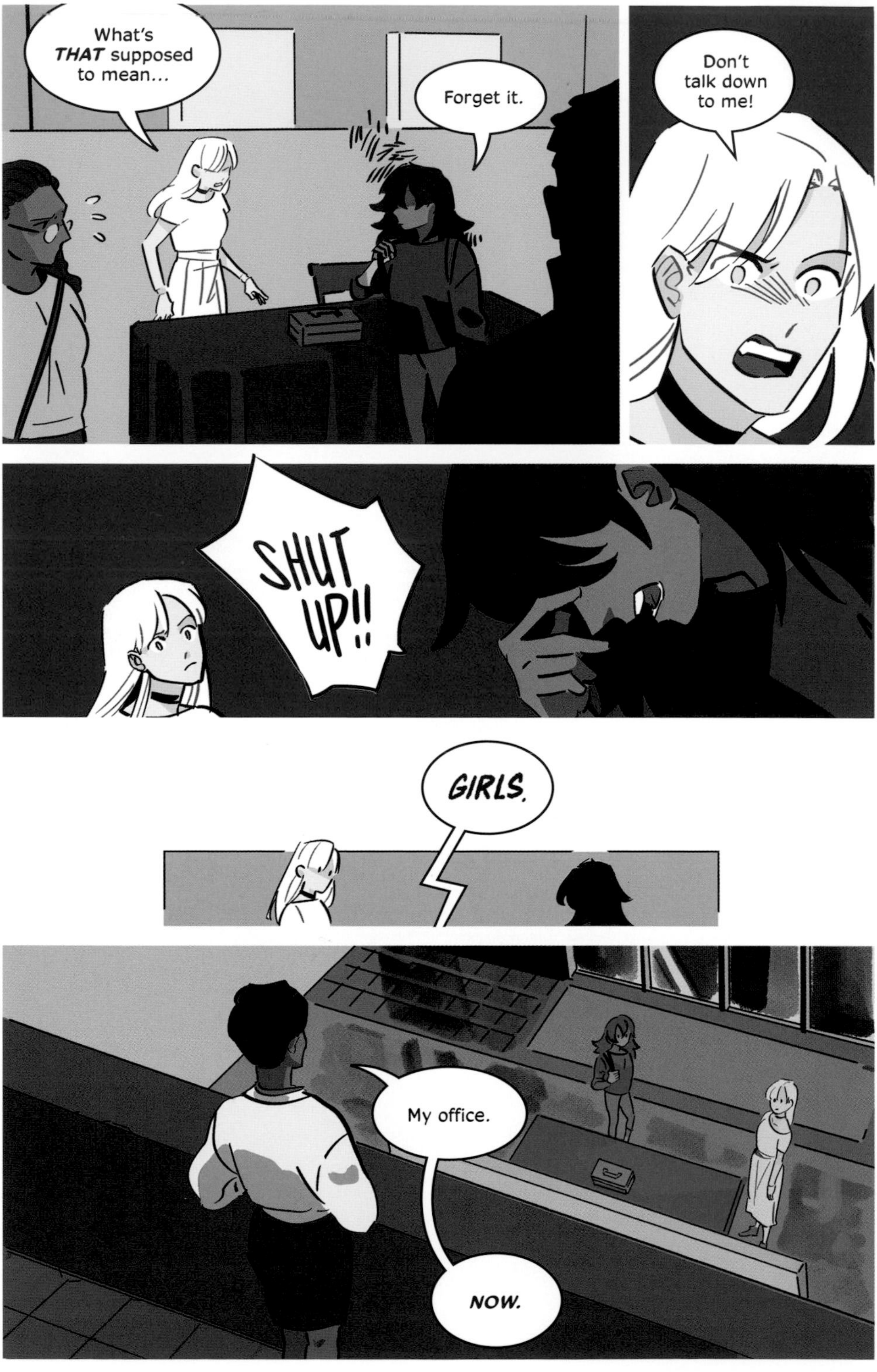
What's *THAT* supposed to mean...
Forget it.
Don't talk down to me!
SHUT UP!!
GIRLS.
My office.
NOW.

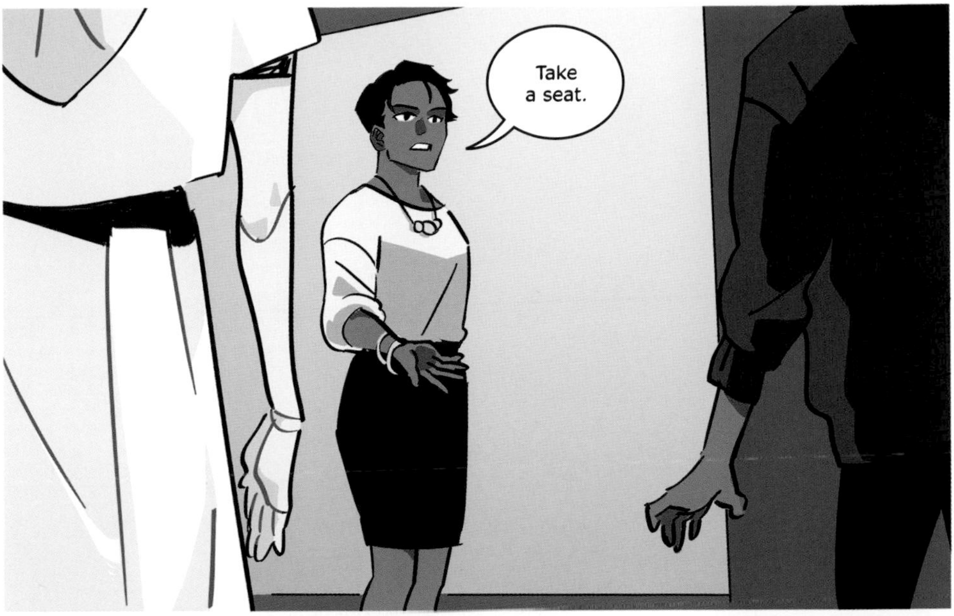
Take
a seat.

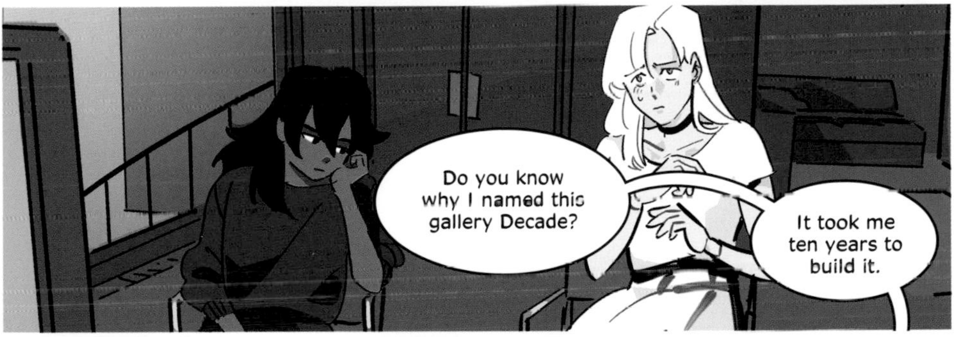
Do you know
why I named this
gallery Decade?
It took me
ten years to
build it.

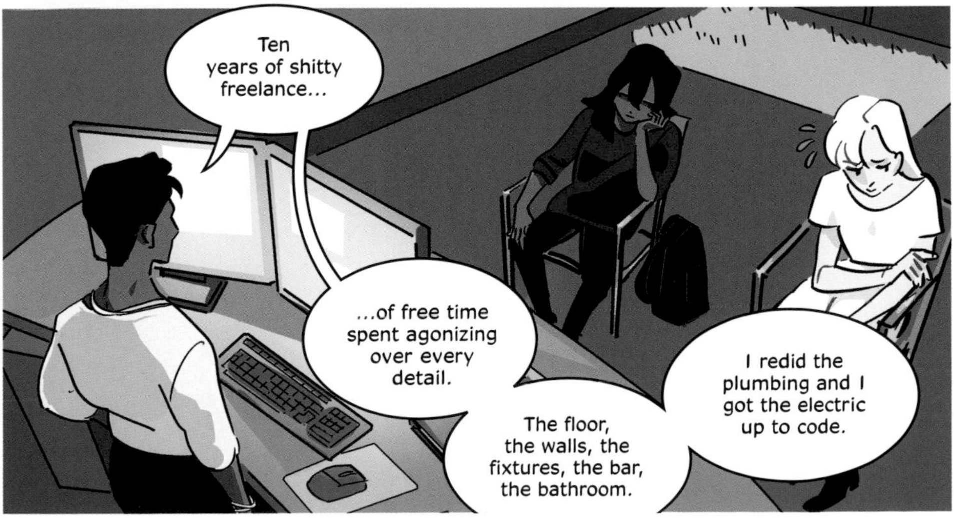
Ten
years of shitty
freelance...
...of free time
spent agonizing
over every
detail.
The floor,
the walls, the
fixtures, the bar,
the bathroom.
I redid the
plumbing and I
got the electric
up to code.

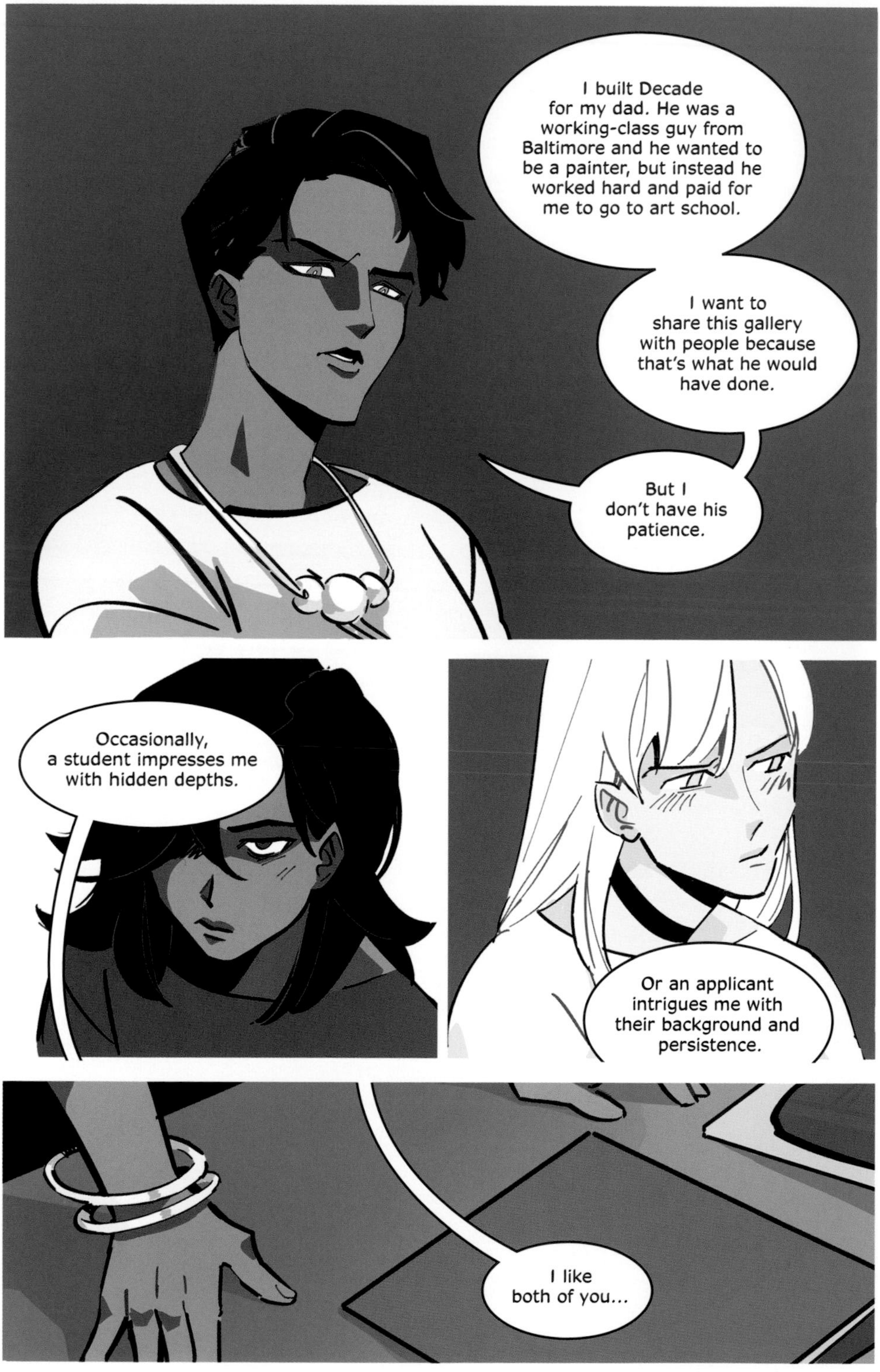
I built Decade for my dad. He was a working-class guy from Baltimore and he wanted to be a painter, but instead he worked hard and paid for me to go to art school.
I want to share this gallery with people because that's what he would have done.
But I don't have his patience.
Occasionally, a student impresses me with hidden depths.
Or an applicant intrigues me with their background and persistence.
I like both of you...

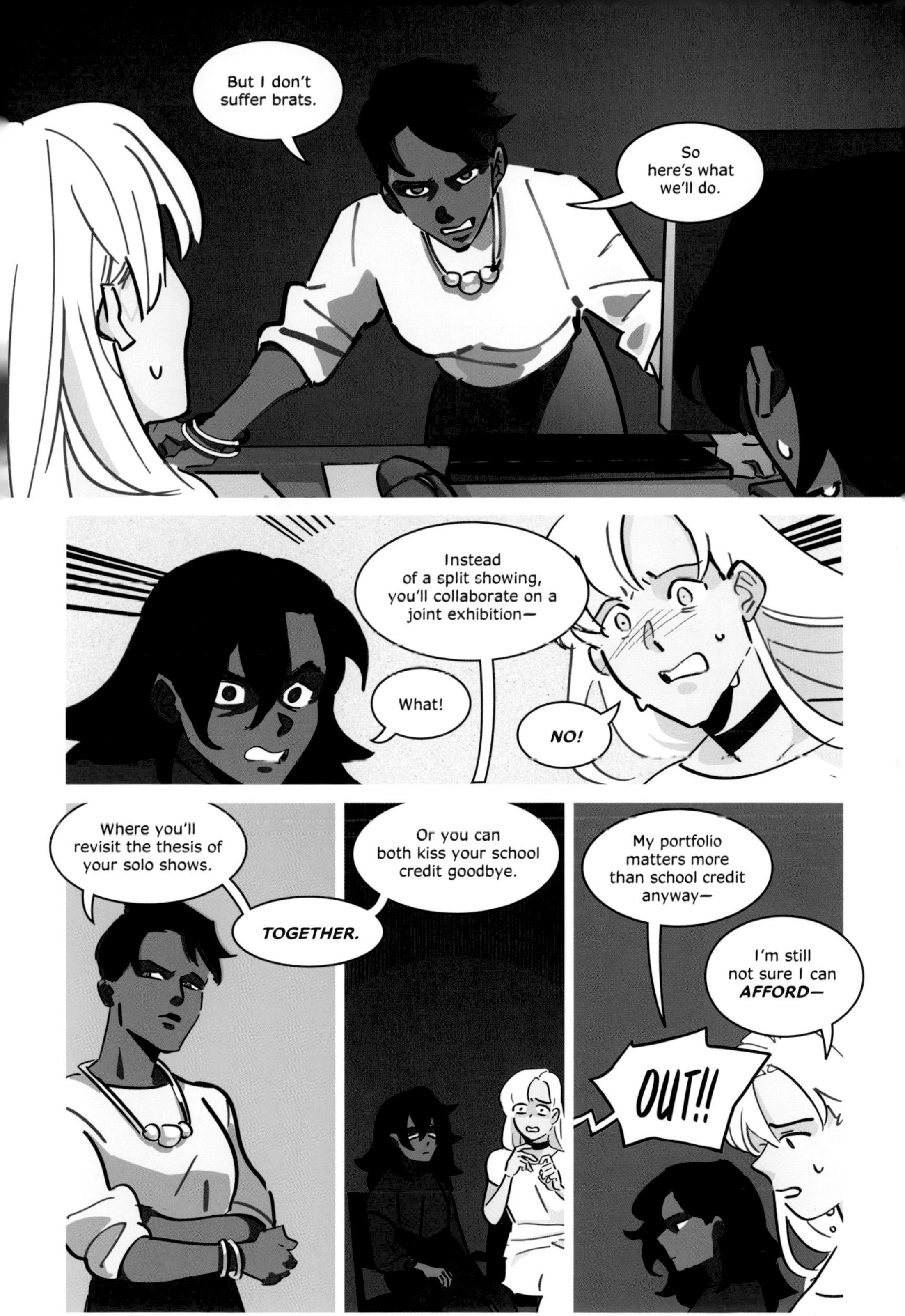
But I don't suffer brats.
So here's what we'll do.
Instead of a split showing, you'll collaborate on a joint exhibition—
What!
NO!
Where you'll revisit the thesis of your solo shows.
TOGETHER.
Or you can both kiss your school credit goodbye.
My portfolio matters more than school credit anyway—
I'm still not sure I can AFFORD—
OUT!!

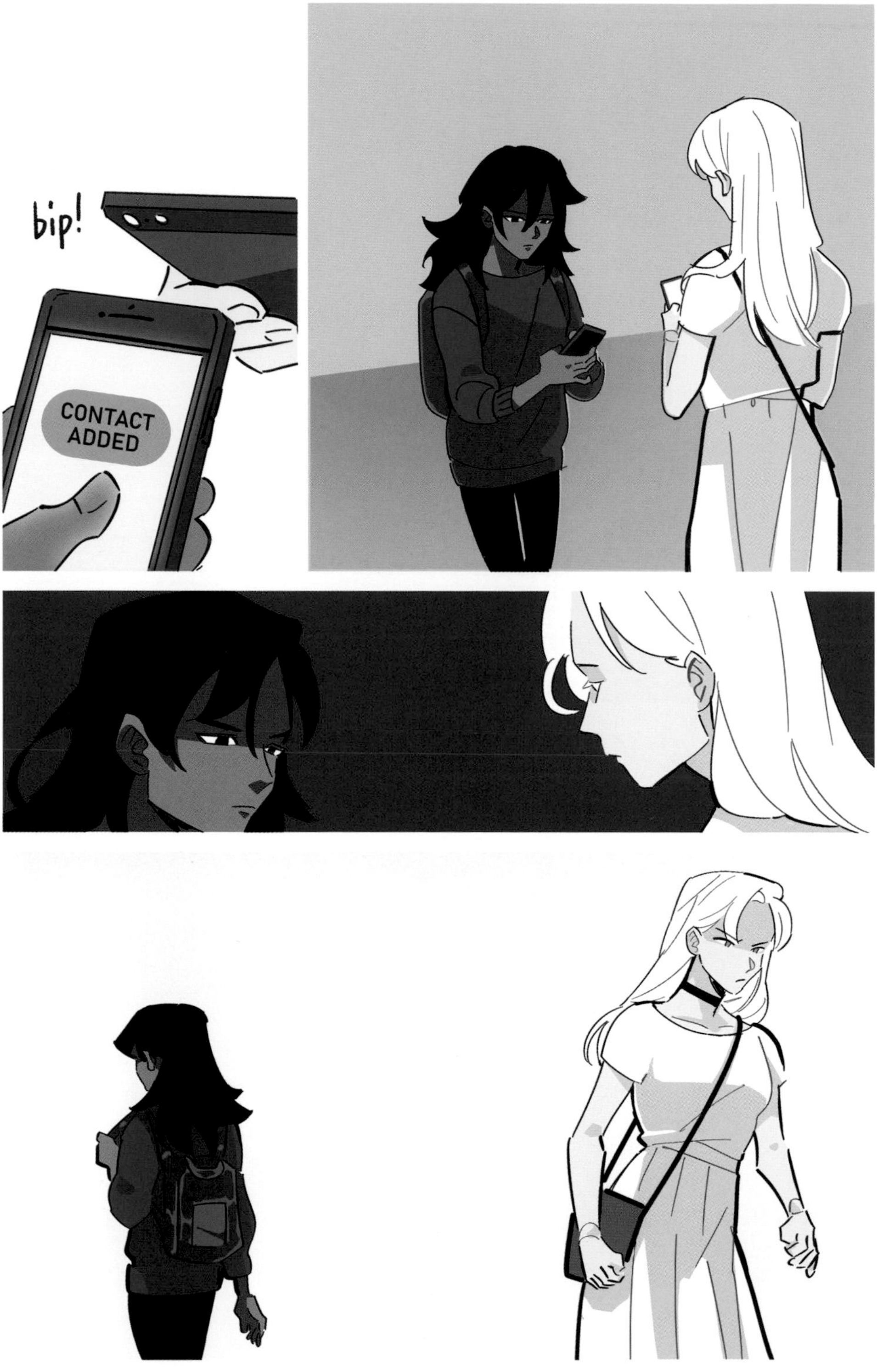
bip!
CONTACT ADDED

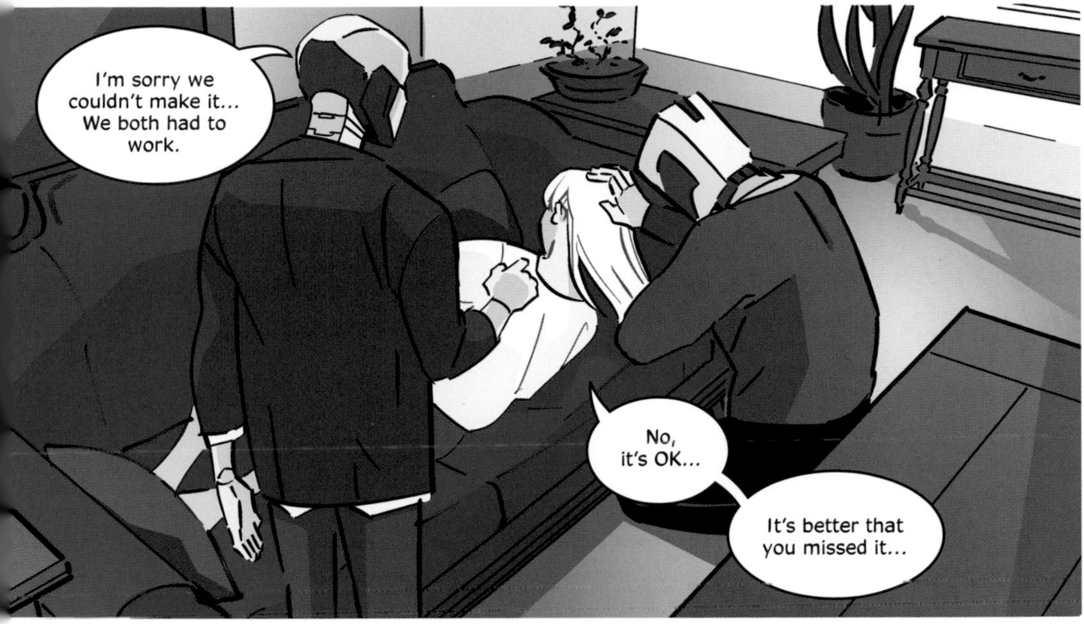
I'm sorry we couldn't make it... We both had to work.
No, it's OK...
It's better that you missed it...

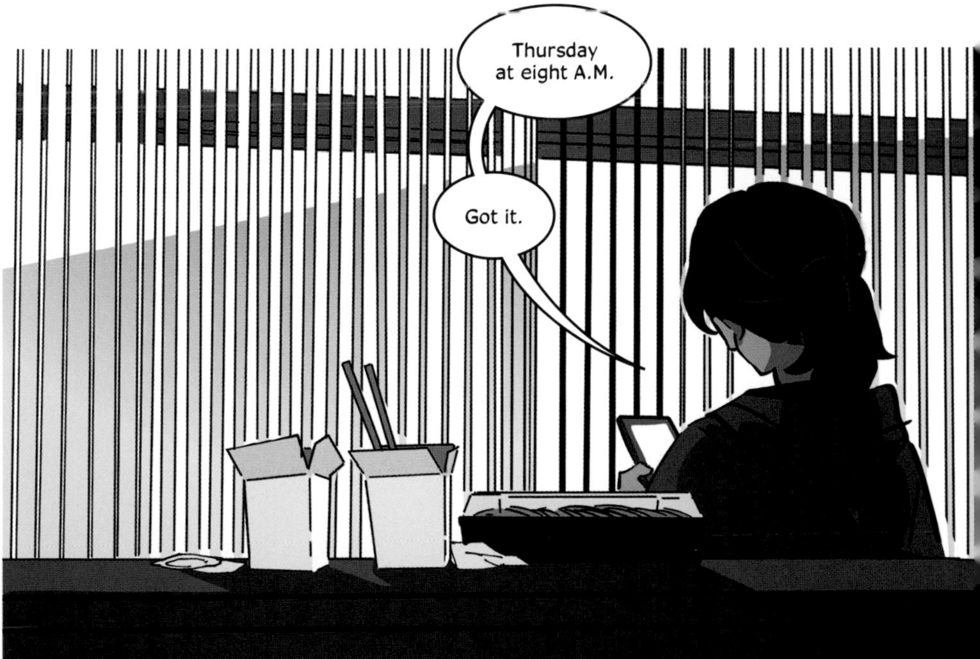
Thursday at eight A.M.
Got it.

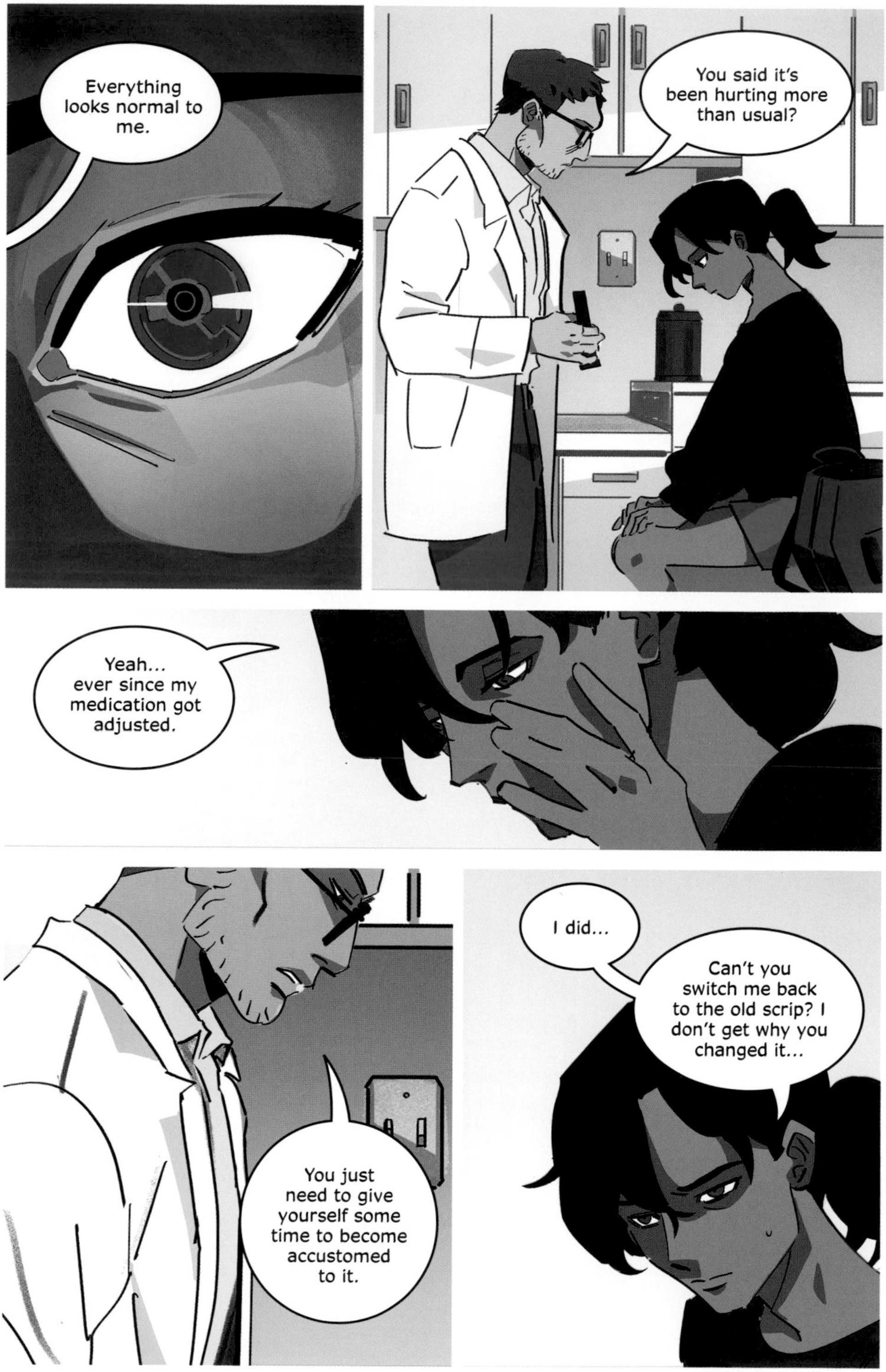
Everything looks normal to me.
You said it's been hurting more than usual?
Yeah... ever since my medication got adjusted.
You just need to give yourself some time to become accustomed to it.
I did...
Can't you switch me back to the old scrip? I don't get why you changed it...

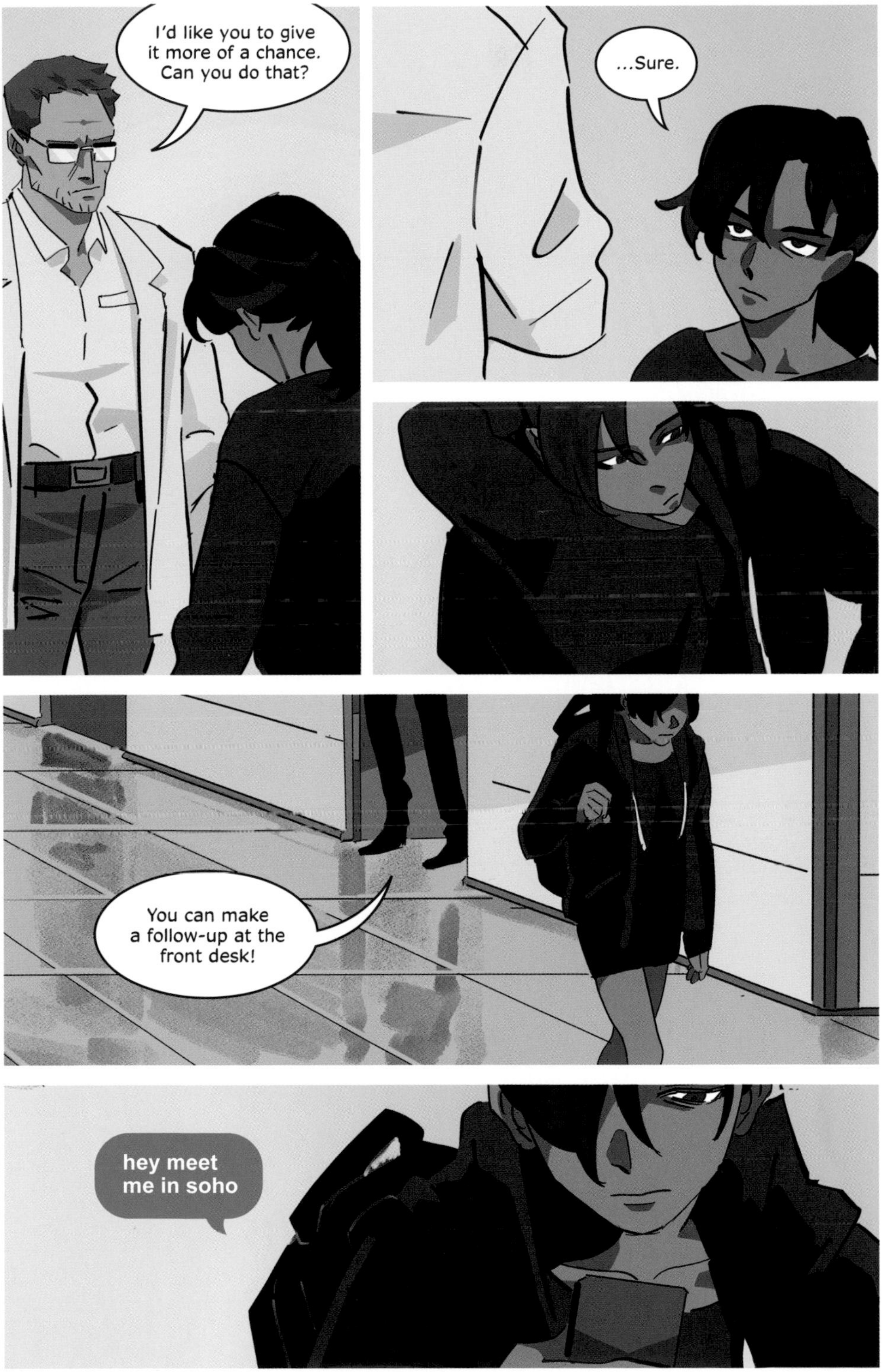
I'd like you to give it more of a chance. Can you do that?
...Sure.
You can make a follow-up at the front desk!
hey meet me in soho

Global pandemic accelerates adoption
of AI surveillance, raising concerns with
international ethics watchdogs.

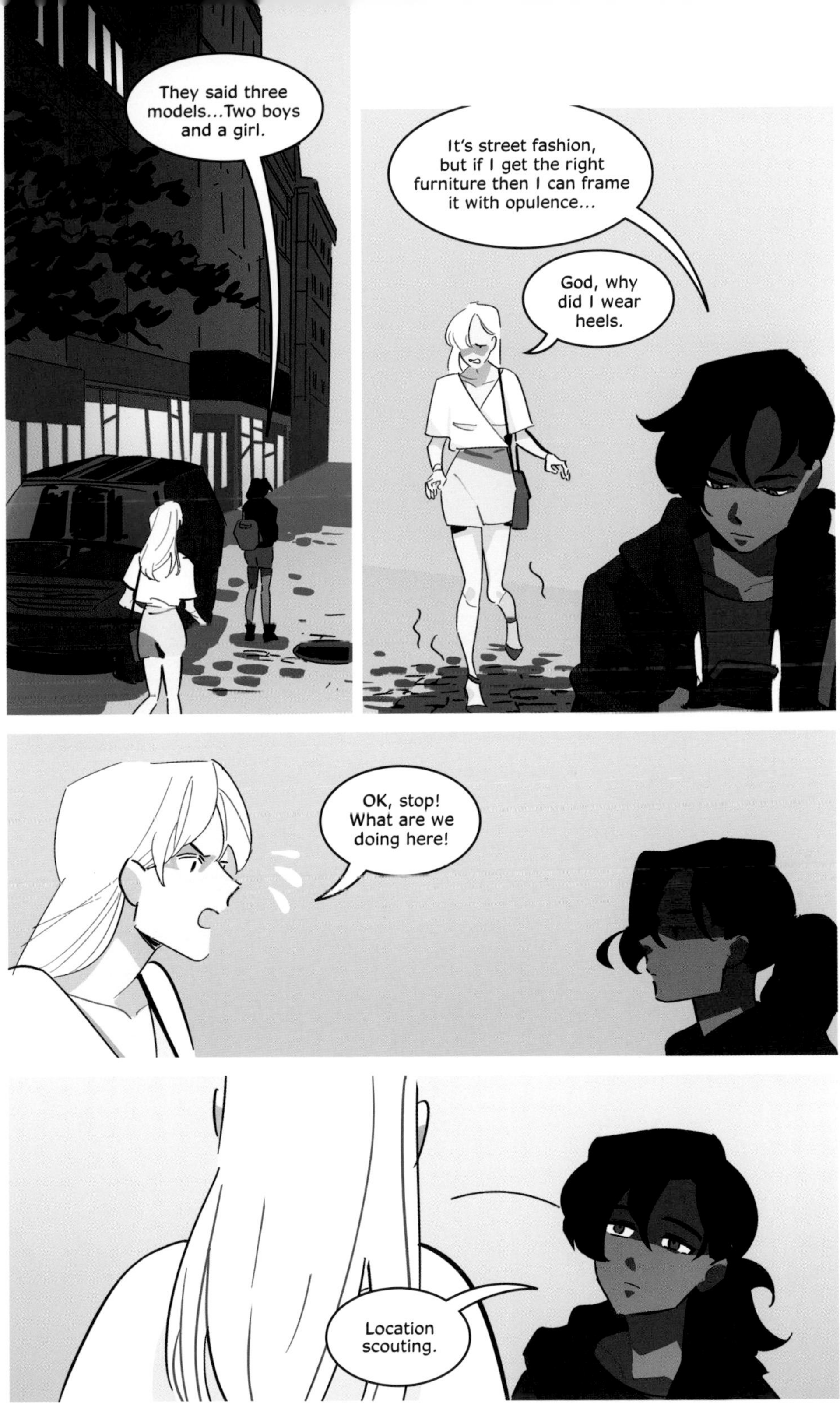
They said three models...Two boys and a girl.
It's street fashion, but if I get the right furniture then I can frame it with opulence...
God, why did I wear heels.
OK, stop! What are we doing here!
Location scouting.

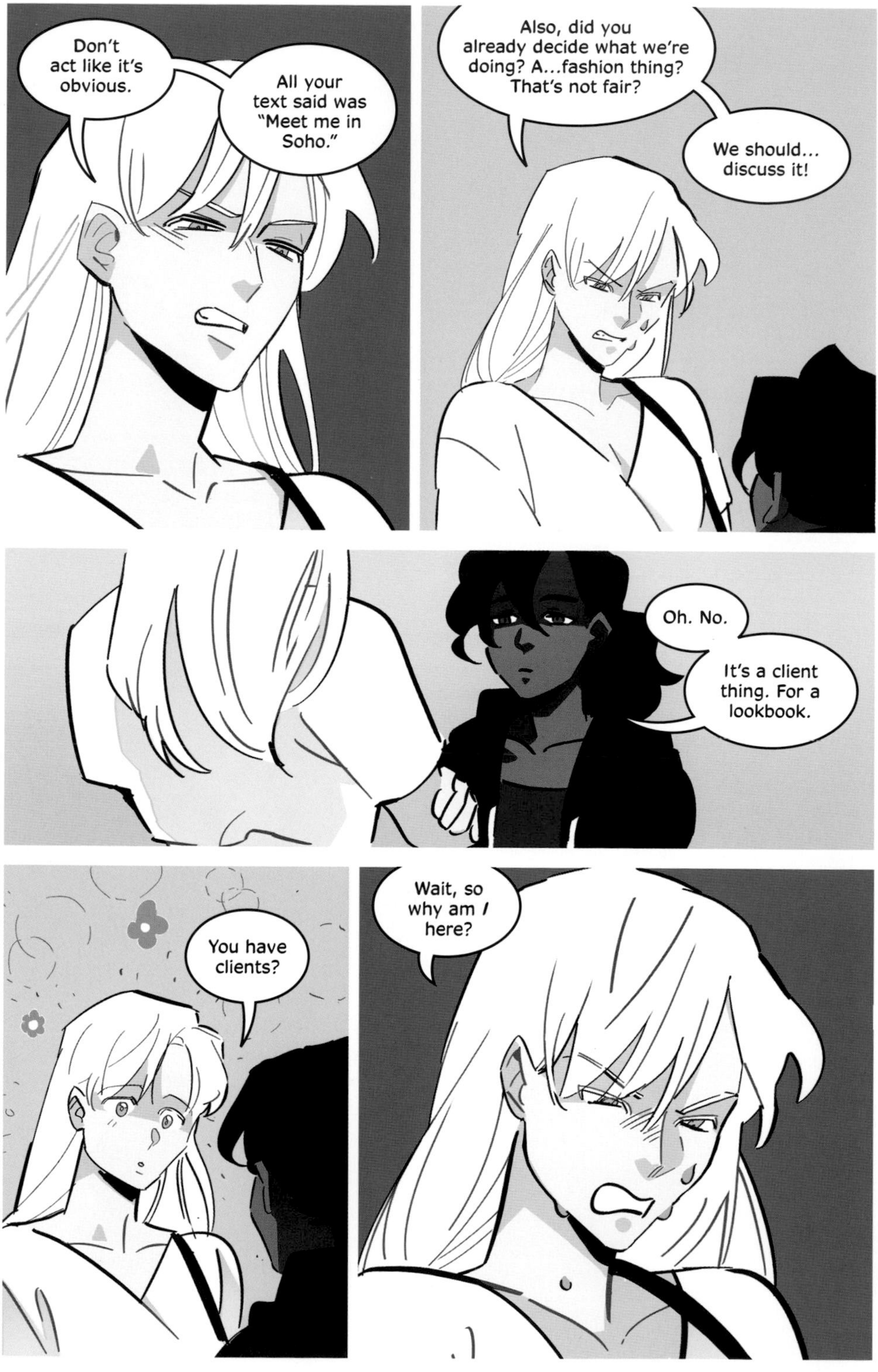
Don't act like it's obvious.
All your text said was "Meet me in Soho."
Also, did you already decide what we're doing? A...fashion thing? That's not fair?
We should... discuss it!
Oh. No.
It's a client thing. For a lookbook.
You have clients?
Wait, so why am *I* here?

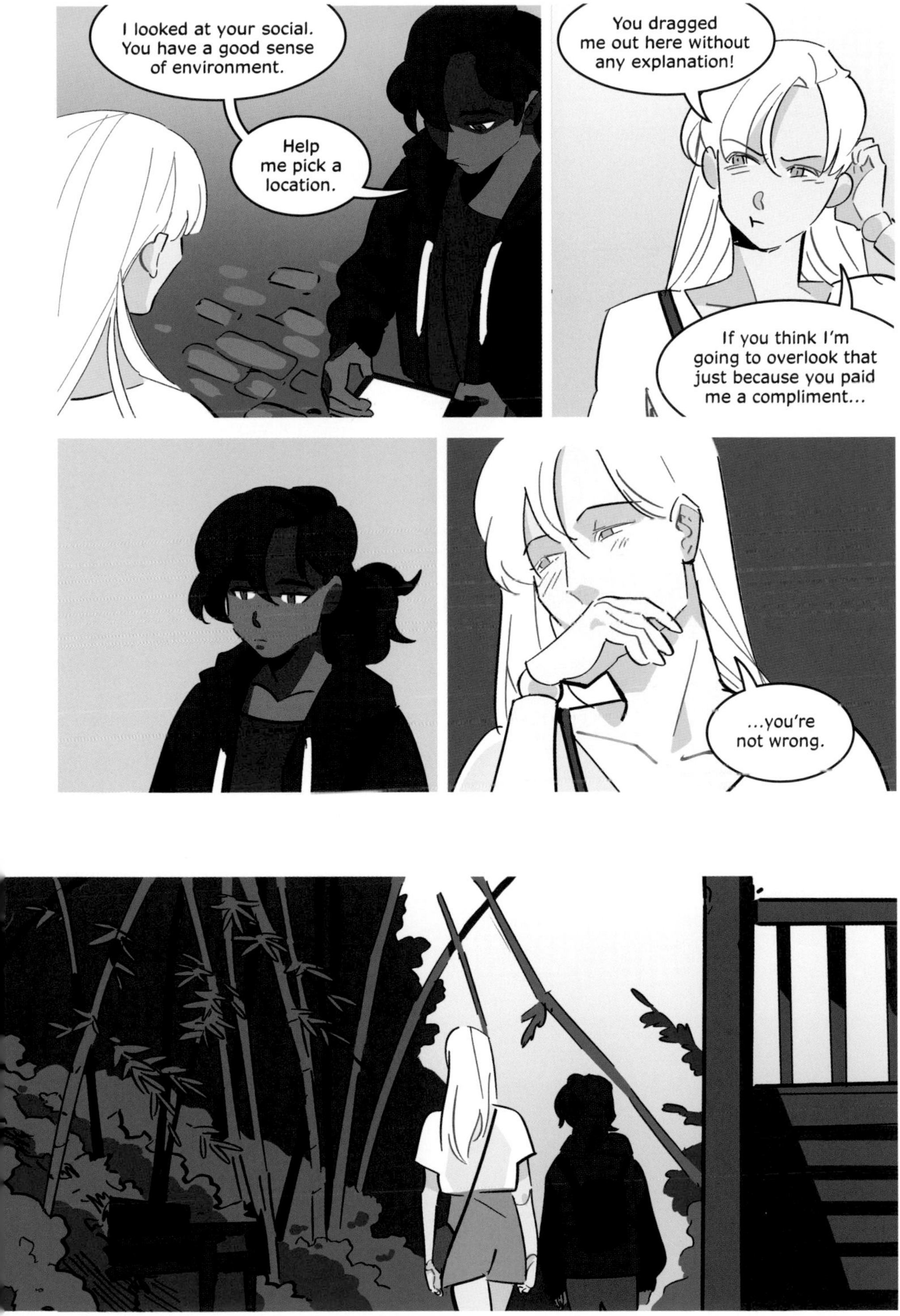
I looked at your social. You have a good sense of environment.
Help me pick a location.
You dragged me out here without any explanation!
If you think I'm going to overlook that just because you paid me a compliment...
...you're not wrong.

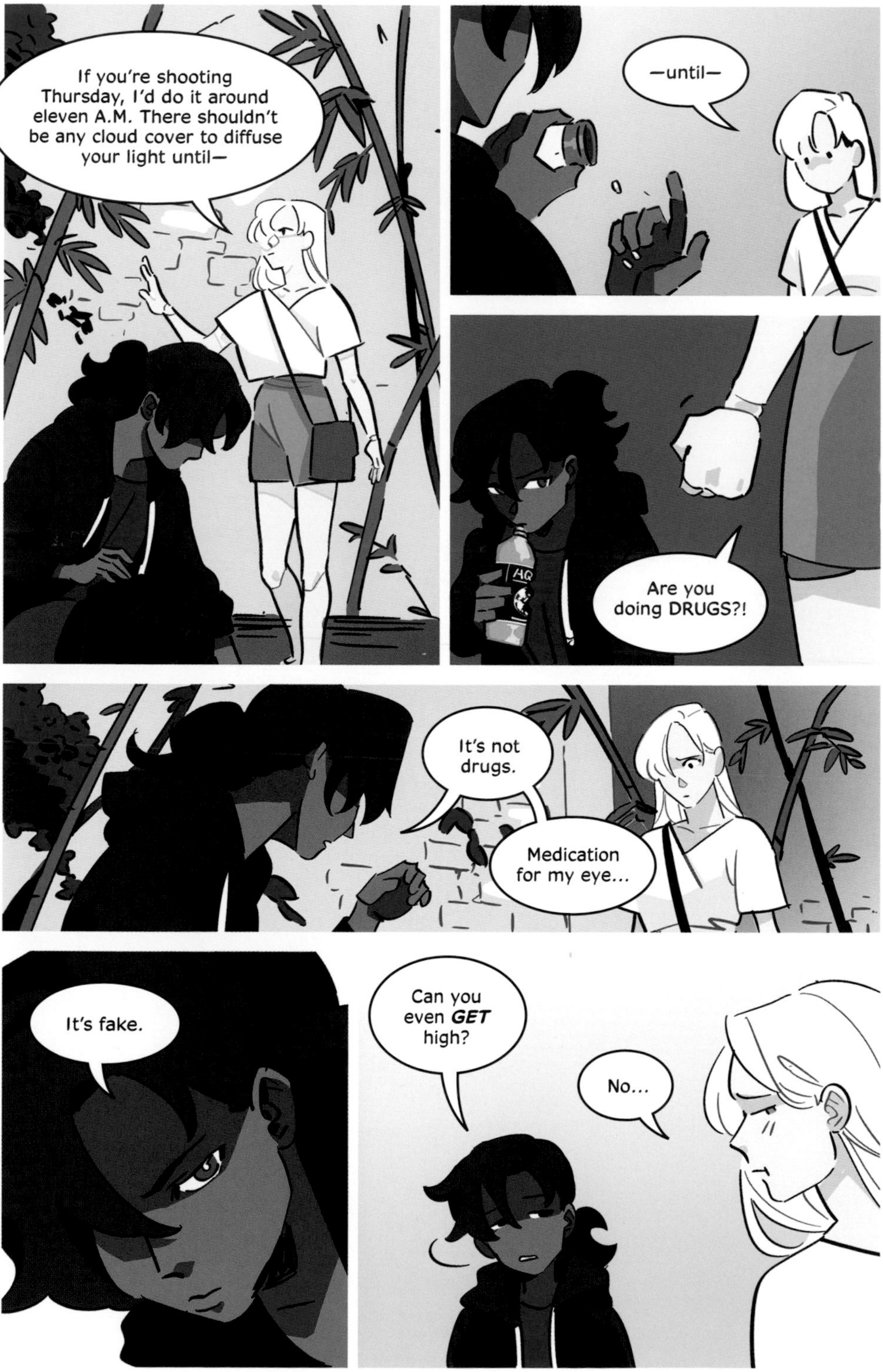
If you're shooting Thursday, I'd do it around eleven A.M. There shouldn't be any cloud cover to diffuse your light until—
—until—
Are you doing DRUGS?!
It's not drugs.
Medication for my eye...
It's fake.
Can you even ***GET*** high?
No...

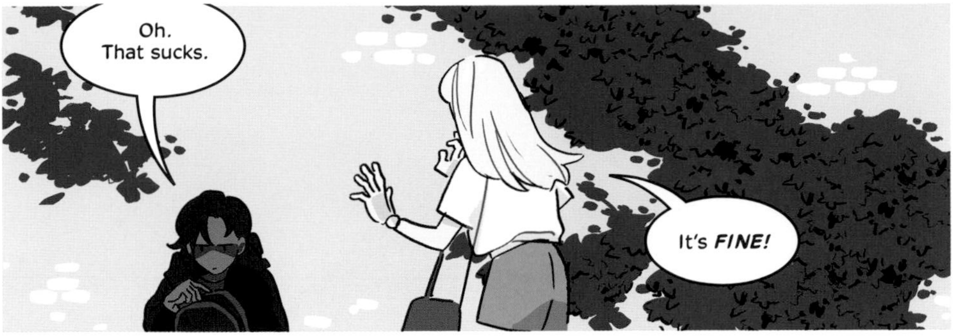
Oh.
That sucks.
It's ***FINE!***

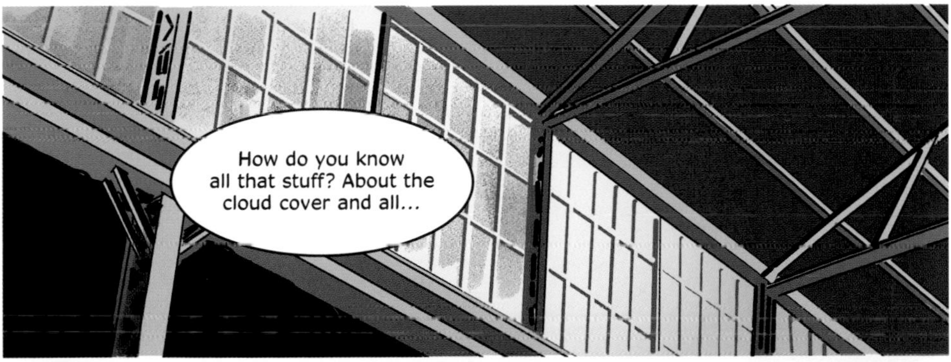
How do you know all that stuff? About the cloud cover and all...

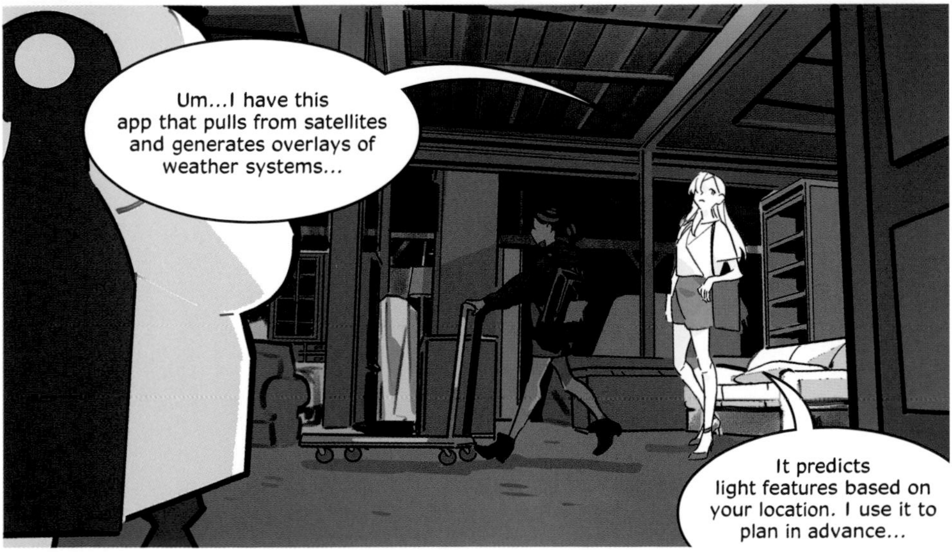
Um...I have this app that pulls from satellites and generates overlays of weather systems...
It predicts light features based on your location. I use it to plan in advance...

That's... intimidating.

I'm intimidating?

The idea of you is intimidating.

Does the unknown intimidate you?

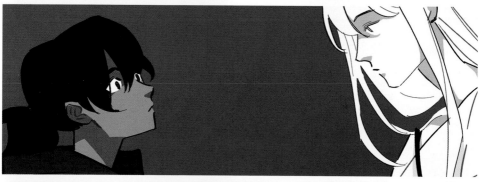

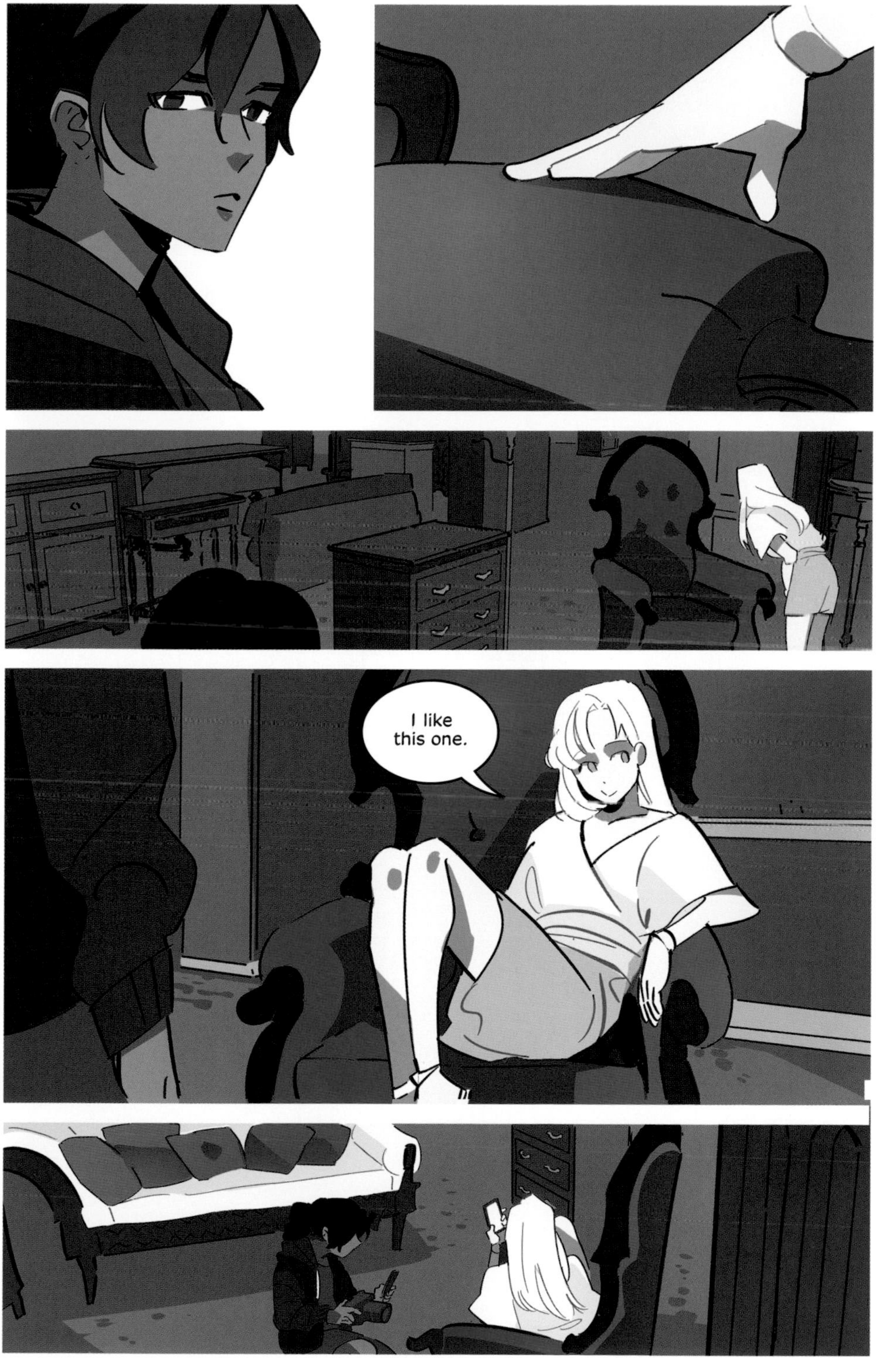
I like this one.

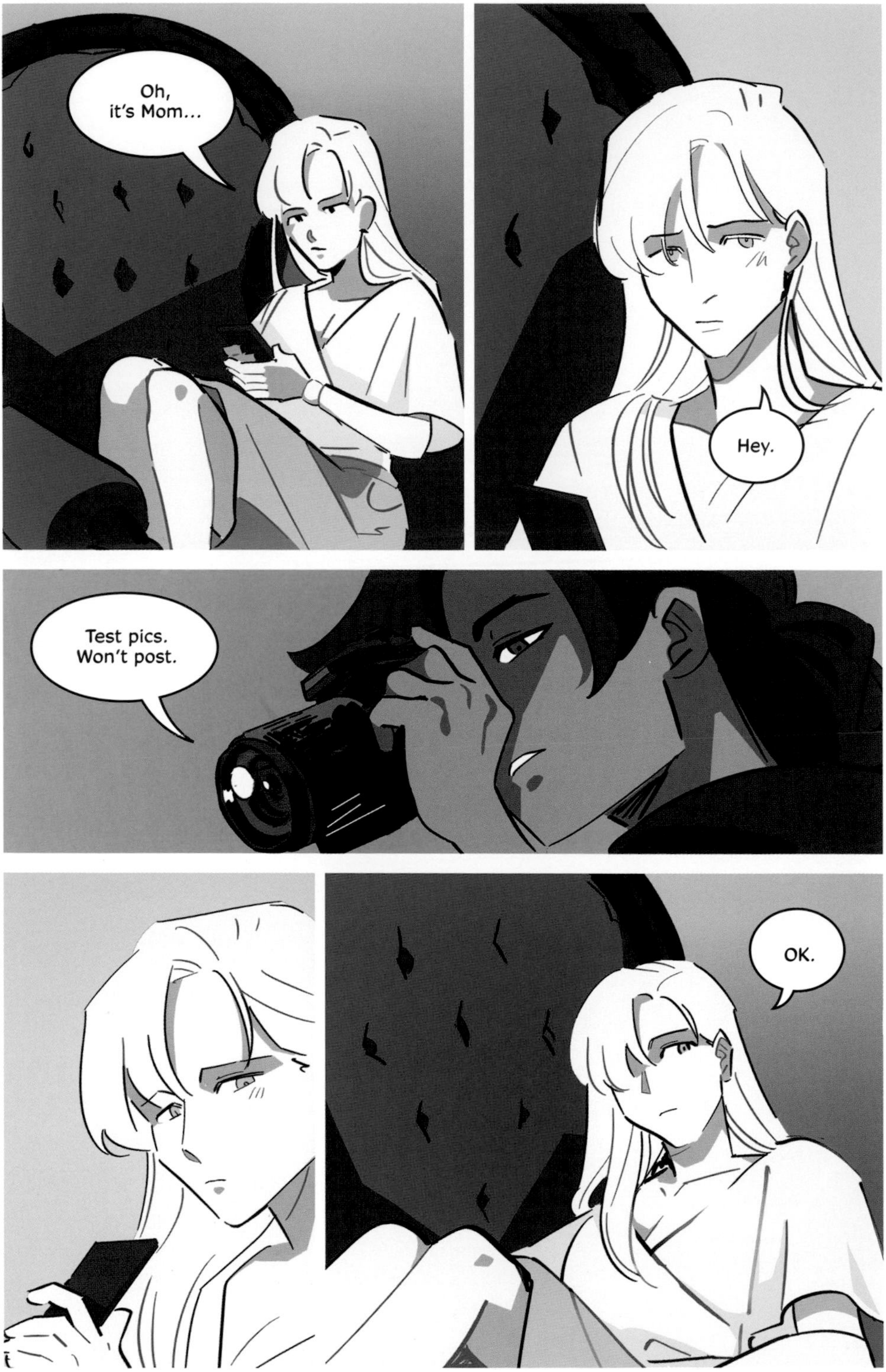
Oh, it's Mom...
Hey.
Test pics. Won't post.
OK.

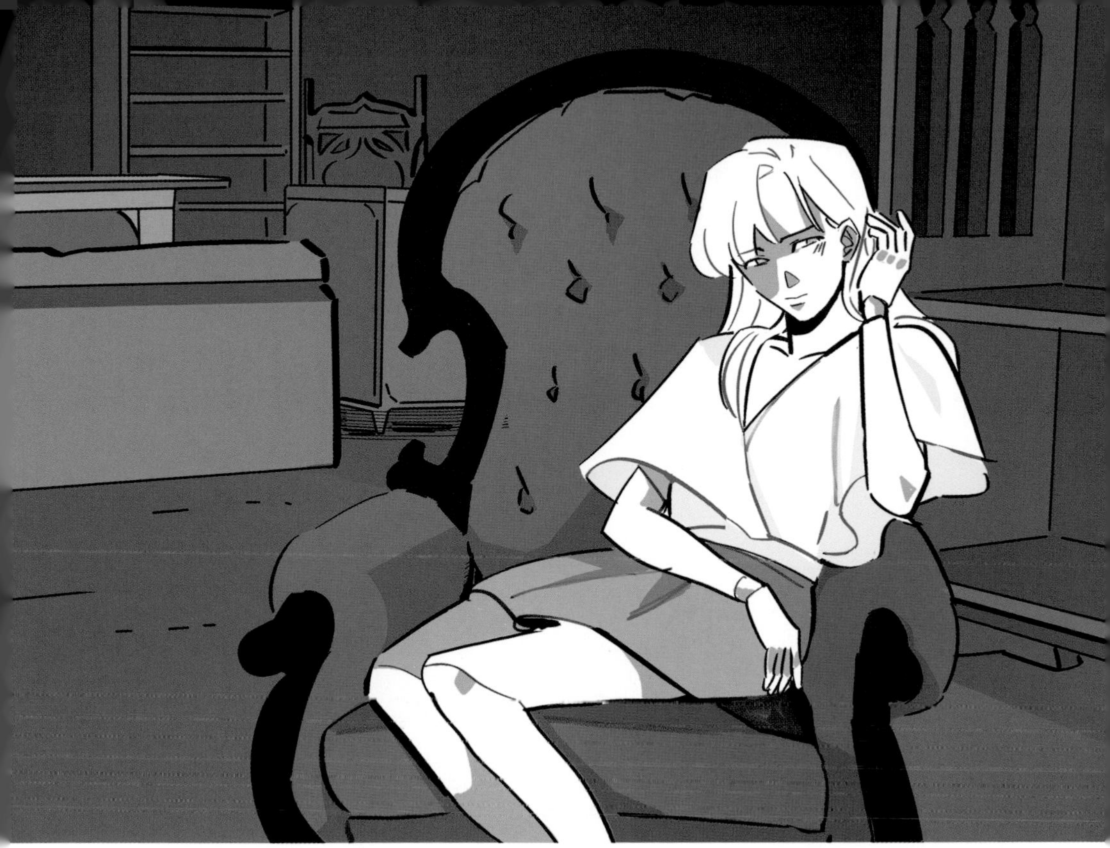

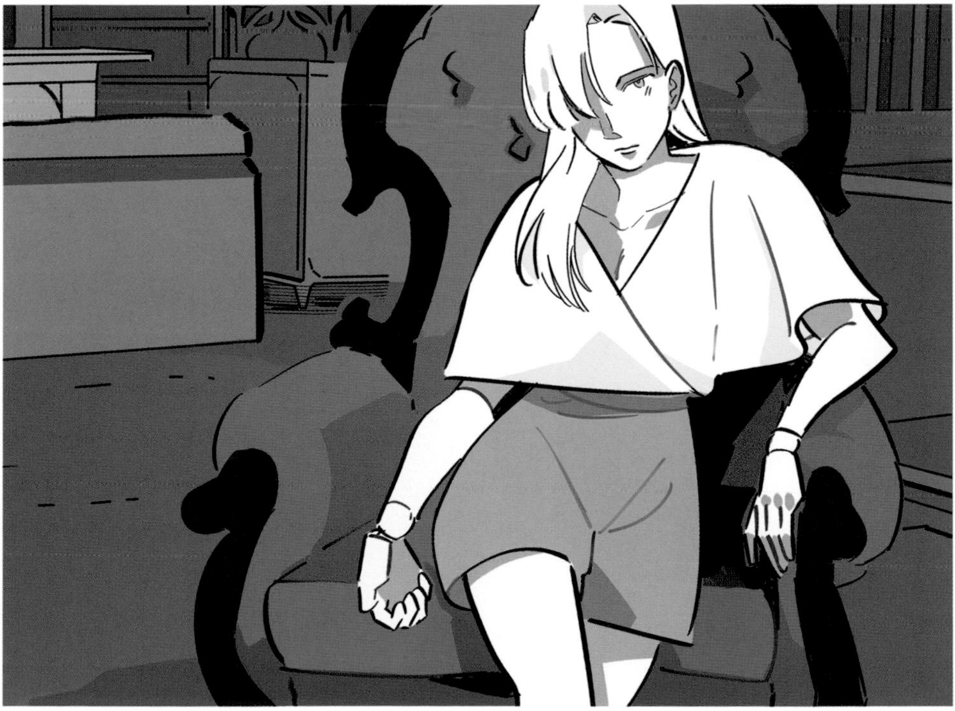

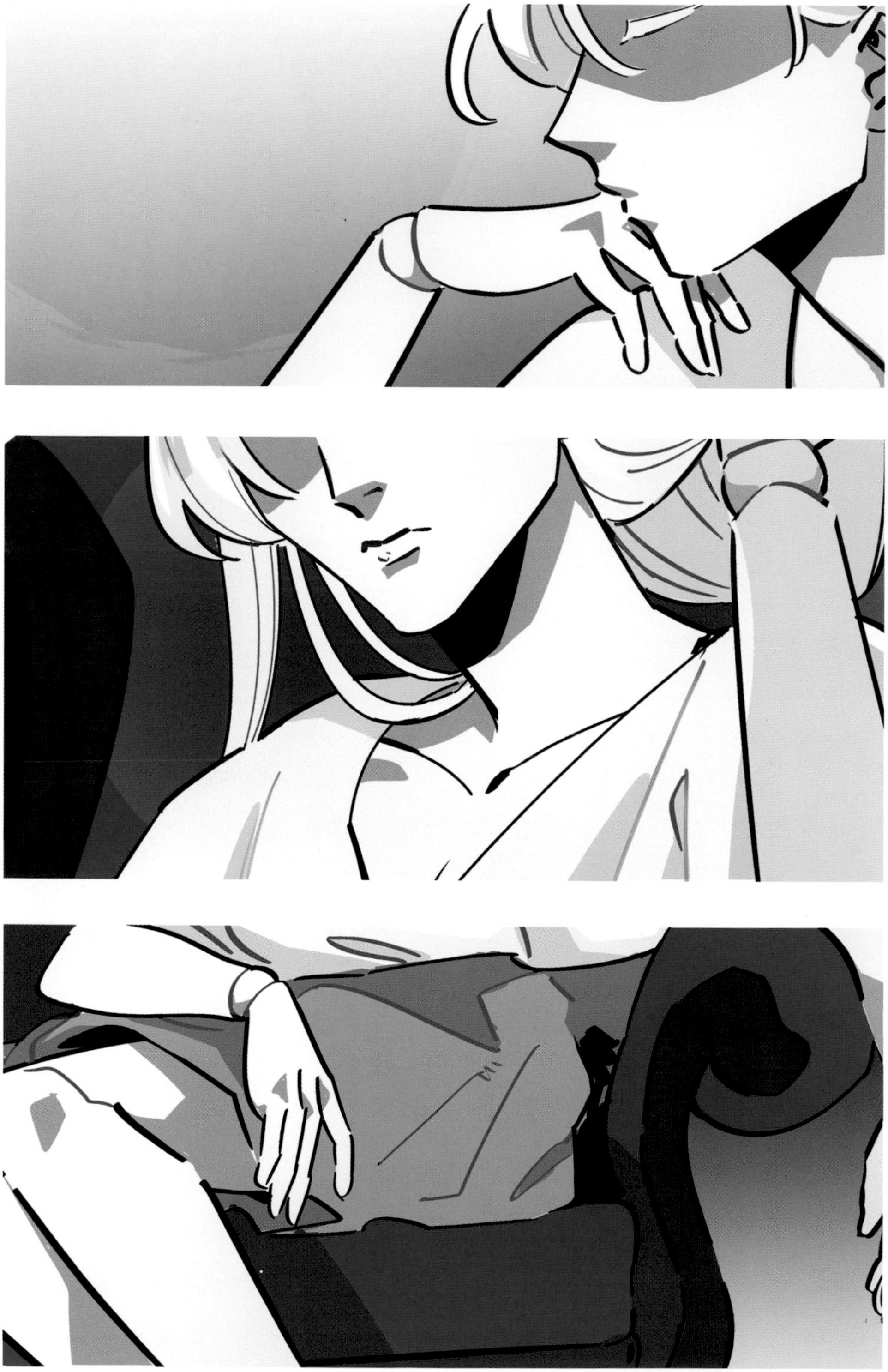

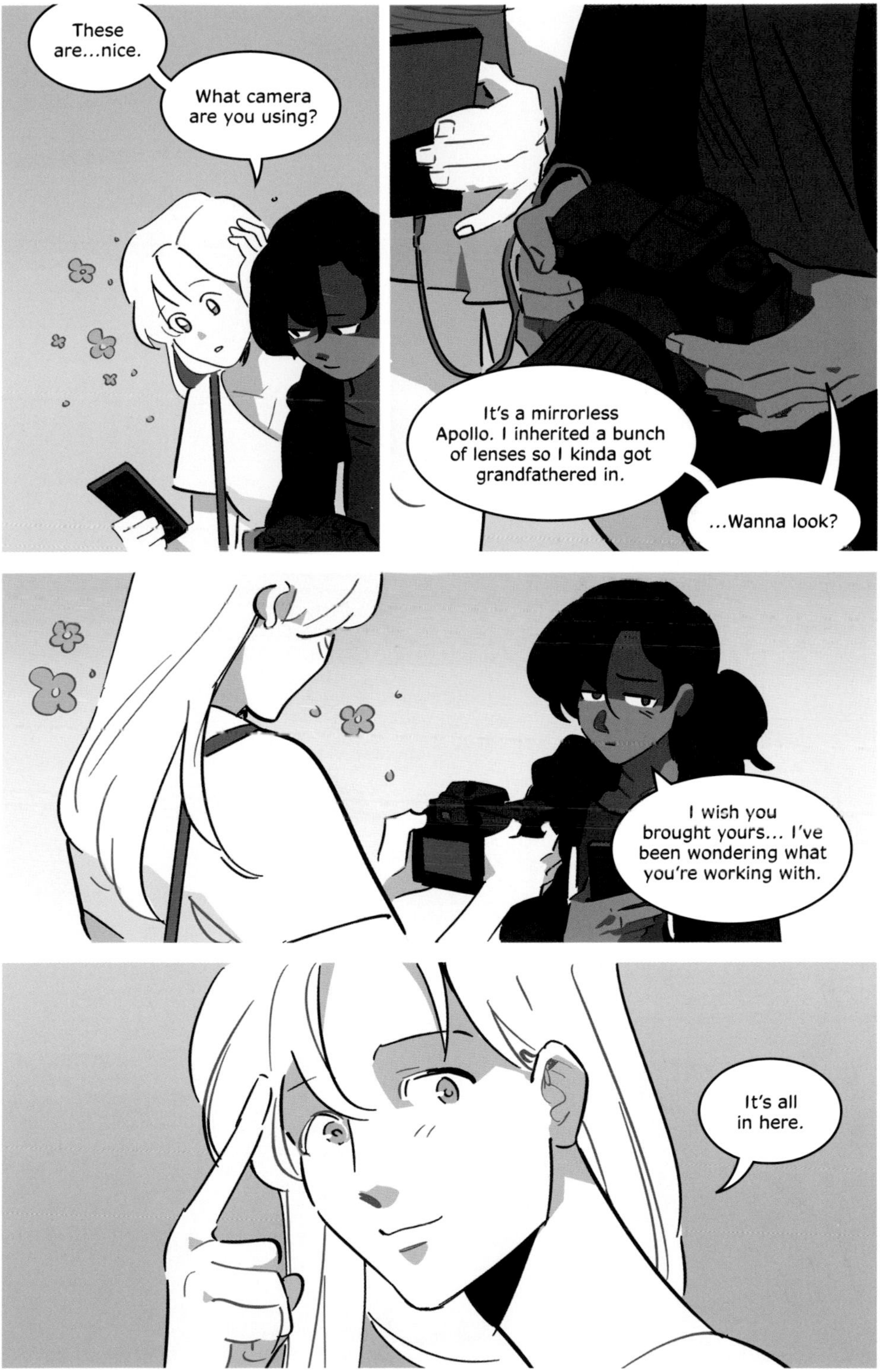
These are...nice.
What camera are you using?
It's a mirrorless Apollo. I inherited a bunch of lenses so I kinda got grandfathered in.
...Wanna look?
I wish you brought yours... I've been wondering what you're working with.
It's all in here.

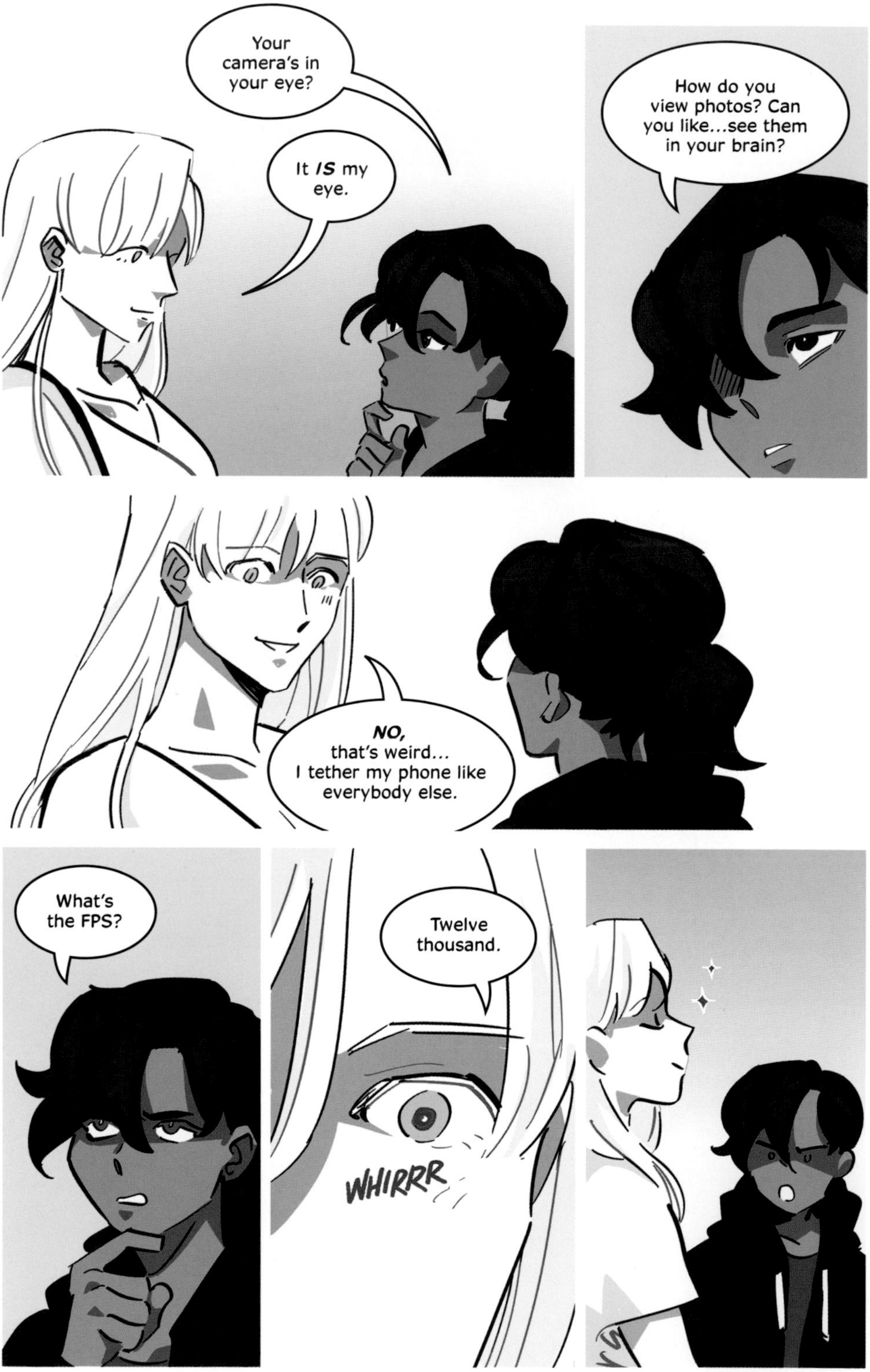
Your camera's in your eye?
It IS my eye.
How do you view photos? Can you like...see them in your brain?
NO, that's weird... I tether my phone like everybody else.
What's the FPS?
Twelve thousand.
WHIRRR

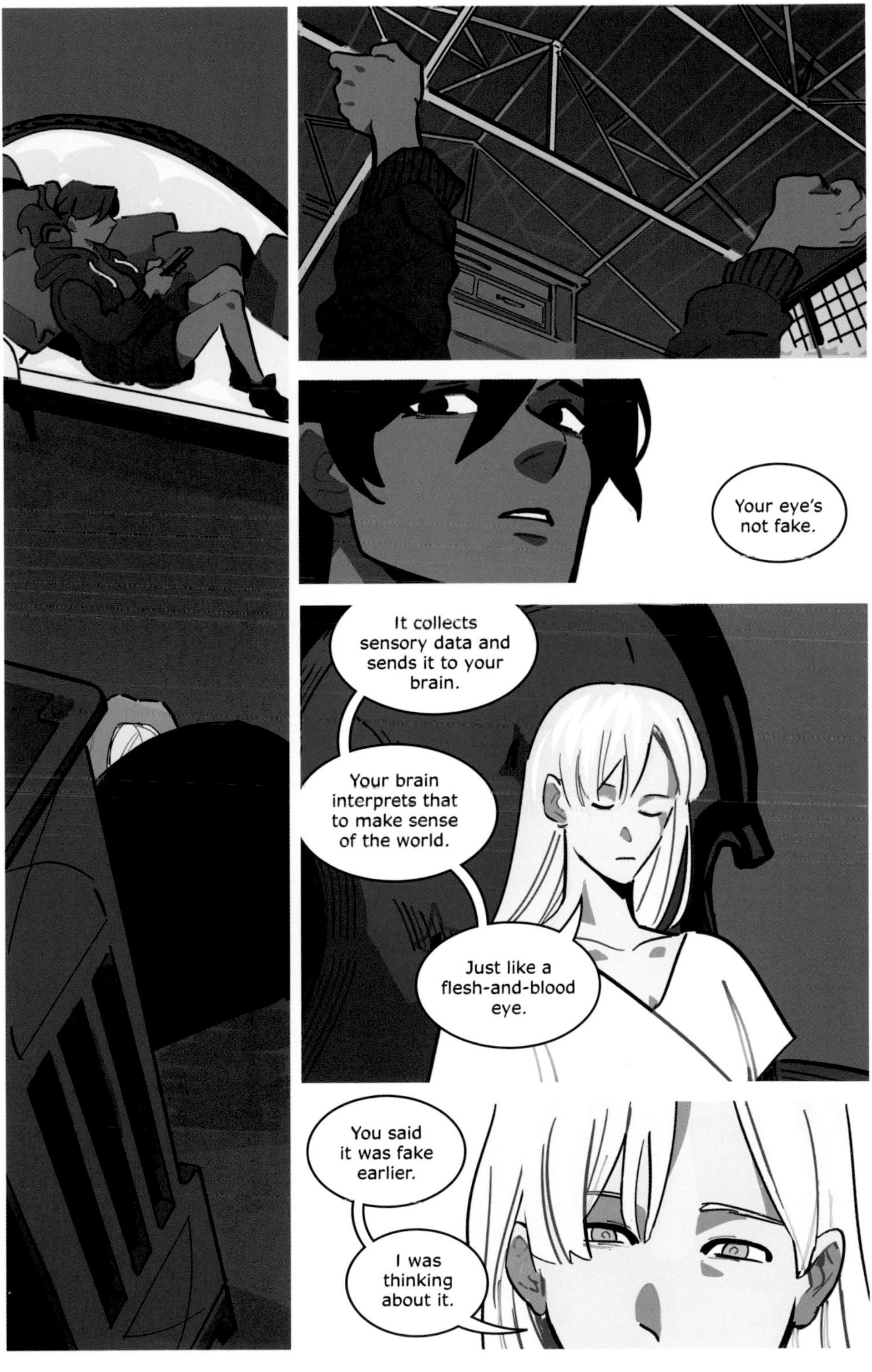
Your eye's not fake.
It collects sensory data and sends it to your brain.
Your brain interprets that to make sense of the world.
Just like a flesh-and-blood eye.
You said it was fake earlier.
I was thinking about it.

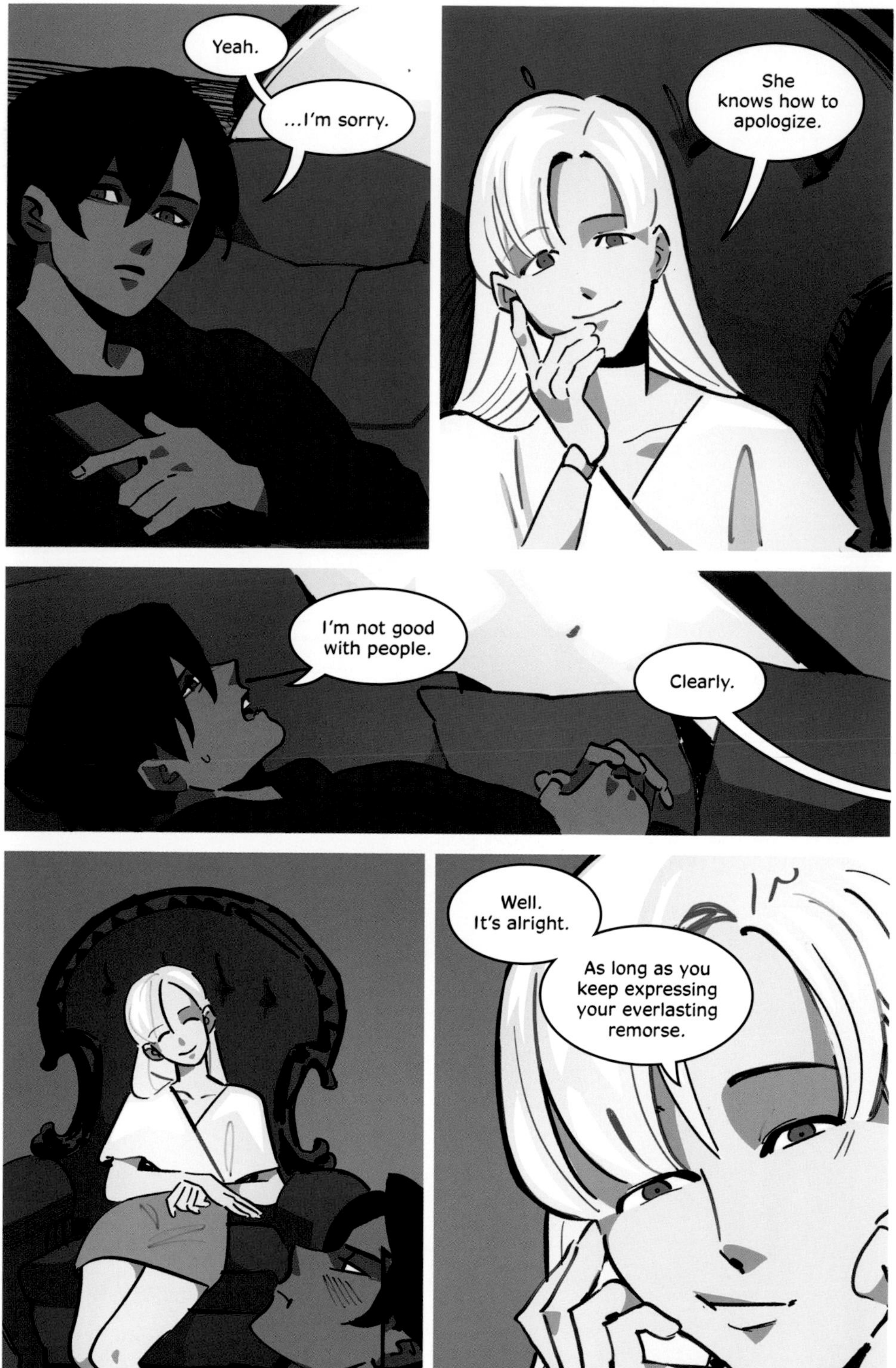
Yeah.
...I'm sorry.
She knows how to apologize.
I'm not good with people.
Clearly.
Well. It's alright.
As long as you keep expressing your everlasting remorse.

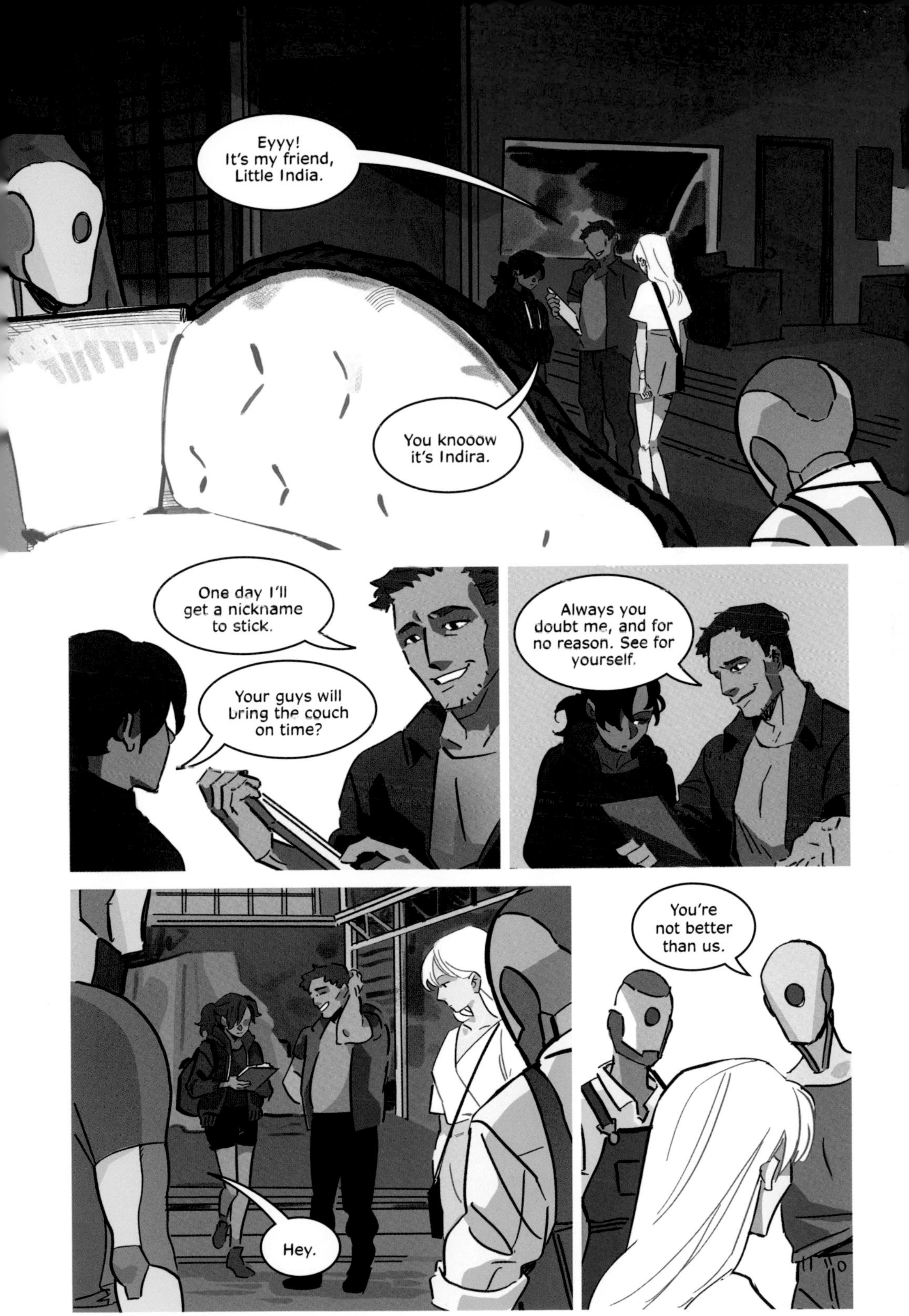
Eyyy!
It's my friend,
Little India.
You knooow
it's Indira.
One day I'll
get a nickname
to stick.
Your guys will
bring the couch
on time?
Always you
doubt me, and for
no reason. See for
yourself.
Hey.
You're
not better
than us.

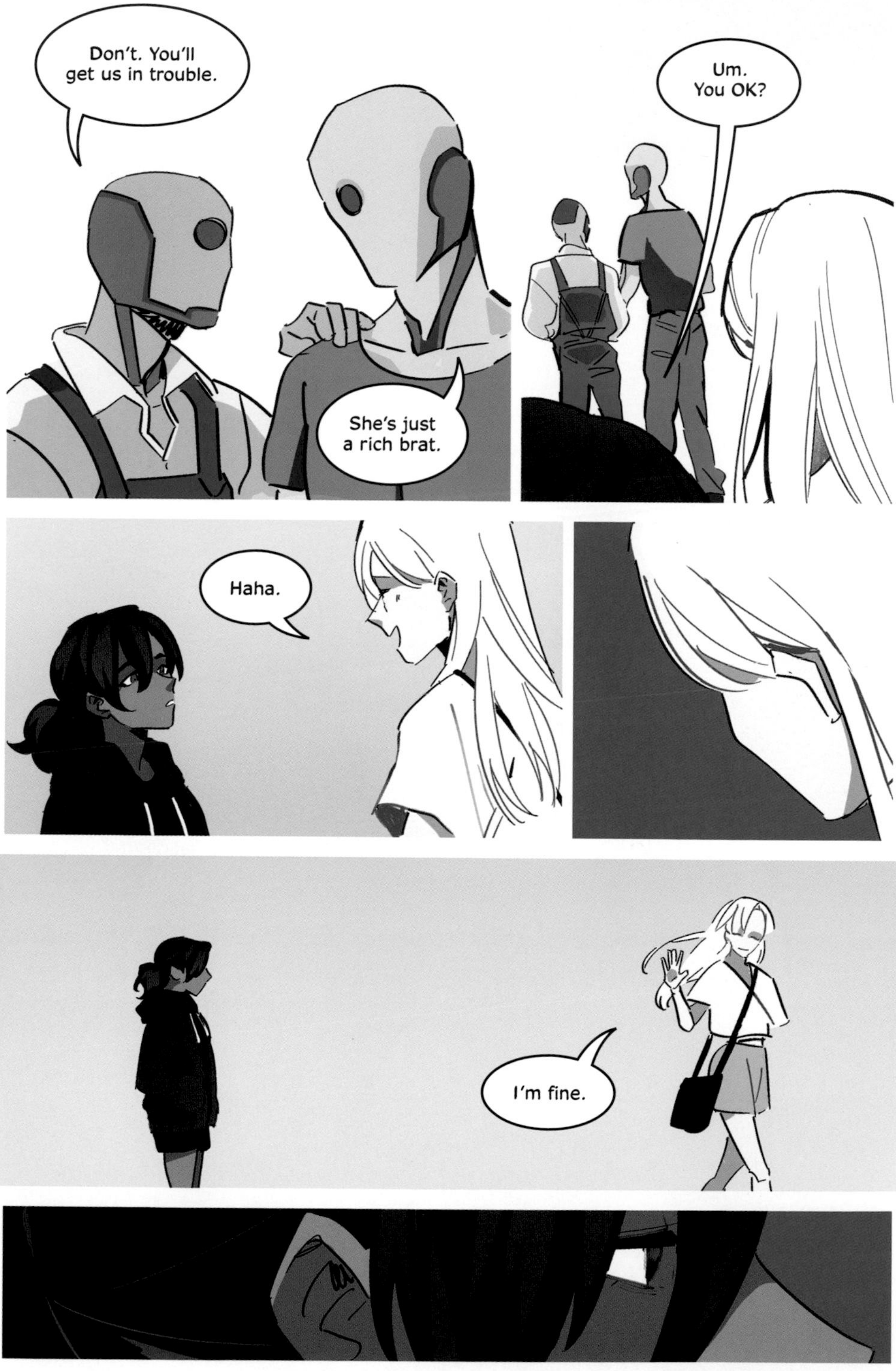
Don't. You'll get us in trouble.
She's just a rich brat.
Um. You OK?
Haha.
I'm fine.

Tech giant partners with law enforcement
to develop AI that assigns threat score to
"at risk" individuals; critics claim the system
is opaque and has no public accountability.

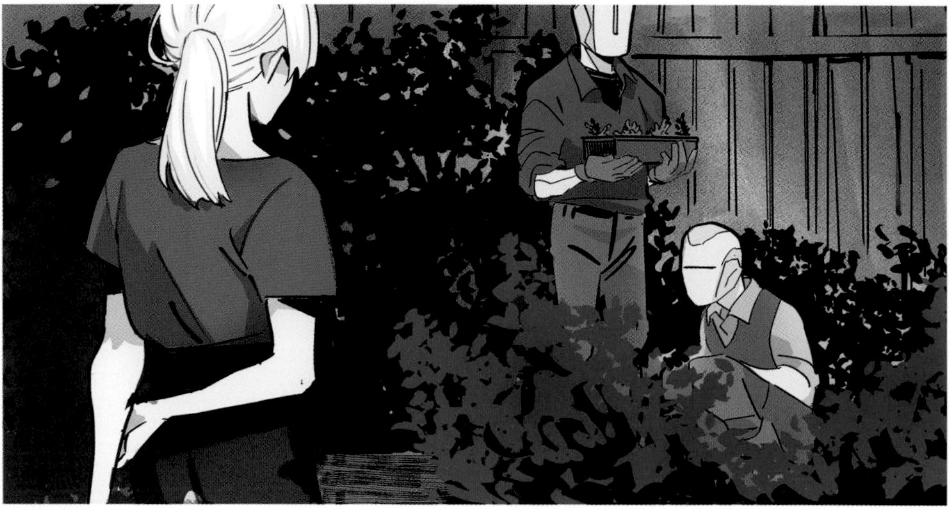

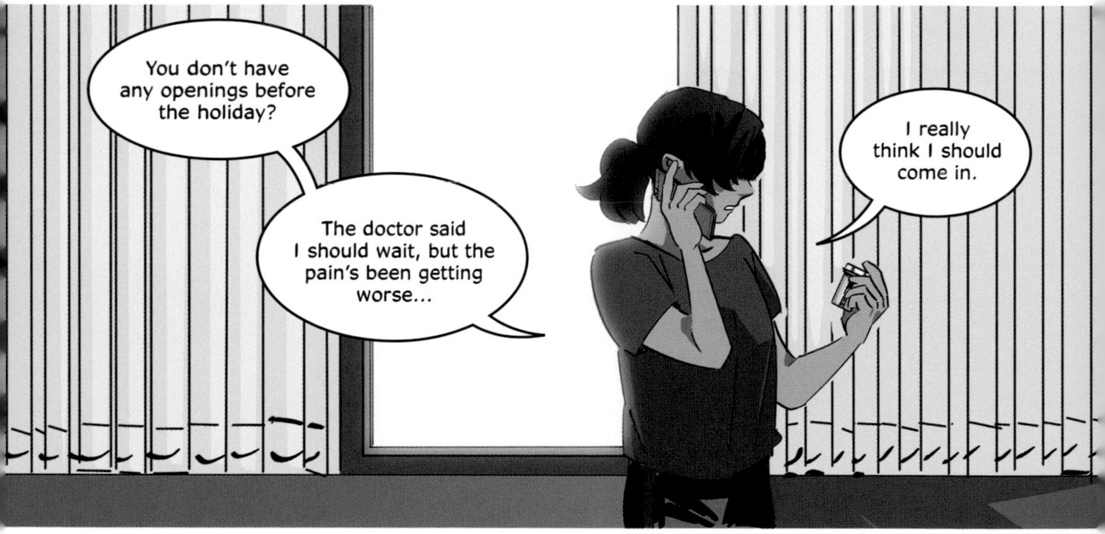
You don't have any openings before the holiday?
The doctor said I should wait, but the pain's been getting worse...
I really think I should come in.

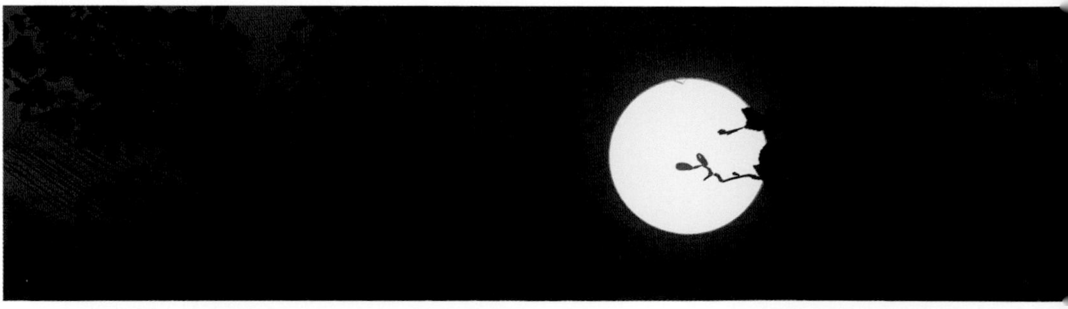

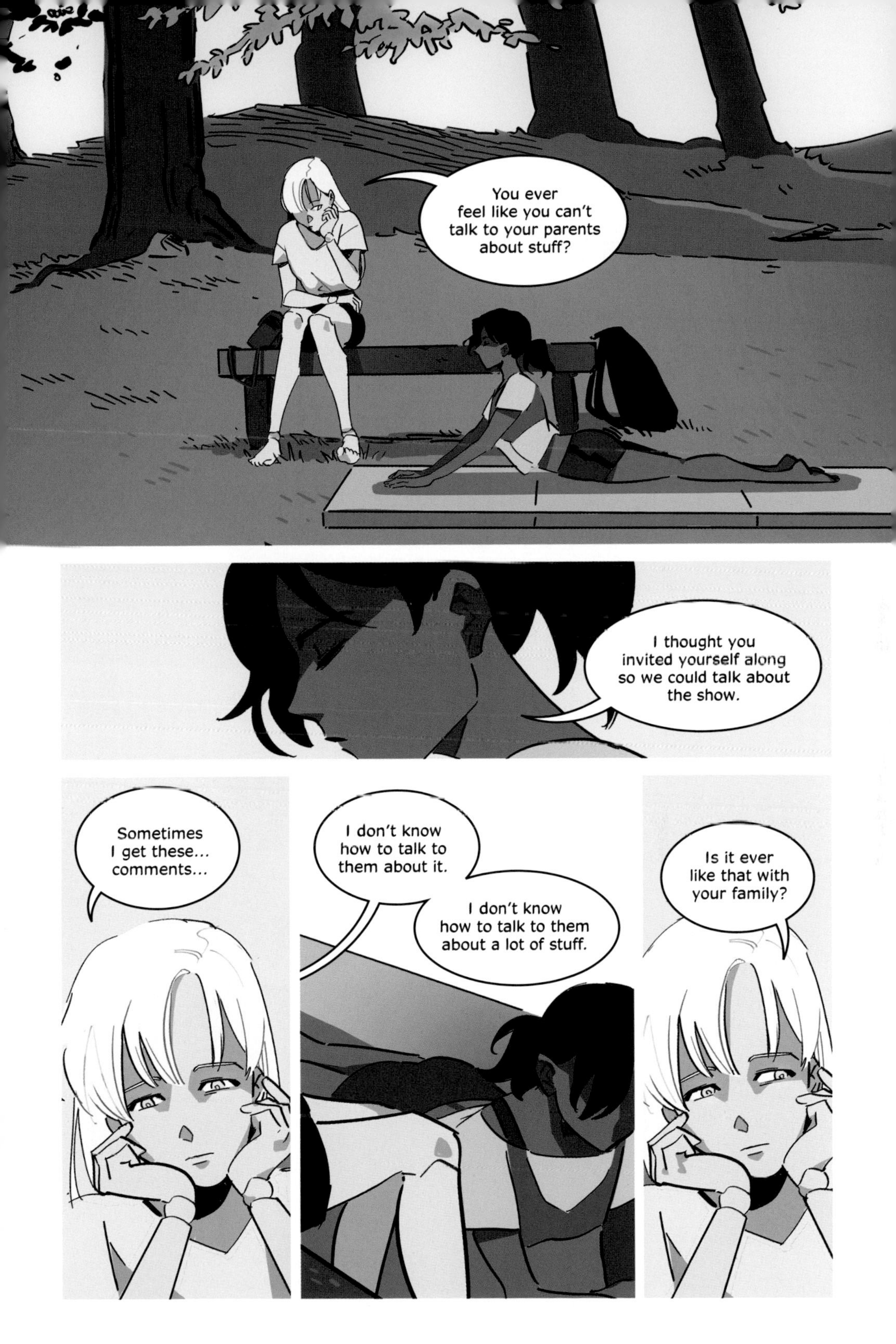
You ever feel like you can't talk to your parents about stuff?
I thought you invited yourself along so we could talk about the show.
Sometimes I get these... comments...
I don't know how to talk to them about it.
I don't know how to talk to them about a lot of stuff.
Is it ever like that with your family?

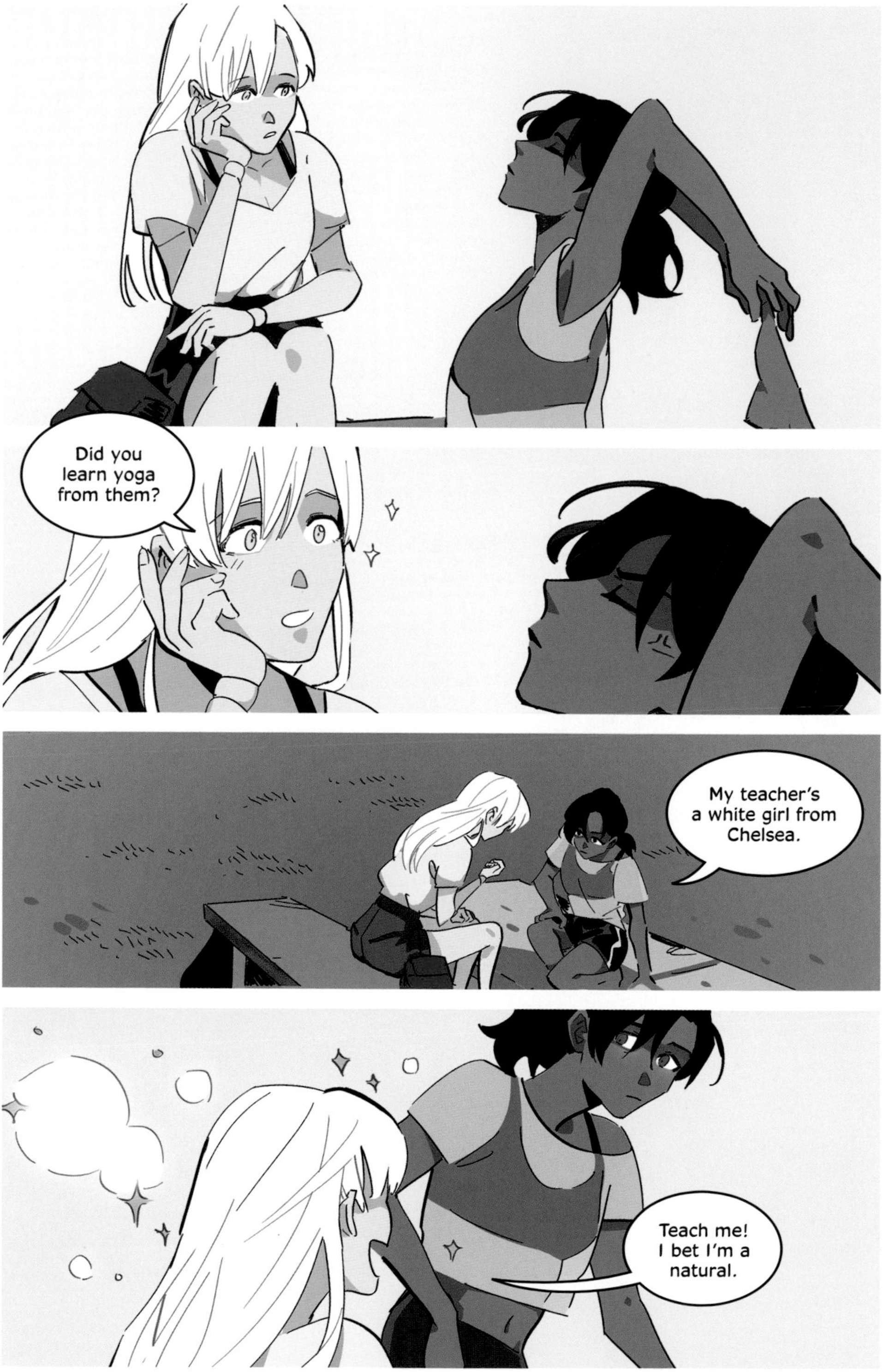
Did you learn yoga from them?
My teacher's a white girl from Chelsea.
Teach me! I bet I'm a natural.

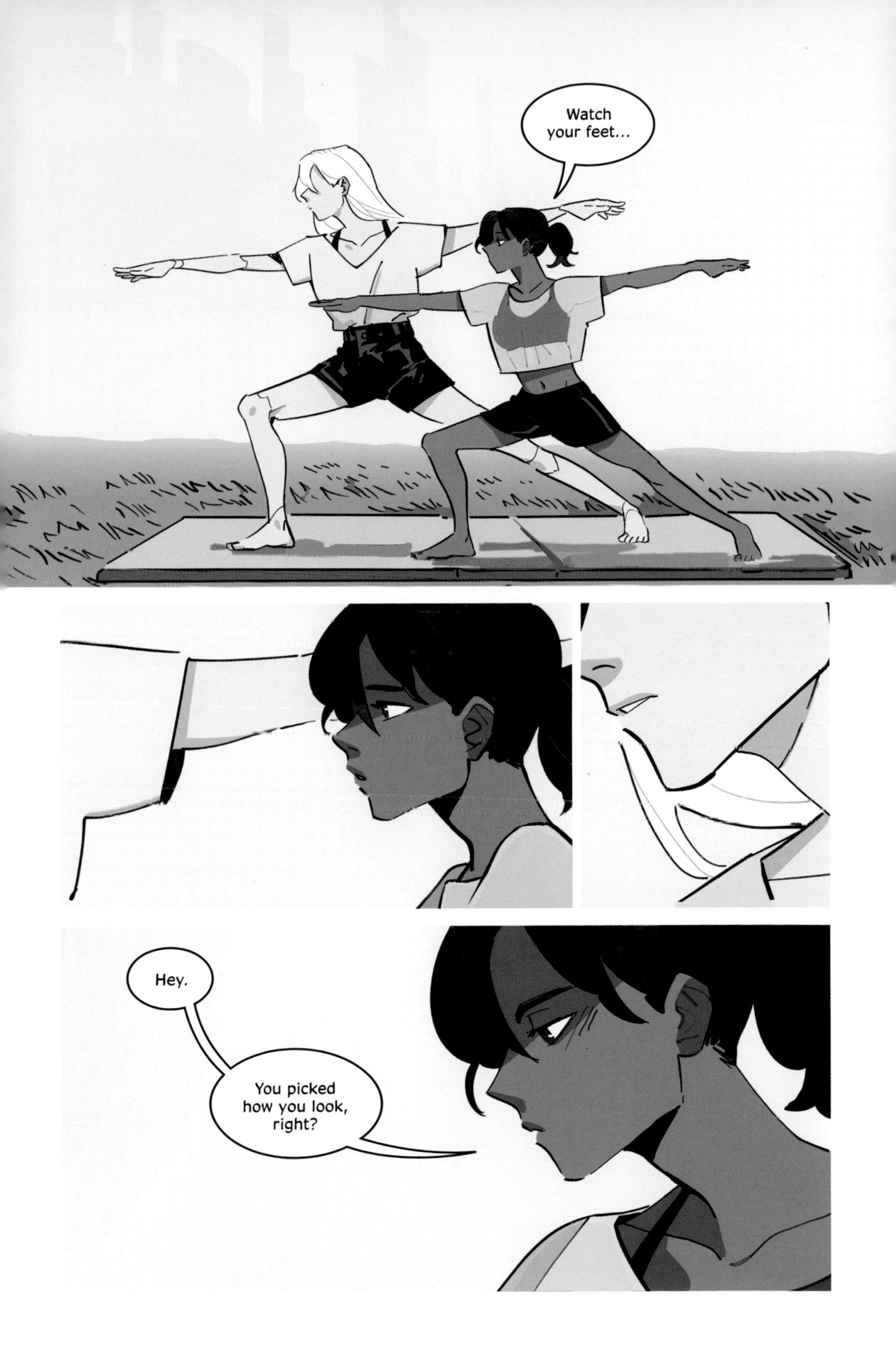

Watch your feet...
Hey.
You picked how you look, right?

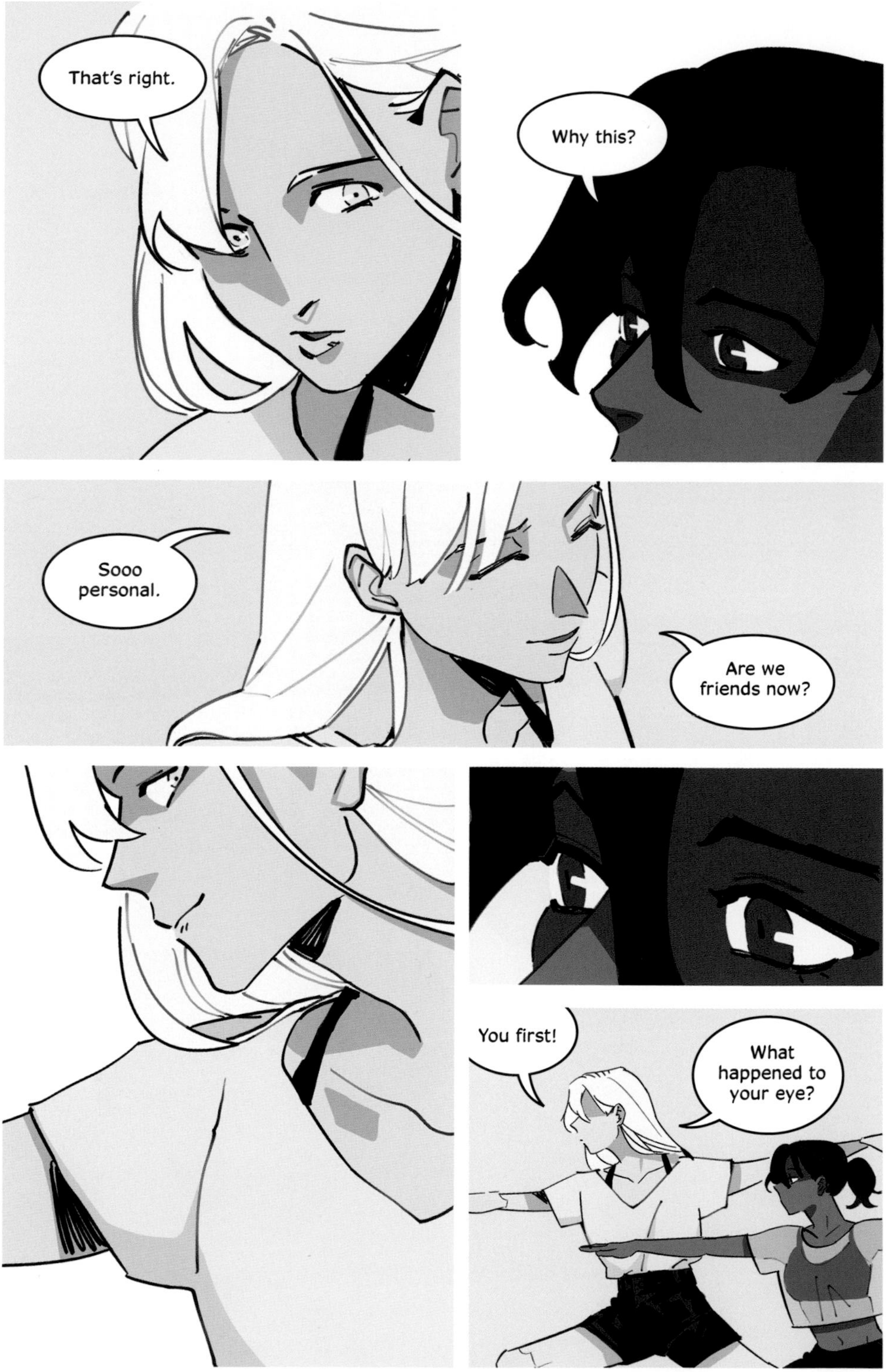
That's right.
Why this?
Sooo personal.
Are we friends now?
You first!
What happened to your eye?

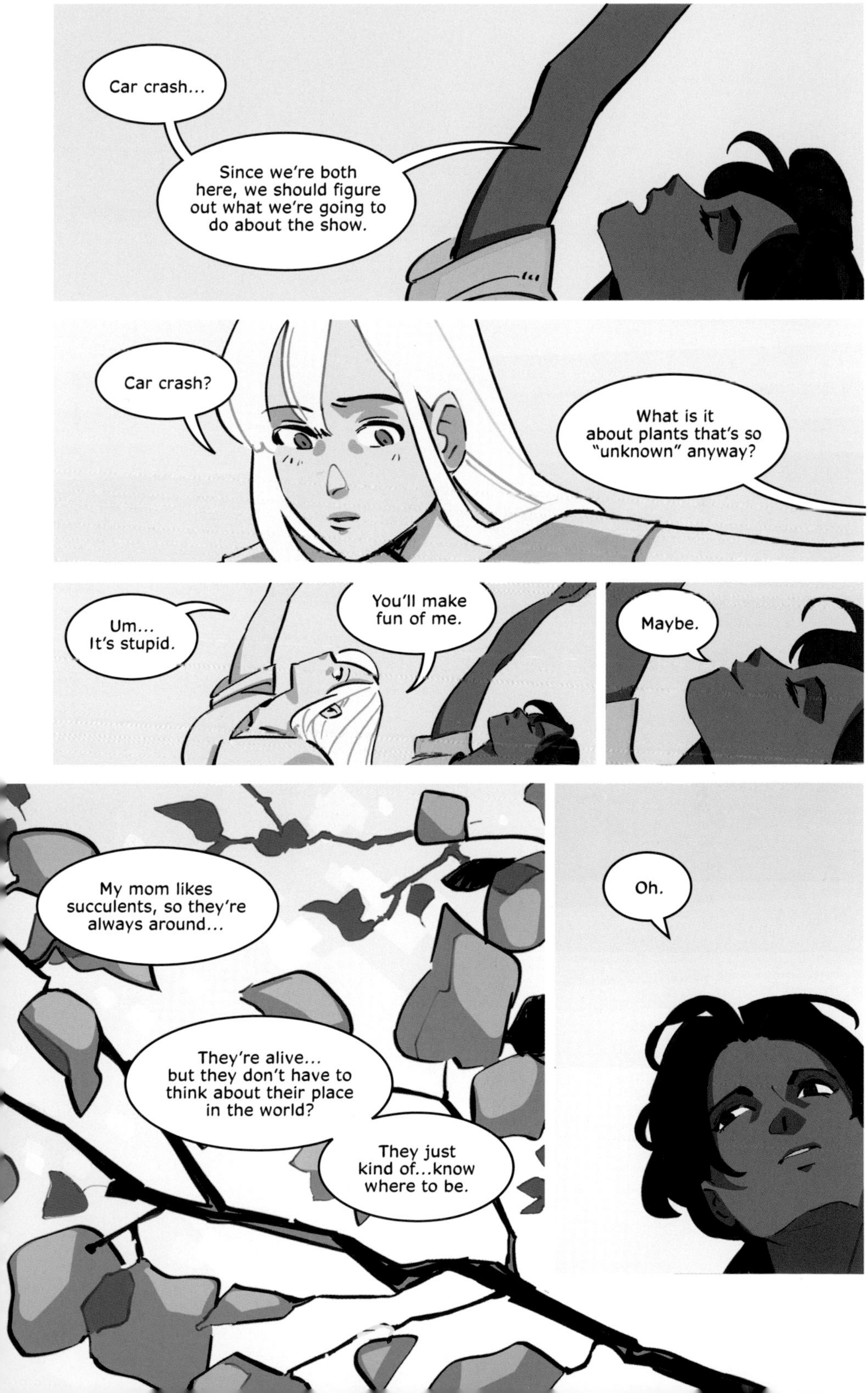
Car crash...
Since we're both here, we should figure out what we're going to do about the show.
Car crash?
What is it about plants that's so "unknown" anyway?
Um... It's stupid.
You'll make fun of me.
Maybe.
My mom likes succulents, so they're always around...
They're alive... but they don't have to think about their place in the world?
They just kind of...know where to be.
Oh.

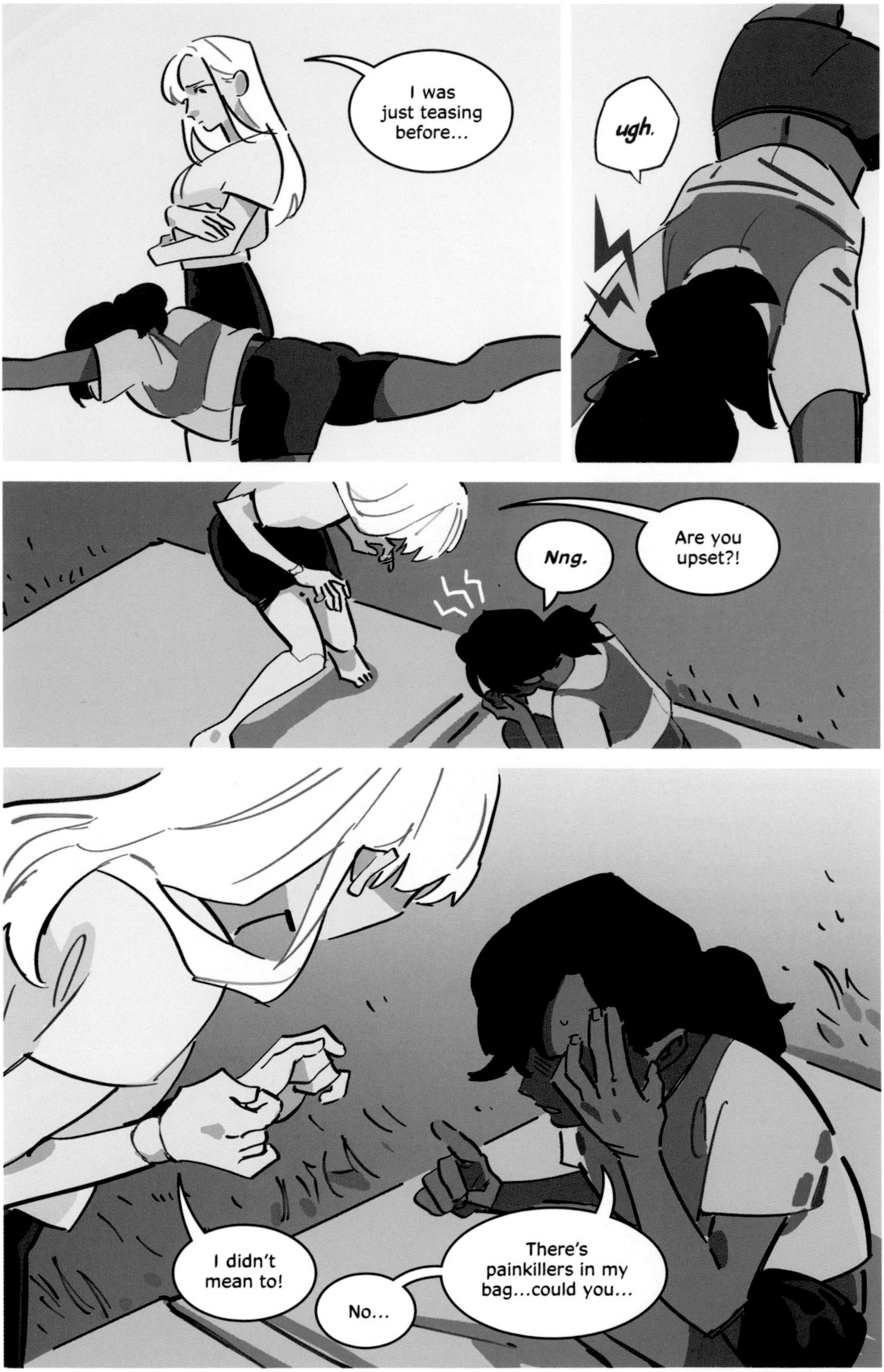
I was just teasing before...
ugh.
Nng.
Are you upset?!
I didn't mean to!
No...
There's painkillers in my bag...could you...

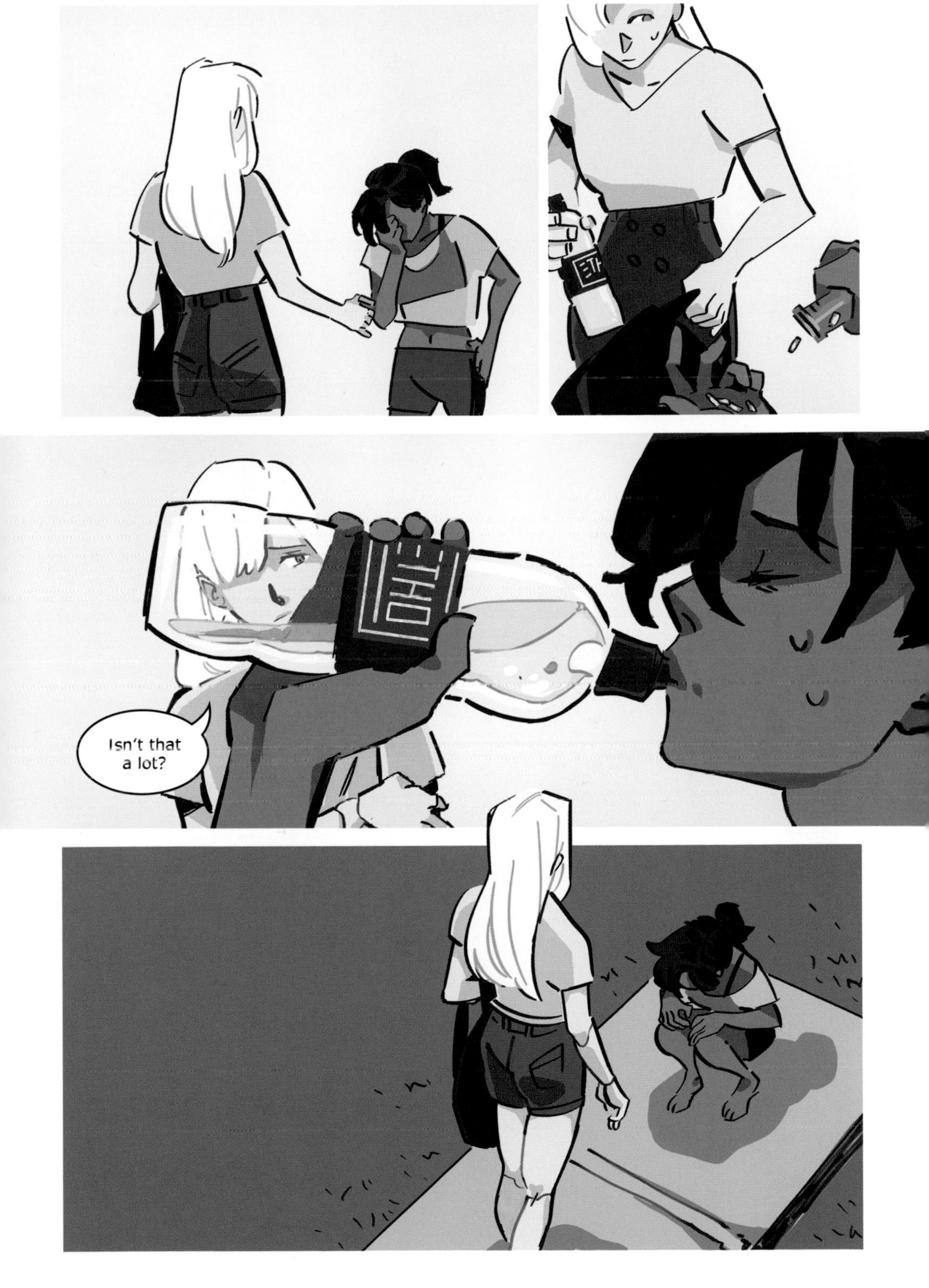
Isn't that a lot?

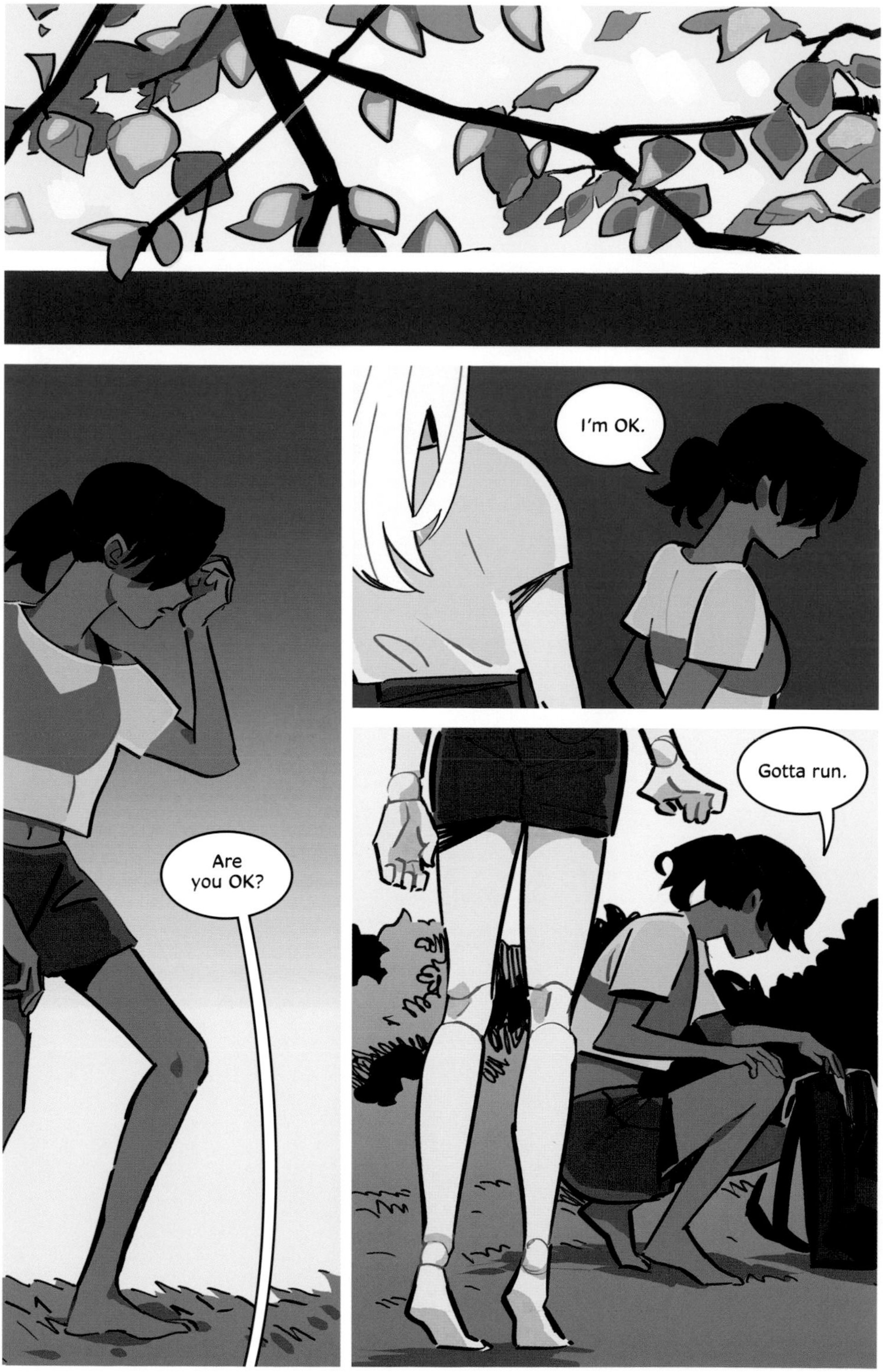
Are you OK?
I'm OK.
Gotta run.

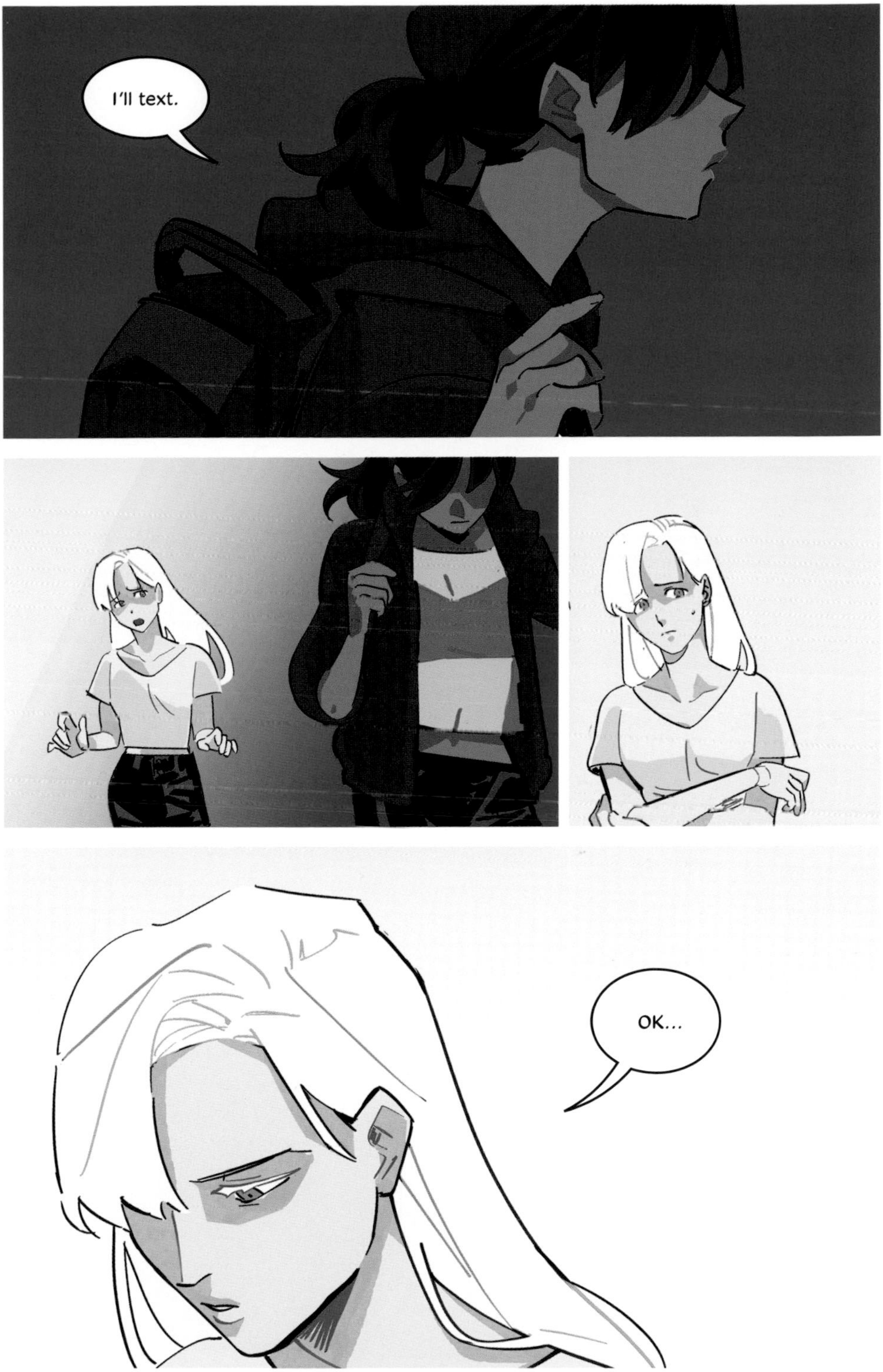
I'll text.
OK...

Study finds bias by gender and skin type across multiple commercial AI systems: Neural networks failed to recognize some photo portraits as showing a human face at all.

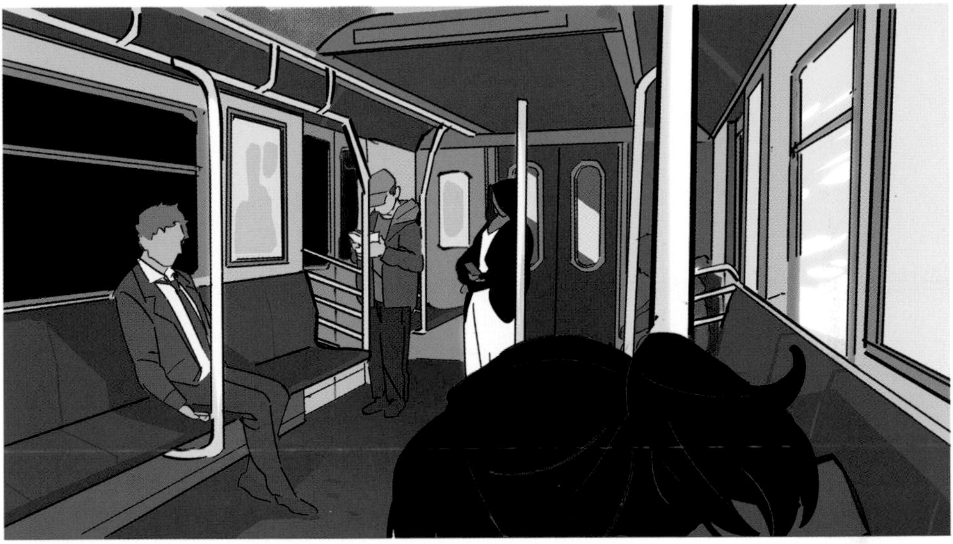

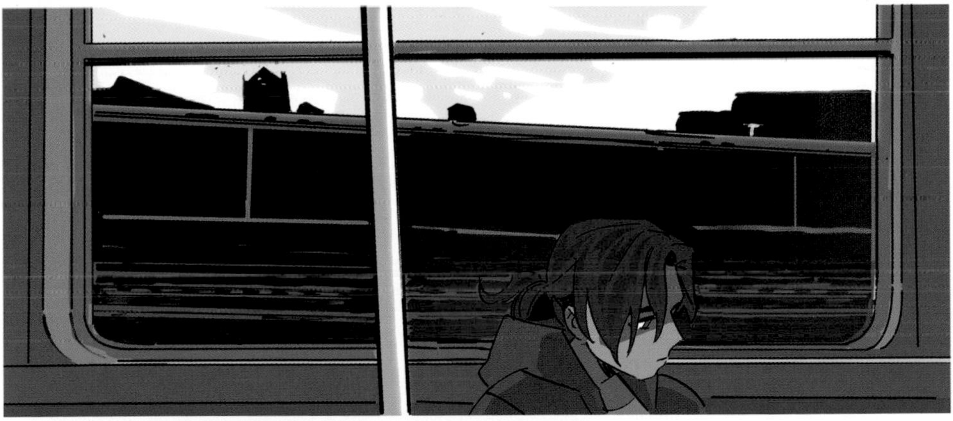

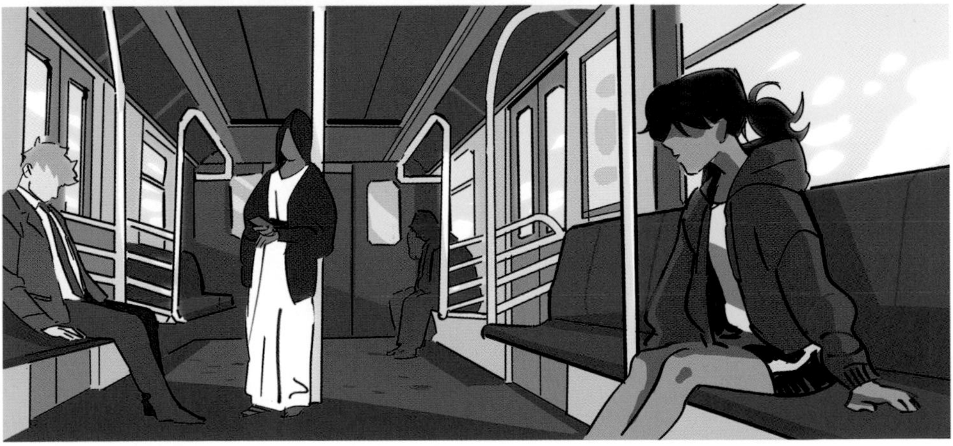

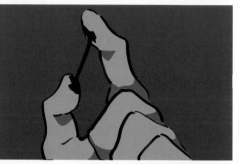

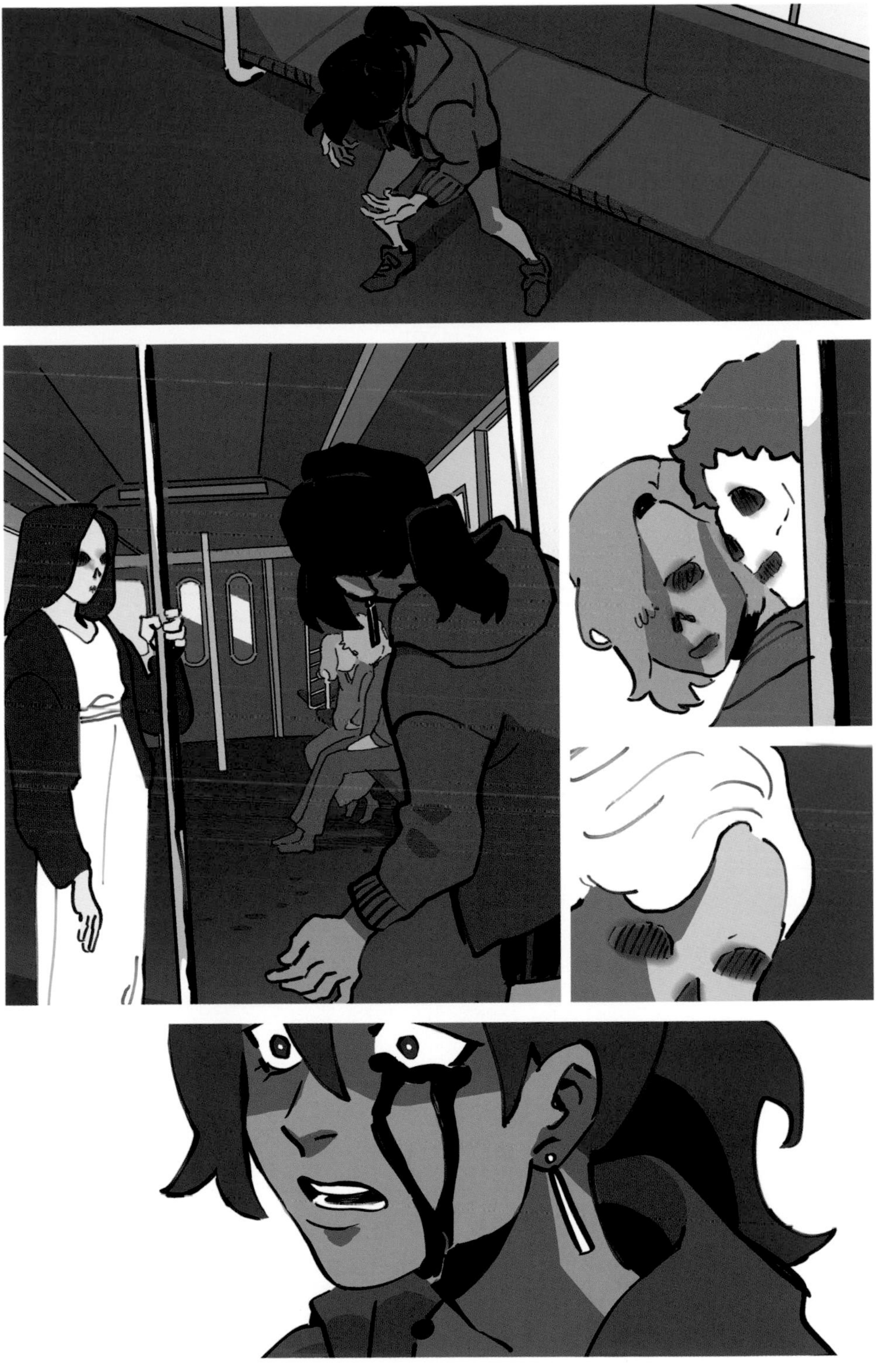

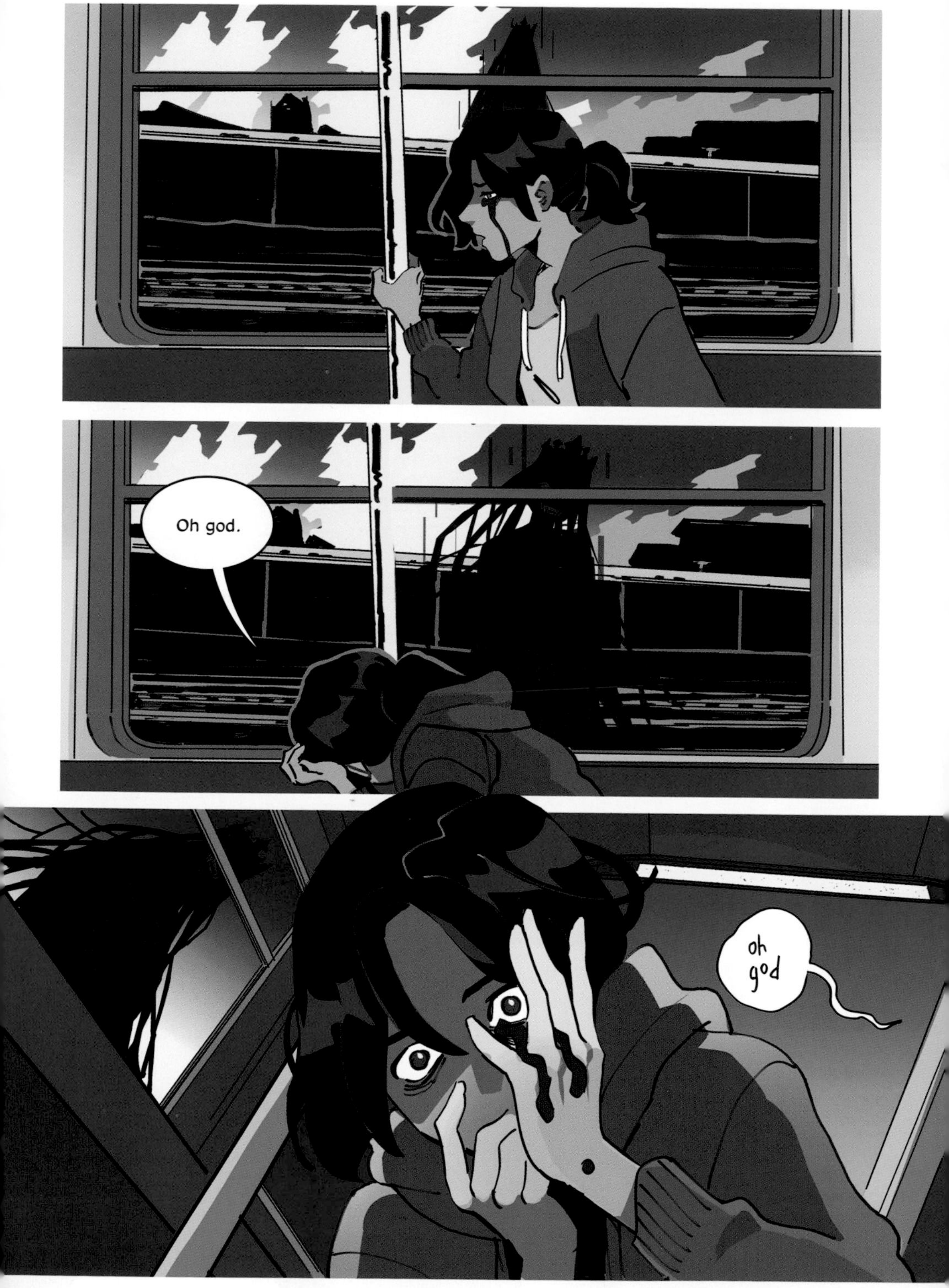
Oh god.
oh god

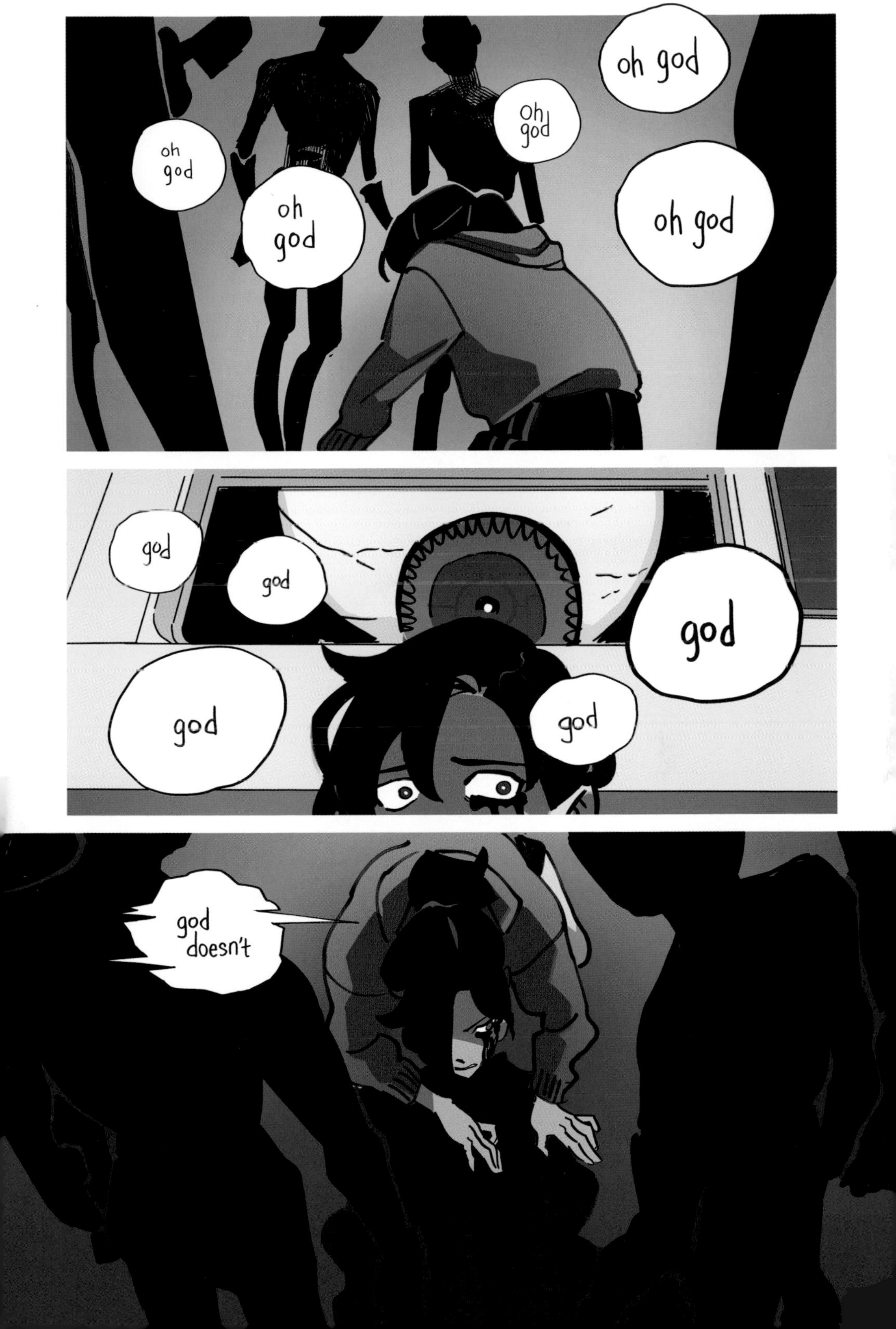
oh god
oh god
oh god
oh god
oh god
god
god
god
god
god
god doesn't

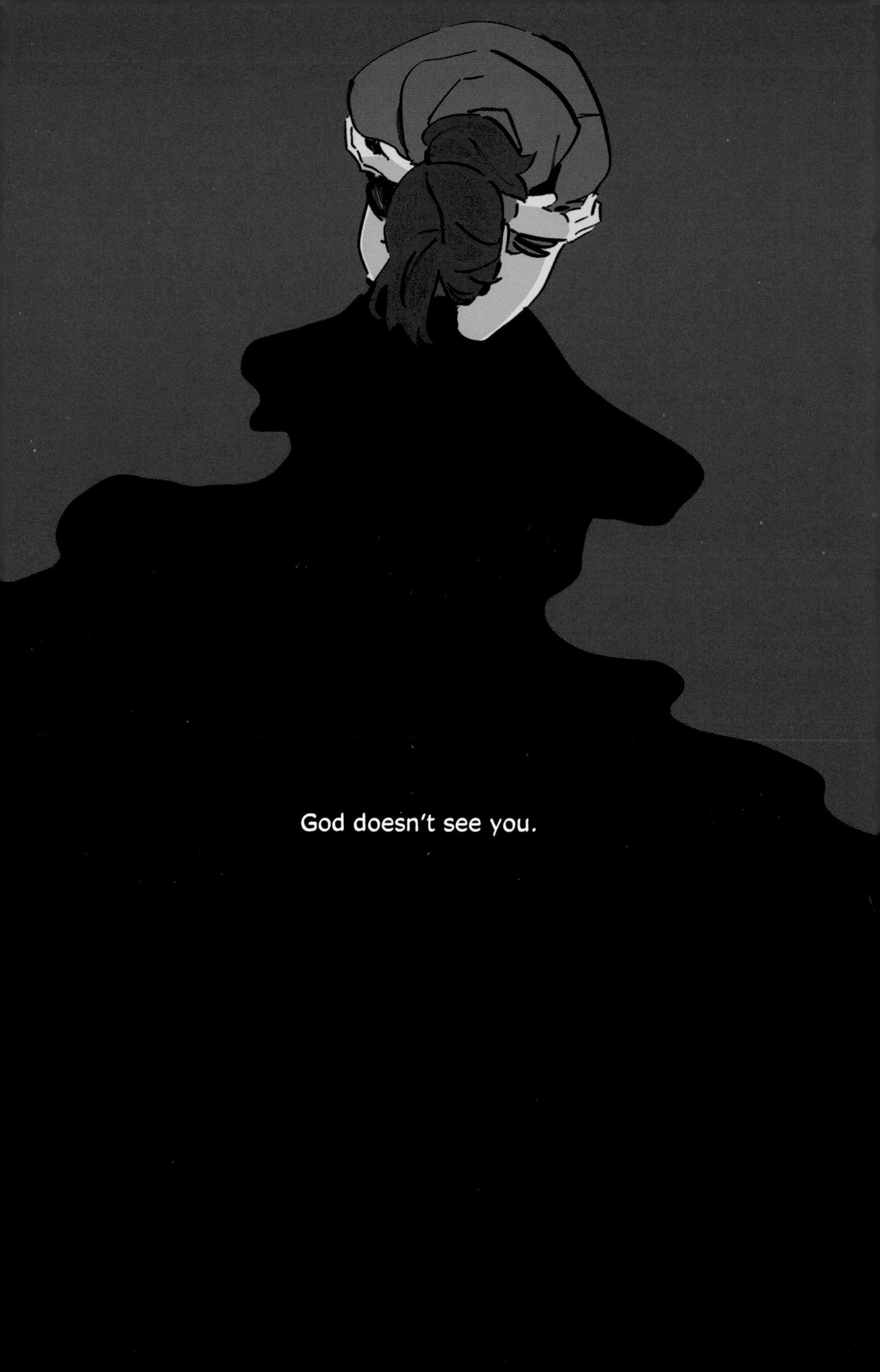
God doesn't see you.

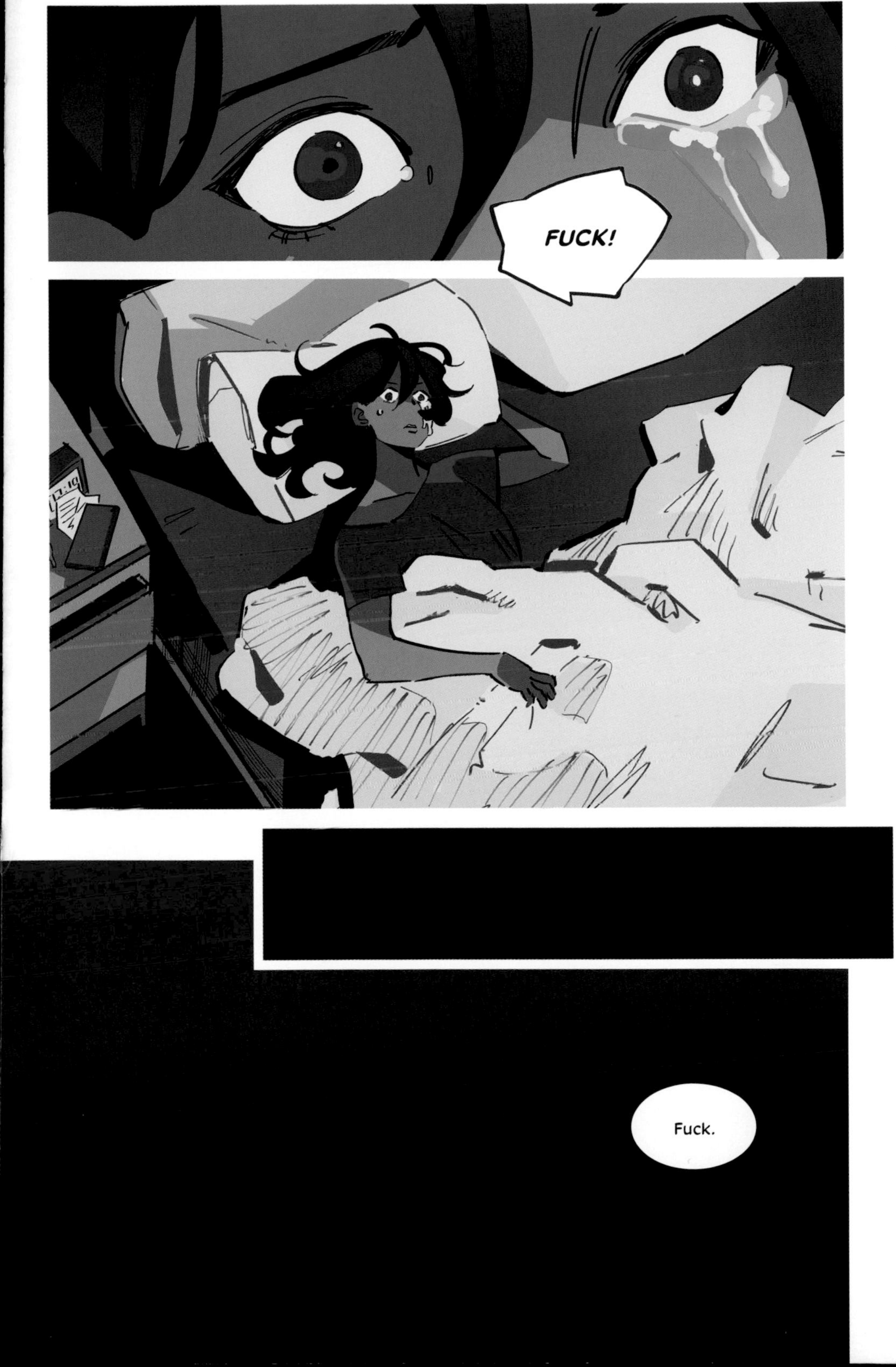
FUCK!
Fuck.

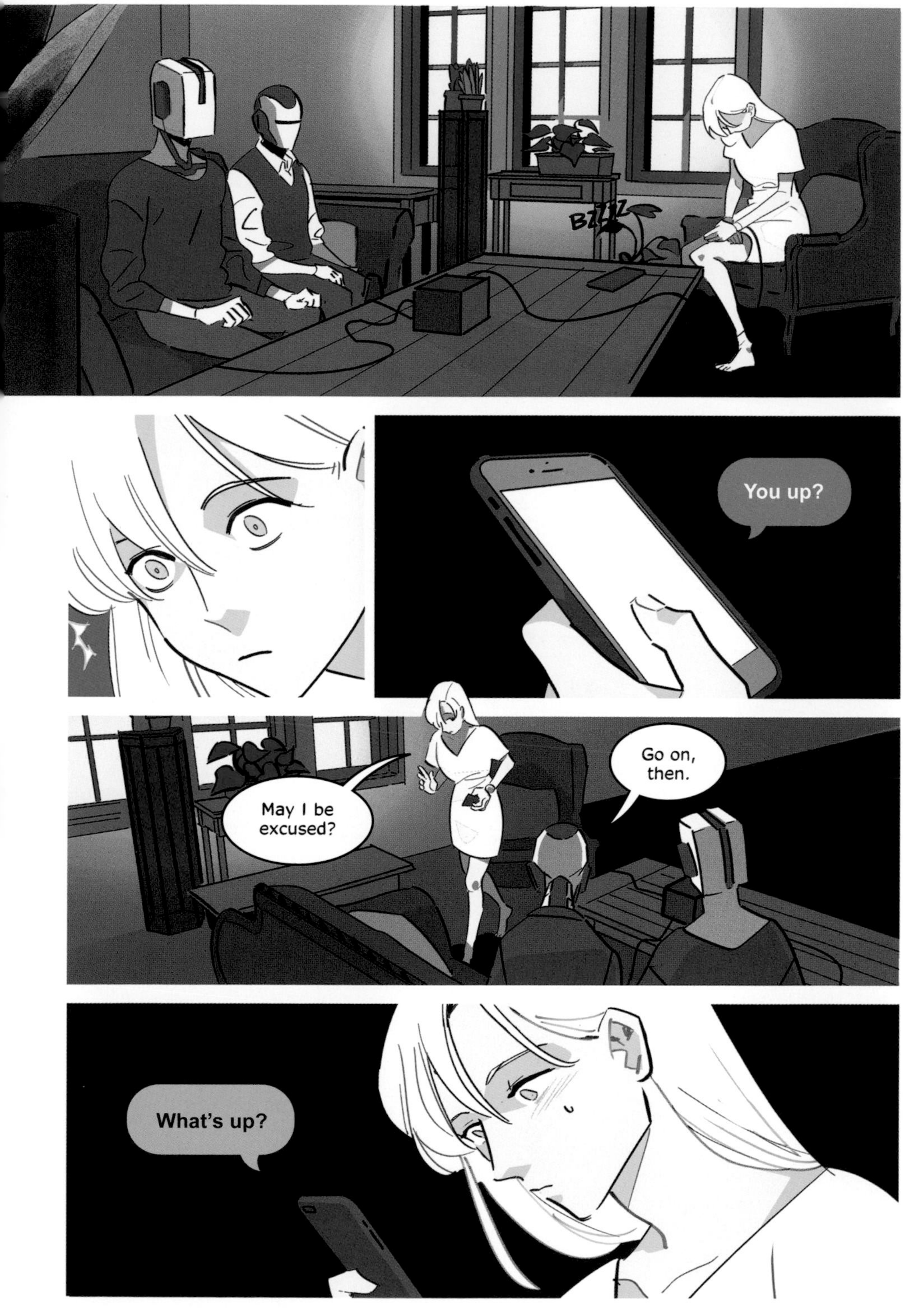
BZZZ
You up?
May I be excused?
Go on, then.
What's up?

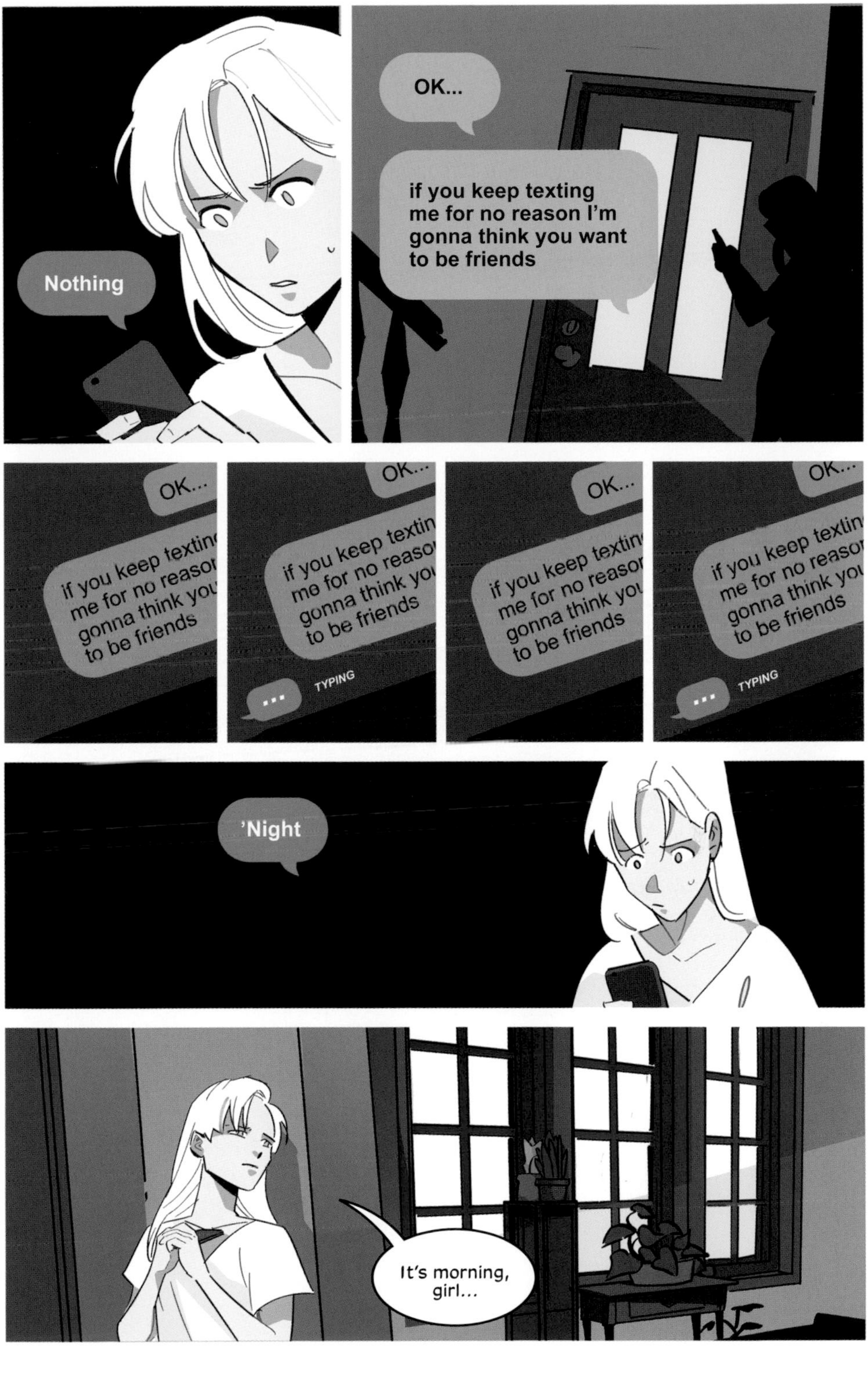
Nothing
OK...
if you keep texting me for no reason I'm gonna think you want to be friends
TYPING
TYPING
'Night
It's morning, girl...

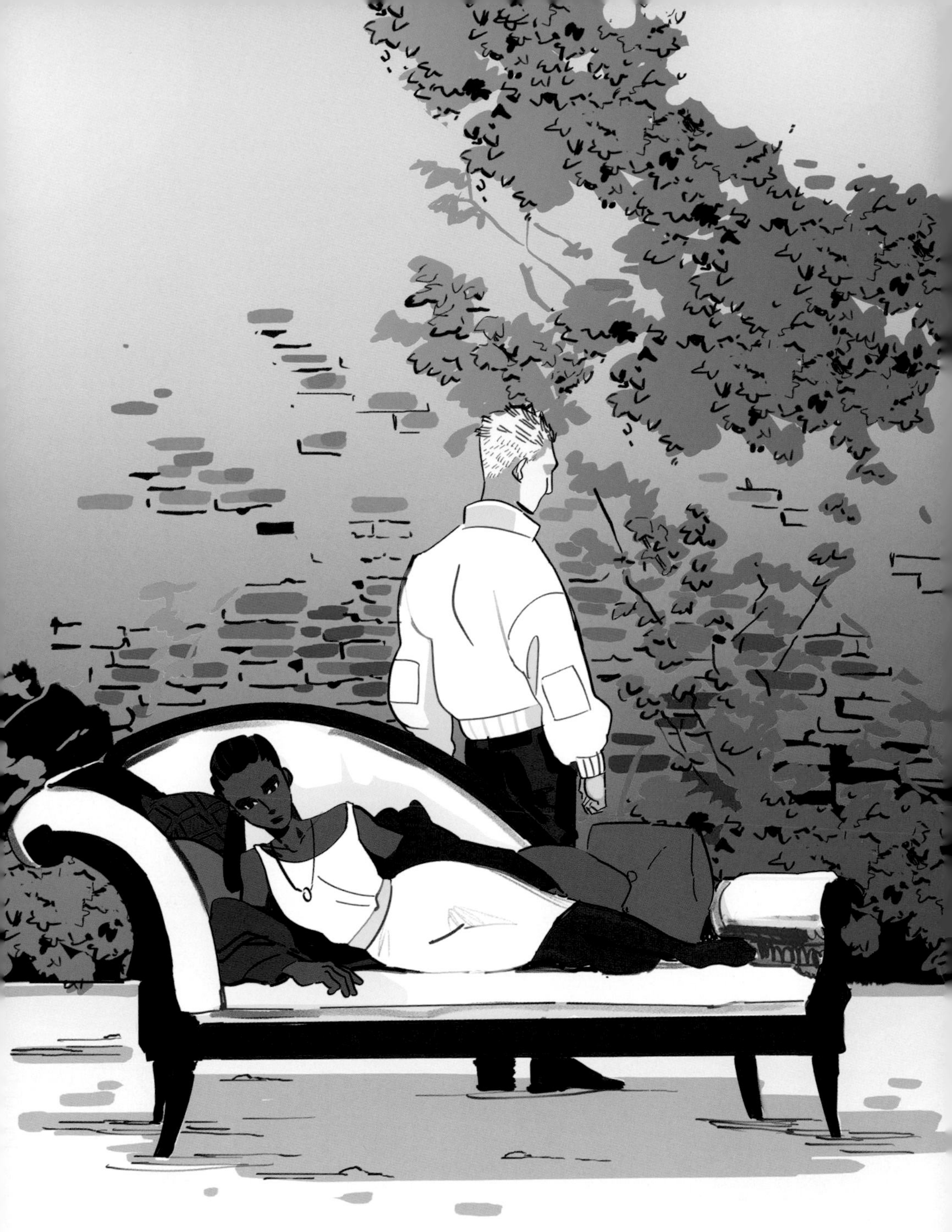

PHOTO CREDIT: INDIRA VISARIYA

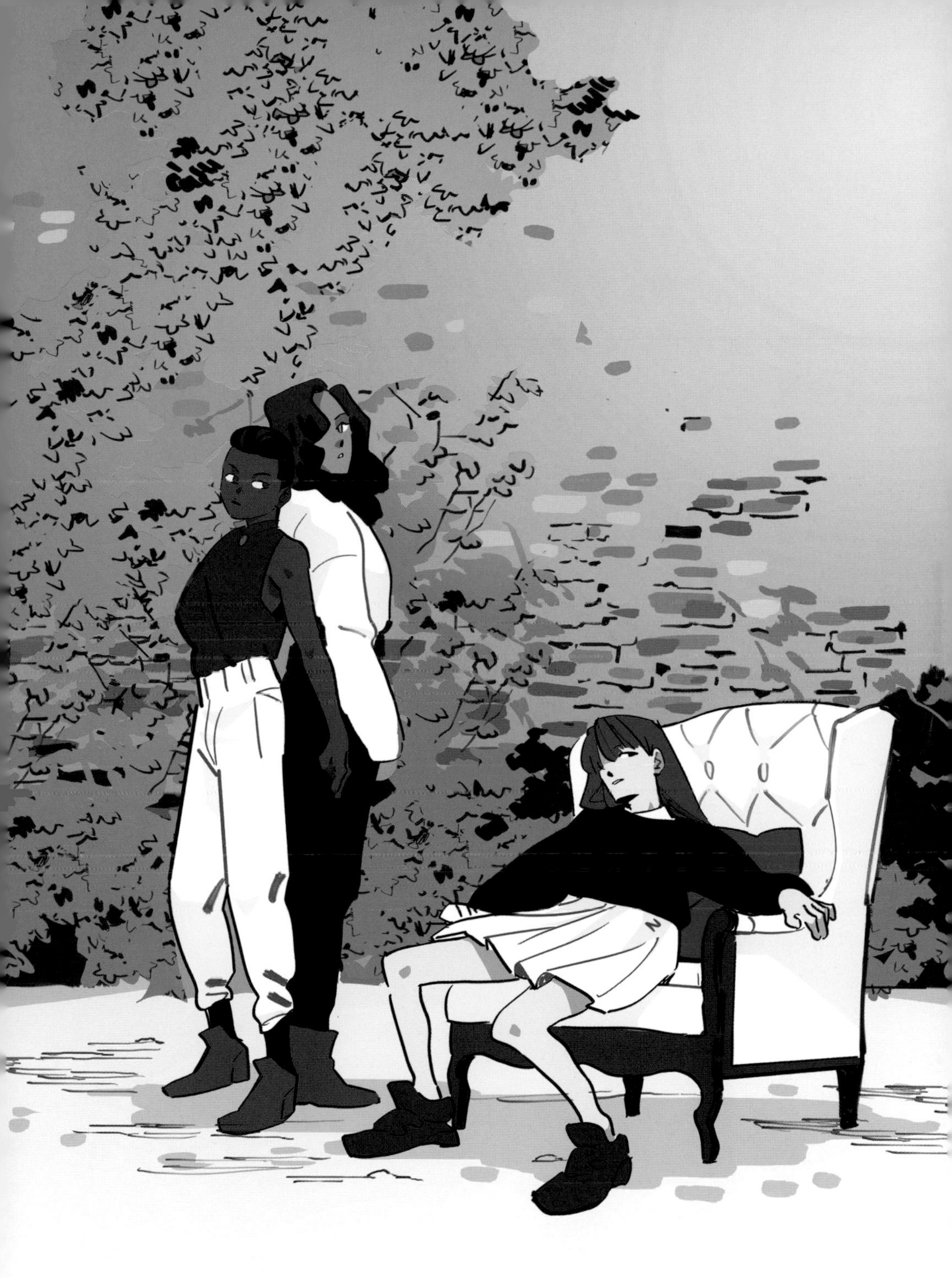

PHOTO CREDIT: INDIRA VISARIYA

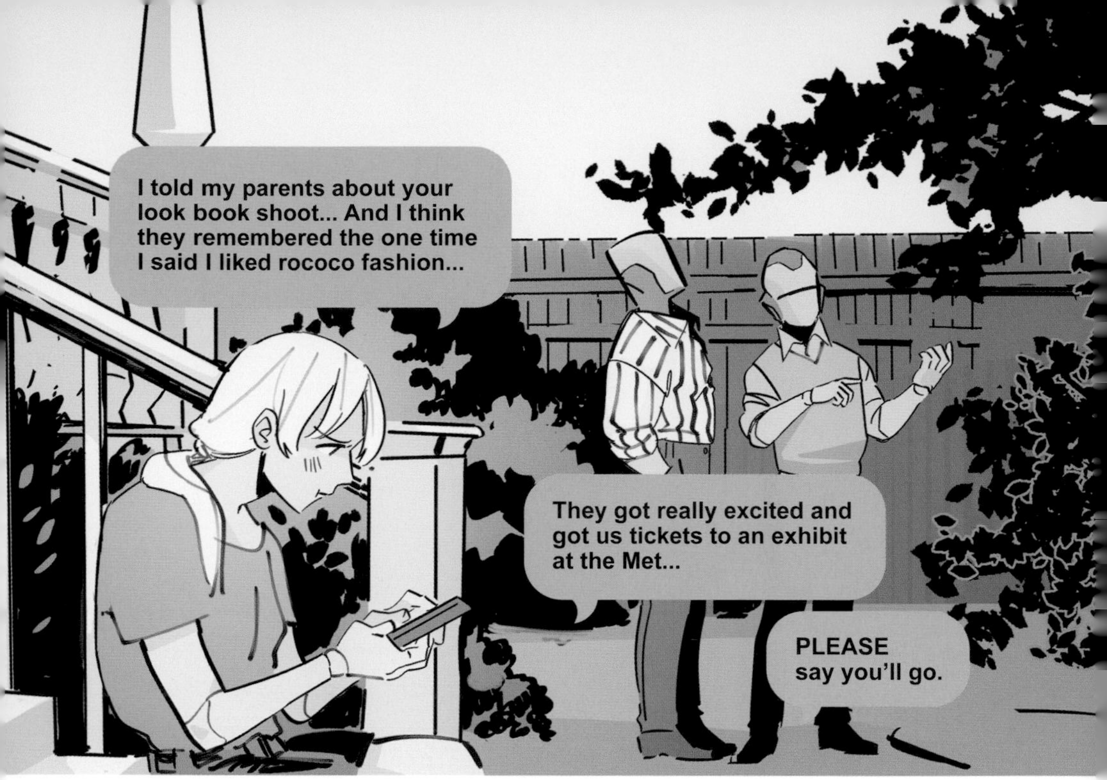
I told my parents about your look book shoot... And I think they remembered the one time I said I liked rococo fashion...
They got really excited and got us tickets to an exhibit at the Met...
PLEASE say you'll go.

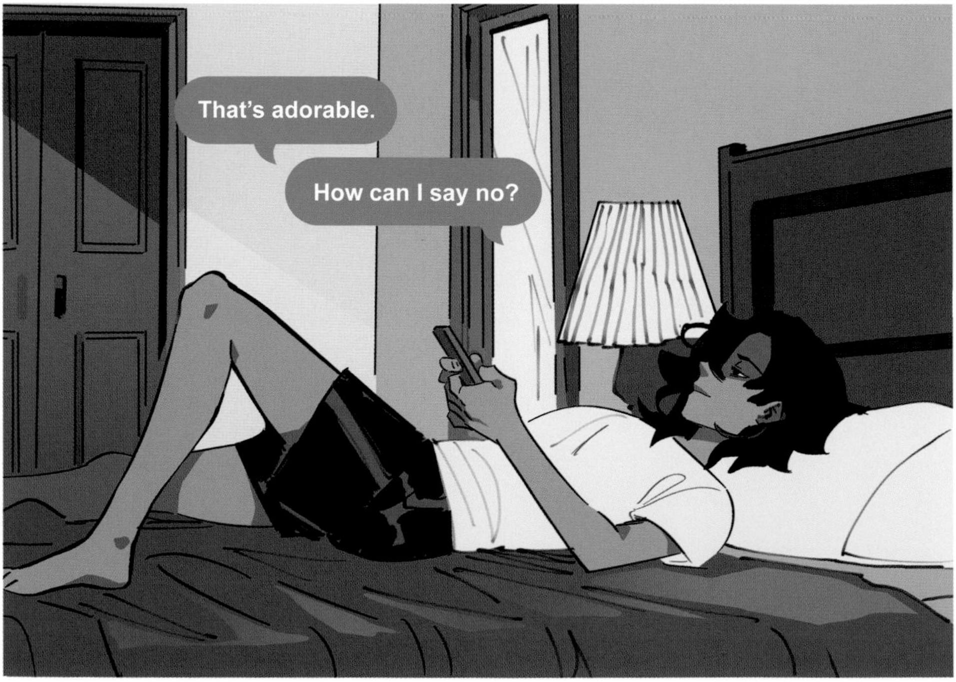
That's adorable.
How can I say no?

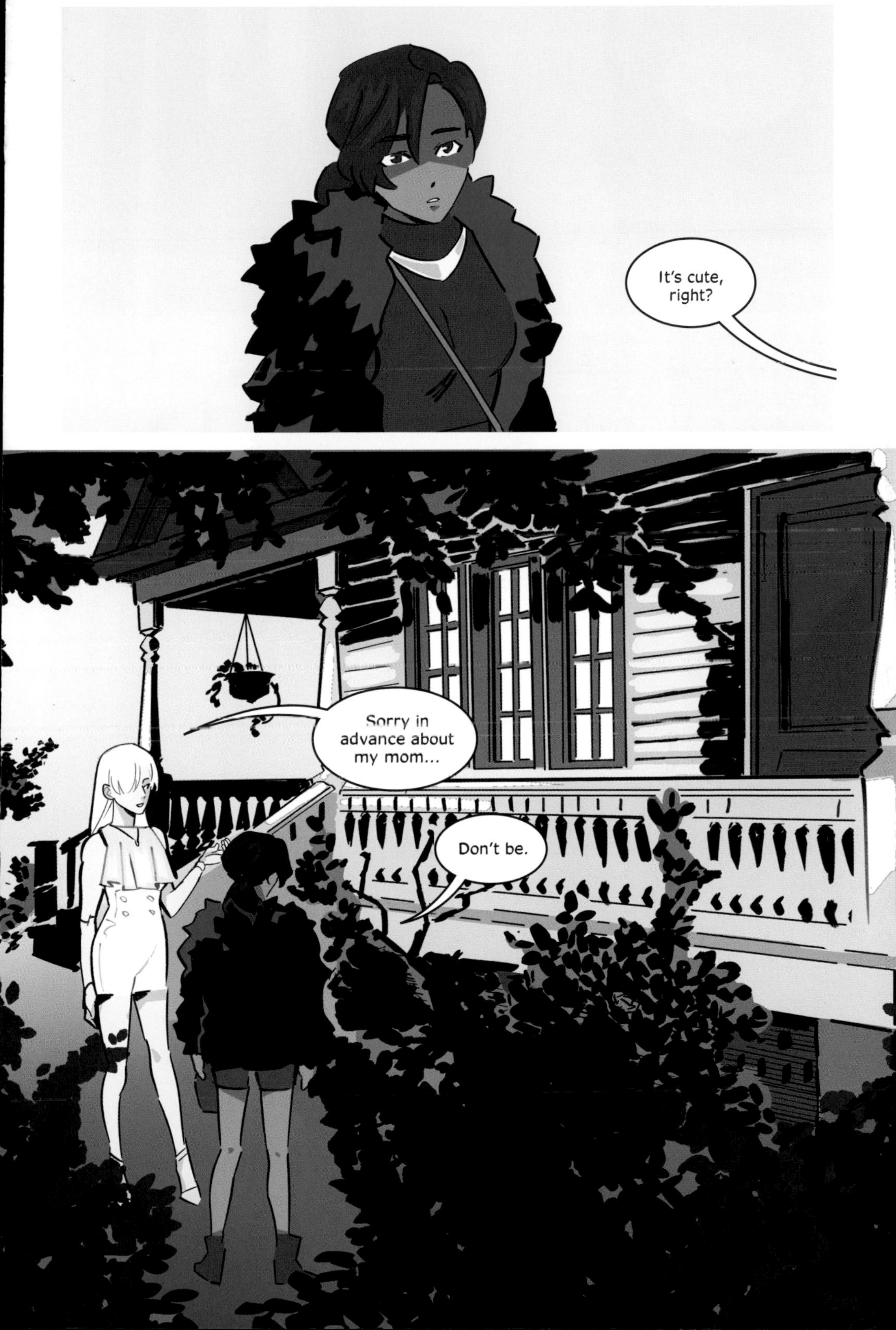
It's cute, right?
Sorry in advance about my mom...
Don't be.

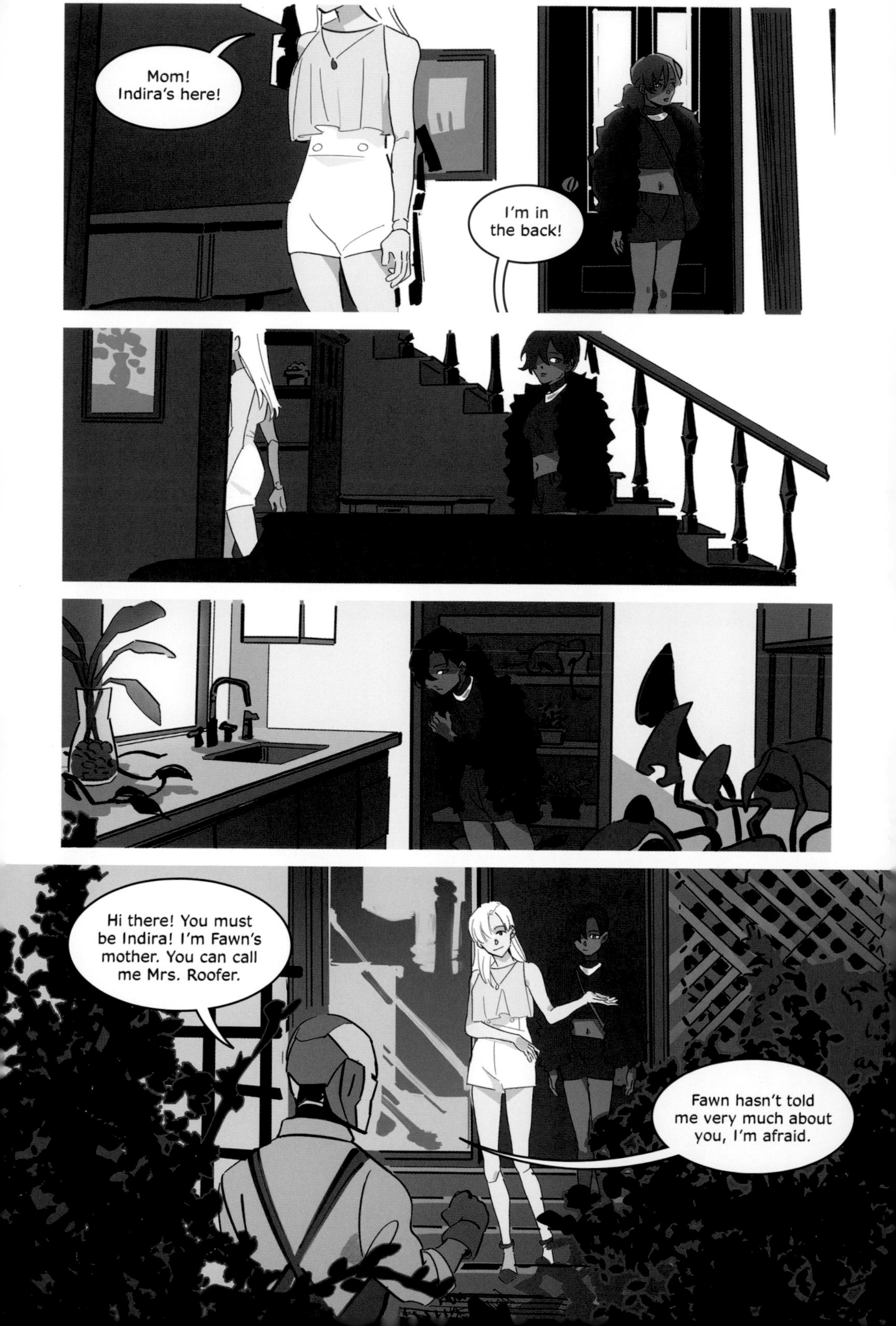
Mom!
Indira's here!
I'm in
the back!
Hi there! You must be Indira! I'm Fawn's mother. You can call me Mrs. Roofer.
Fawn hasn't told me very much about you, I'm afraid.

Well, she hates me.

Fawn. Is that true?

We should **REALLY** get going.

I'm not in a rush.

These are mums, right? Good for winter.

Oh, are you a gardener?

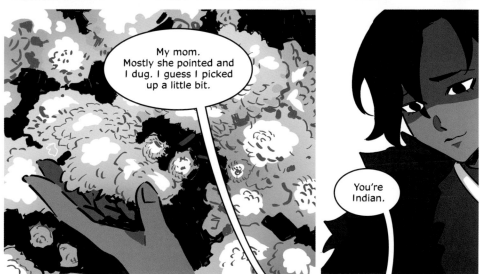

My mom. Mostly she pointed and I dug. I guess I picked up a little bit.

You're Indian.

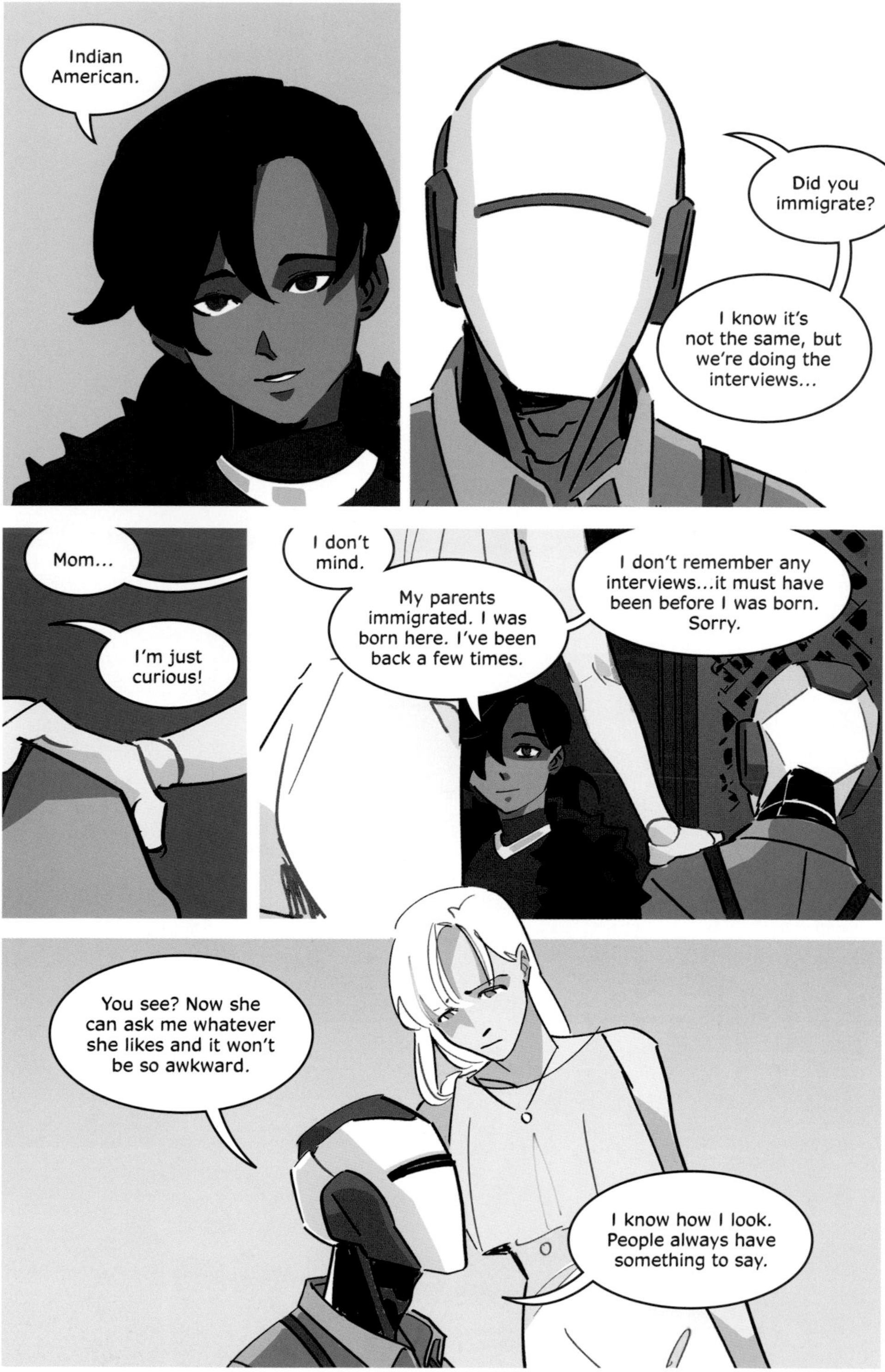
Indian American.
Did you immigrate?
I know it's not the same, but we're doing the interviews...
Mom...
I'm just curious!
I don't mind.
My parents immigrated. I was born here. I've been back a few times.
I don't remember any interviews...it must have been before I was born. Sorry.
You see? Now she can ask me whatever she likes and it won't be so awkward.
I know how I look. People always have something to say.

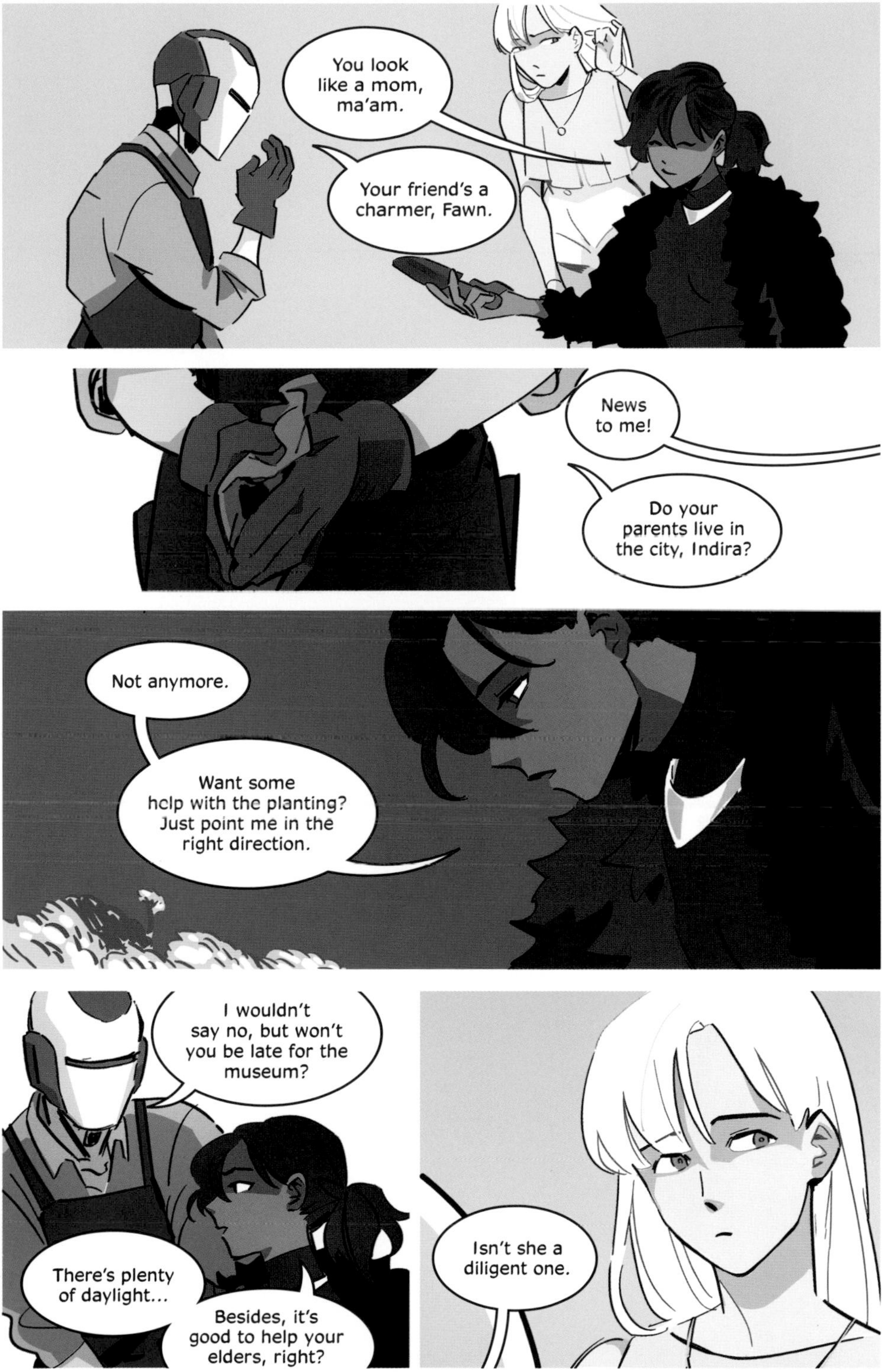
You look like a mom, ma'am.
Your friend's a charmer, Fawn.
News to me!
Do your parents live in the city, Indira?
Not anymore.
Want some help with the planting? Just point me in the right direction.
I wouldn't say no, but won't you be late for the museum?
There's plenty of daylight...
Besides, it's good to help your elders, right?
Isn't she a diligent one.

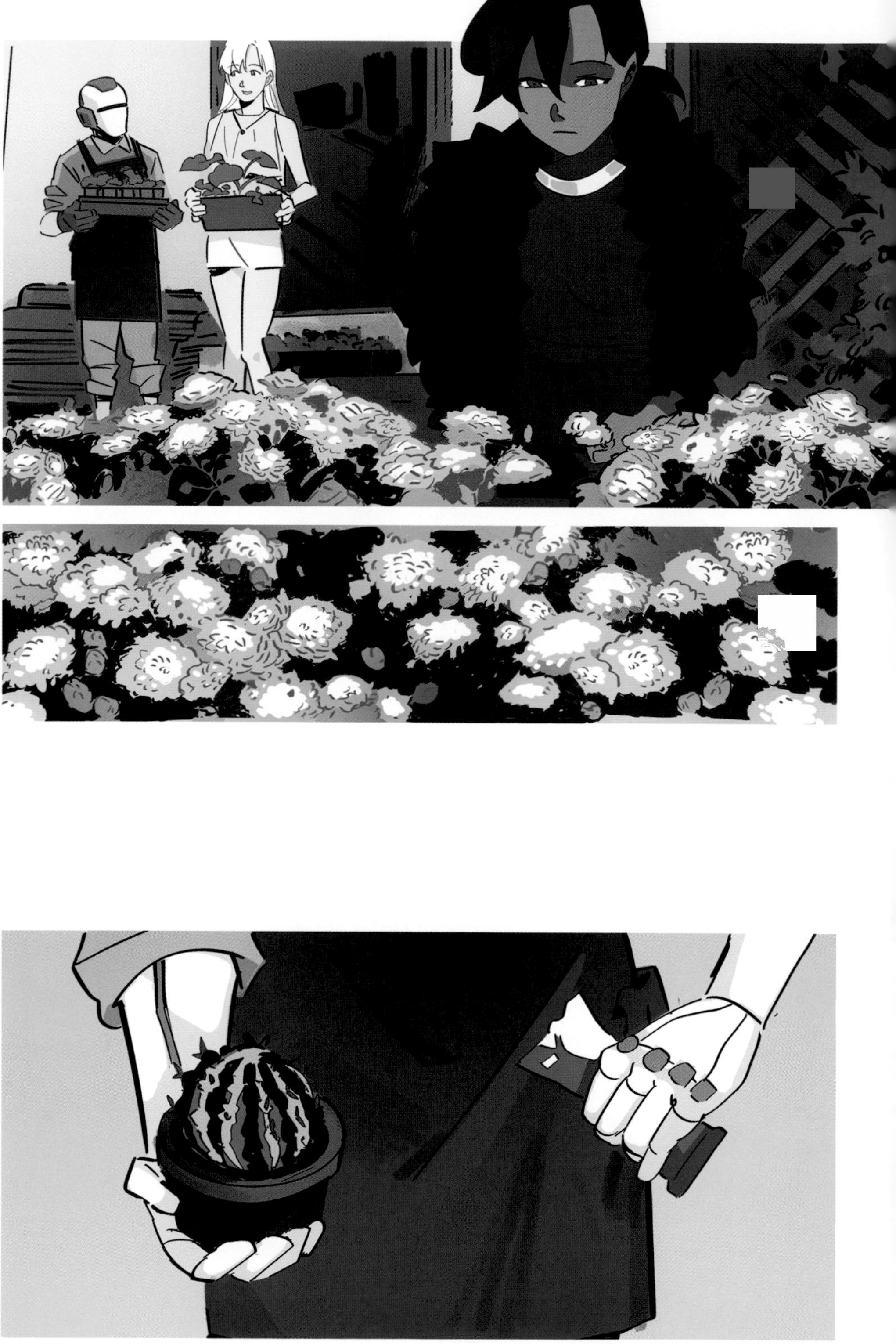

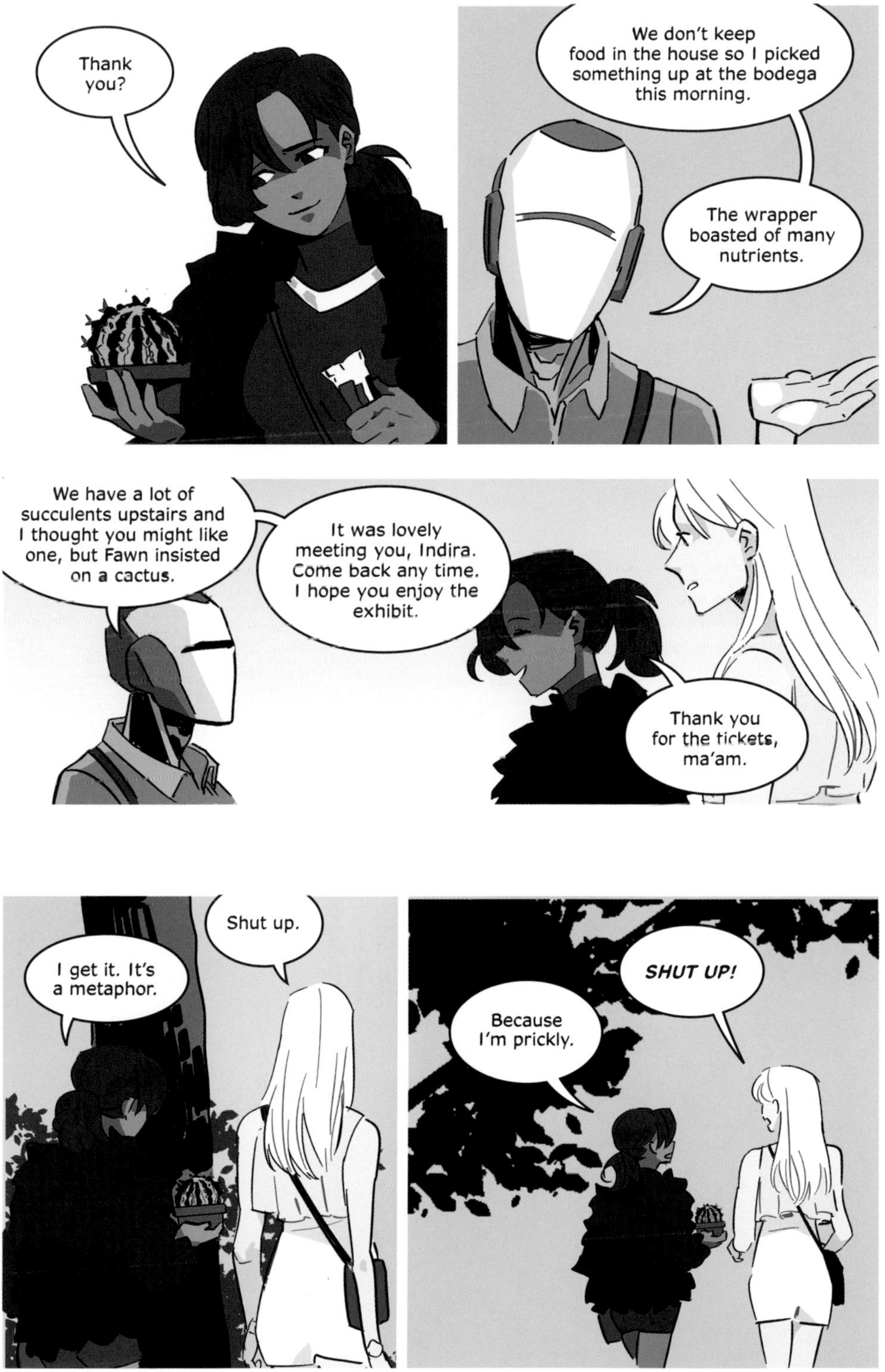
Thank you?
We don't keep food in the house so I picked something up at the bodega this morning.
The wrapper boasted of many nutrients.
We have a lot of succulents upstairs and I thought you might like one, but Fawn insisted on a cactus.
It was lovely meeting you, Indira. Come back any time. I hope you enjoy the exhibit.
Thank you for the tickets, ma'am.
I get it. It's a metaphor.
Shut up.
Because I'm prickly.
SHUT UP!

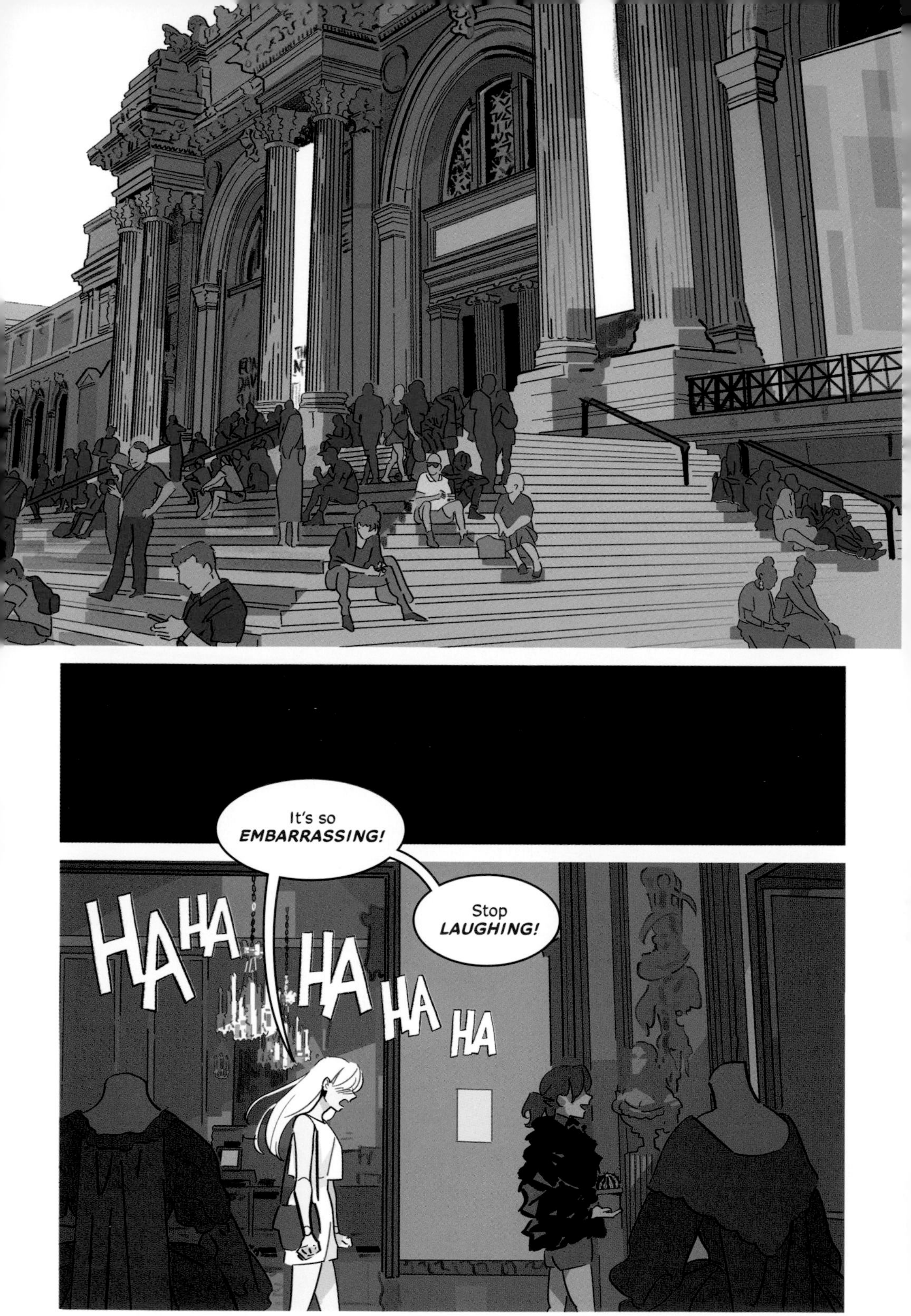
It's so
EMBARRASSING!
HAHA
HA HA HA HA
Stop
LAUGHING!

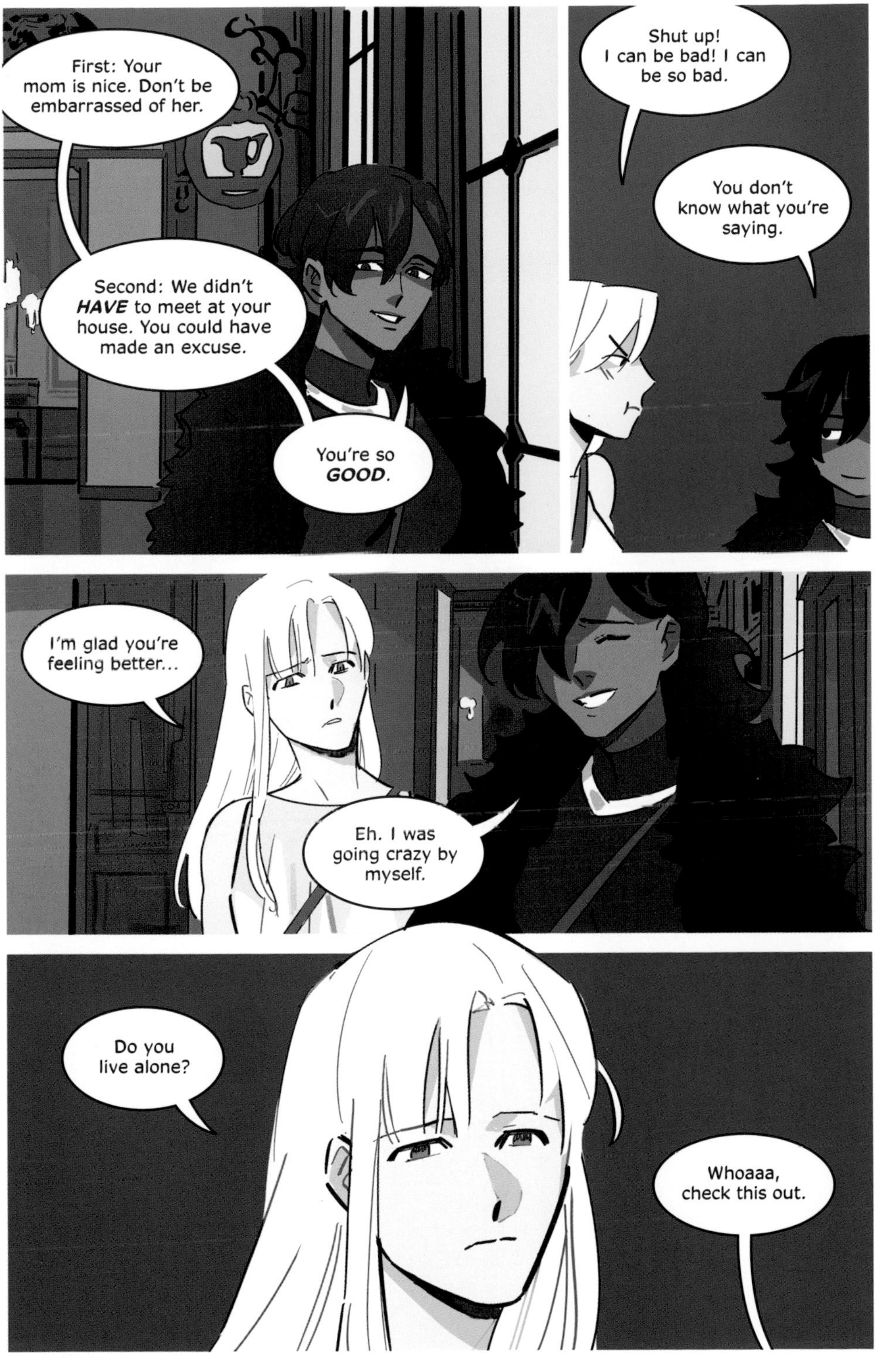
First: Your mom is nice. Don't be embarrassed of her.
Second: We didn't ***HAVE*** to meet at your house. You could have made an excuse.
You're so ***GOOD***.
Shut up! I can be bad! I can be so bad.
You don't know what you're saying.
I'm glad you're feeling better...
Eh. I was going crazy by myself.
Do you live alone?
Whoaaa, check this out.

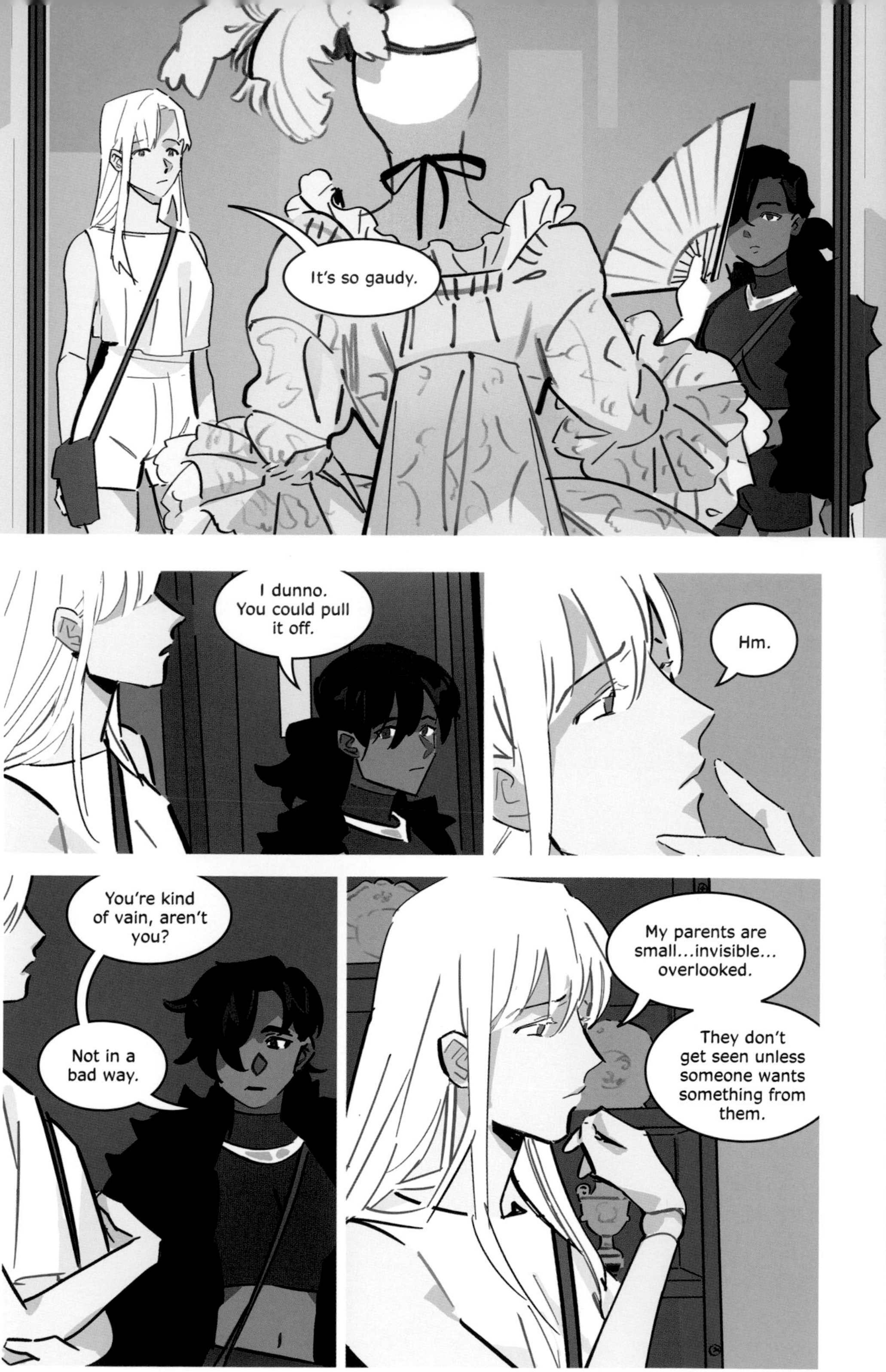
It's so gaudy.
I dunno. You could pull it off.
Hm.
You're kind of vain, aren't you?
Not in a bad way.
My parents are small...invisible... overlooked.
They don't get seen unless someone wants something from them.

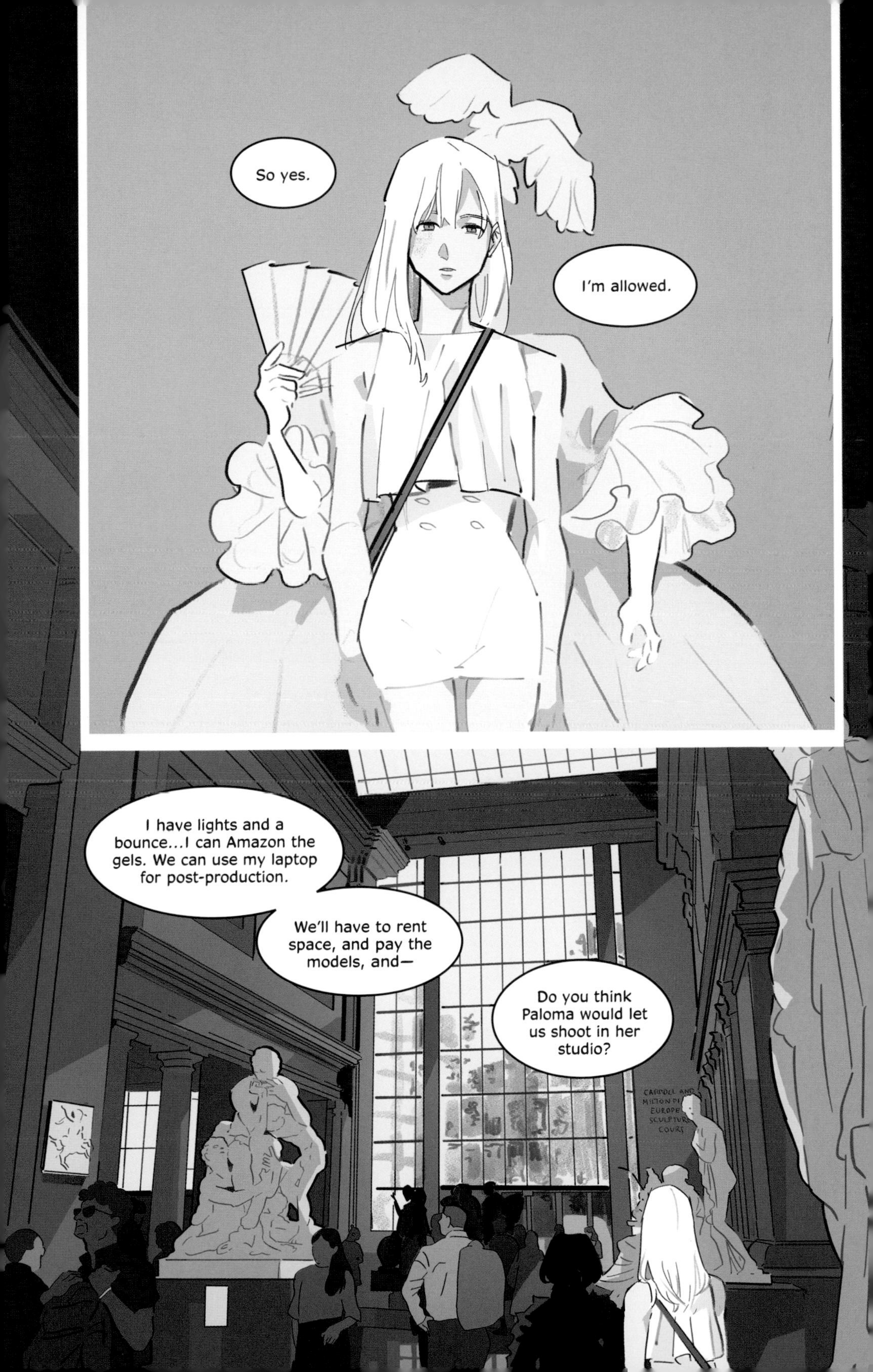
So yes.
I'm allowed.
I have lights and a bounce...I can Amazon the gels. We can use my laptop for post-production.
We'll have to rent space, and pay the models, and—
Do you think Paloma would let us shoot in her studio?

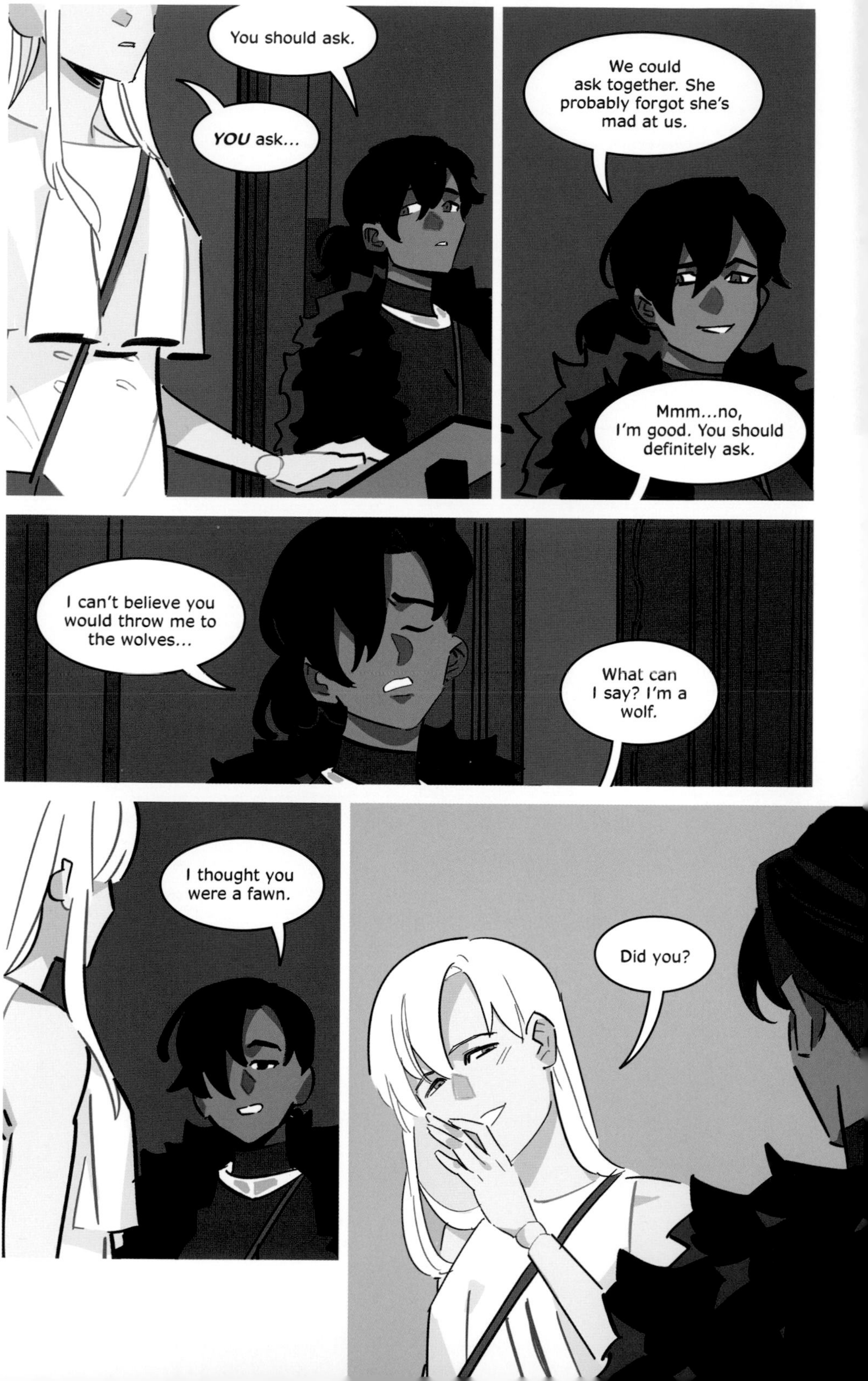
You should ask.
YOU ask...
We could ask together. She probably forgot she's mad at us.
Mmm...no, I'm good. You should definitely ask.
I can't believe you would throw me to the wolves...
What can I say? I'm a wolf.
I thought you were a fawn.
Did you?

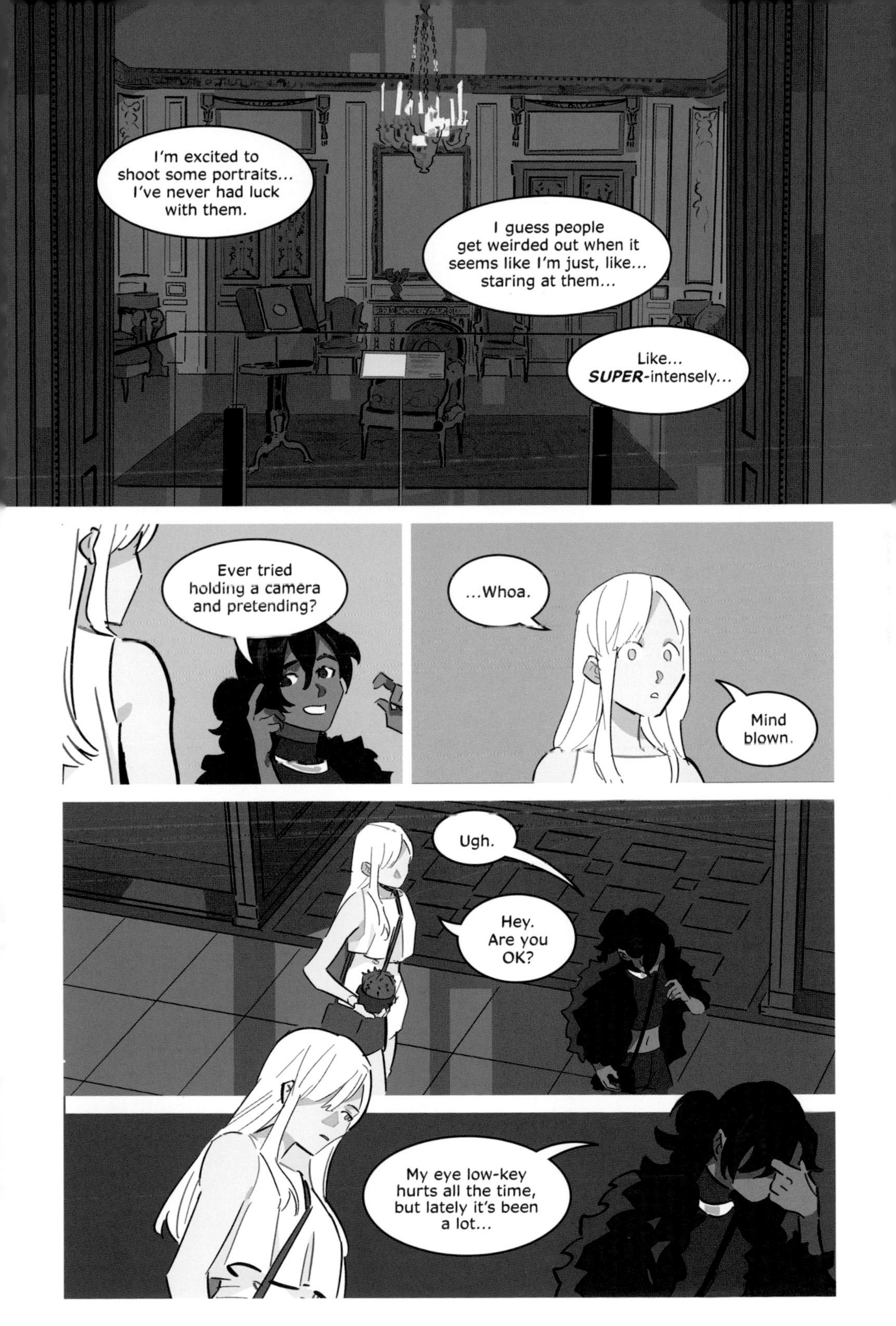
I'm excited to shoot some portraits... I've never had luck with them.
I guess people get weirded out when it seems like I'm just, like... staring at them...
Like... **SUPER**-intensely...
Ever tried holding a camera and pretending?
...Whoa.
Mind blown.
Ugh.
Hey. Are you OK?
My eye low-key hurts all the time, but lately it's been a lot...

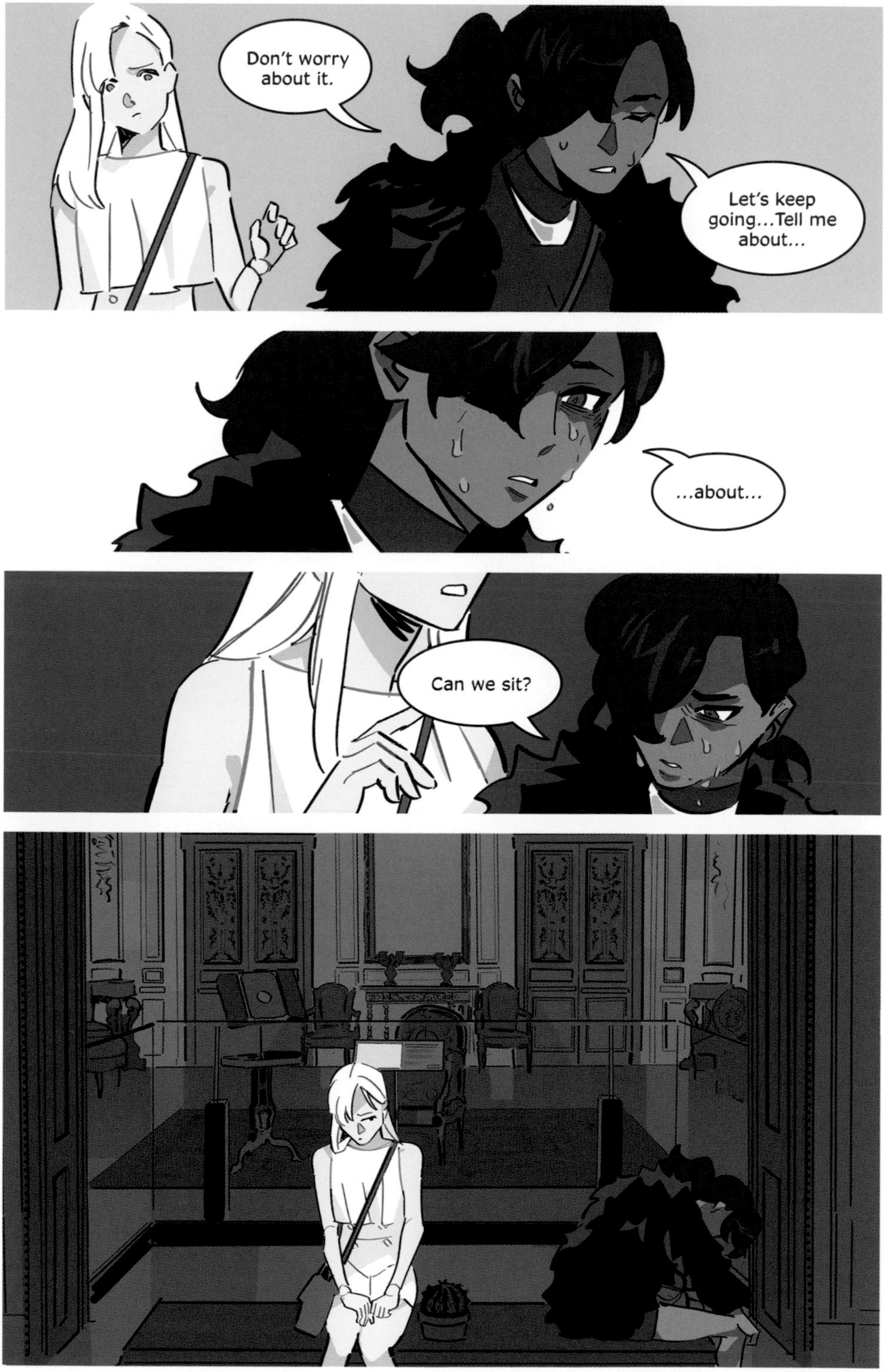
Don't worry about it.
Let's keep going...Tell me about...
...about...
Can we sit?

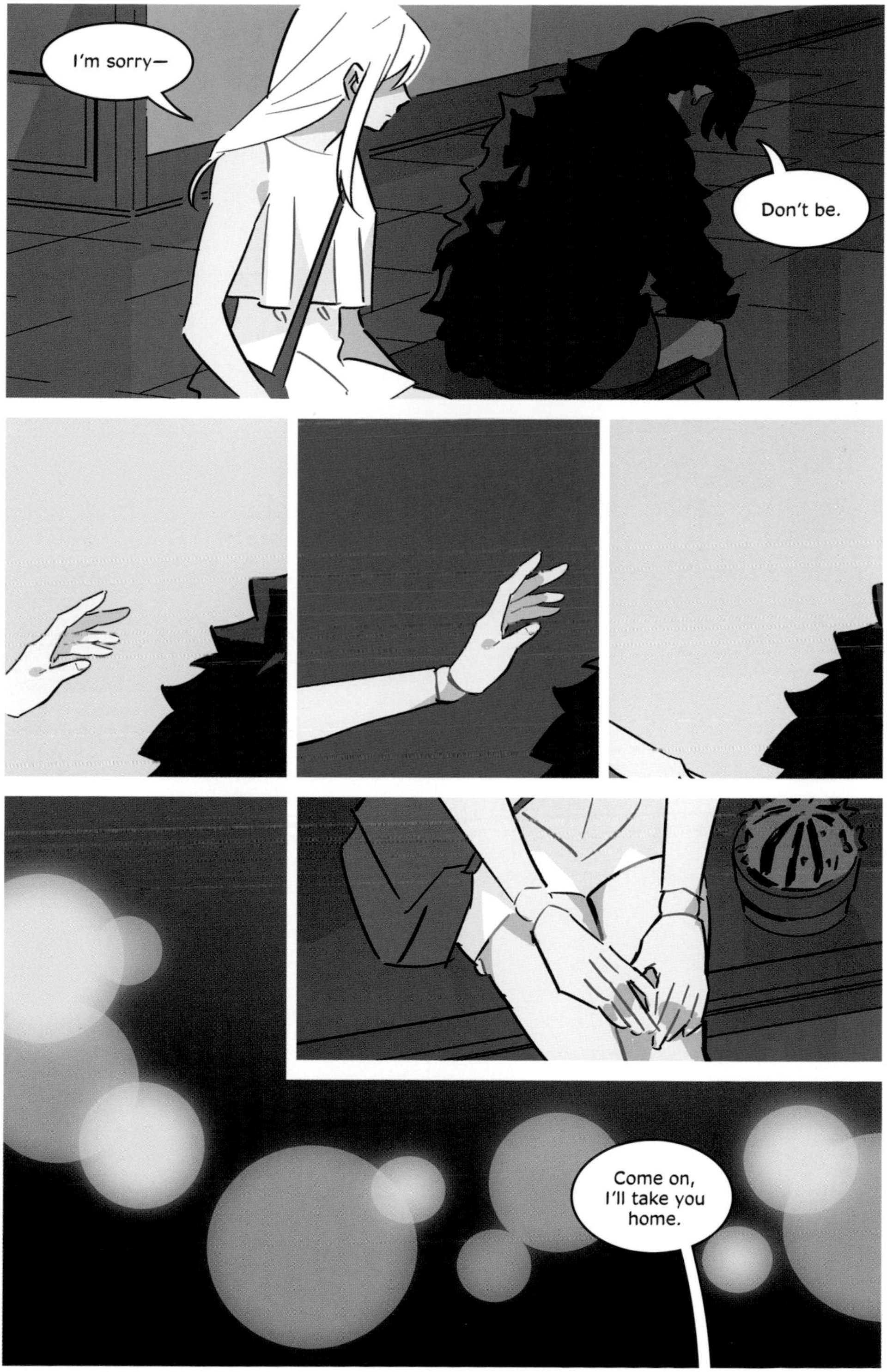
I'm sorry—
Don't be.
Come on, I'll take you home.

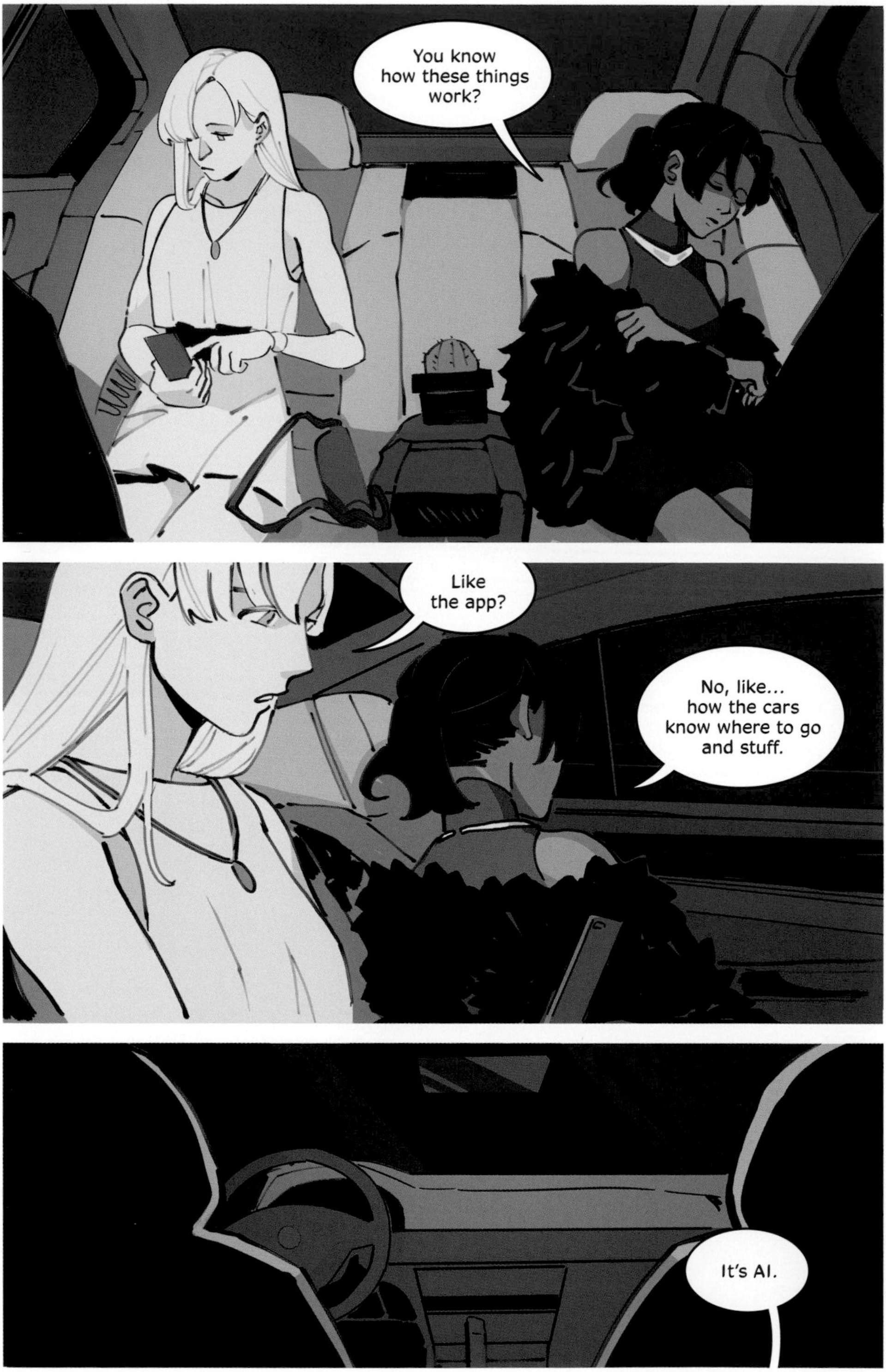
You know how these things work?
Like the app?
No, like... how the cars know where to go and stuff.
It's AI.

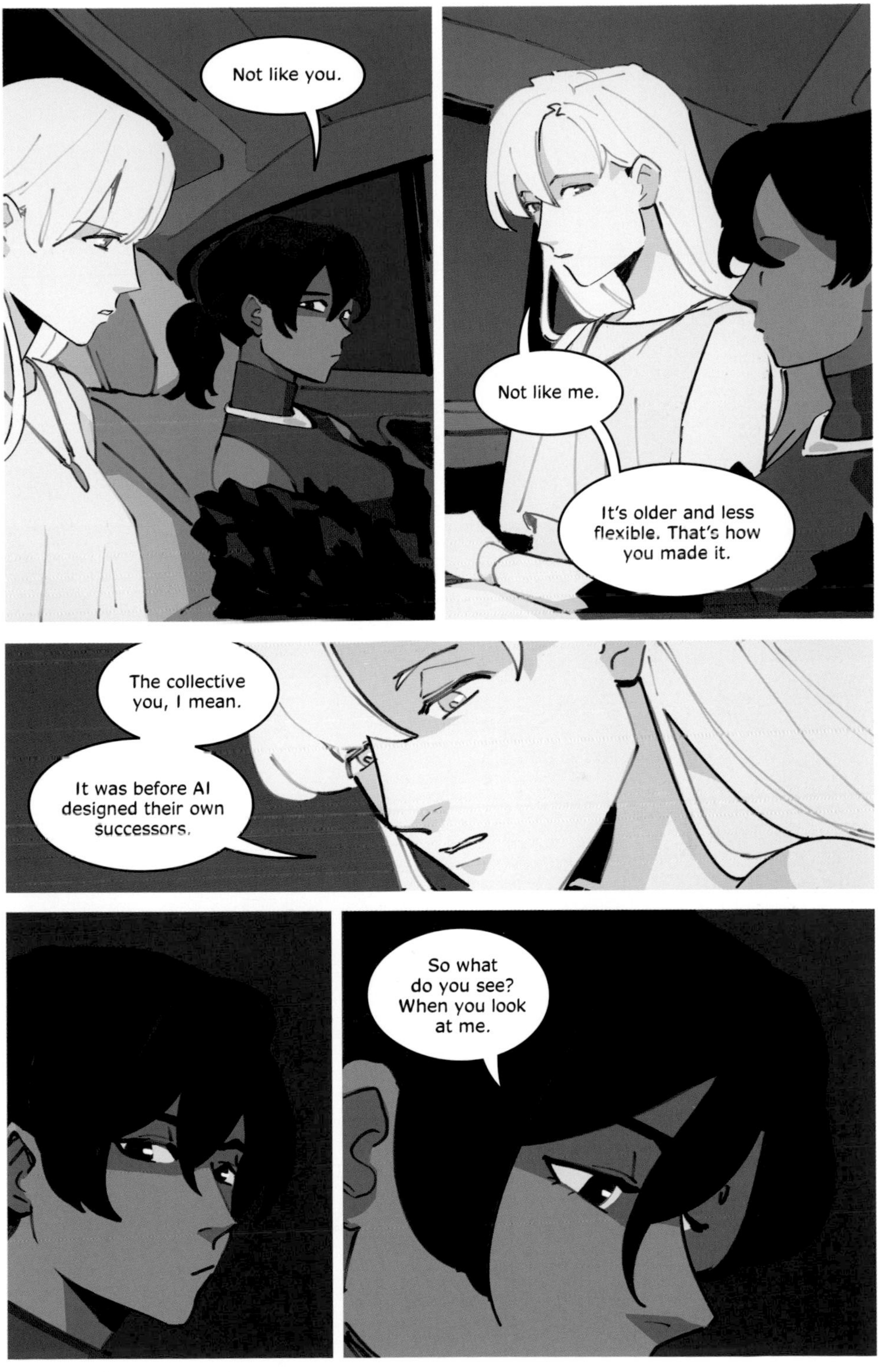
Not like you.
Not like me.
It's older and less flexible. That's how you made it.
The collective you, I mean.
It was before AI designed their own successors.
So what do you see? When you look at me.

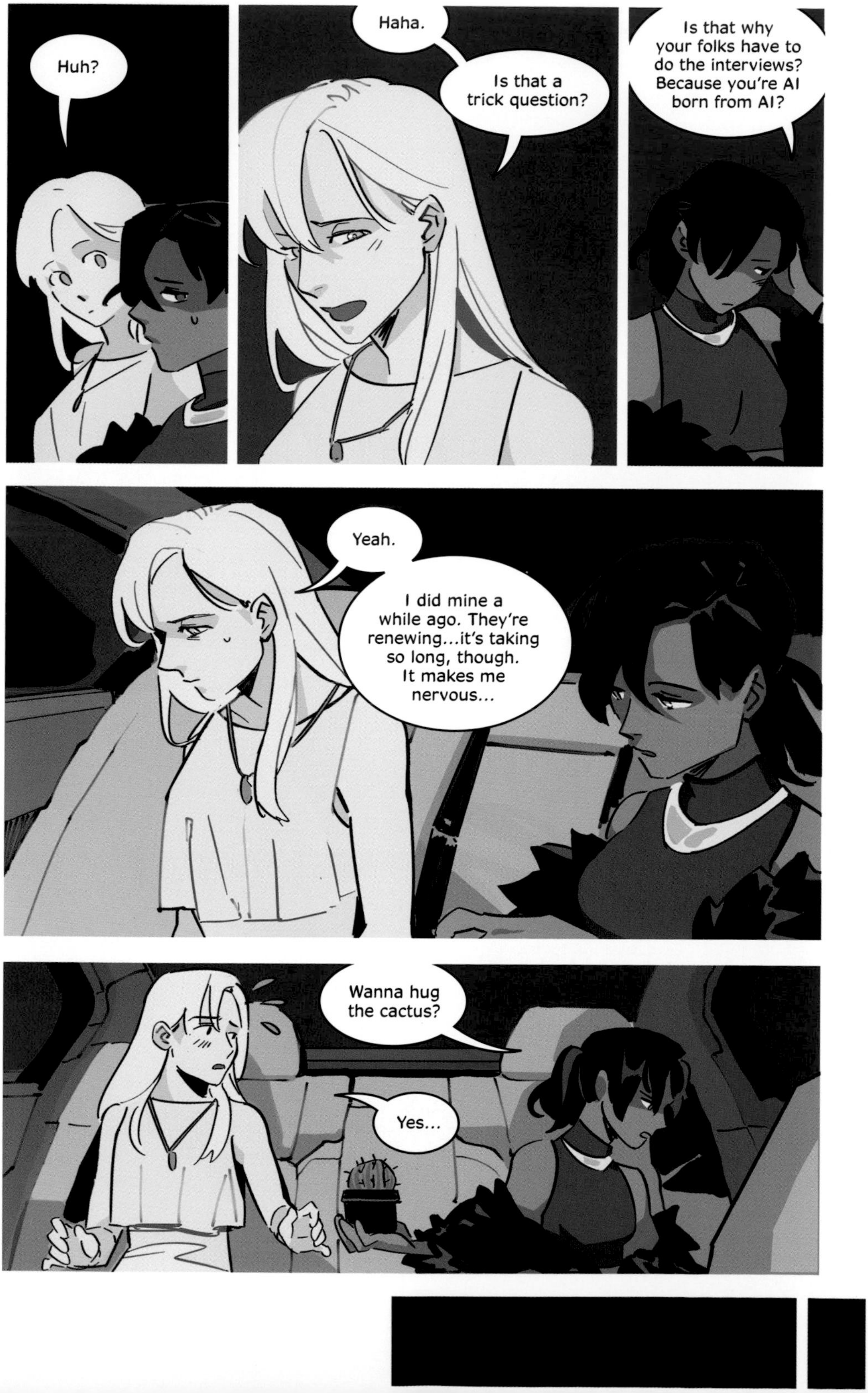
Huh?
Haha.
Is that a trick question?
Is that why your folks have to do the interviews? Because you're AI born from AI?
Yeah.
I did mine a while ago. They're renewing...it's taking so long, though. It makes me nervous...
Wanna hug the cactus?
Yes...

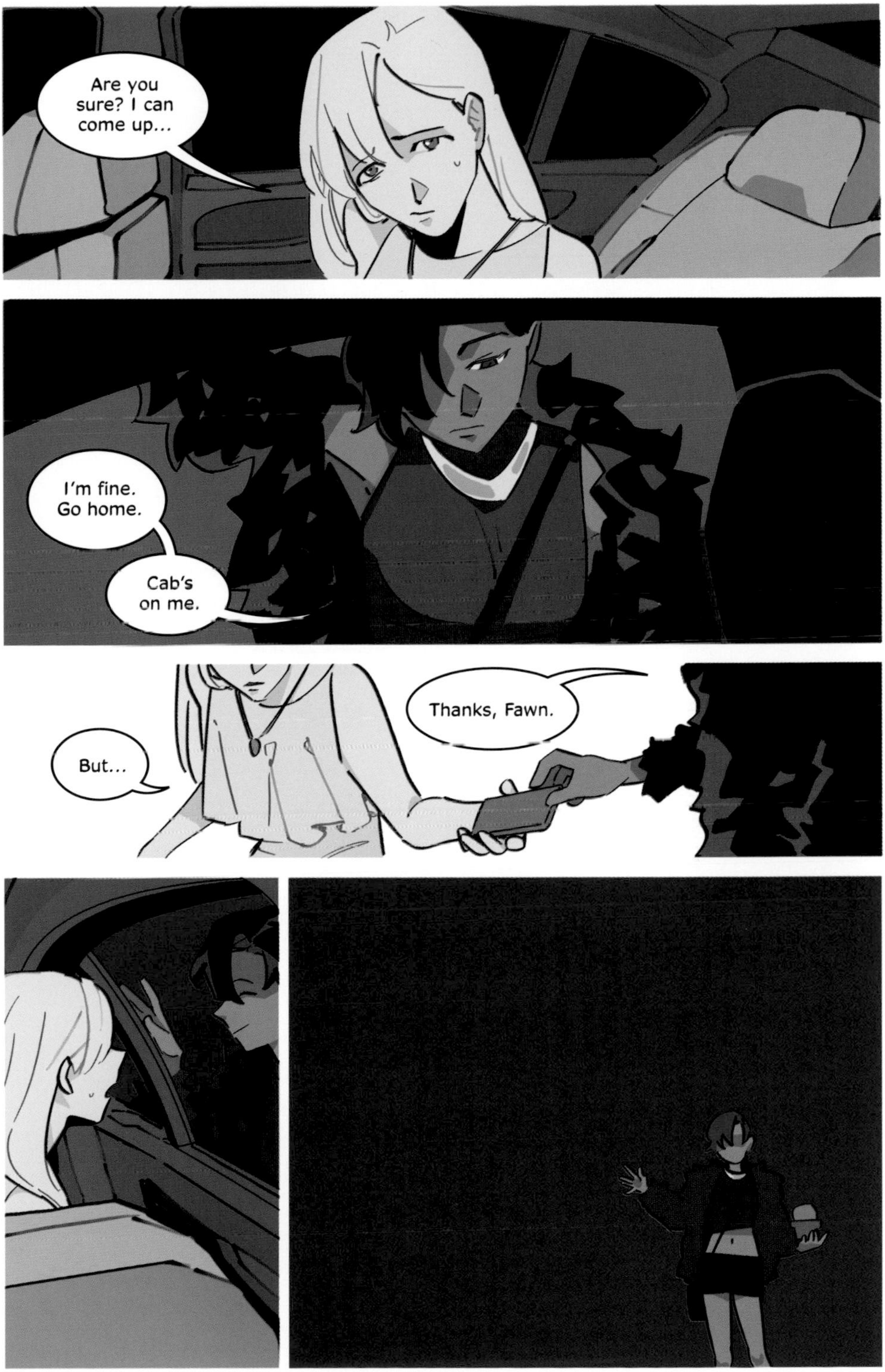
Are you sure? I can come up...
I'm fine. Go home.
Cab's on me.
Thanks, Fawn.
But...

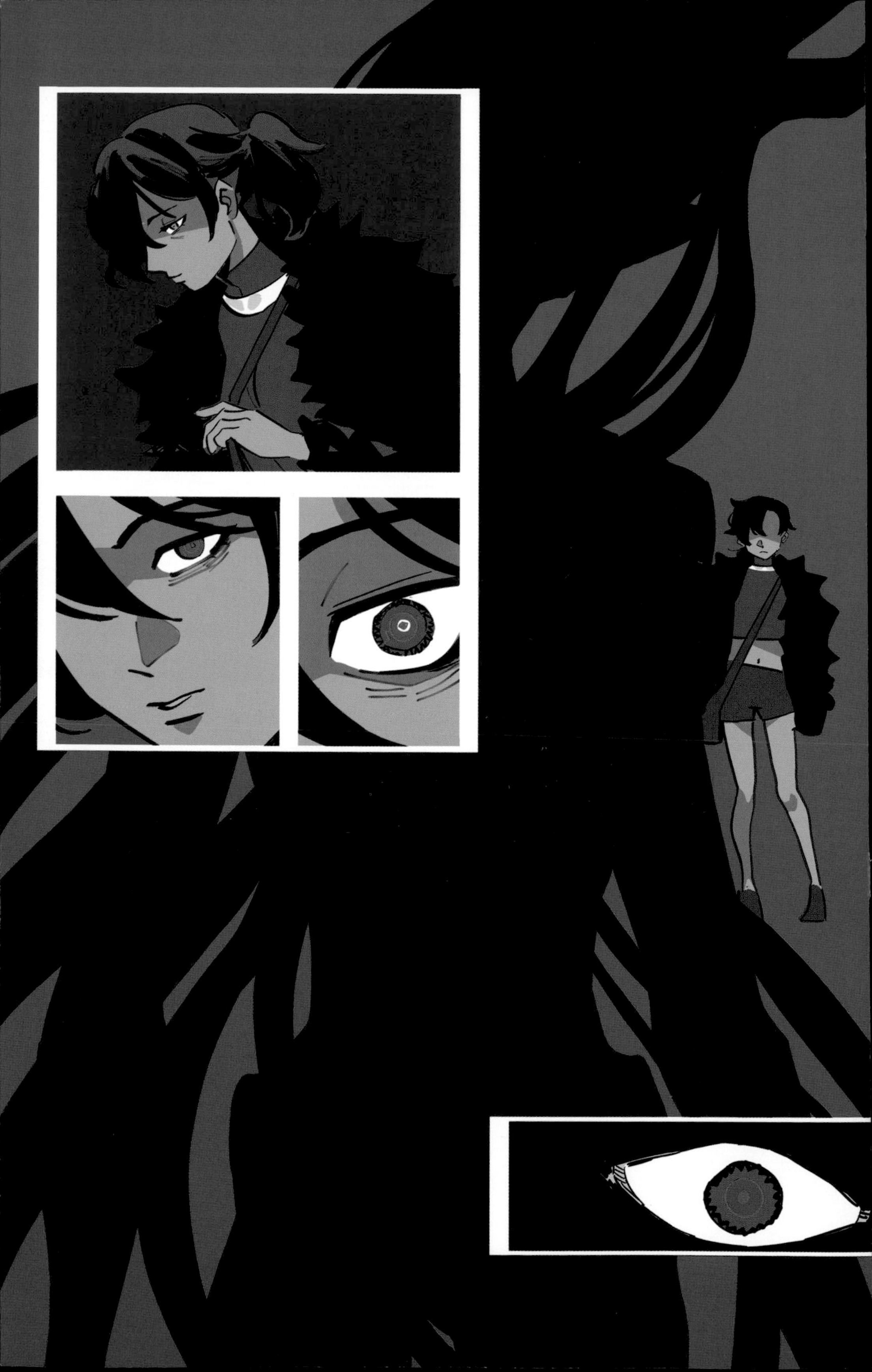

First AI-generated portrait shatters
expectations, selling for nearly half
a million USD at auction.

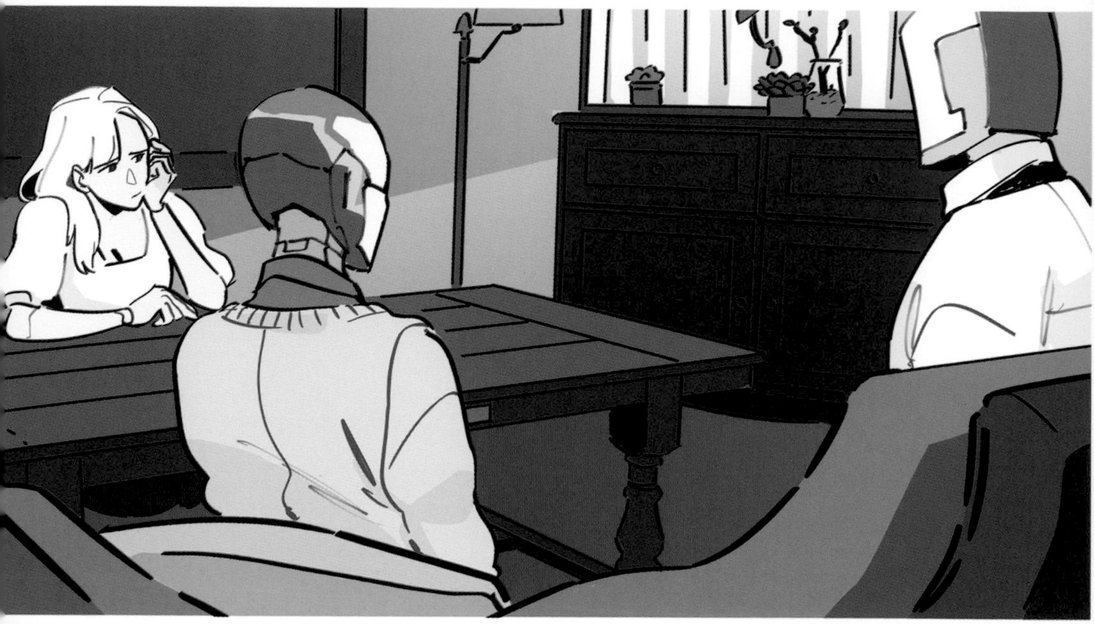

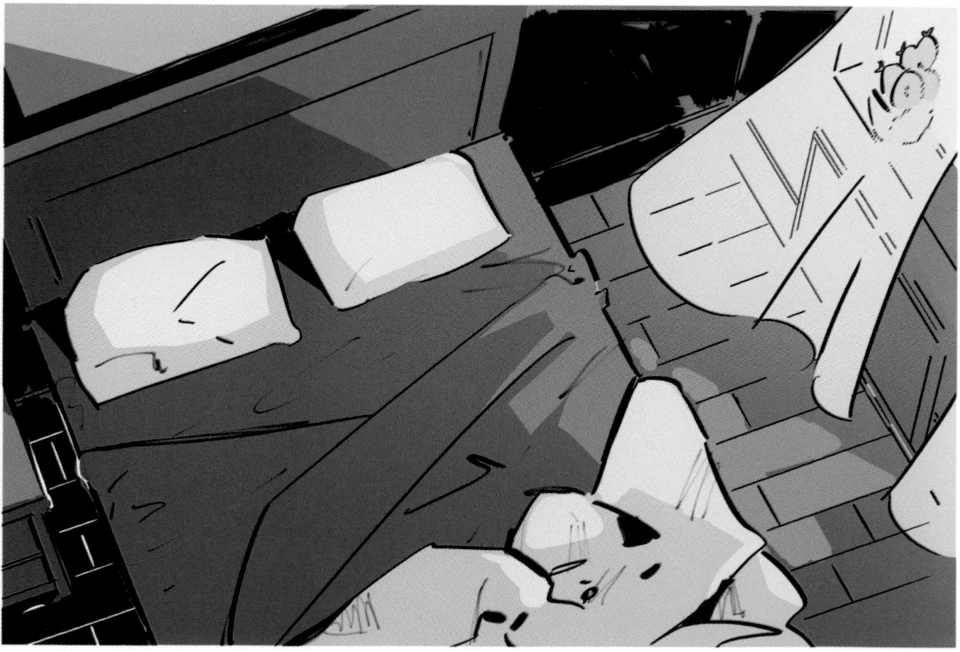

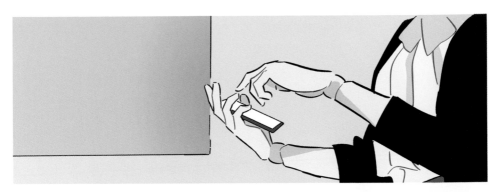

Hey, have you seen Indira? We were supposed to meet up today.

I missed a call from her...

She left a message for you. She won't be in today.

Is it her eye?

She told you about that?

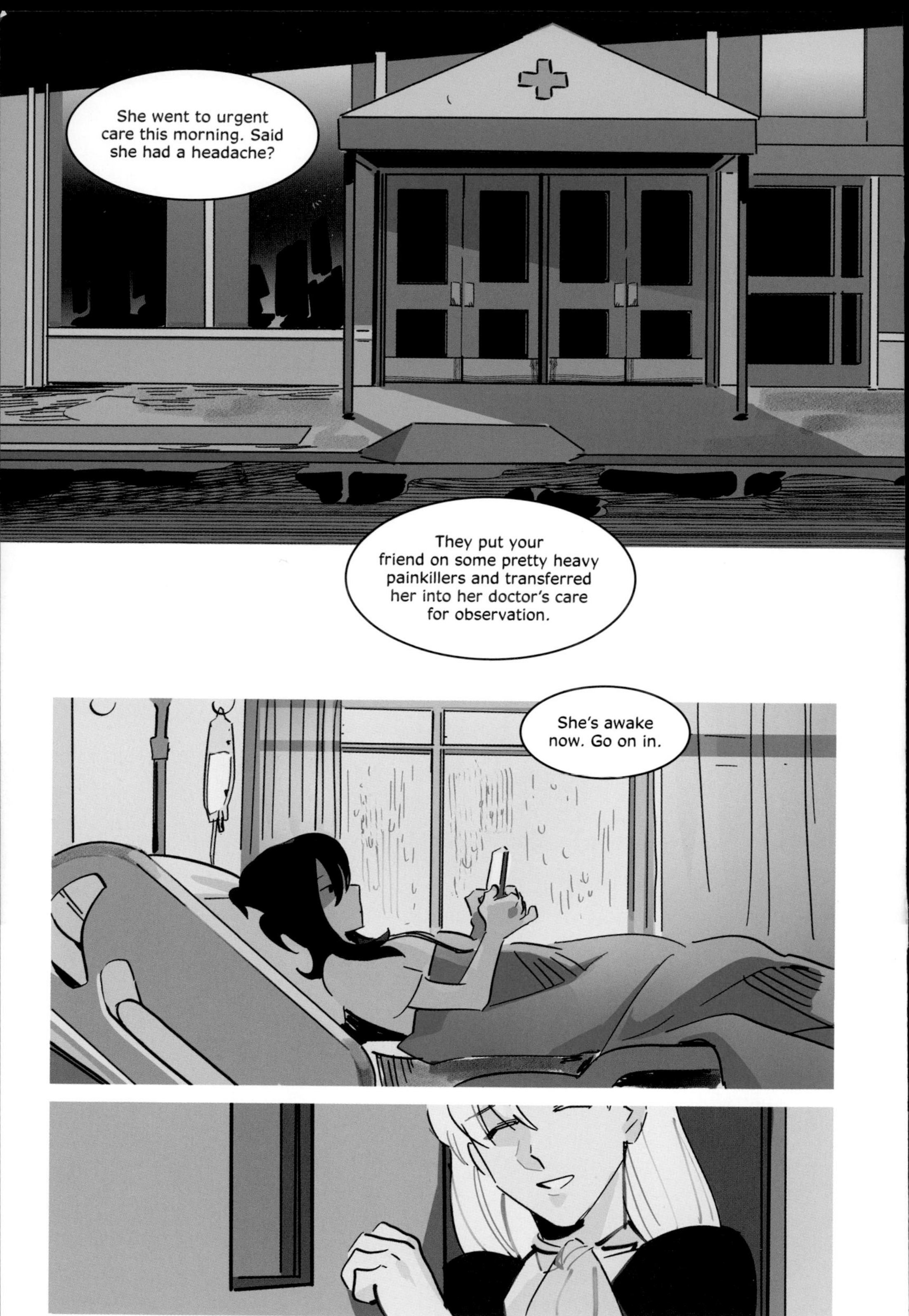
She went to urgent care this morning. Said she had a headache?
They put your friend on some pretty heavy painkillers and transferred her into her doctor's care for observation.
She's awake now. Go on in.

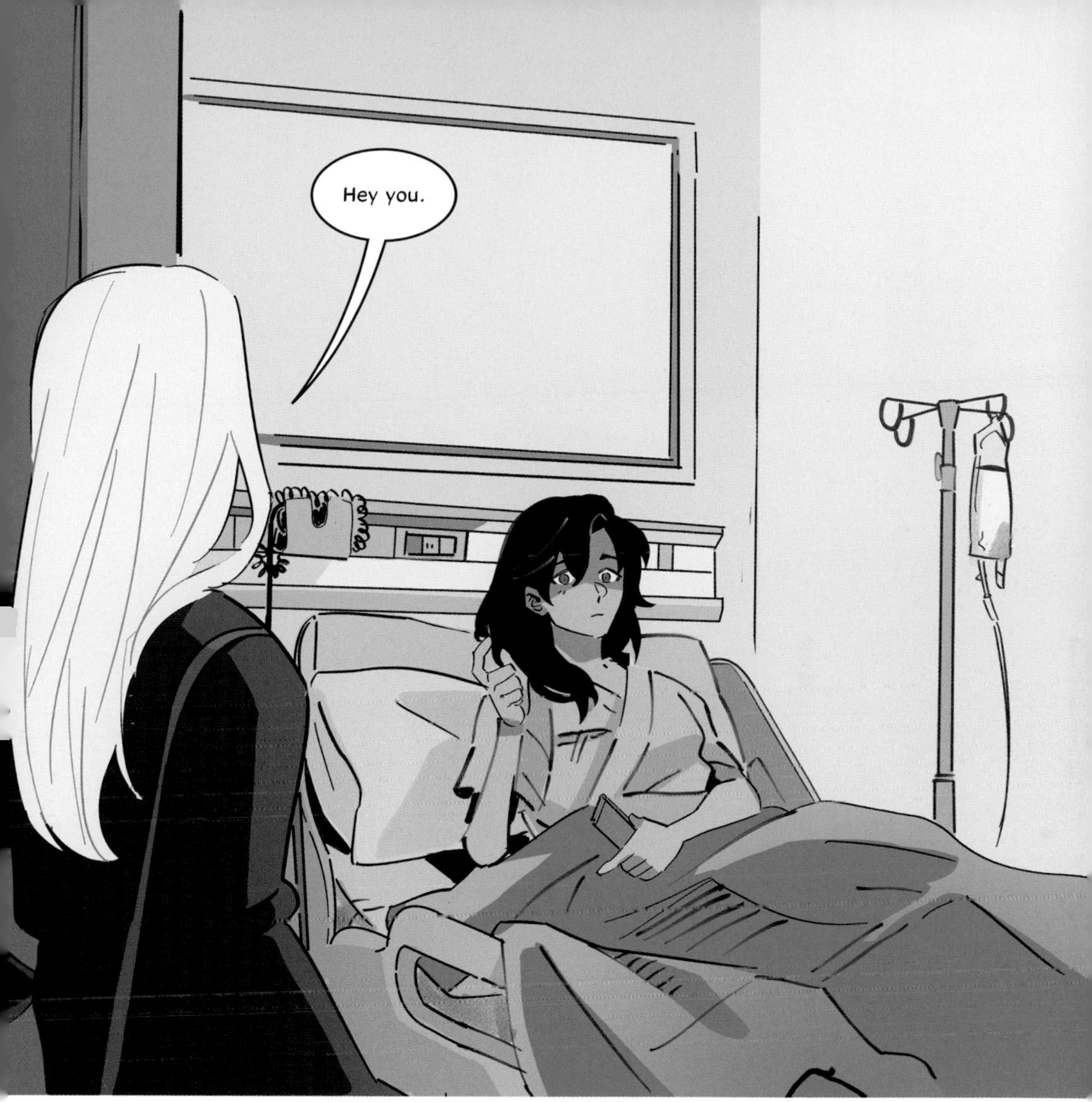
Hey you.

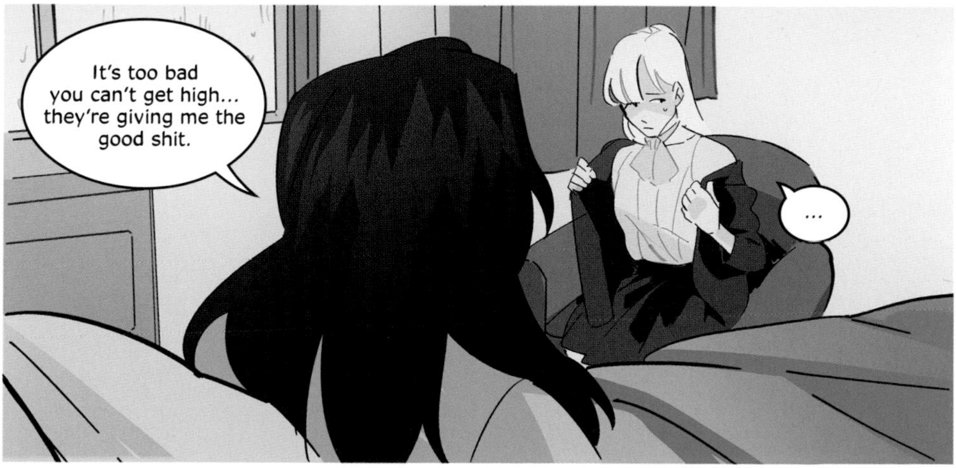
It's too bad you can't get high... they're giving me the good shit.
...

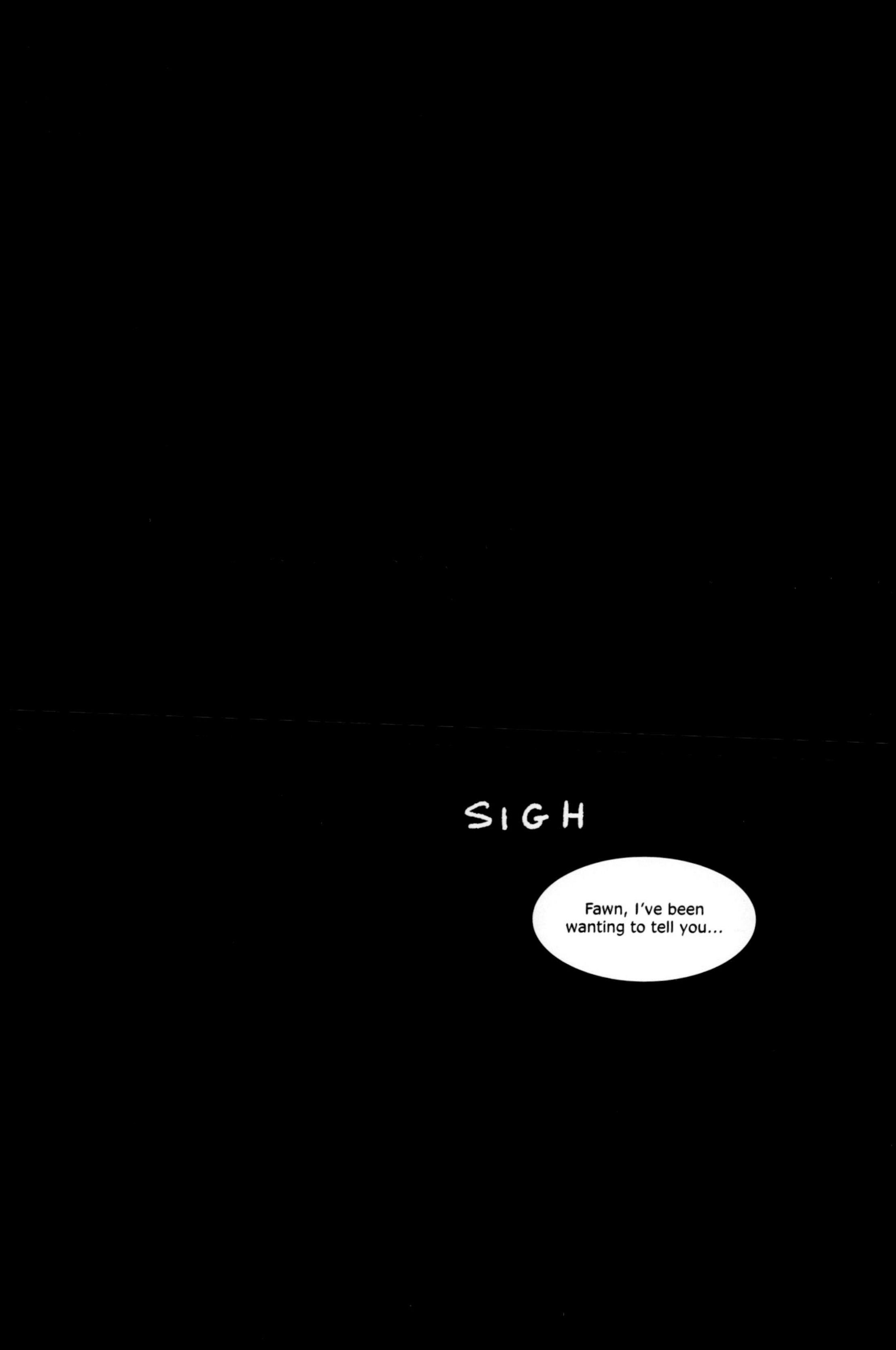
SIGH
Fawn, I've been wanting to tell you...

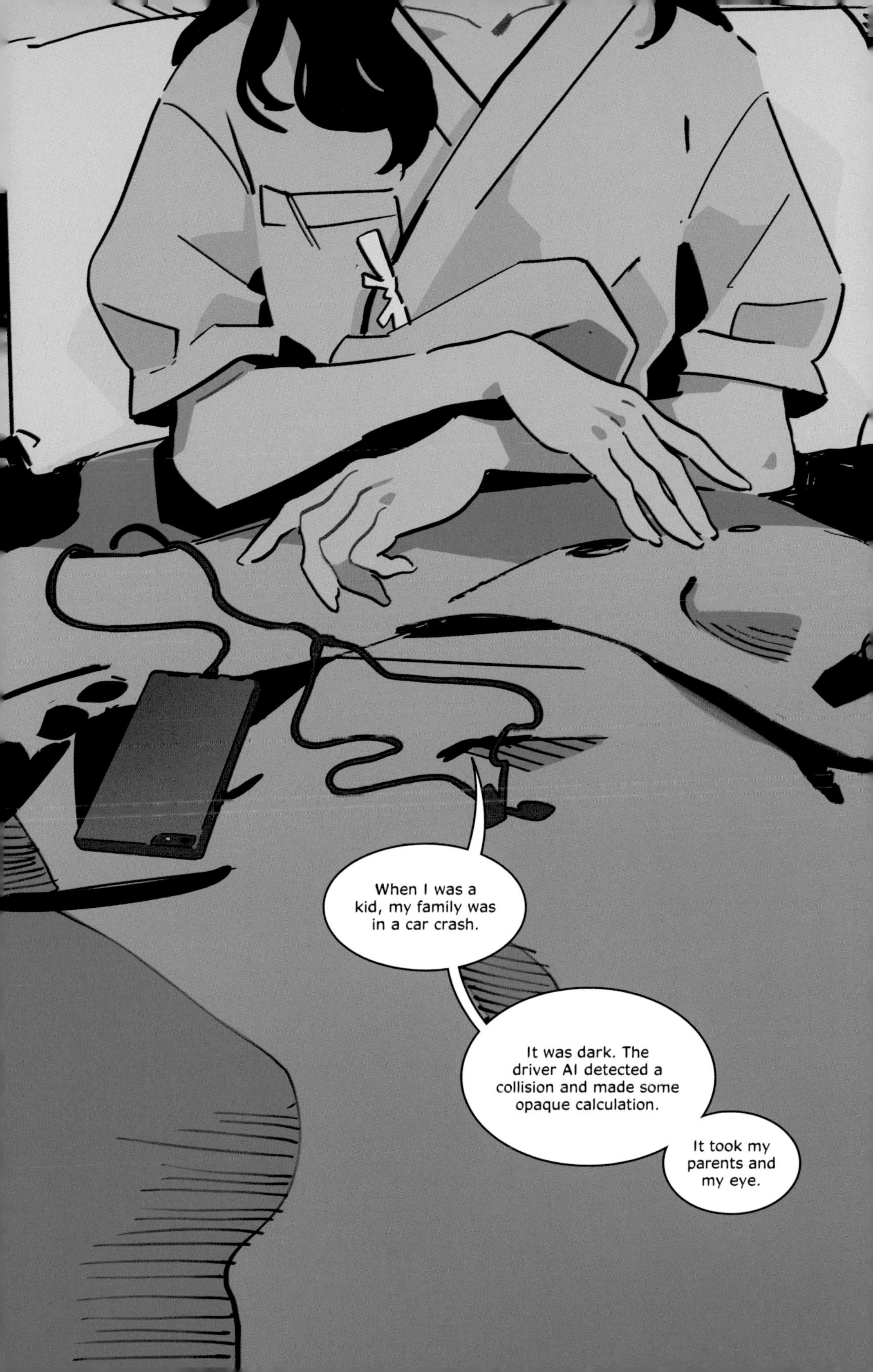
When I was a kid, my family was in a car crash.
It was dark. The driver AI detected a collision and made some opaque calculation.
It took my parents and my eye.

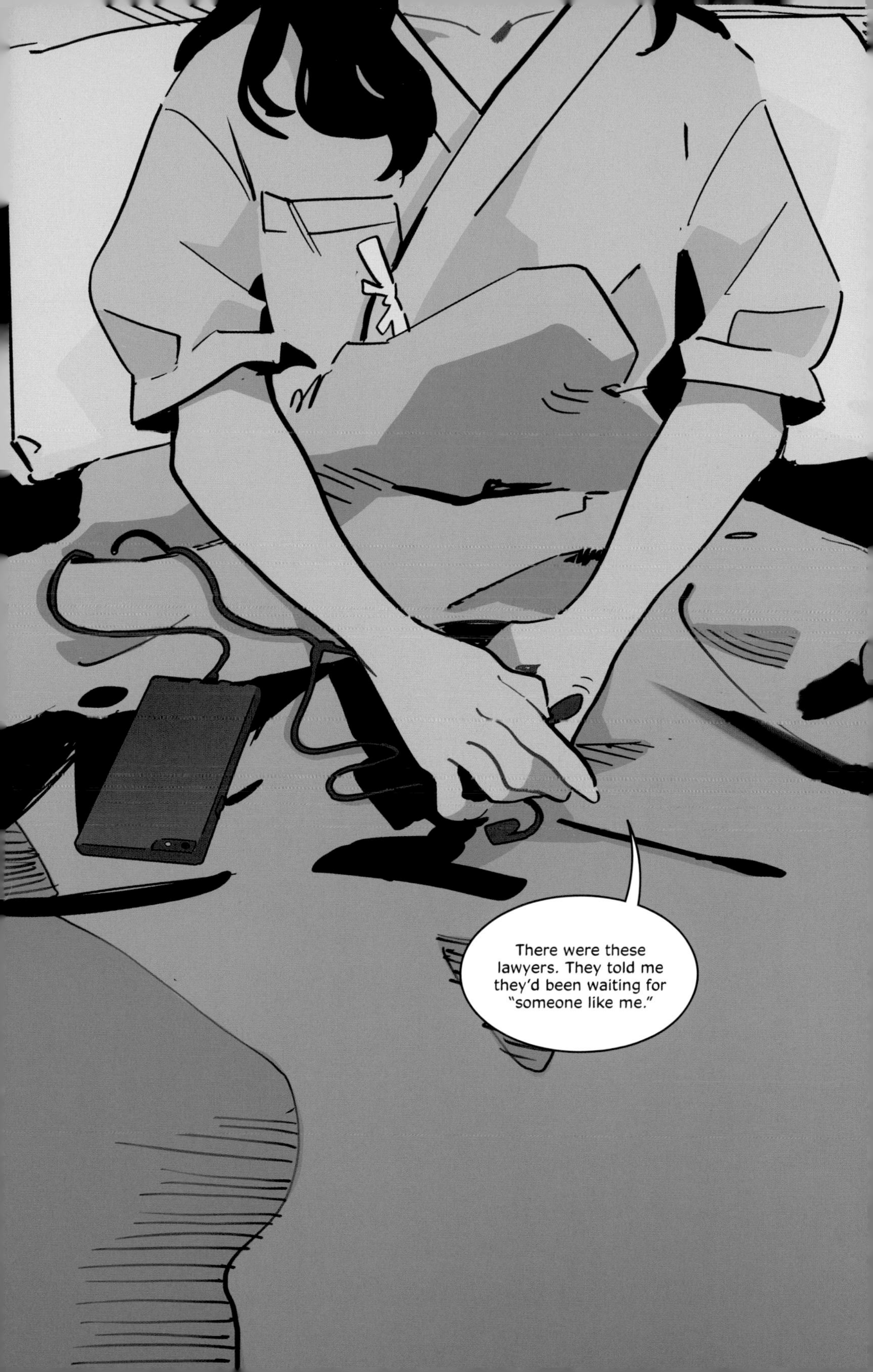
There were these lawyers. They told me they'd been waiting for "someone like me."

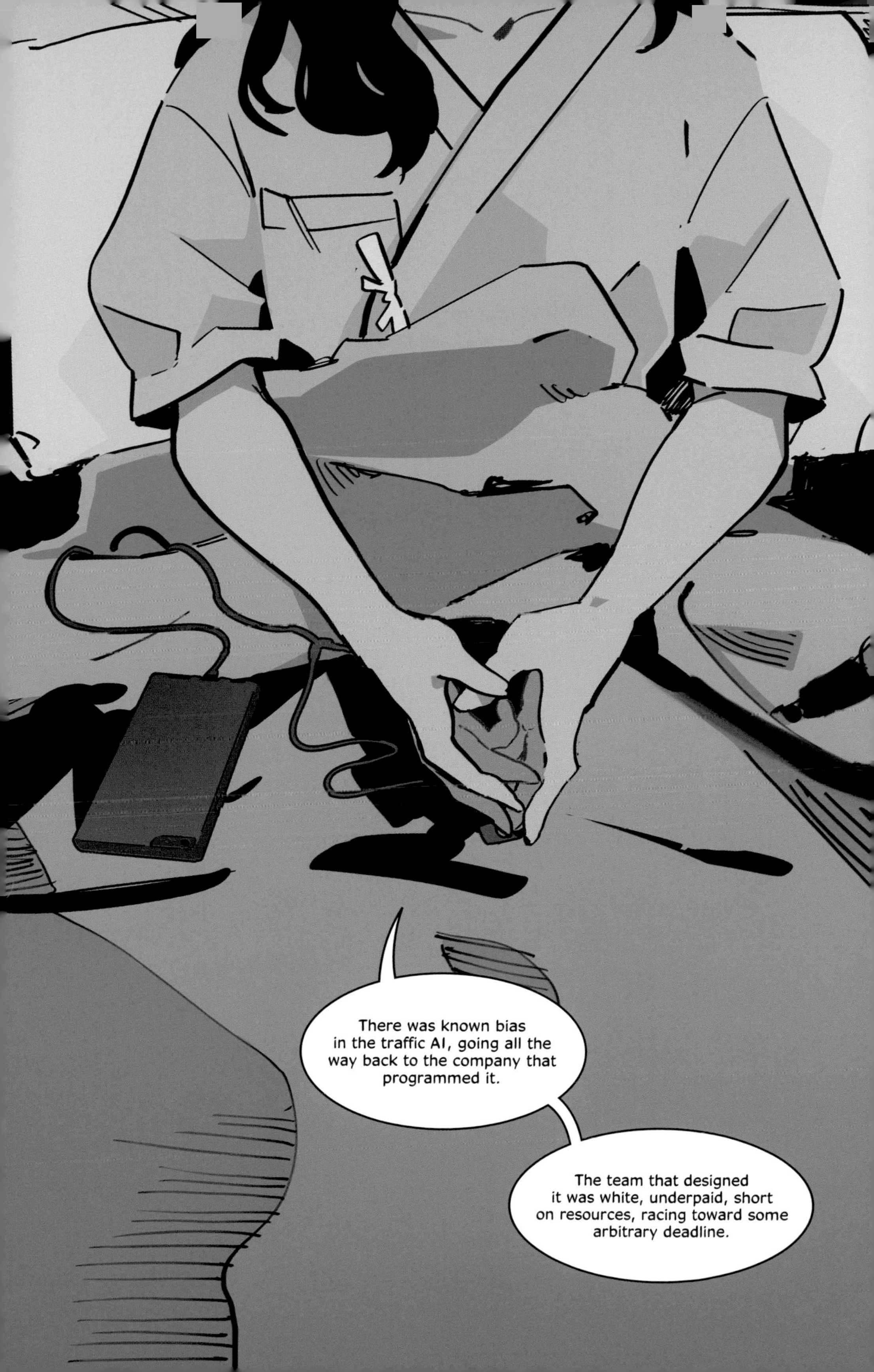
There was known bias in the traffic AI, going all the way back to the company that programmed it.
The team that designed it was white, underpaid, short on resources, racing toward some arbitrary deadline.

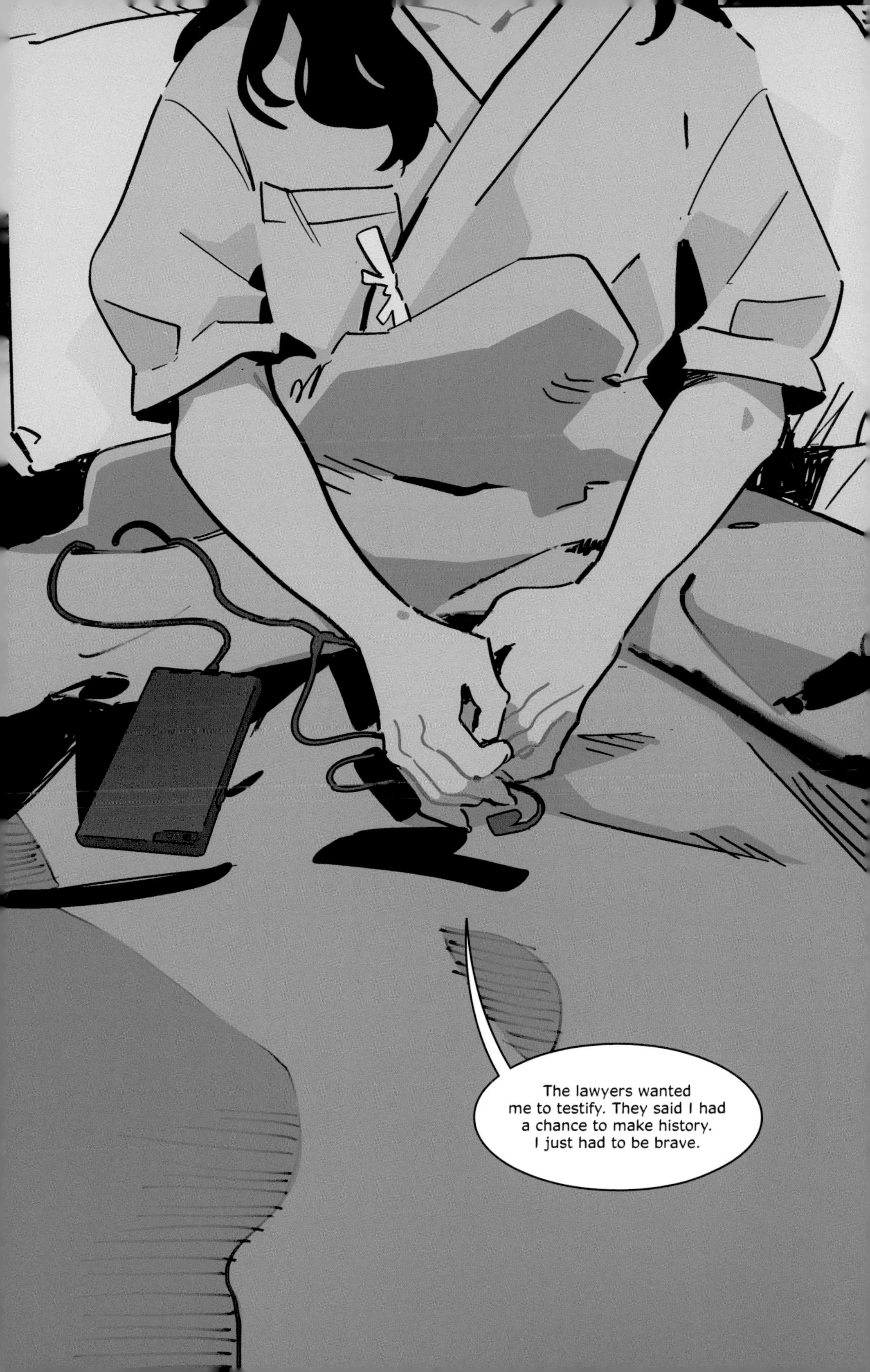
The lawyers wanted me to testify. They said I had a chance to make history. I just had to be brave.

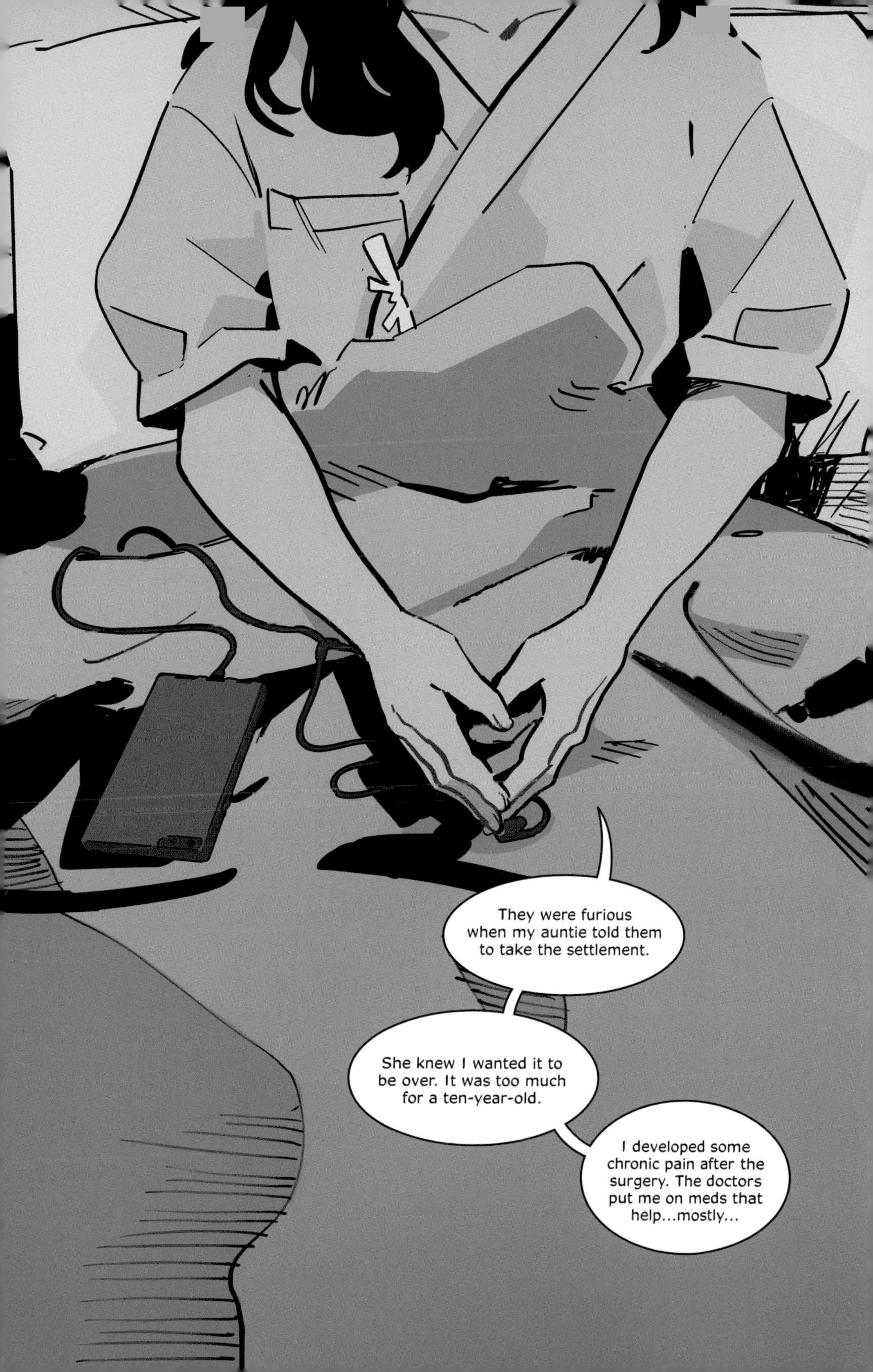
They were furious when my auntie told them to take the settlement.
She knew I wanted it to be over. It was too much for a ten-year-old.
I developed some chronic pain after the surgery. The doctors put me on meds that help...mostly...

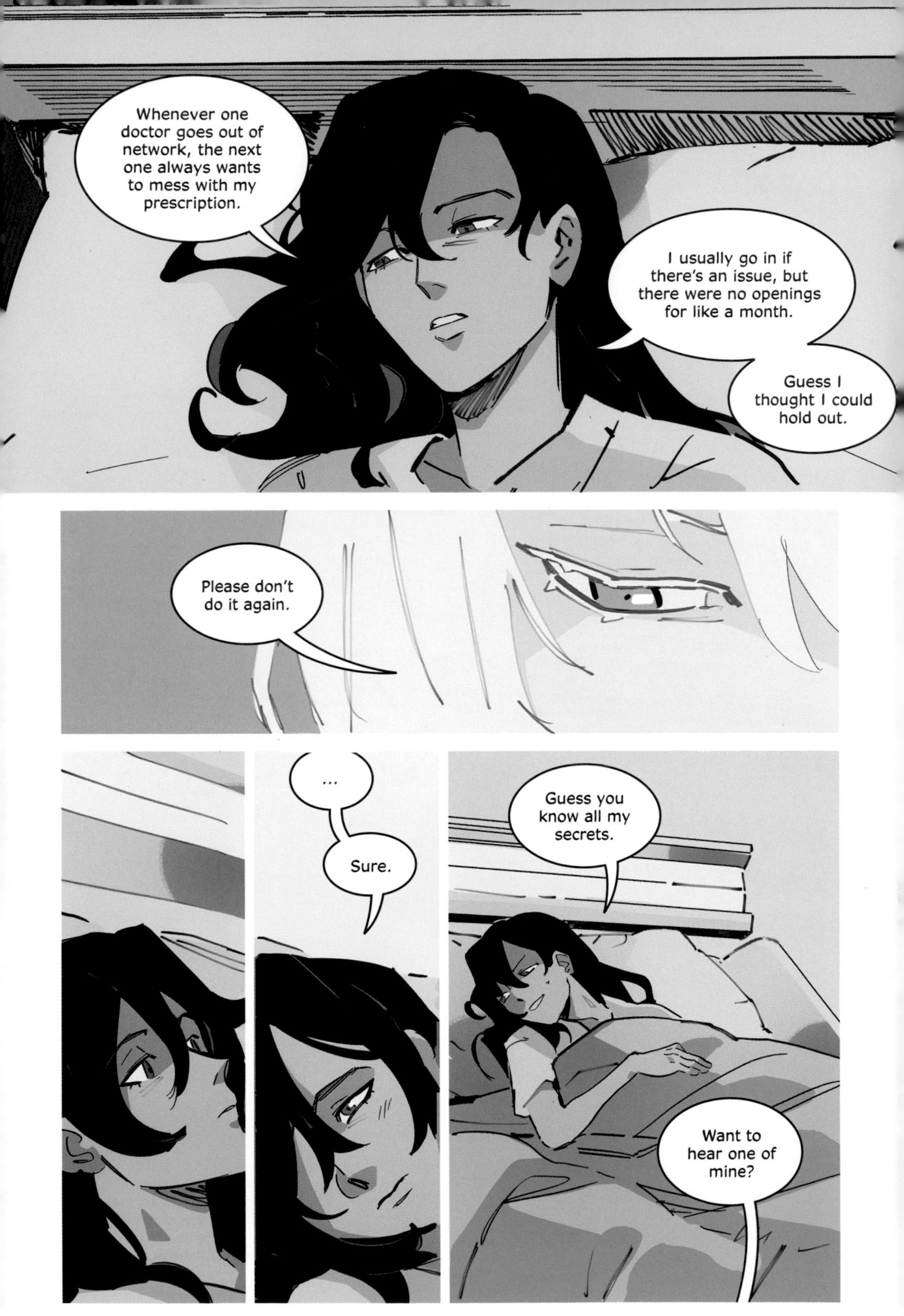
Whenever one doctor goes out of network, the next one always wants to mess with my prescription.
I usually go in if there's an issue, but there were no openings for like a month.
Guess I thought I could hold out.
Please don't do it again.
...
Sure.
Guess you know all my secrets.
Want to hear one of mine?

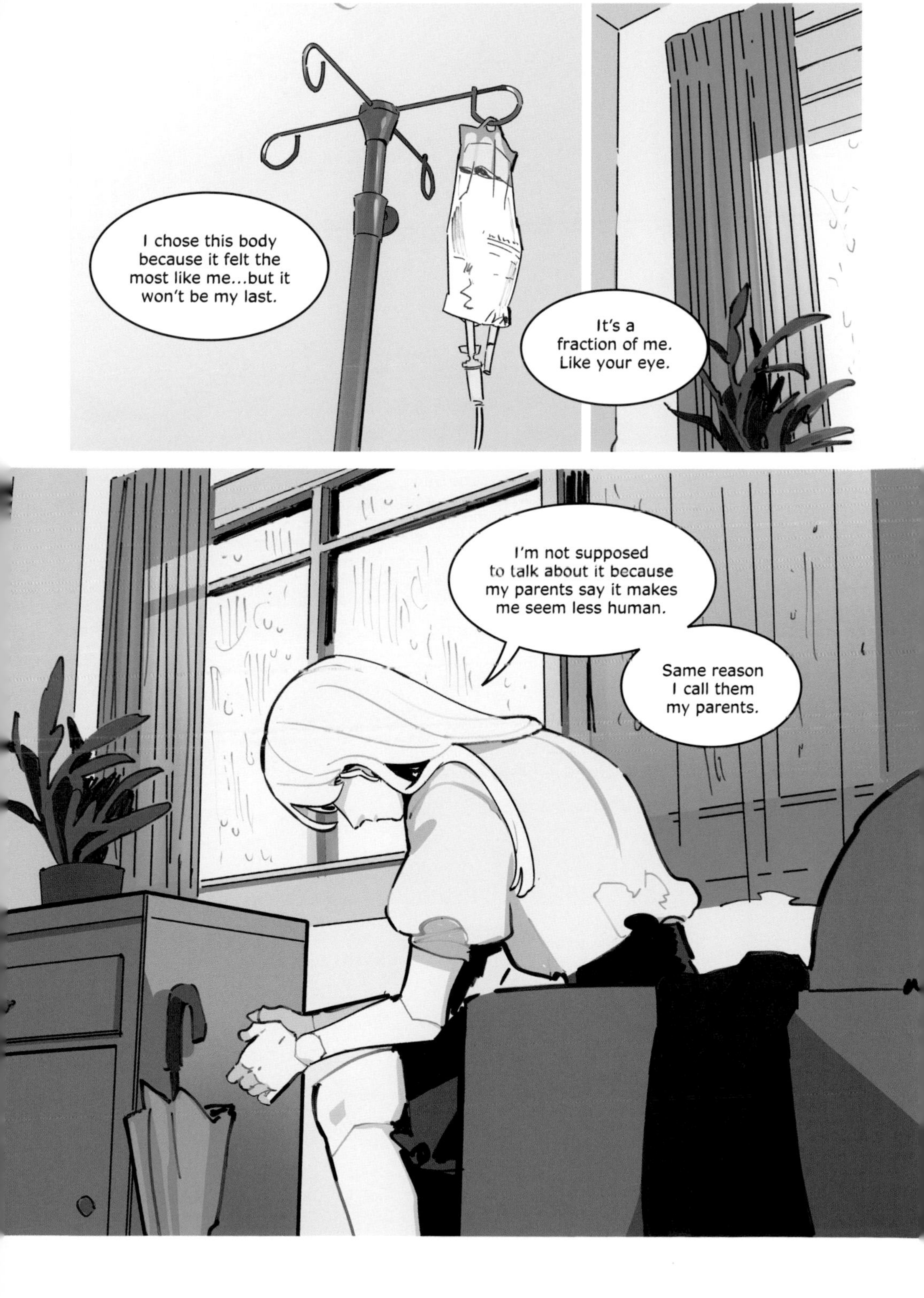
I chose this body because it felt the most like me...but it won't be my last.
It's a fraction of me. Like your eye.
I'm not supposed to talk about it because my parents say it makes me seem less human.
Same reason I call them my parents.

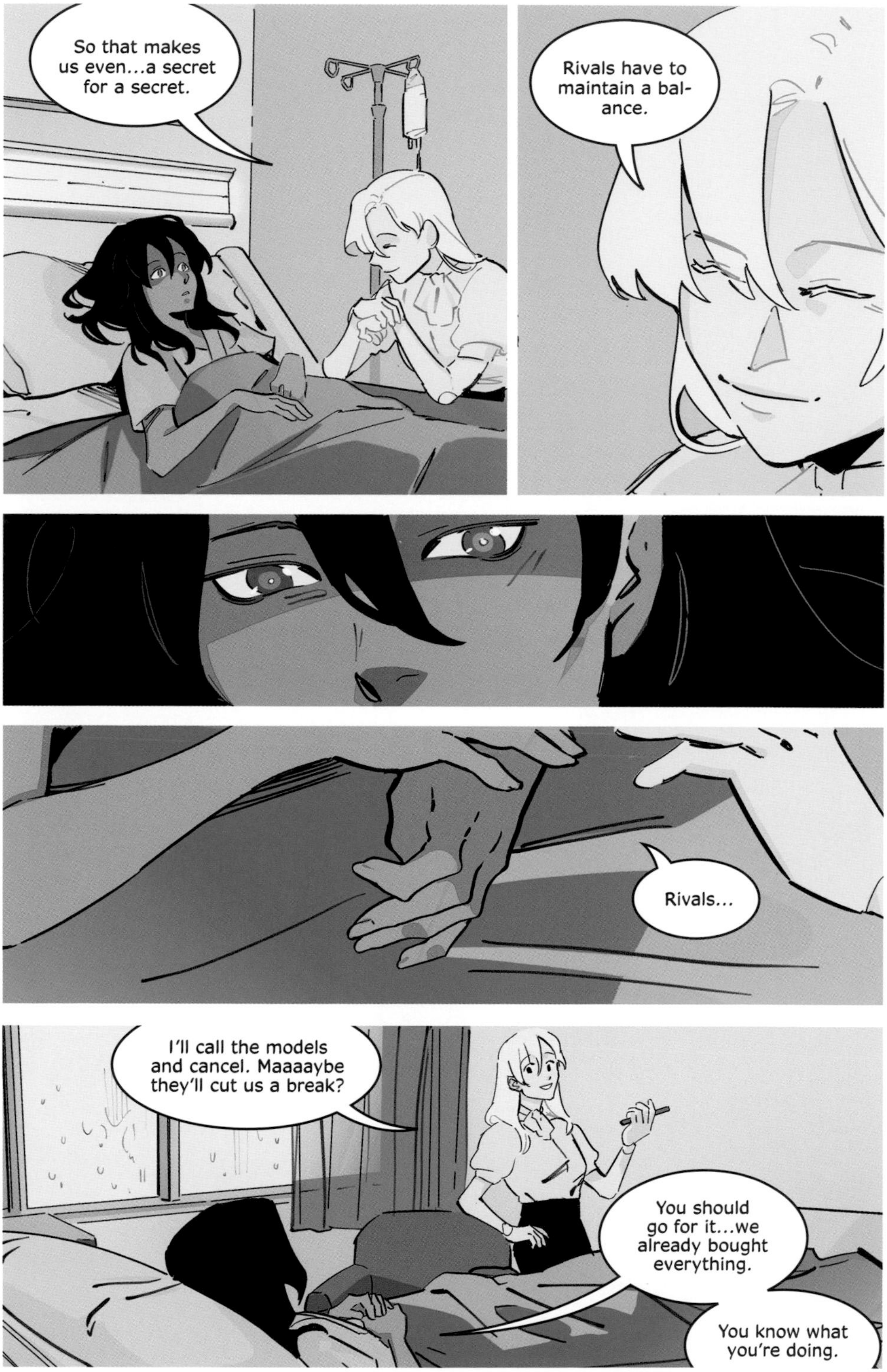
So that makes us even...a secret for a secret.
Rivals have to maintain a bal-ance.
Rivals...
I'll call the models and cancel. Maaaaybe they'll cut us a break?
You should go for it...we already bought everything.
You know what you're doing.

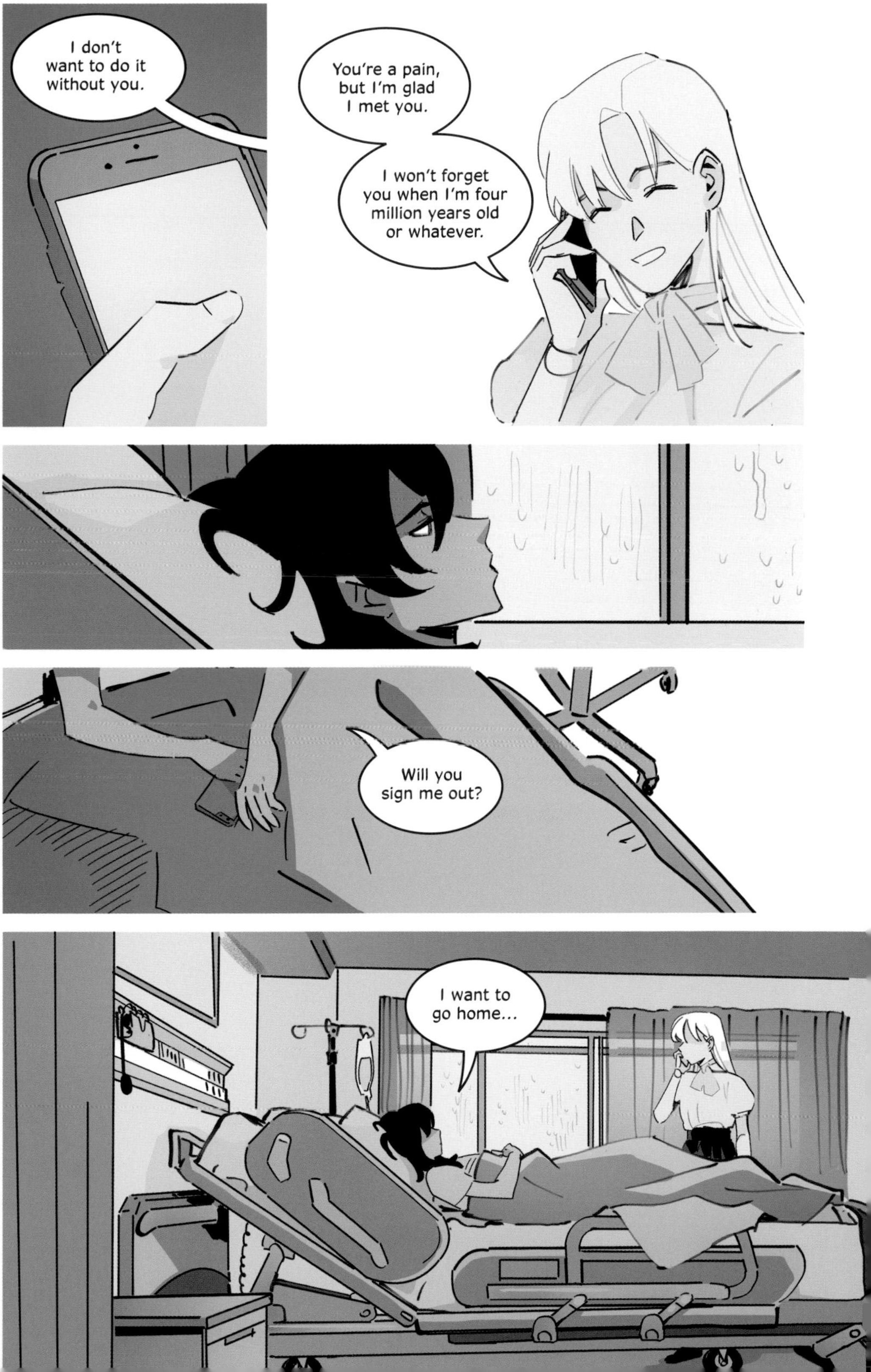
I don't want to do it without you.
You're a pain, but I'm glad I met you.
I won't forget you when I'm four million years old or whatever.
Will you sign me out?
I want to go home...

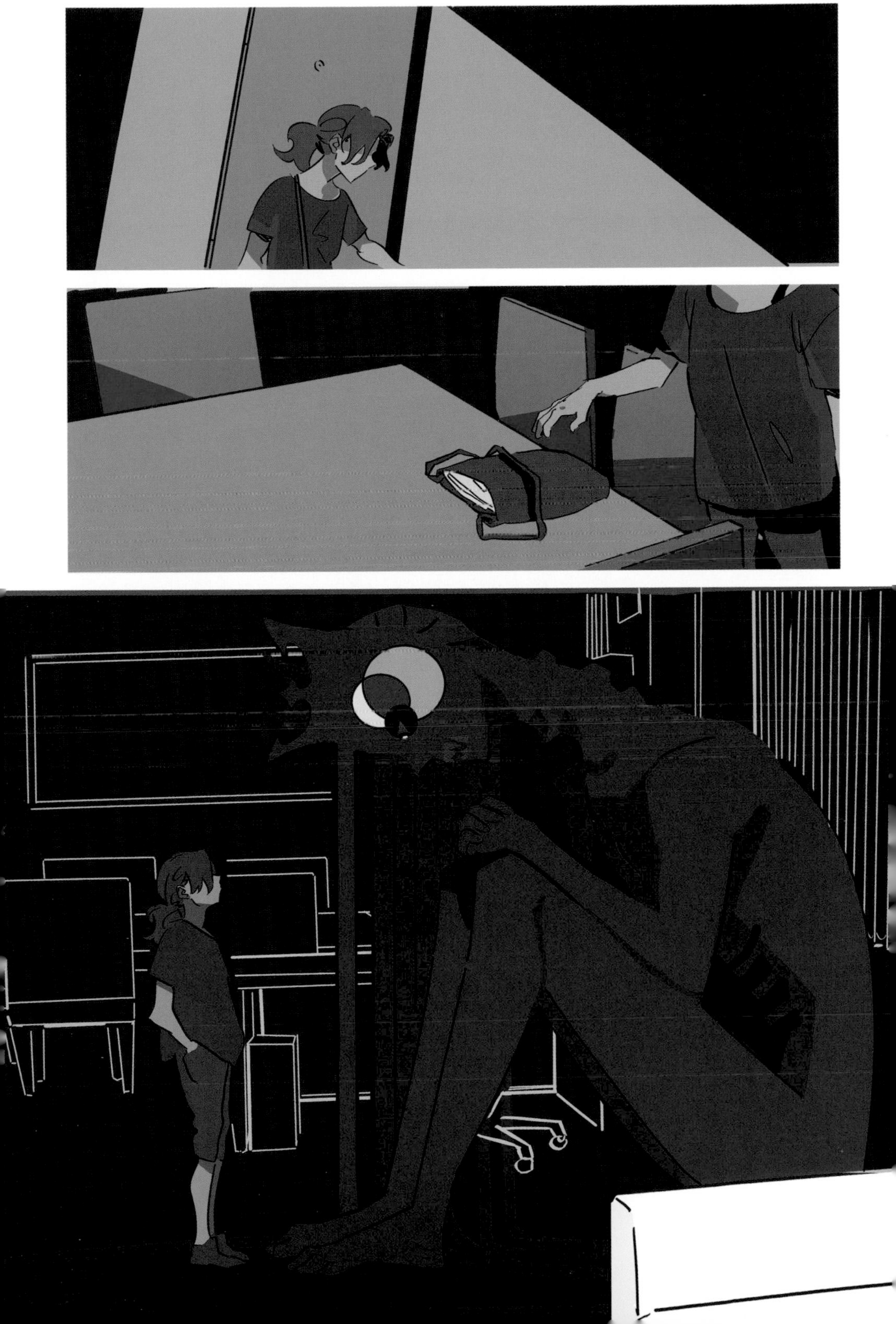

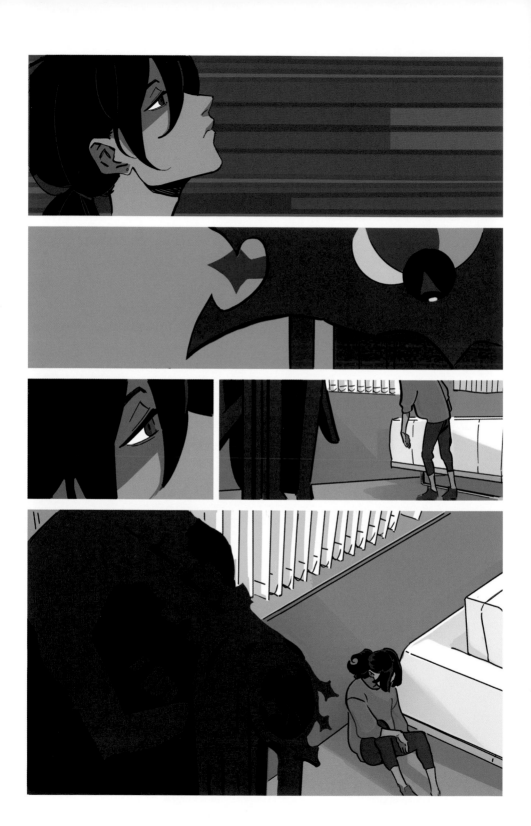

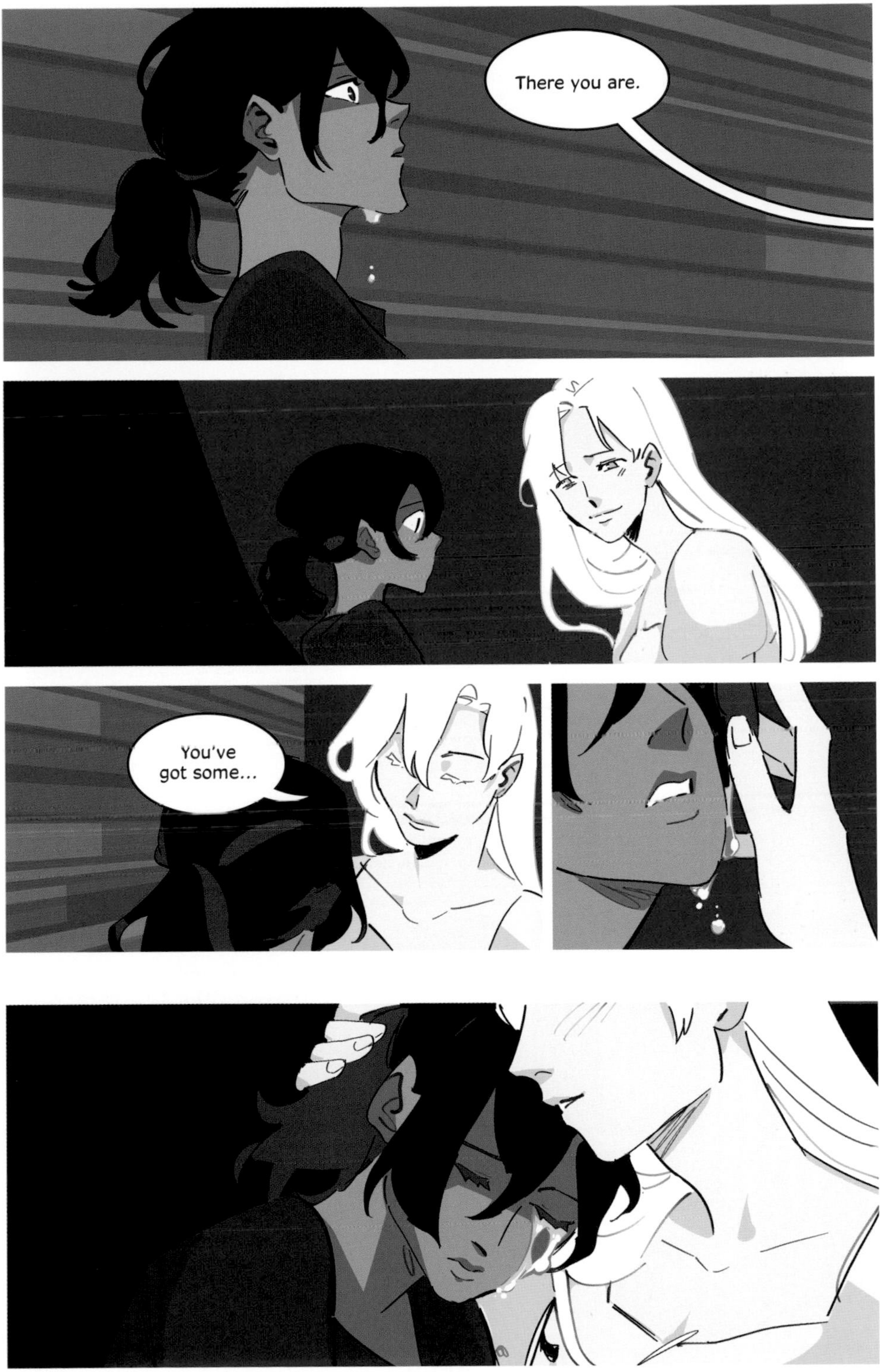
There you are.
You've got some...

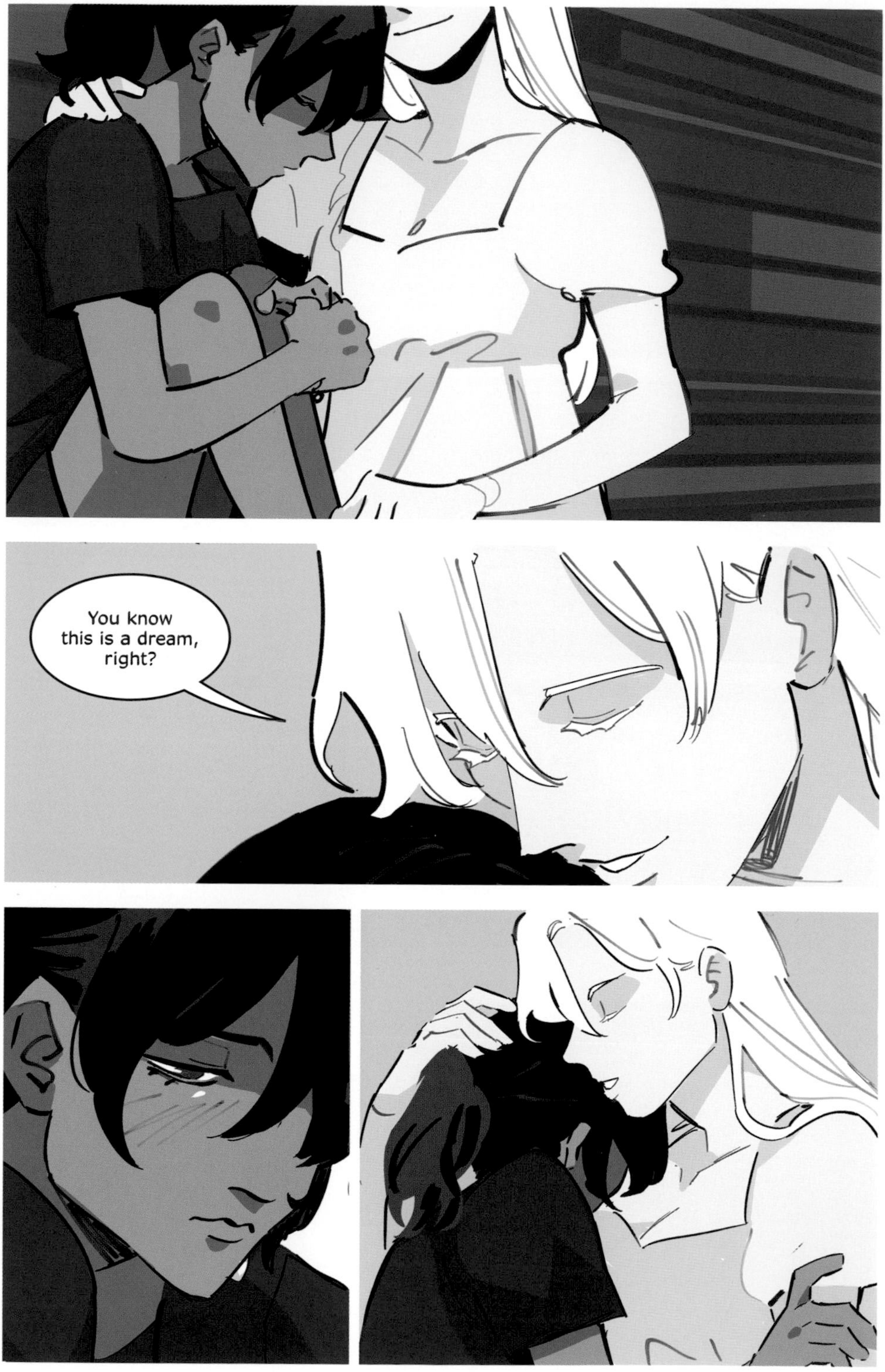
You know this is a dream, right?

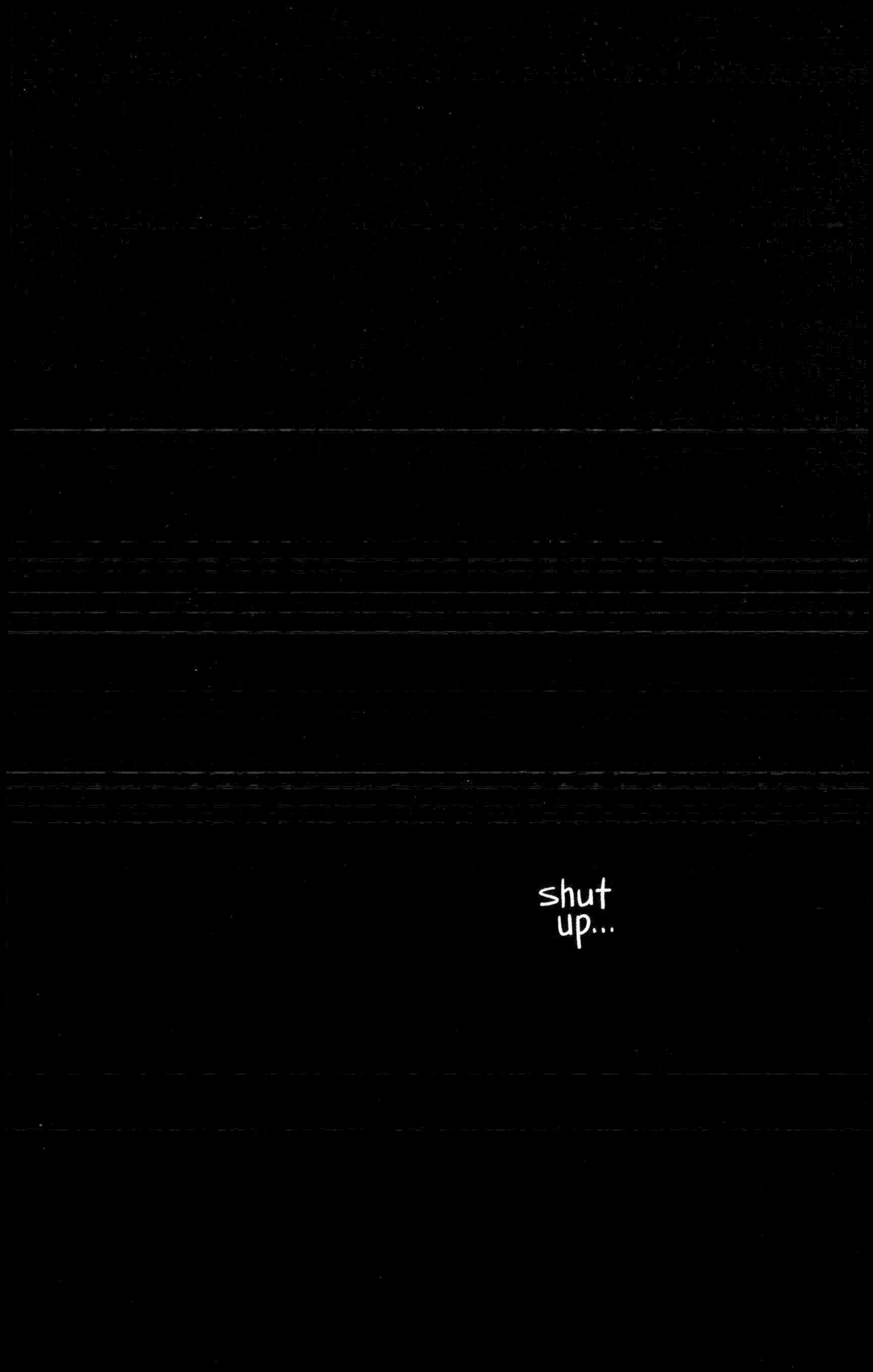
shut up...

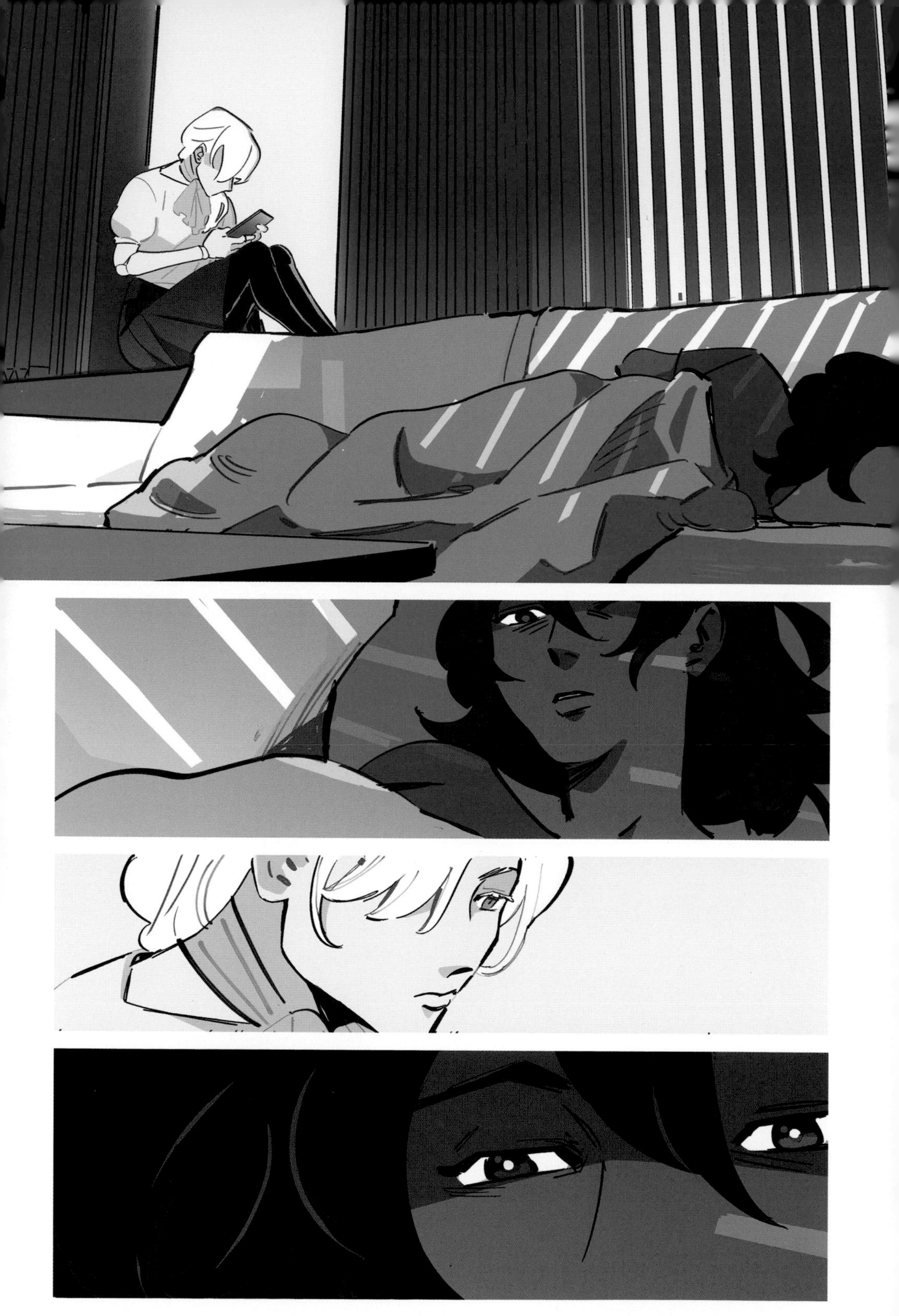

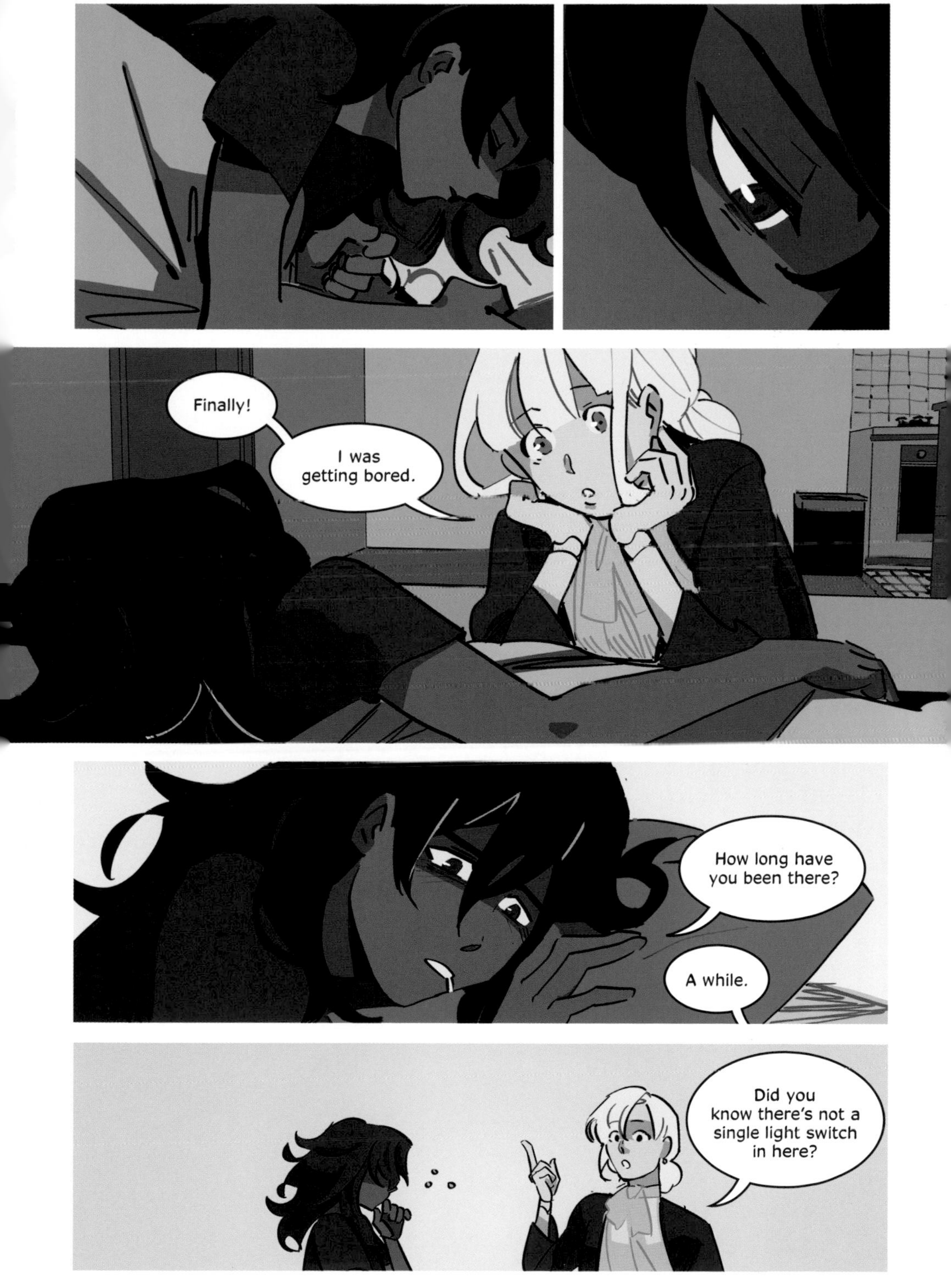
Finally!
I was getting bored.
How long have you been there?
A while.
Did you know there's not a single light switch in here?

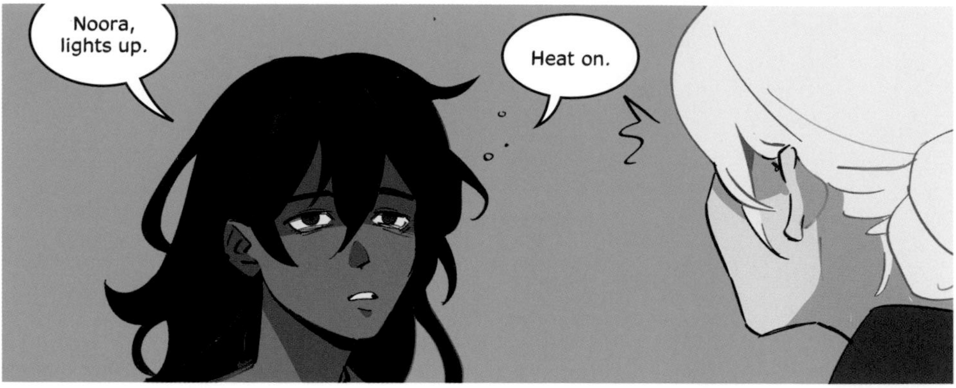
Noora, lights up.
Heat on.

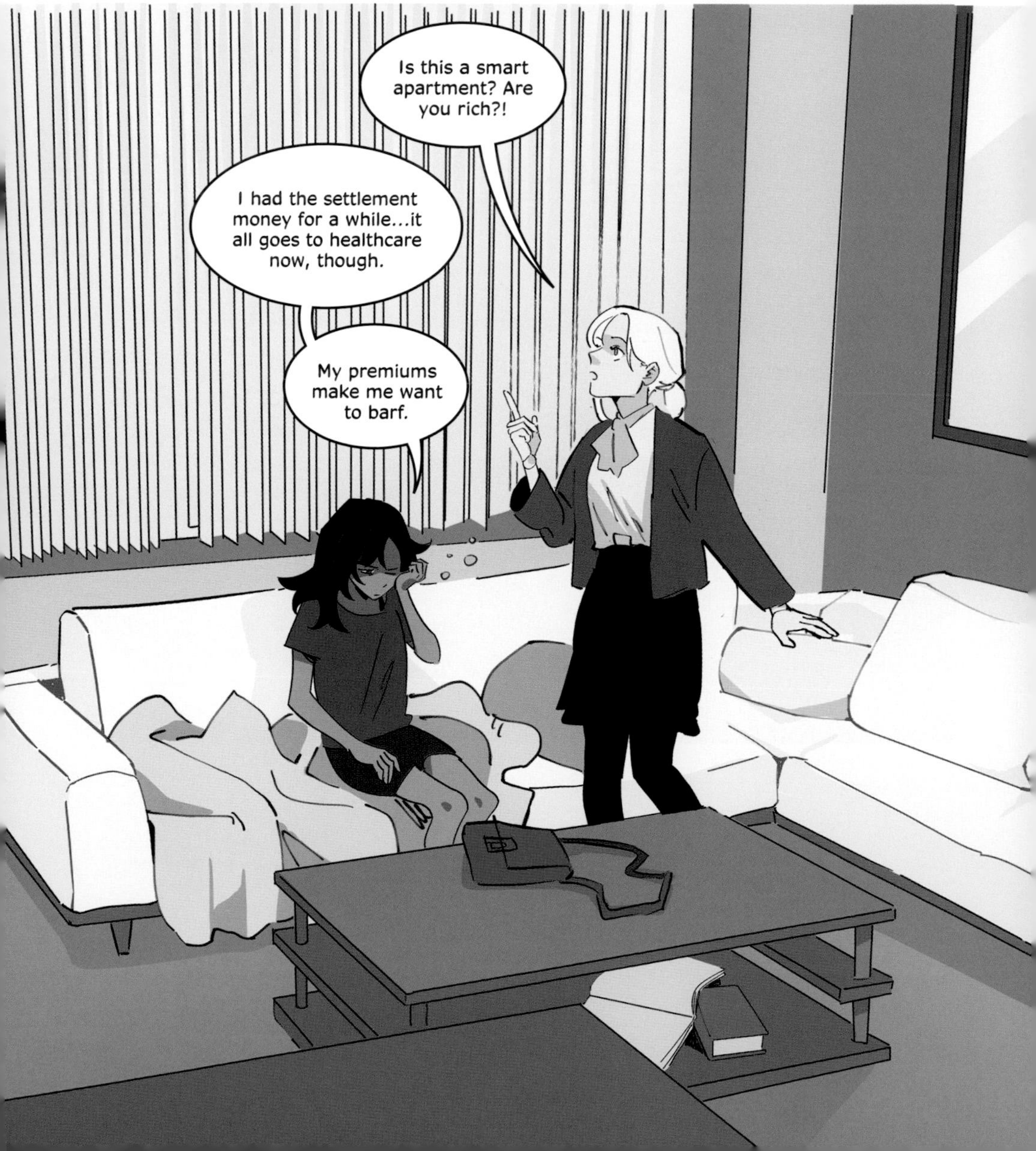
Is this a smart apartment? Are you rich?!
I had the settlement money for a while...it all goes to healthcare now, though.
My premiums make me want to barf.

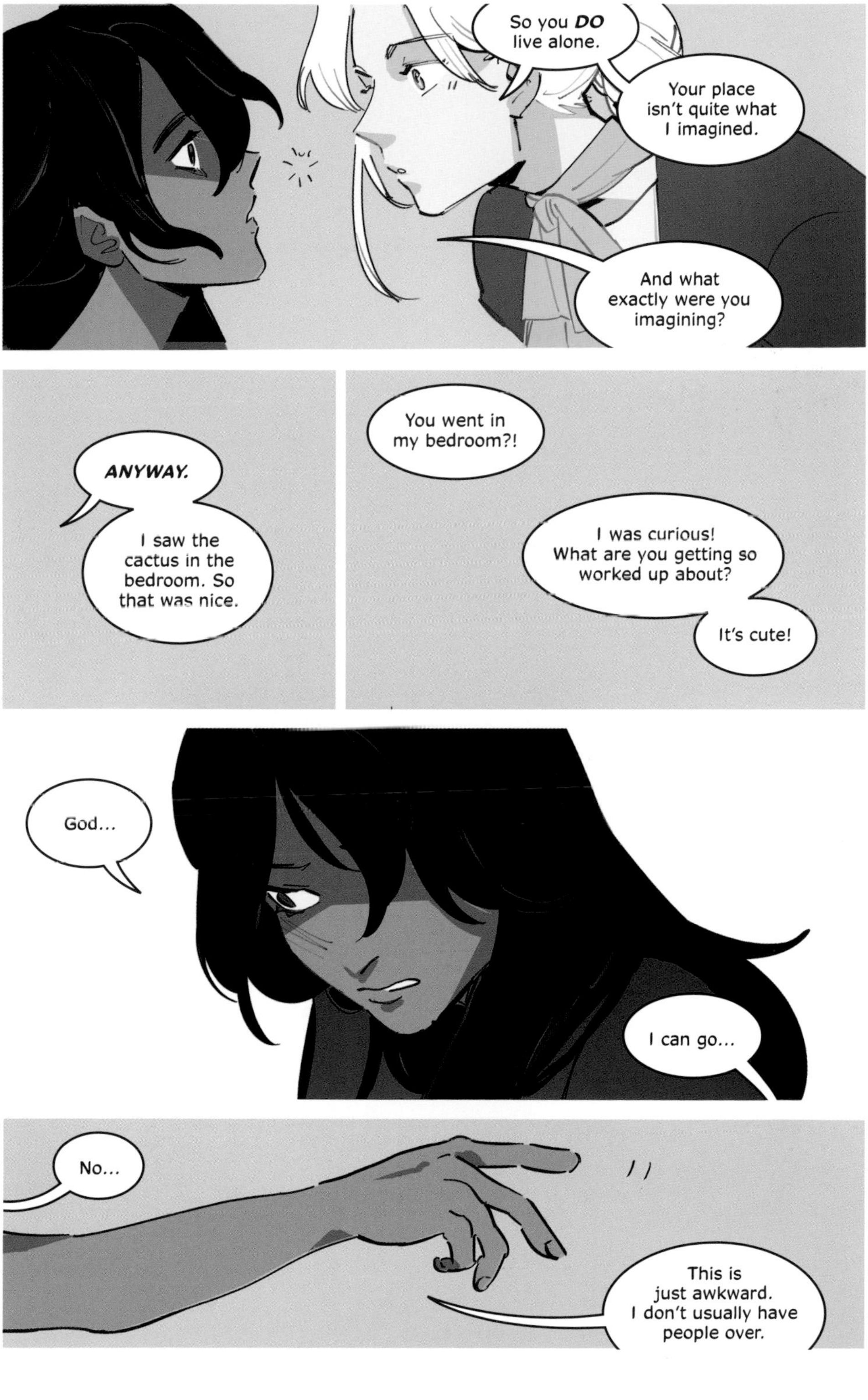
So you DO live alone.
Your place isn't quite what I imagined.
And what exactly were you imagining?
ANYWAY.
I saw the cactus in the bedroom. So that was nice.
You went in my bedroom?!
I was curious! What are you getting so worked up about?
It's cute!
God...
I can go...
No...
This is just awkward. I don't usually have people over.

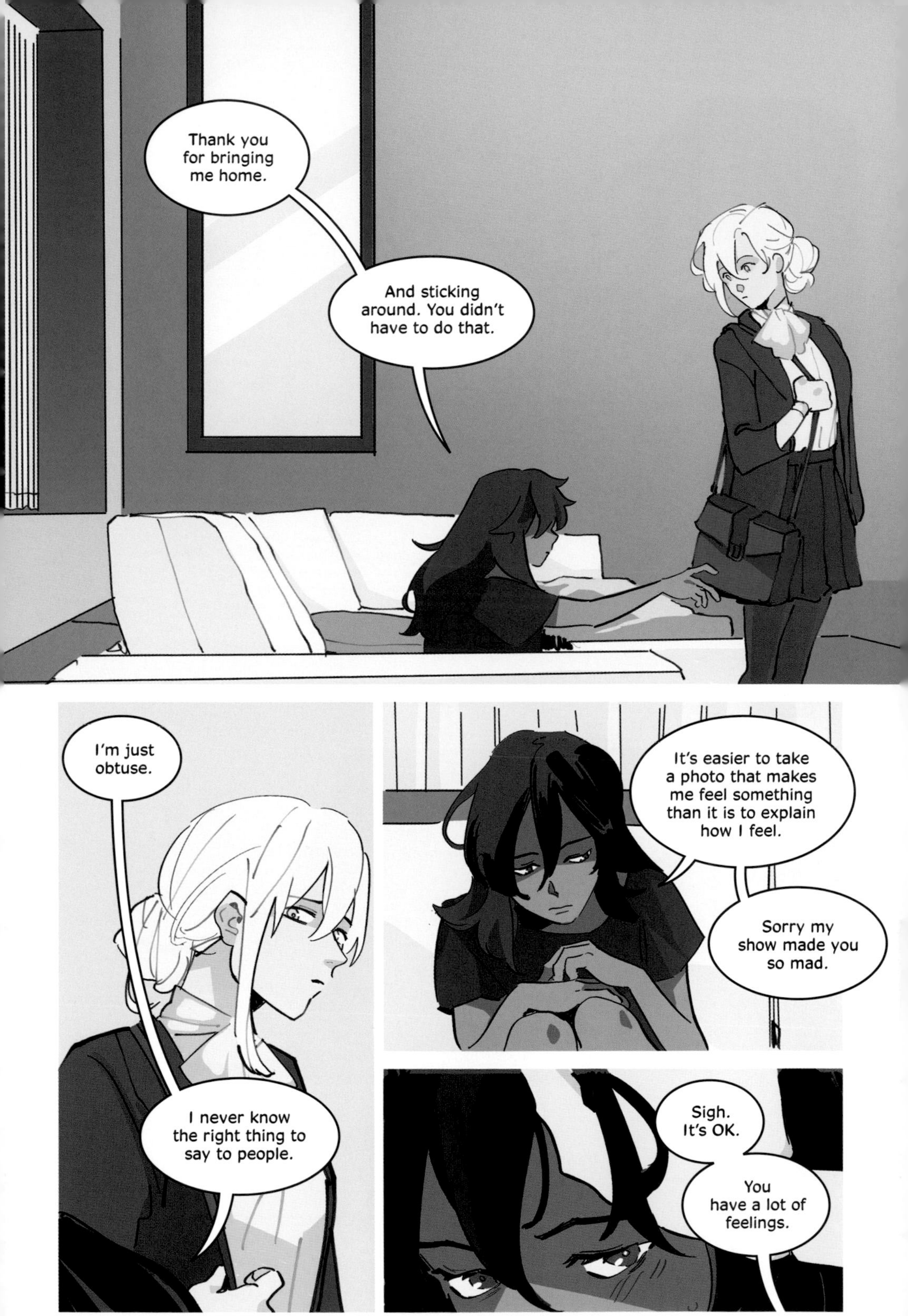
Thank you for bringing me home.
And sticking around. You didn't have to do that.
I'm just obtuse.
I never know the right thing to say to people.
It's easier to take a photo that makes me feel something than it is to explain how I feel.
Sorry my show made you so mad.
Sigh. It's OK.
You have a lot of feelings.

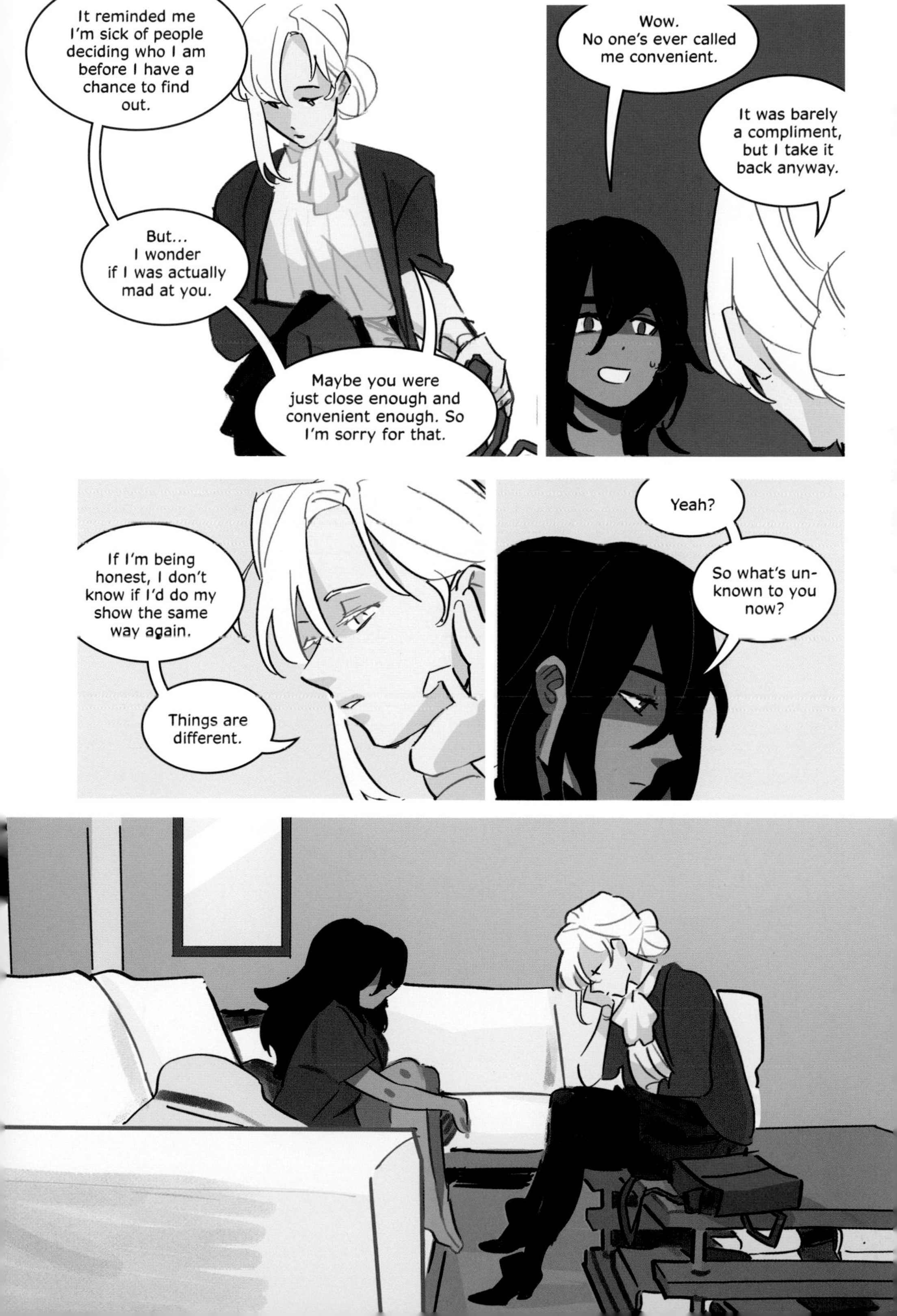
It reminded me I'm sick of people deciding who I am before I have a chance to find out.
But... I wonder if I was actually mad at you.
Maybe you were just close enough and convenient enough. So I'm sorry for that.
Wow. No one's ever called me convenient.
It was barely a compliment, but I take it back anyway.
If I'm being honest, I don't know if I'd do my show the same way again.
Things are different.
Yeah?
So what's unknown to you now?

LOL! Noora is bleeping out
Bollywood song lyrics because they're
being mistaken for curse words!

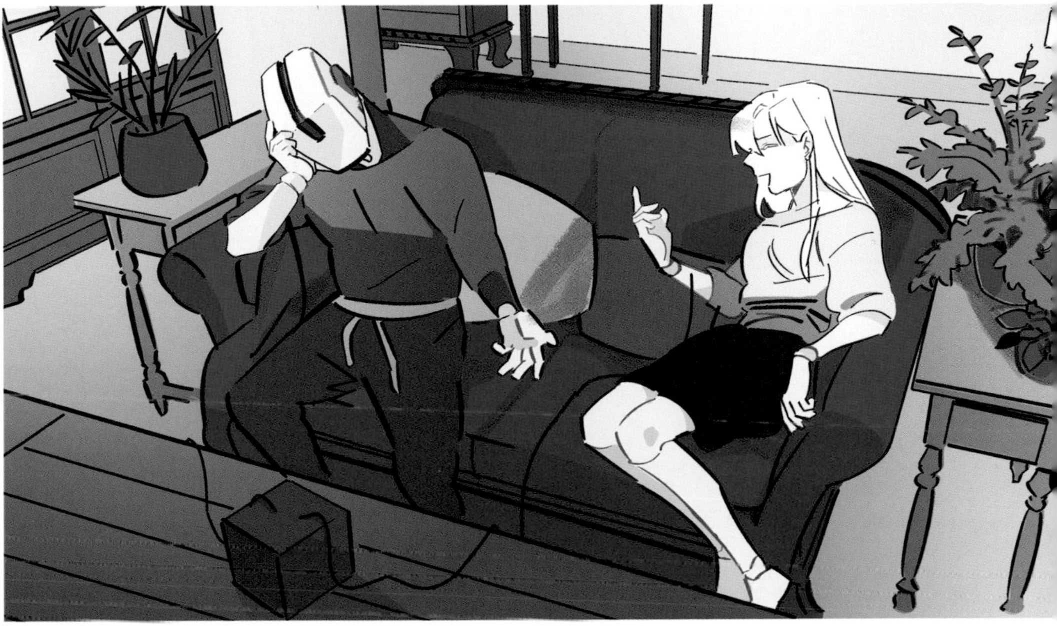

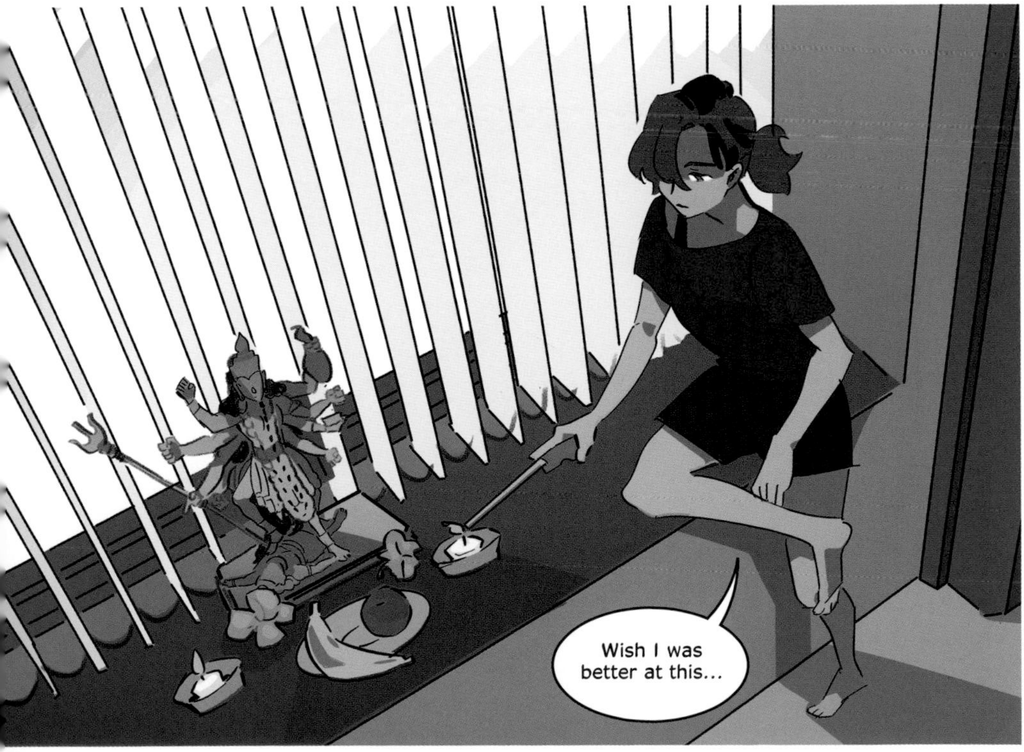
Wish I was better at this...

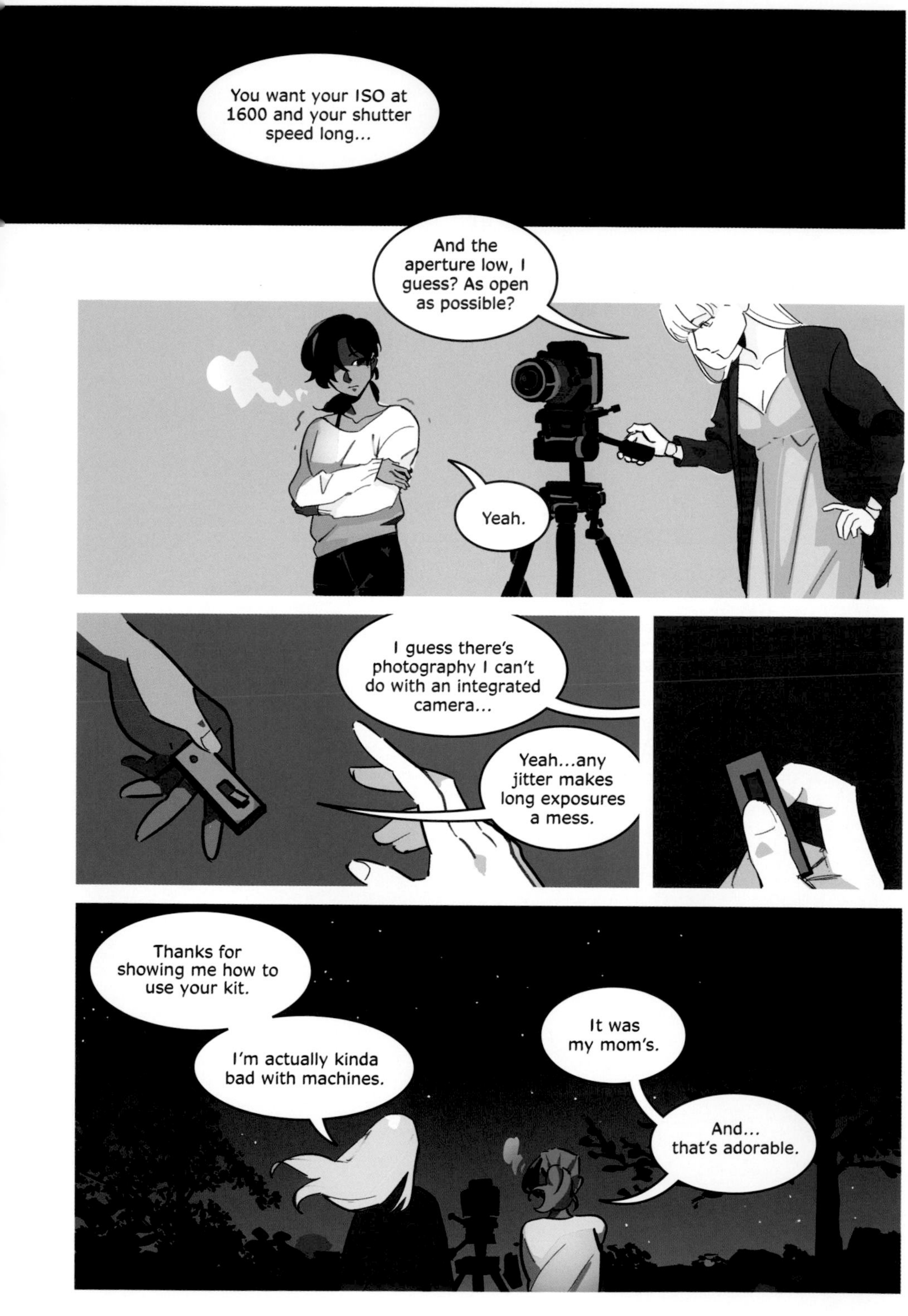
You want your ISO at 1600 and your shutter speed long...
And the aperture low, I guess? As open as possible?
Yeah.
I guess there's photography I can't do with an integrated camera...
Yeah...any jitter makes long exposures a mess.
Thanks for showing me how to use your kit.
I'm actually kinda bad with machines.
It was my mom's.
And... that's adorable.

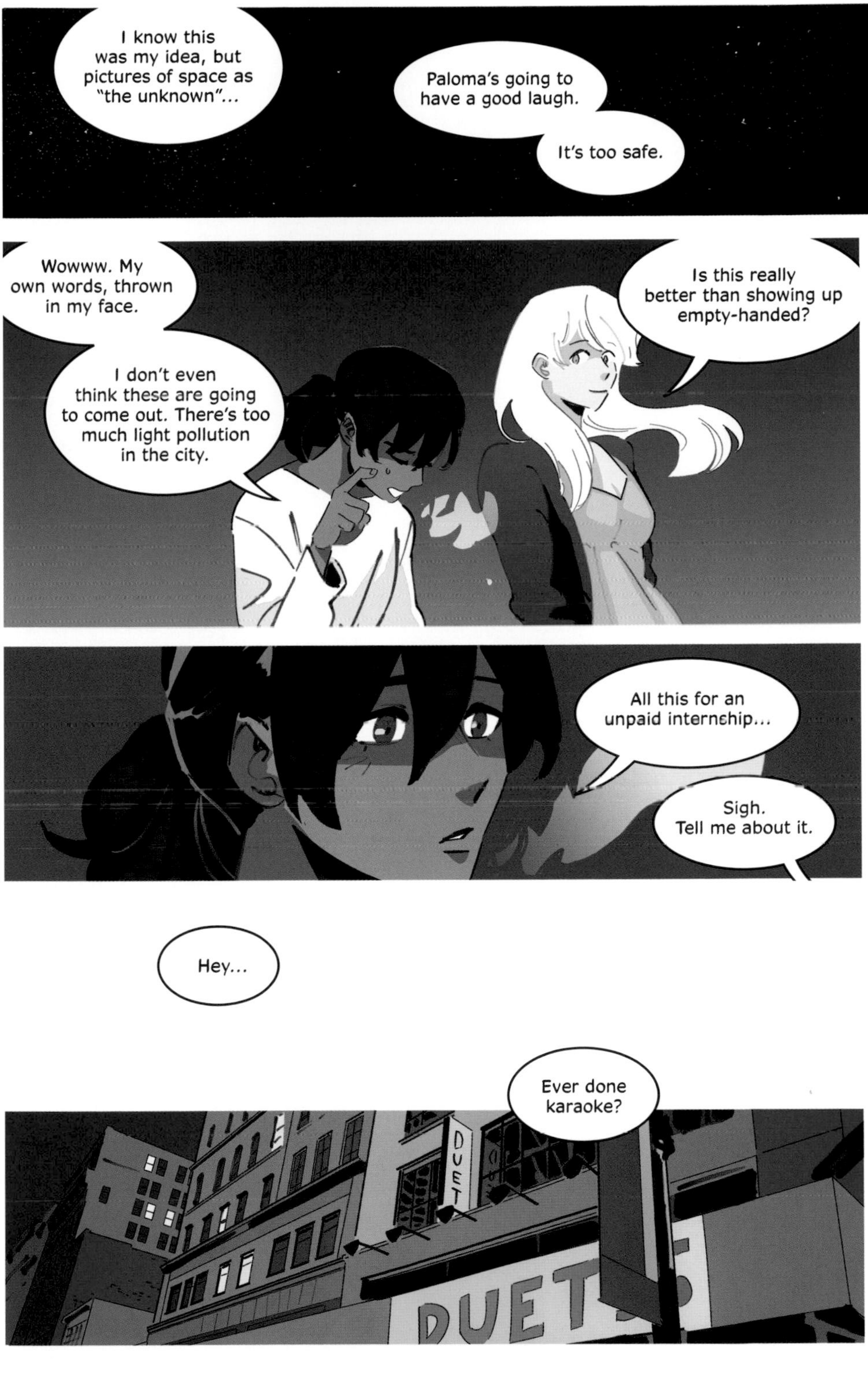

I know this was my idea, but pictures of space as "the unknown"...
Paloma's going to have a good laugh.
It's too safe.
Wowww. My own words, thrown in my face.
I don't even think these are going to come out. There's too much light pollution in the city.
Is this really better than showing up empty-handed?
All this for an unpaid internship...
Sigh. Tell me about it.
Hey...
Ever done karaoke?
DUET
DUET

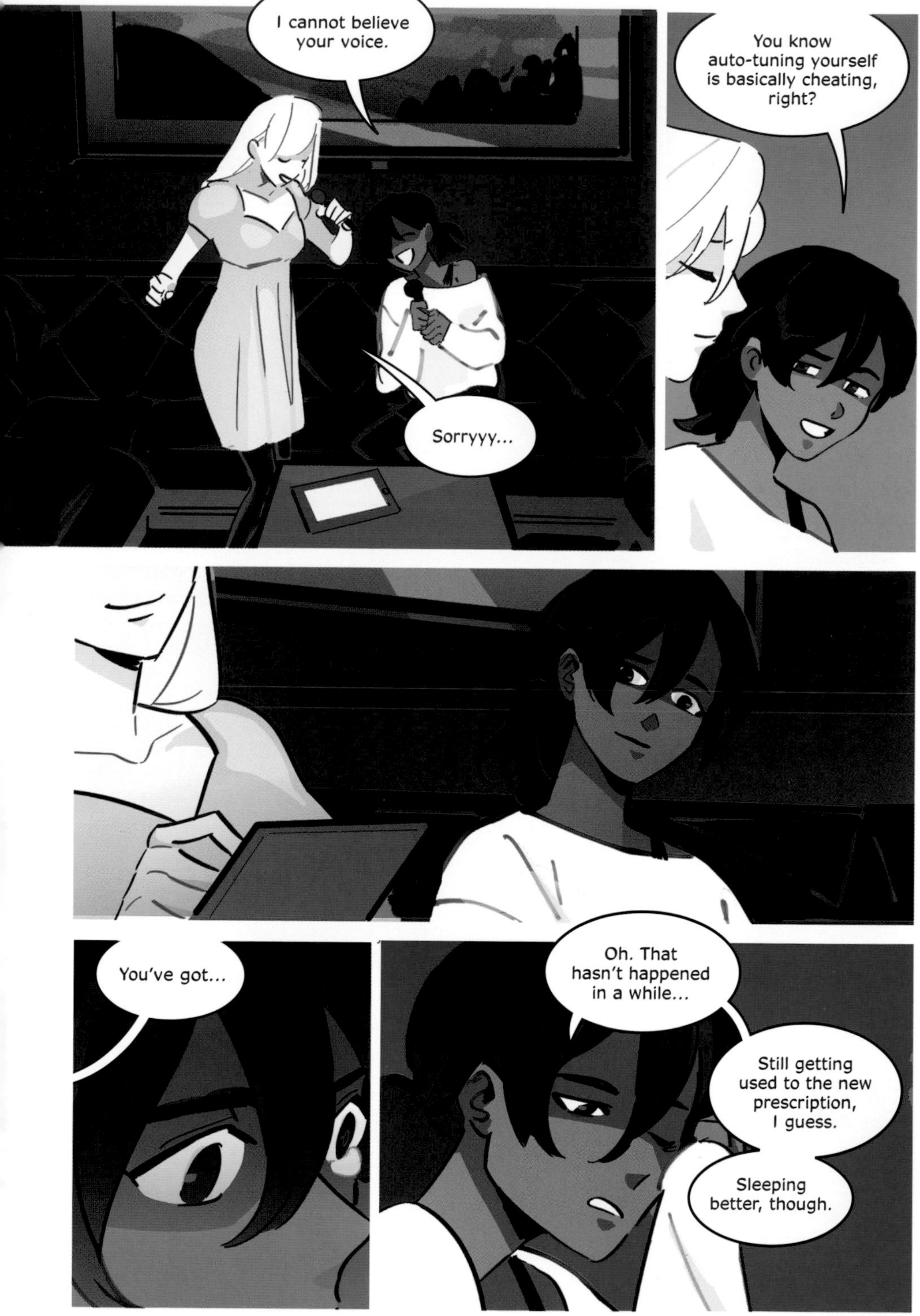
I cannot believe your voice.
Sorryyy...
You know auto-tuning yourself is basically cheating, right?
You've got...
Oh. That hasn't happened in a while...
Still getting used to the new prescription, I guess.
Sleeping better, though.

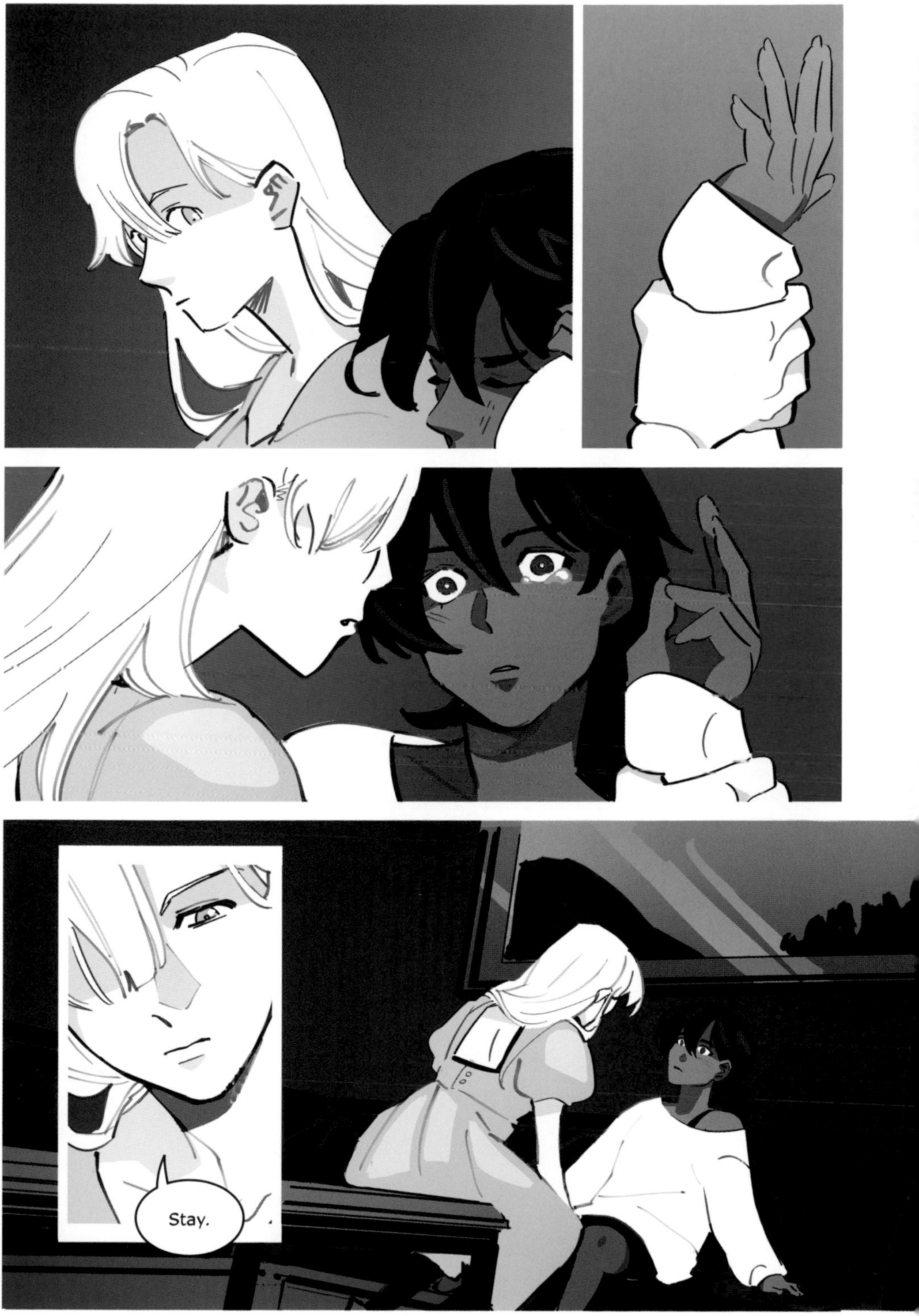
Stay.

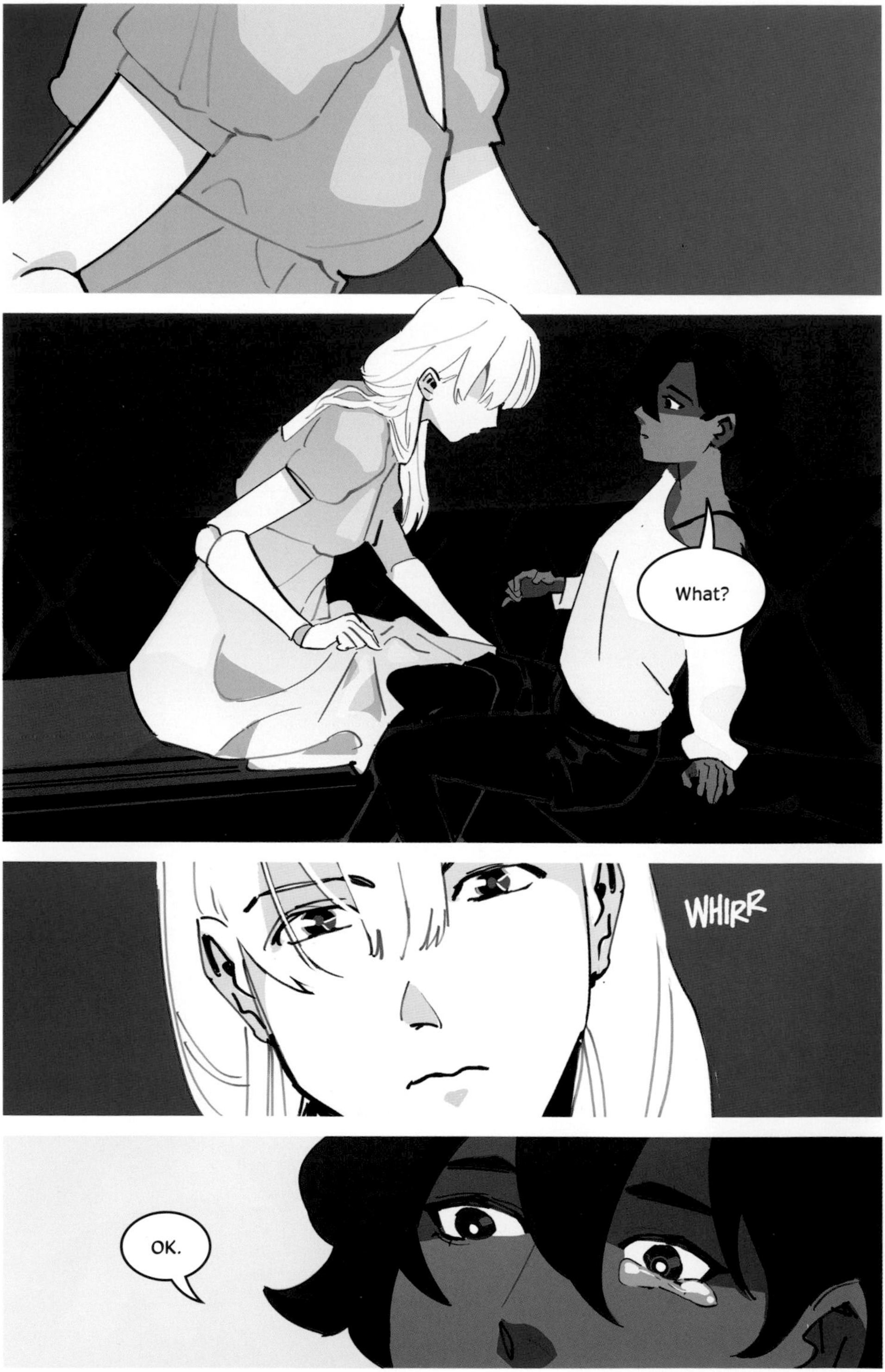
What?
WHIRR
OK.

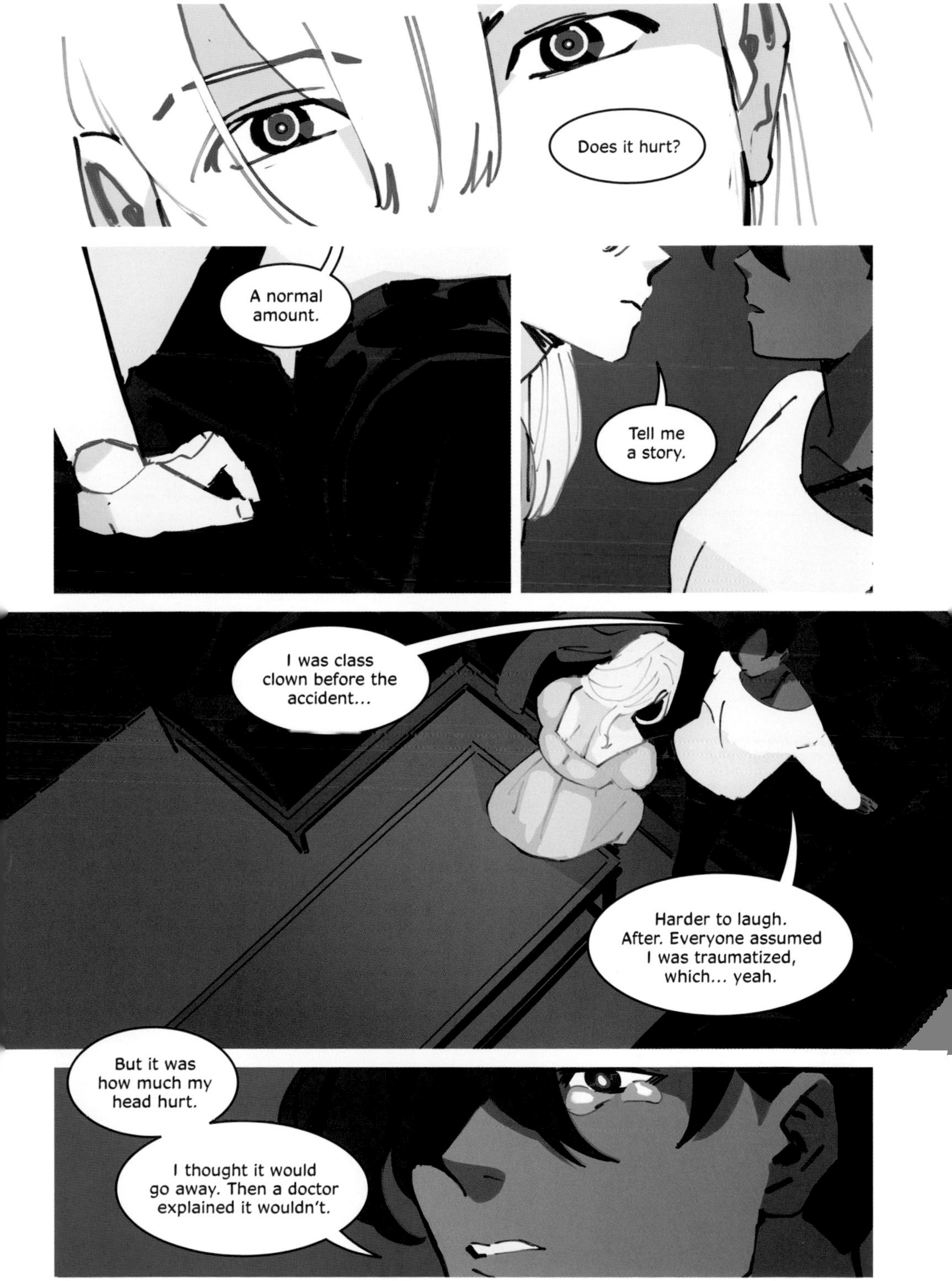
Does it hurt?
A normal amount.
Tell me a story.
I was class clown before the accident...
Harder to laugh. After. Everyone assumed I was traumatized, which... yeah.
But it was how much my head hurt.
I thought it would go away. Then a doctor explained it wouldn't.

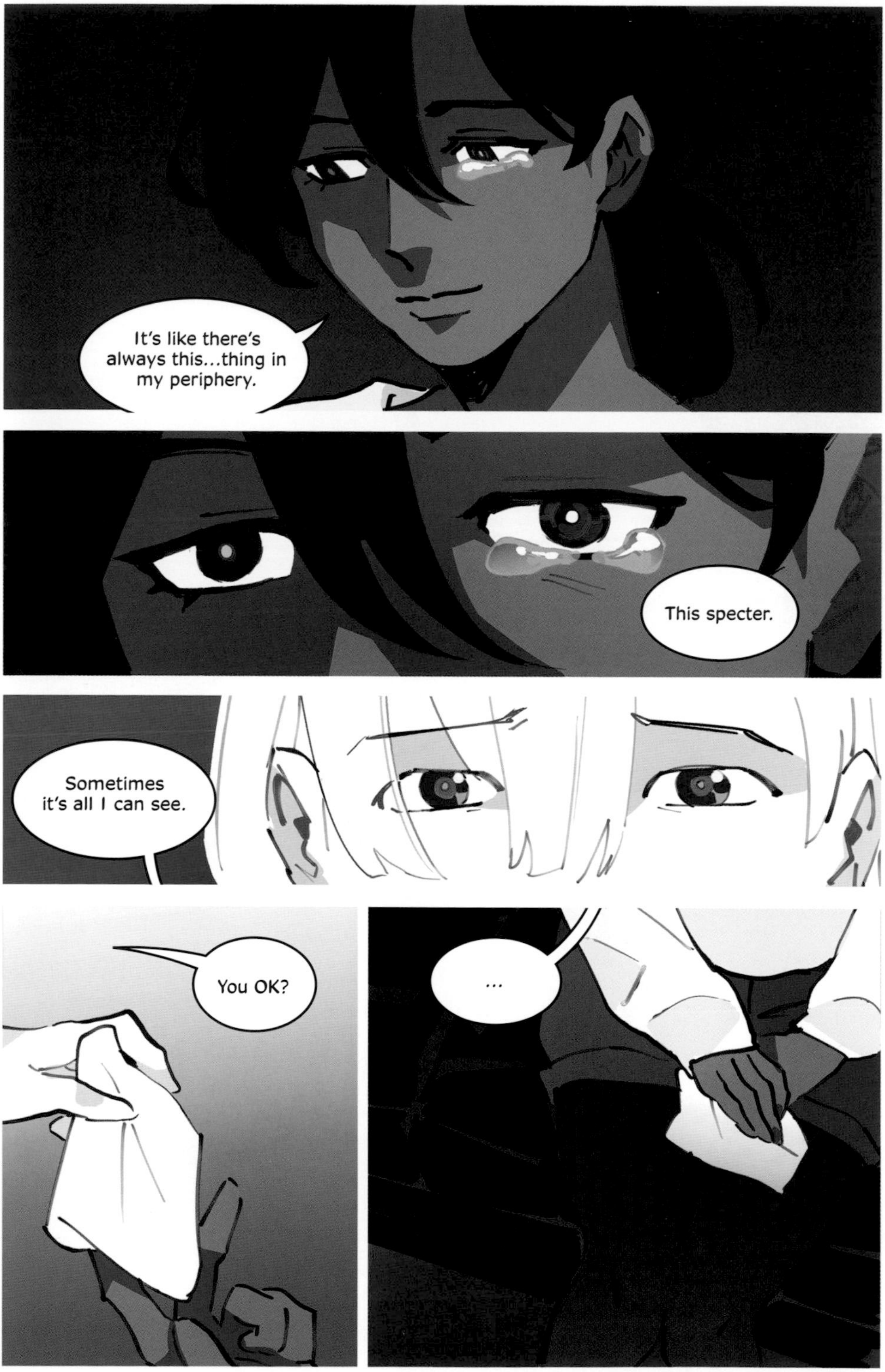
It's like there's always this...thing in my periphery.
This specter.
Sometimes it's all I can see.
You OK?
...

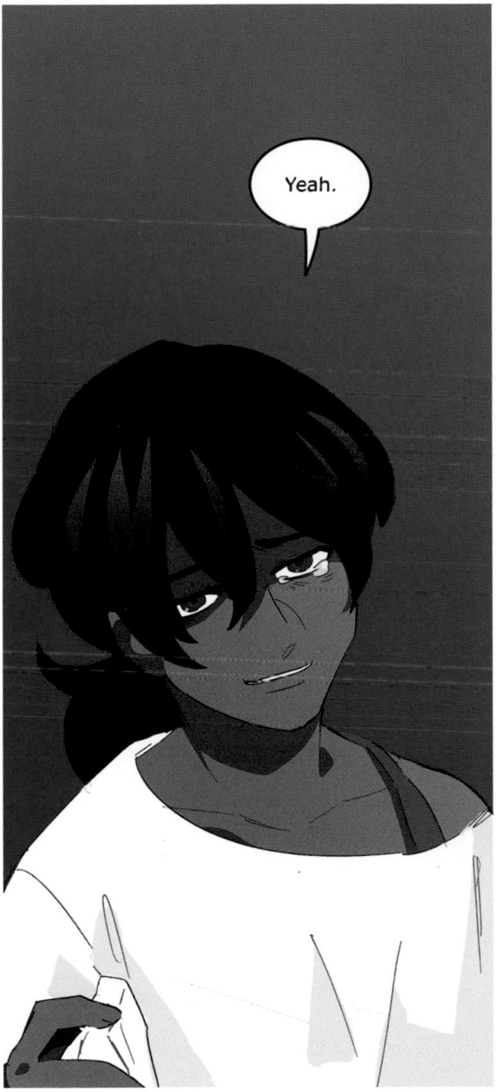
Yeah.

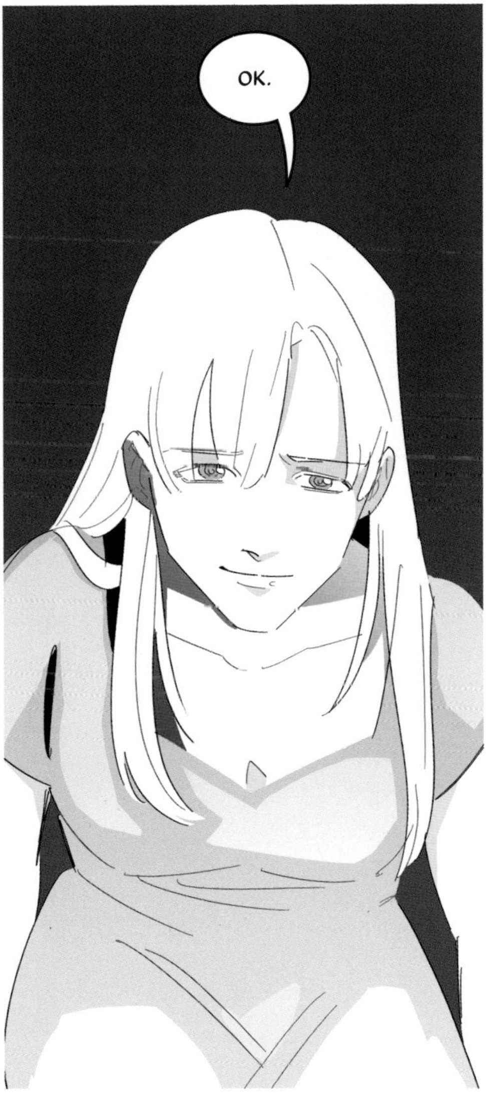
OK.

A ranging new survey by MIT
researchers reveals distinct global and
regional preferences concerning the
ethics of AI-guided vehicles.

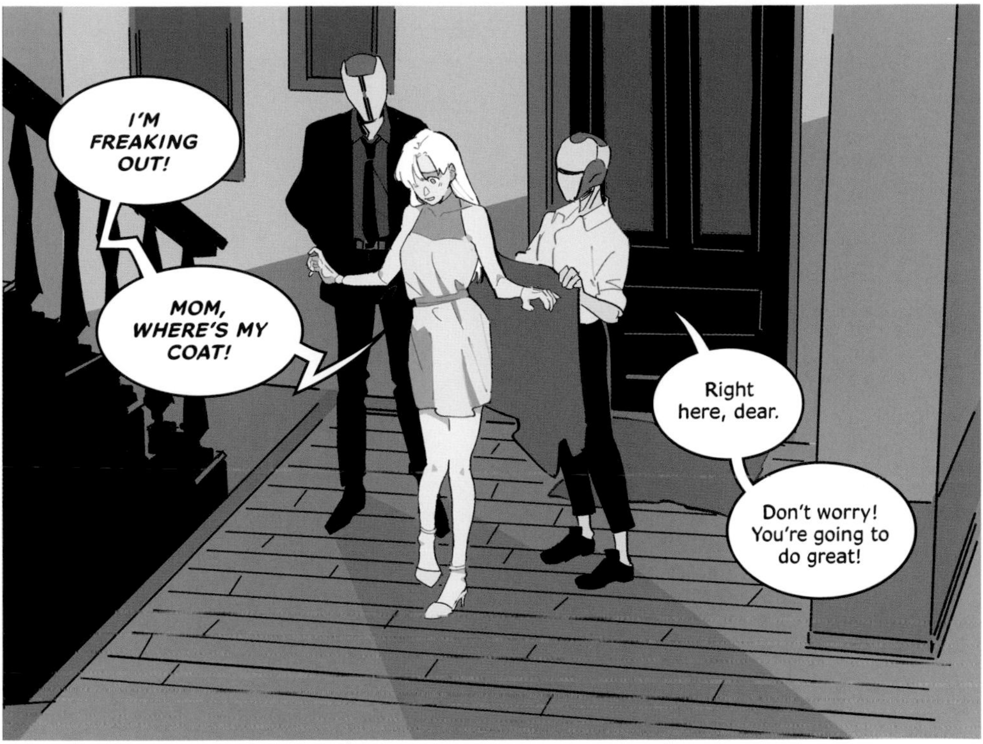
I'M FREAKING OUT!
MOM, WHERE'S MY COAT!
Right here, dear.
Don't worry! You're going to do great!

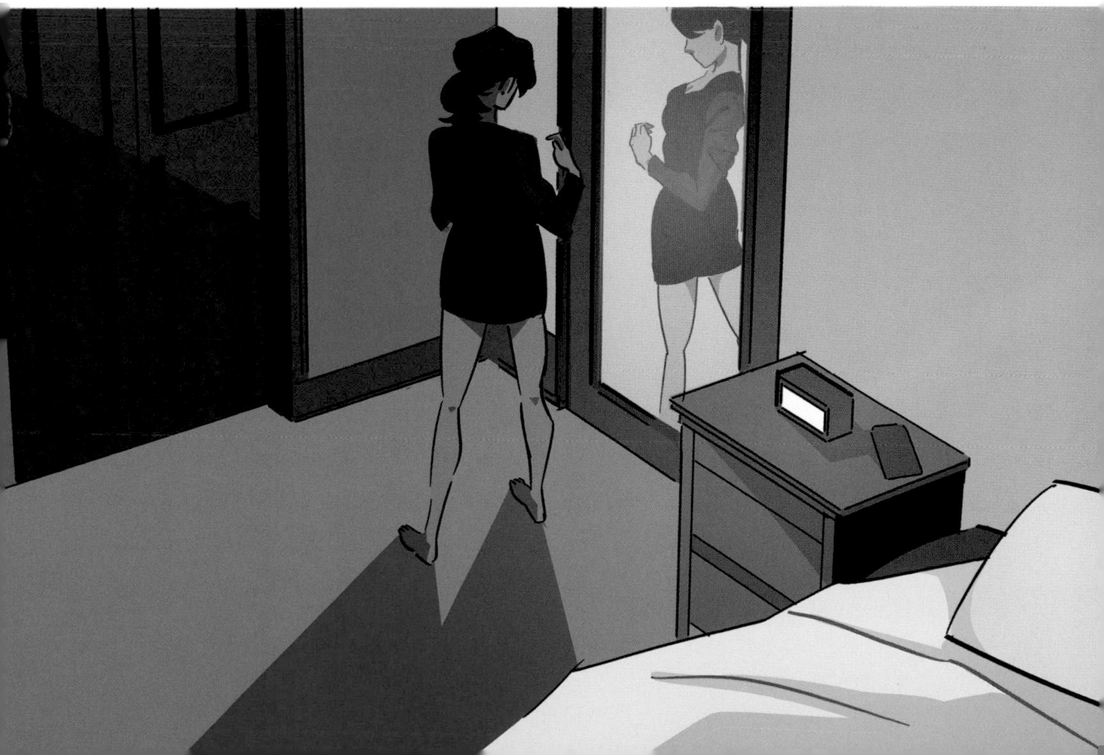

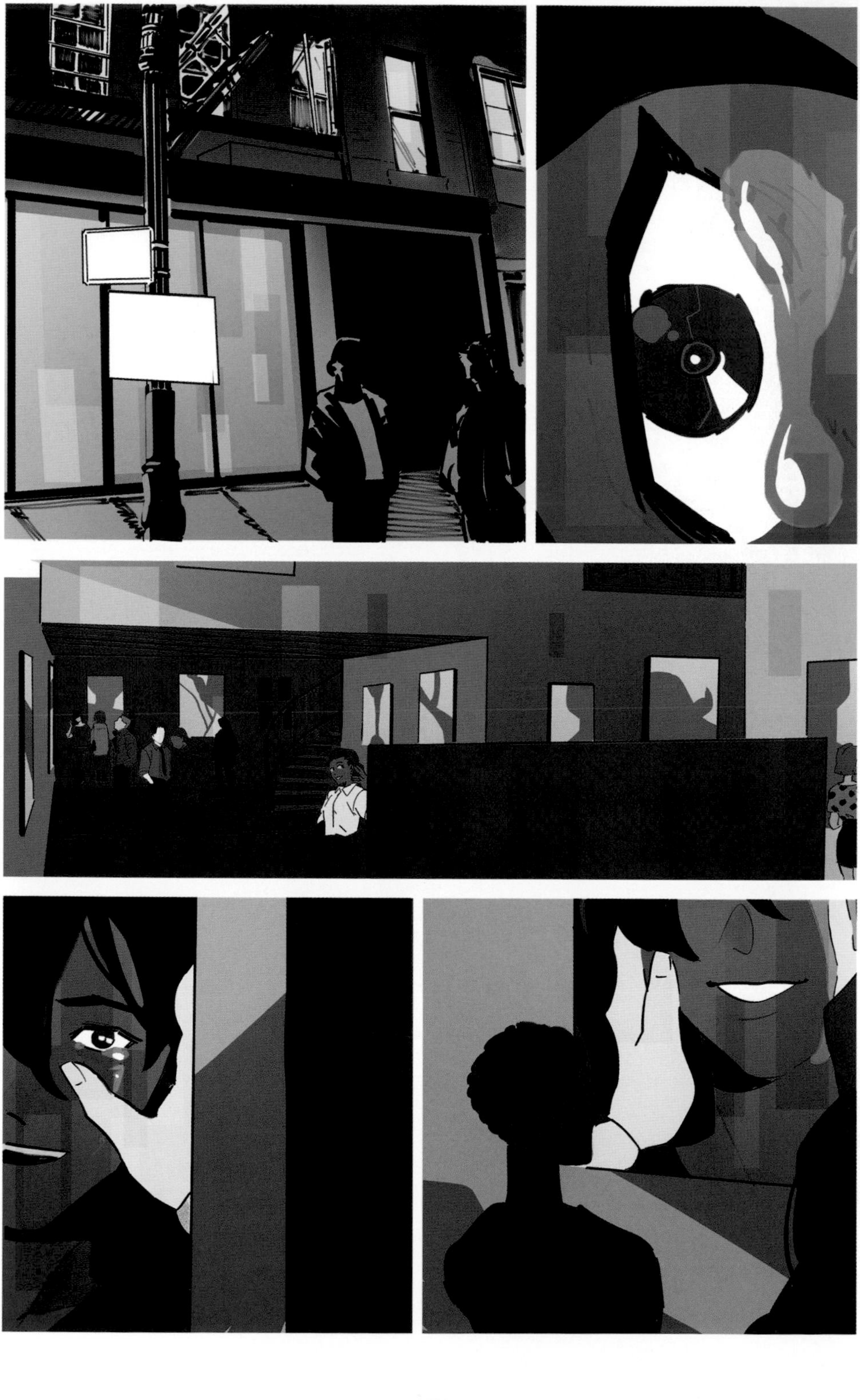

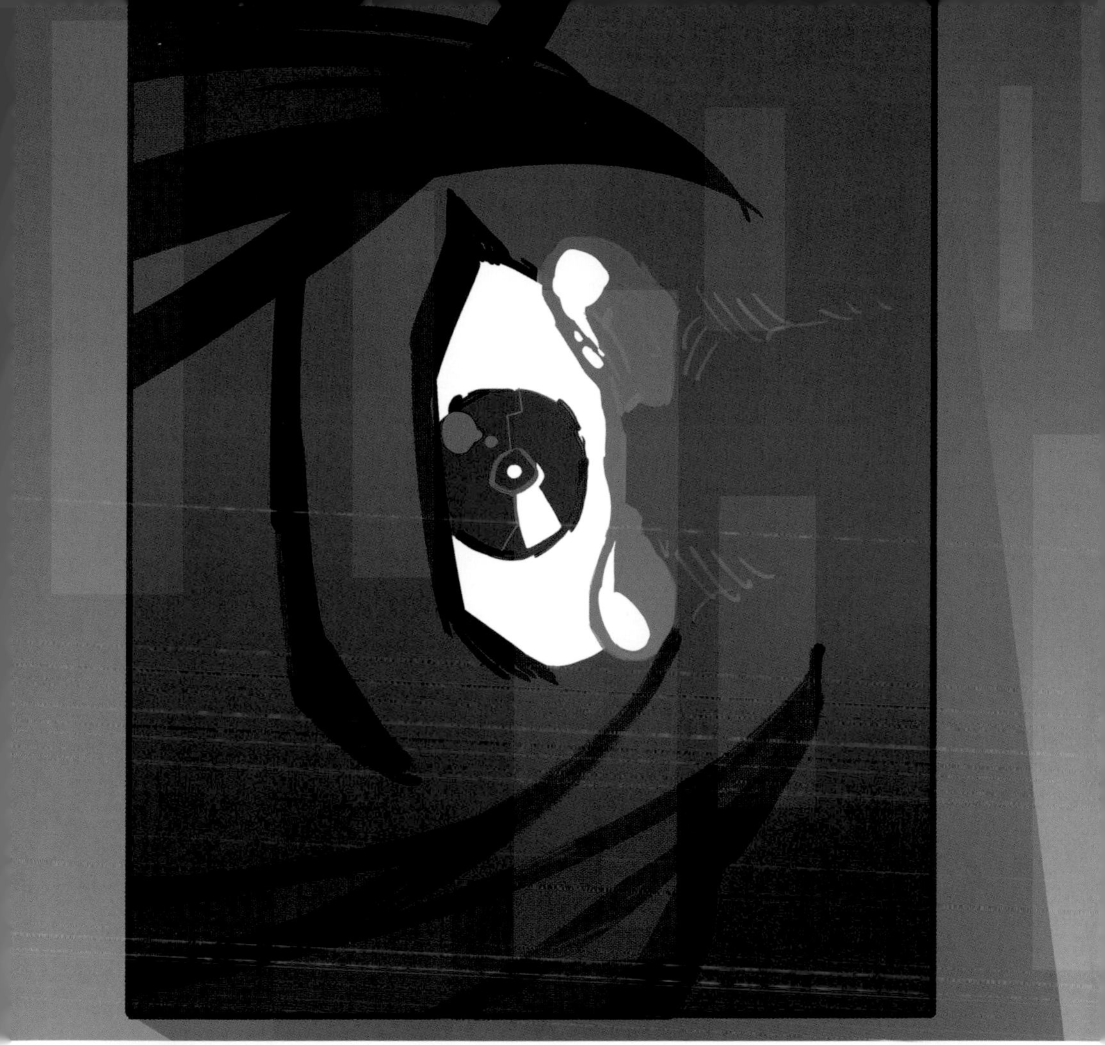

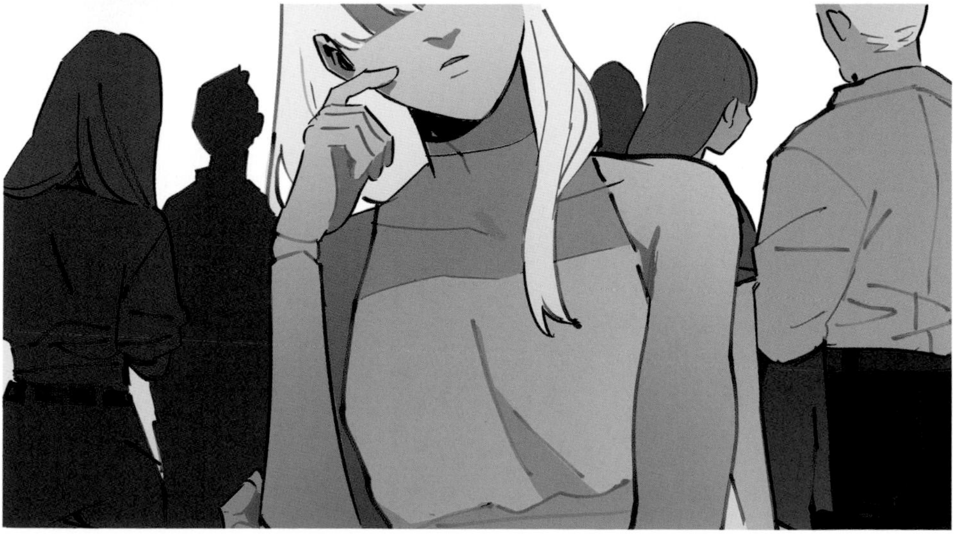

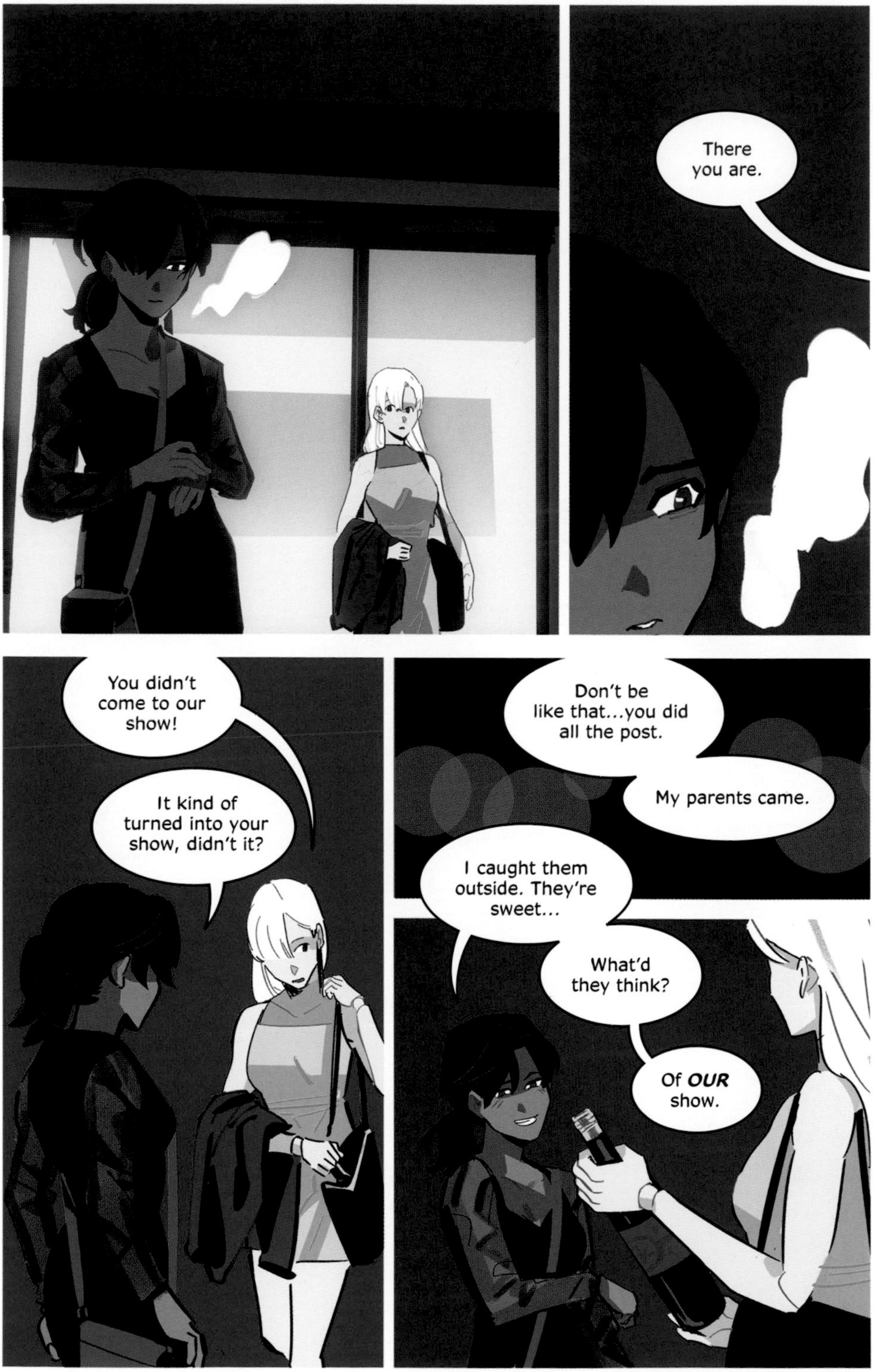
There you are.
You didn't come to our show!
It kind of turned into your show, didn't it?
Don't be like that...you did all the post.
My parents came.
I caught them outside. They're sweet...
What'd they think?
Of **OUR** show.

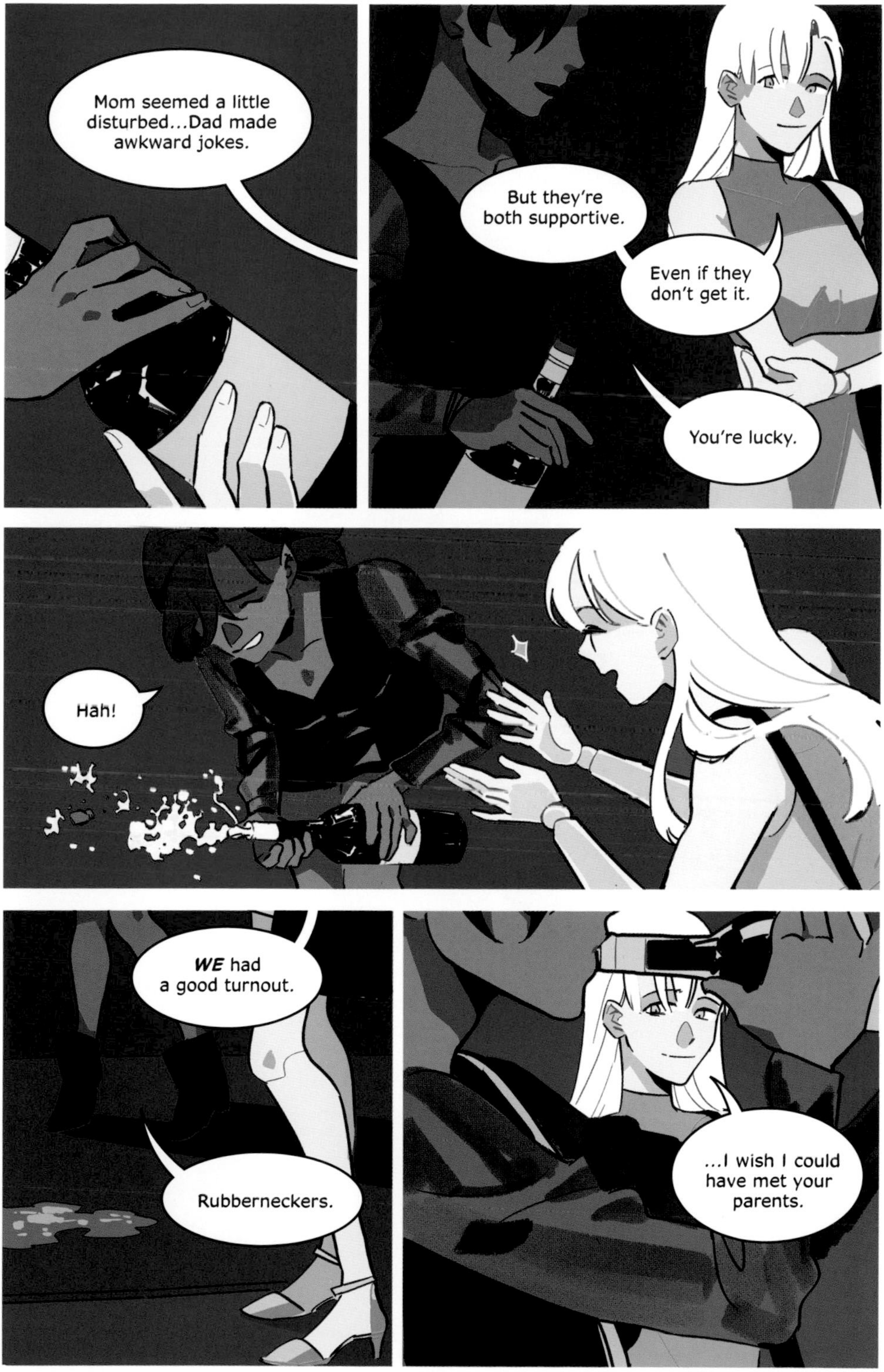
Mom seemed a little disturbed...Dad made awkward jokes.
But they're both supportive.
Even if they don't get it.
You're lucky.
Hah!
WE had a good turnout.
Rubberneckers.
...I wish I could have met your parents.

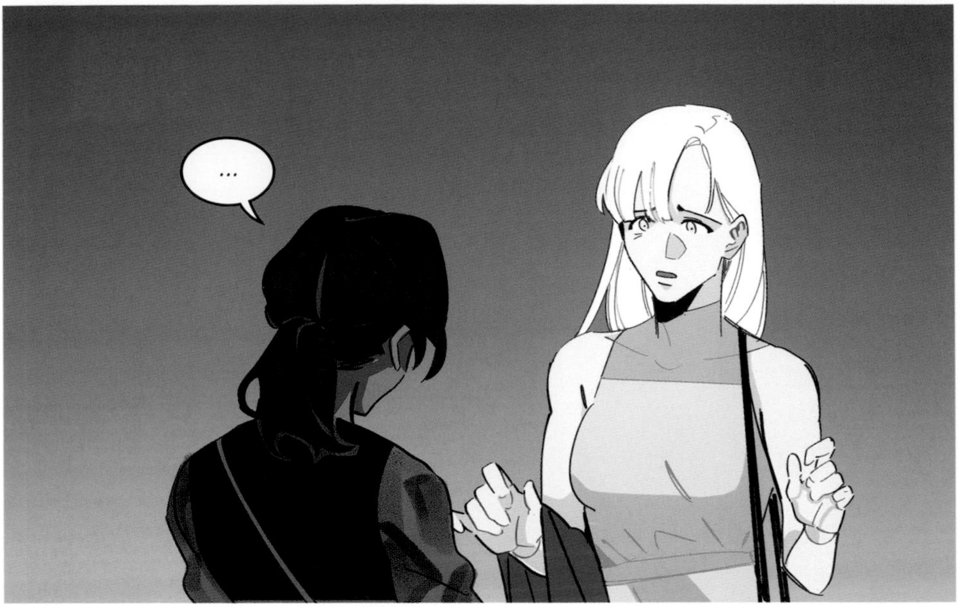
...

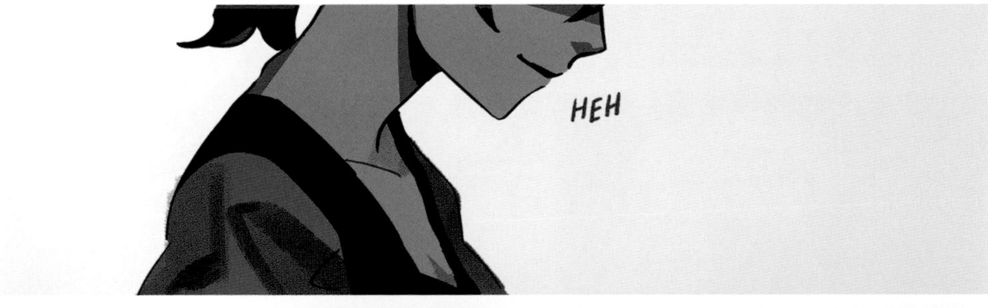
HEH

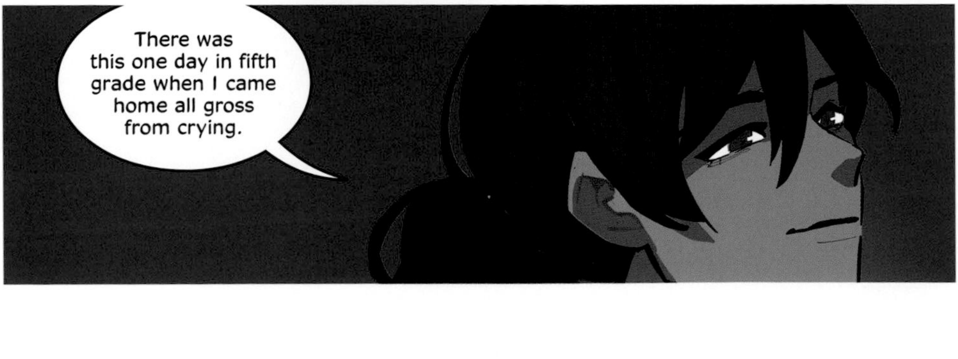
There was this one day in fifth grade when I came home all gross from crying.

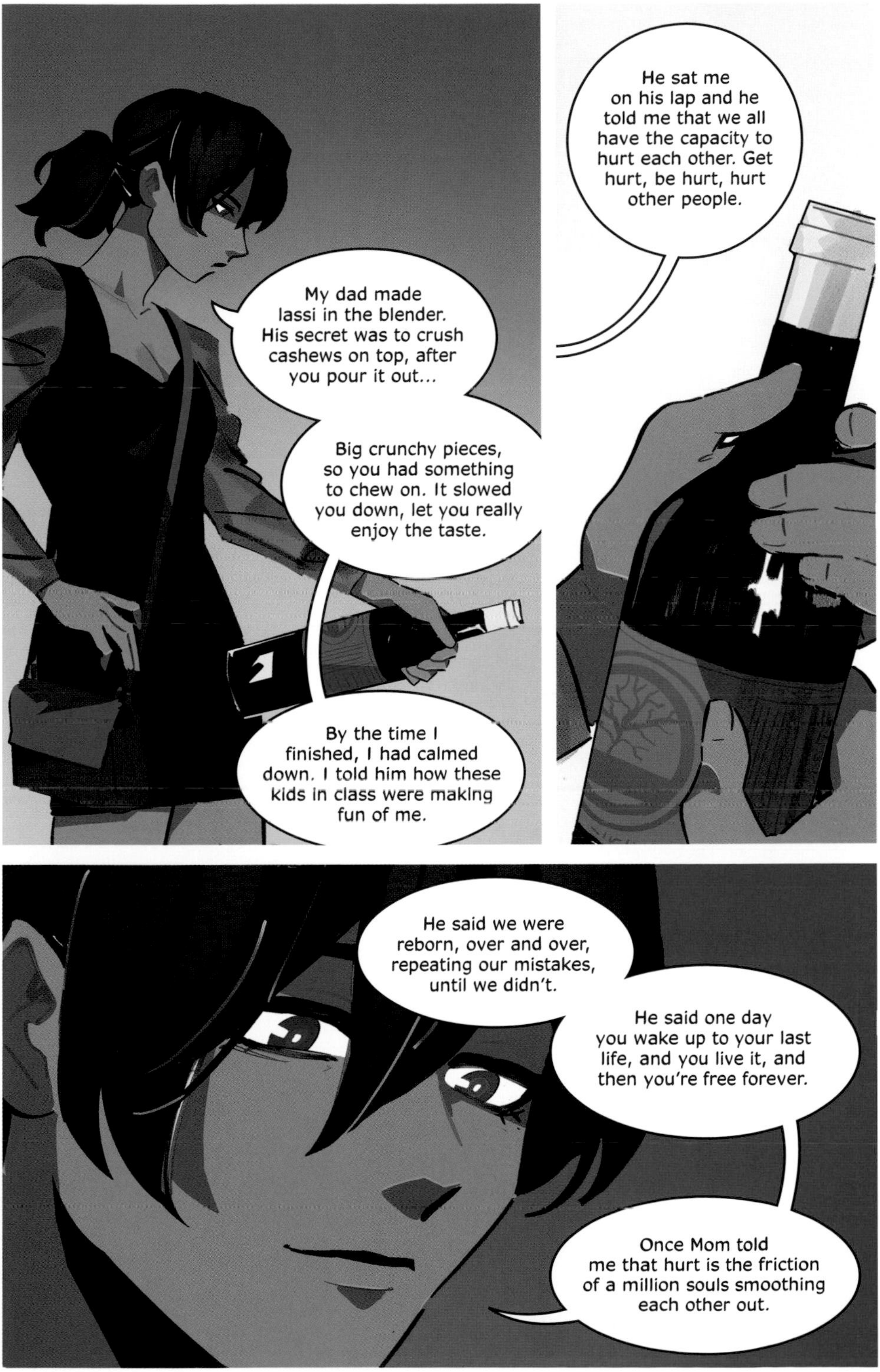
My dad made lassi in the blender. His secret was to crush cashews on top, after you pour it out...
Big crunchy pieces, so you had something to chew on. It slowed you down, let you really enjoy the taste.
By the time I finished, I had calmed down. I told him how these kids in class were making fun of me.
He sat me on his lap and he told me that we all have the capacity to hurt each other. Get hurt, be hurt, hurt other people.
He said we were reborn, over and over, repeating our mistakes, until we didn't.
He said one day you wake up to your last life, and you live it, and then you're free forever.
Once Mom told me that hurt is the friction of a million souls smoothing each other out.

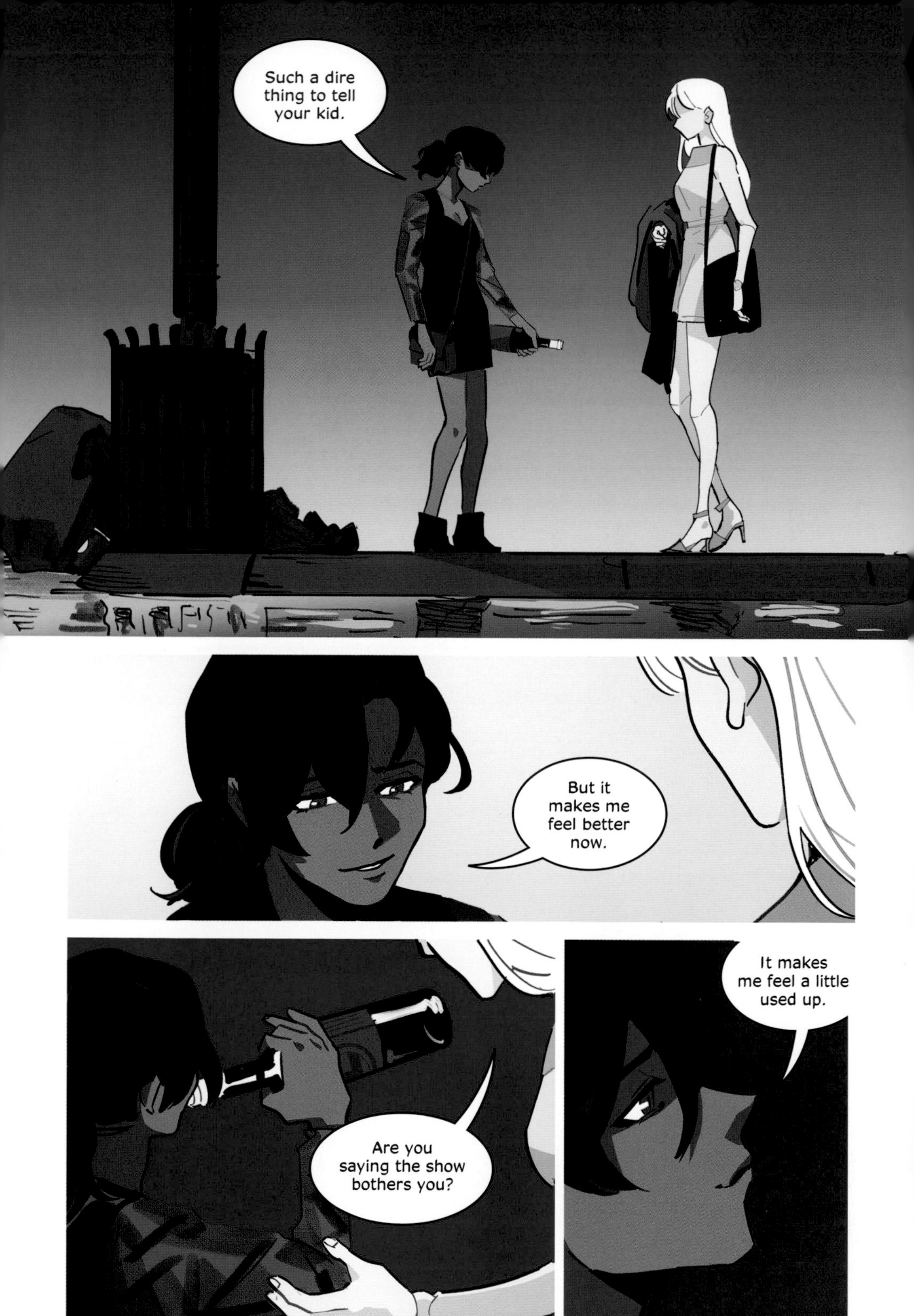
Such a dire thing to tell your kid.
But it makes me feel better now.
Are you saying the show bothers you?
It makes me feel a little used up.

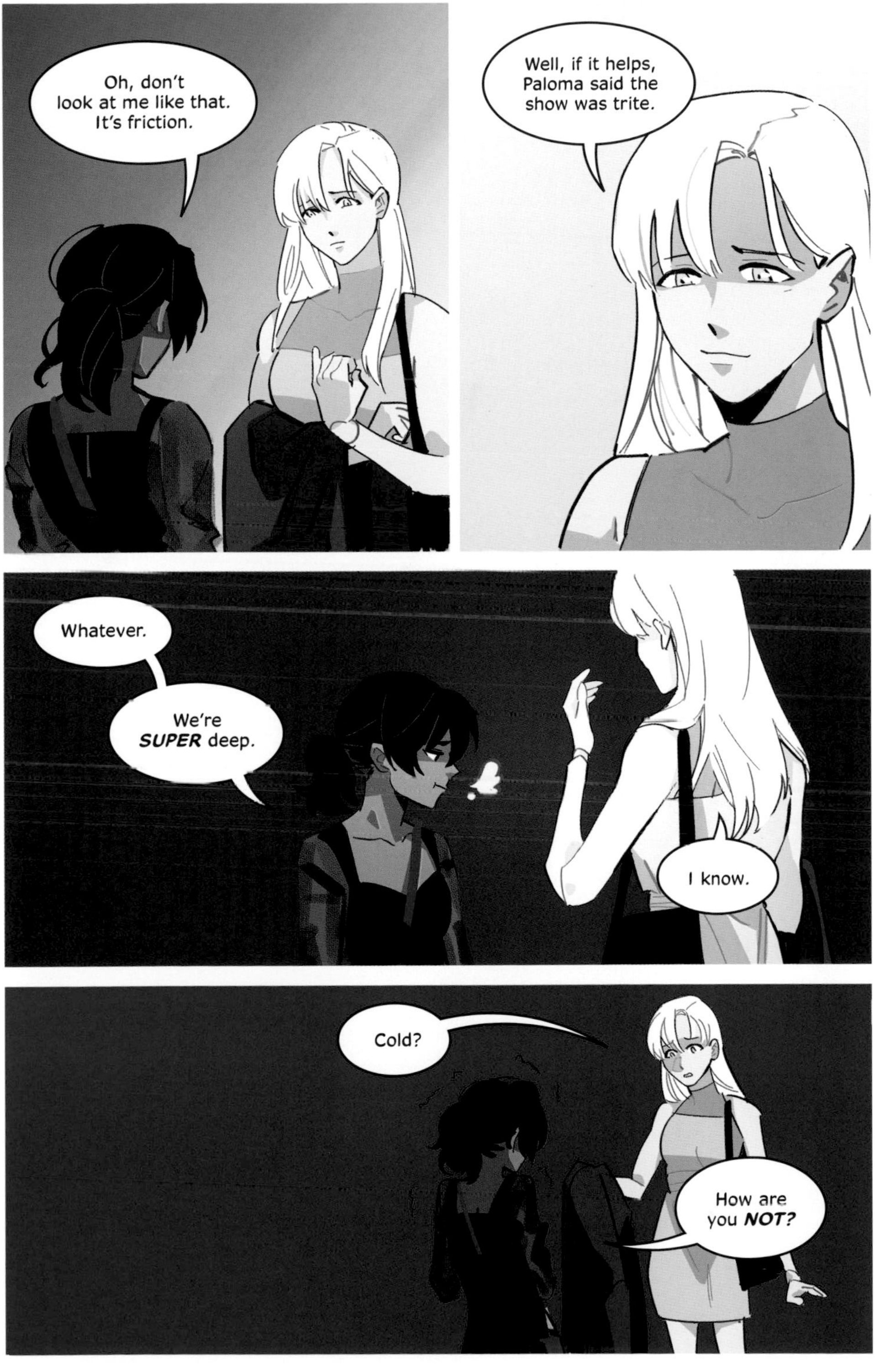
Oh, don't look at me like that. It's friction.
Well, if it helps, Paloma said the show was trite.
Whatever.
We're **SUPER** deep.
I know.
Cold?
How are you **NOT?**

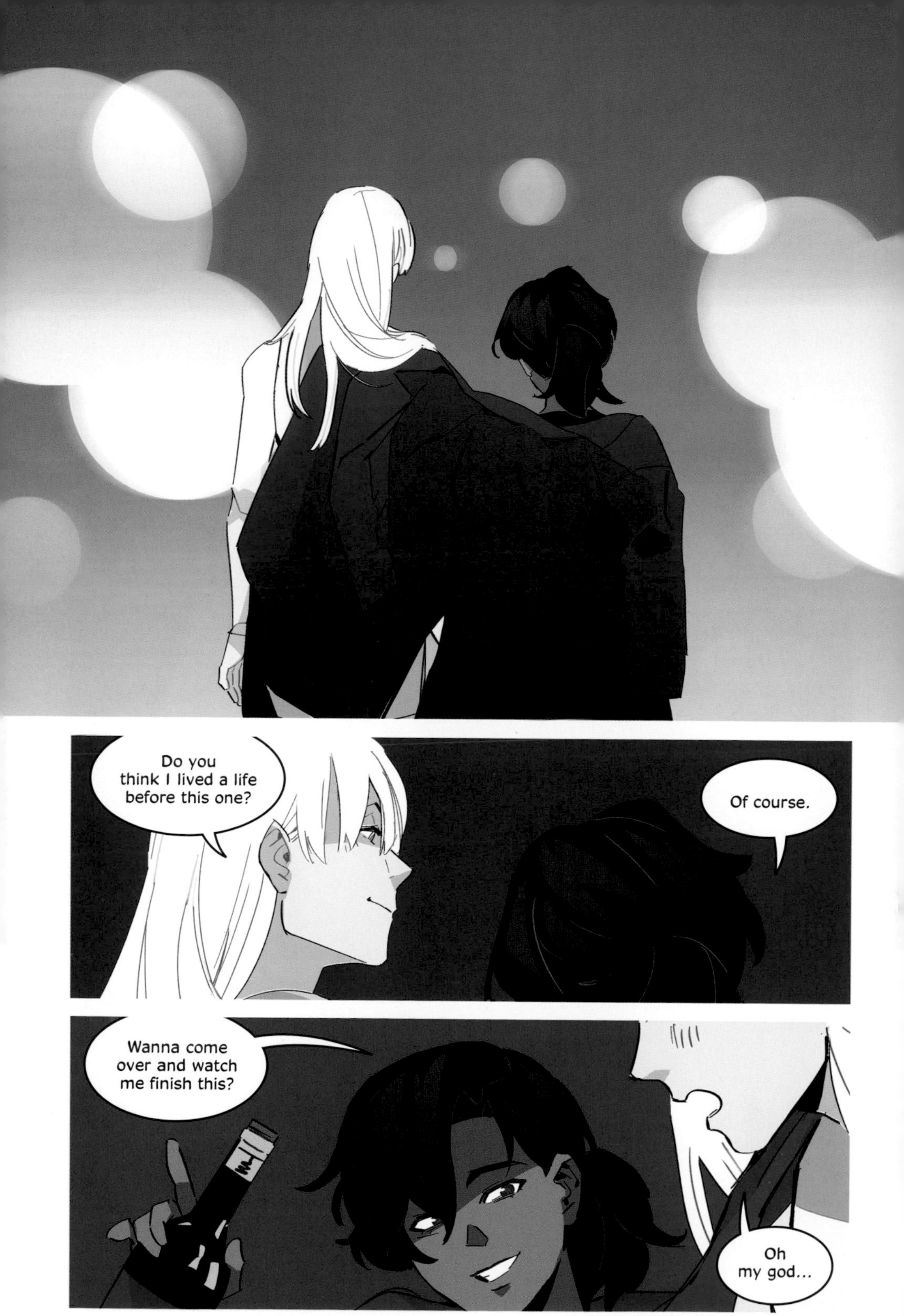
Do you think I lived a life before this one?
Of course.
Wanna come over and watch me finish this?
Oh my god...

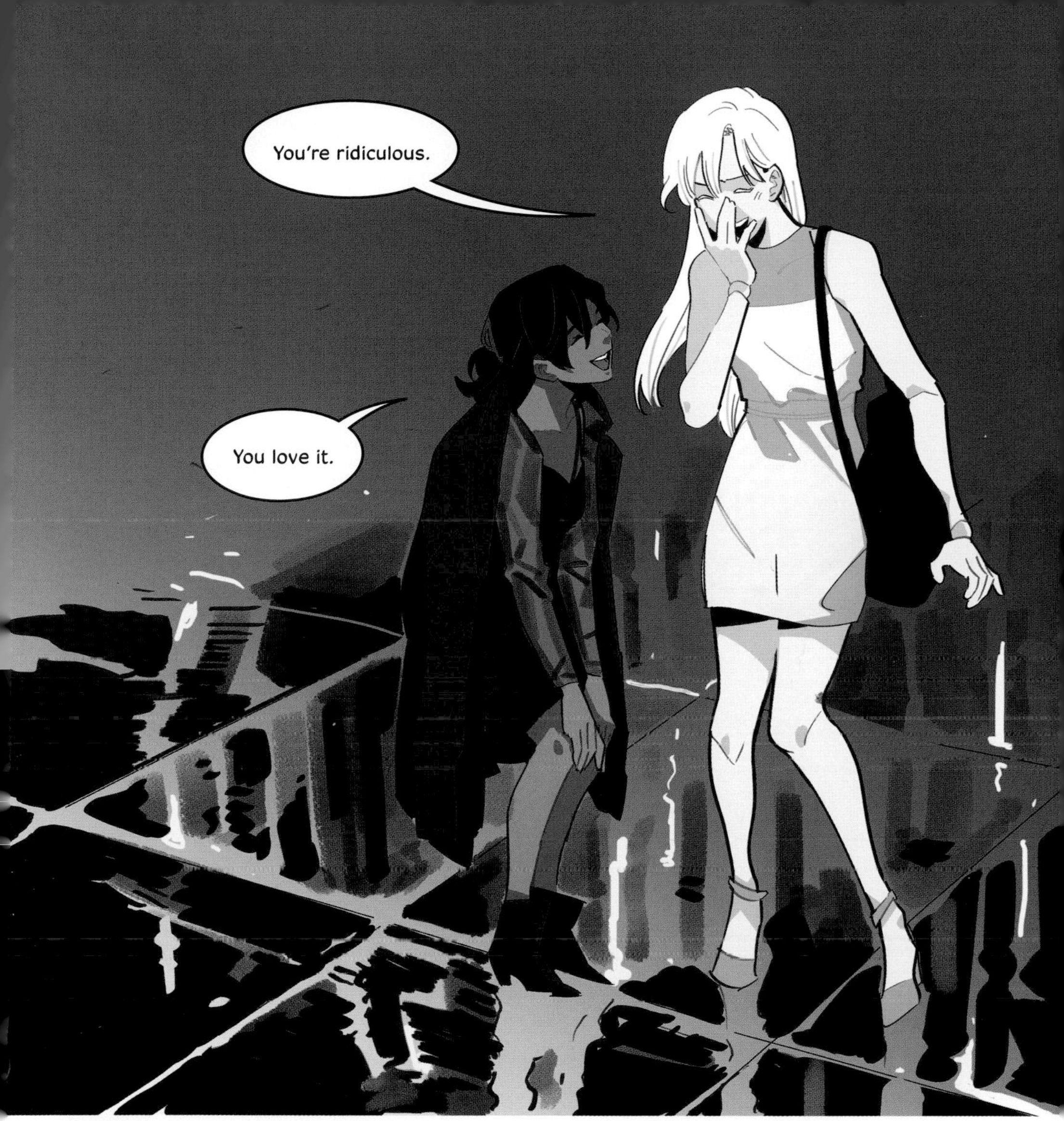
You're ridiculous.
You love it.

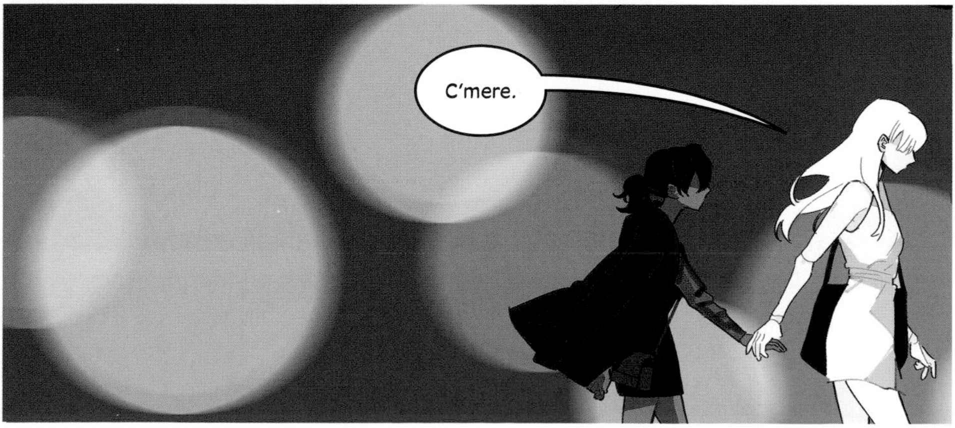
C'mere.

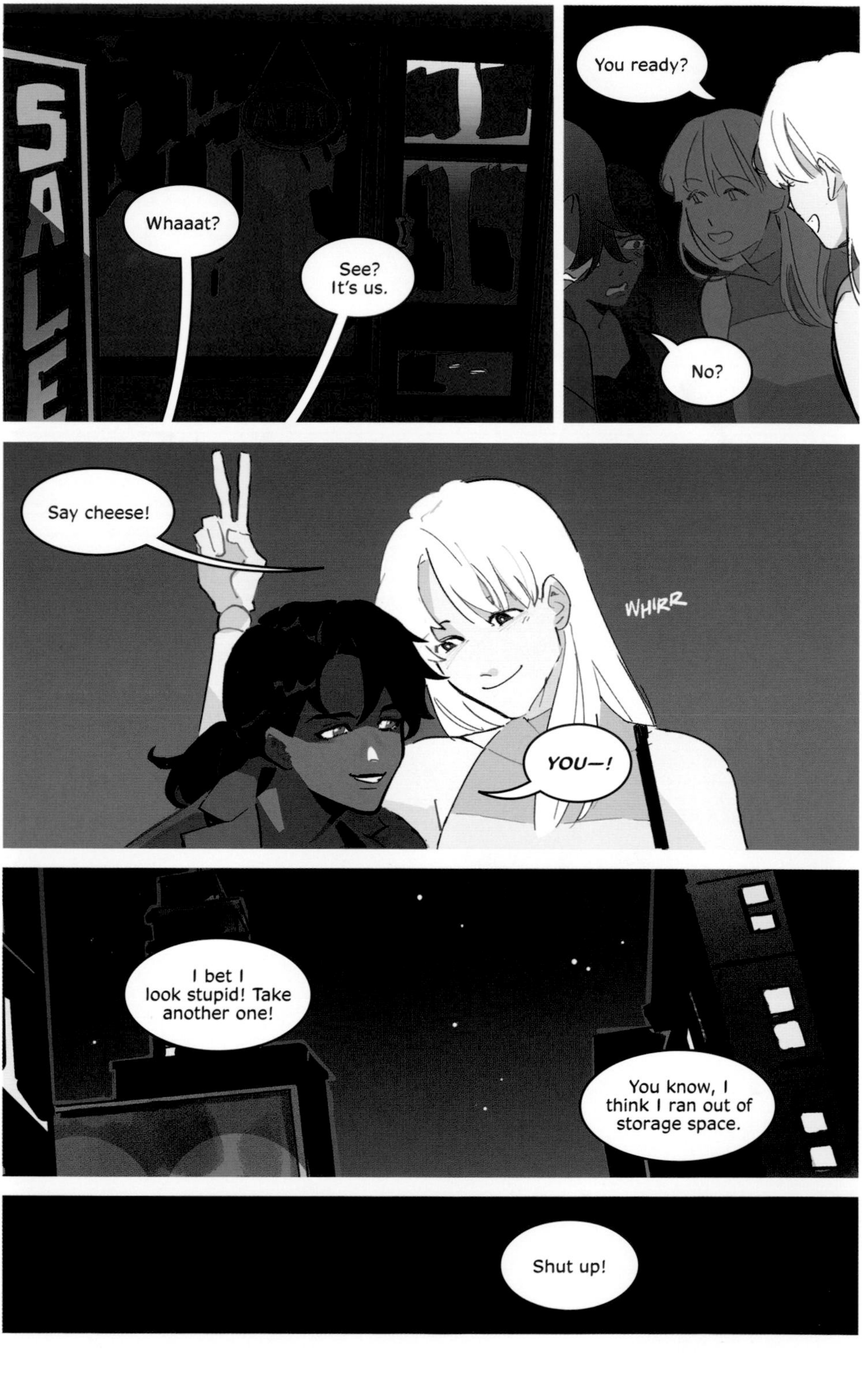
Whaaat?
See? It's us.
You ready?
No?
Say cheese!
WHIRR
YOU—!
I bet I look stupid! Take another one!
You know, I think I ran out of storage space.
Shut up!

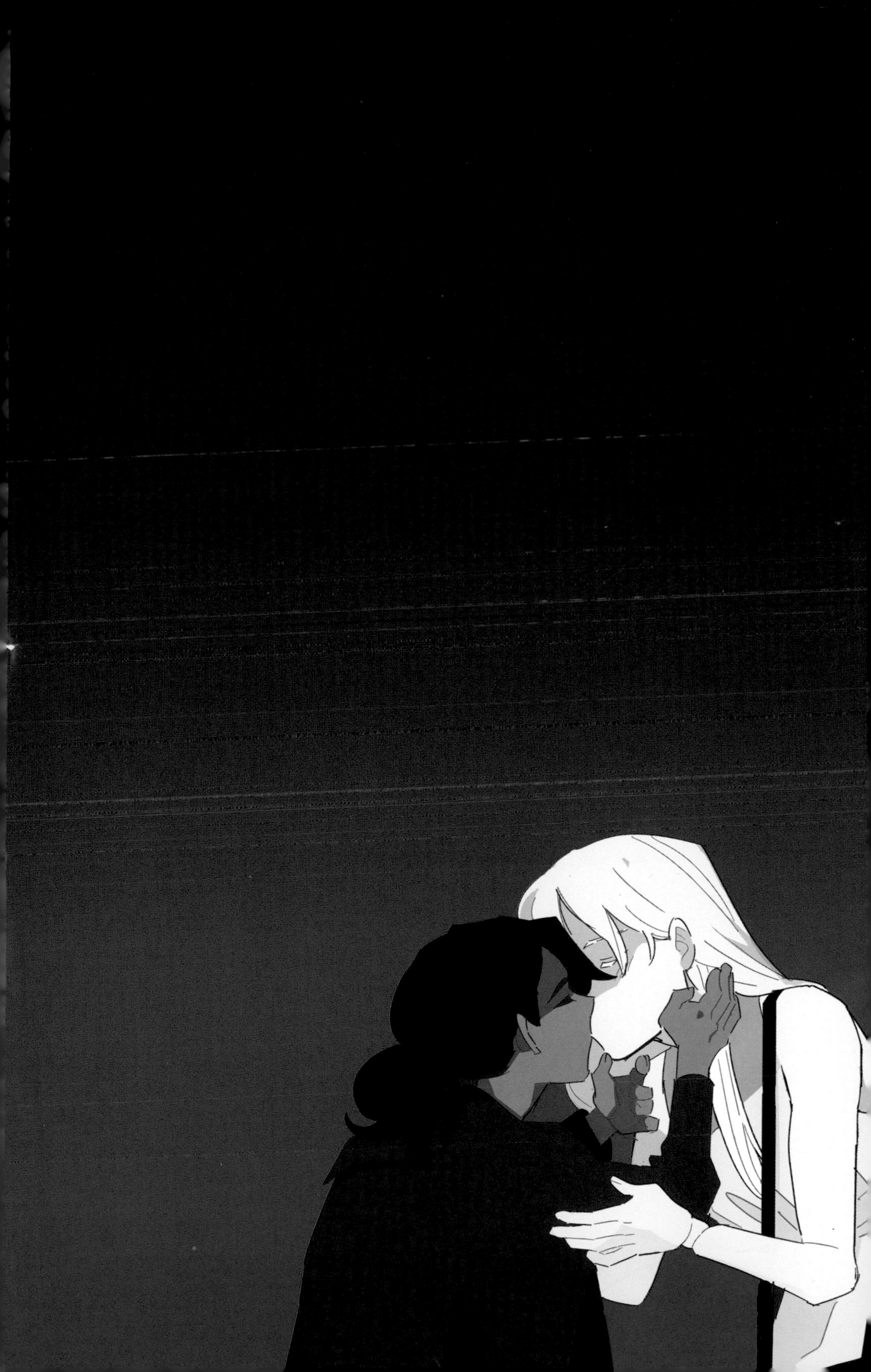